Stab Proof Scarecrows

Stab Proof Scarecrows

Lance Manley

Matador
5 Weir Road
Kibworth Beauchamp
Leicester LE8 0LQ, UK
Tel: (+44) 116 279 2299
Fax: (+44) 116 279 2277
Email: books@troubador.co.uk
Web: www.troubador.co.uk/matador

ISBN 978 1848762 978

British Library Cataloguing in Publication Data.
A catalogue record for this book is available from the British Library.

**363.
2**

Typeset in 11pt Sabon MT by Troubador Publishing Ltd, Leicester, UK
Printed and bound in Great Britain by TJ International Ltd, Padstow, Cornwall

Matador is an imprint of Troubador Publishing Ltd

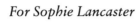

For Sophie Lancaster

ACKNOWLEDGMENTS

Thanks to Dad for his artwork and for saying "either put it behind you or write a book". Stephan for his intervention. Carmen for proving the existence of fate. Johan for his faith in me. Richard W for his continued support long after he had to. Alex H, Simon D, Pete L, Jason D, Oliver T, Robert C, Dave R, and Ian M for being the diamonds in the rough. Tony and John from the QA...and of course to Sergeant Kerwan for being a catalyst for more than he realises.

CONTENTS

"When I compromised my ethics, or swallowed my pride.
It was never through fear or cowardice.
Merely a desire to be accepted".

Lance Manley – November 2008

"Be careful what you wish for.
You may end up stuck with it".

Anonymous

THE SPECIAL CONSTABULARY

Years ago while at university in the north of England I saw a billboard advertising The Specials and 'helping the community'. I'd never heard of this concept before and upon finding out that it was being a cop but for no money I sneered a derisory sneer and asked incredulously just why anyone would want to do THAT job for nothing?

In my early thirties in London I saw so much that pissed me off. So many illegal acts, casual bullying or just discourtesy and rudeness. I had been described as "aggressive and confrontational" in the past but didn't agree with that observation. I liked to think of myself as "assertive and stubborn" and believed that being a Special and training as a cop would allow me to channel that in a positive way. The City of London Police were recruiting for Specials and so were the Metropolitan Police. I applied to both and while the Met didn't get back to me even after two months, COLP replied within a week.

The modern Special Constabulary are a supplementary arm of the UK Police Forces. Specials are volunteer cops who take a condensed Basic Training and are issued with a Warrant Card that gives them all the powers of a Regular officer whether on or off duty. They also have a uniform 99% identical to their Regular counterparts, only differences being that most Forces put 'SC' on the epaulettes above the Force number and higher ranking Specials have different insignia to the Regulars. They receive no money beyond travel and subsistence expenses and no perks apart from those in the Met, British Transport Police or COLP as they get to travel for free on public transport within London with the Warrant Card.

Specials join out of a sense of "wanting to do the right thing". They agree to work a minimum of 200 hours a year (about four per week on average) but can do more if they wish to.

They were like gold dust in the Second World War when they kept the streets of London safe while younger, fitter men were off fighting the Hun.

Nowadays they back up the Regular Force and have a similar rank structure to their paid counterparts. Revered in some Forces, marginalised in others they are populated both by people who have a huge sense of social conscience and those who have personality disorders and like a bit of power. There are also those that come in between the two. It's fairly odd for most people to imagine if they're not part of it or don't know anyone who is.

Picture the scene. You're in your office on a Friday at 5.30pm and you and your colleagues are putting on jackets and coats. Someone says "I'm off for a pint. Anyone fancy joining me?"

Someone else replies "sorry, I'm taking the wife out for dinner."

Another says "I'm off to take the kids to see the new Harry Potter movie".

The Special then pipes up "and I'm going to walk around in the rain and arrest people for no money".

I knew from day one of stepping into the Nick for my interview that Race and Diversity played a HUUUGE part in the role of a modern copper. Even then, with nothing to compare it to it didn't feel proportionate or even RIGHT that there was so much of a swing in the pendulum. At no point in either Force I served in was I ever asked "why do you want to be a Police officer?" The first question they asked me when I was interviewed for both Forces was "when did you last hear a racist, sexist or homophobic remark and what did you do about it?" I also had to fill out a lengthy application form, have a Medical and pass a Fitness test to get into the Specials.

I joined up the following September.

It was always fairly surreal. Having a Police force of such vast numbers patrolling one square mile of London. The City of London is the heart of the British economy. It has a resident population of only 7000 and some of the most powerful companies in the world are based there. It is controlled by the Corporation of London and has a different Lord Mayor to the rest of the capital.

It has 900 Police Officers, about 300 Police Support Employees (PSEs) and around 90 Specials. There are three working Police stations, Snow Hill, Bishopsgate and Wood Street. The former two are the only active stations and have Custody Suites. Wood Street is the HQ for Traffic, Mounted, CCTV, Control Room and ACPO (the top three ranks of Commissioner, Assistant Commissioner and Commander). The warrant card holder is unique in that the badge is gold not silver and has the St. George's shield and cross in the centre. It also has the warrant number in Braille, an addition brought in by blind former Home Secretary David Blunkett. Officers swear allegiance to the Corporation of London and not the Monarch like every other Force, in order to protect England's Wall Street. The uniform they wear is different to the Metropolitan Police in that the checks are red instead of blue.

Day jobs amongst my peers ranged from a Christian missionary, a nanny, a bank director, an accountant, a photograph restorer, a millionaire businessman and me the English teacher.

Some fairly unusual aspects of the Special Constabulary were revealed as time went on.

First of all, any Special no matter what length of service or what rank he holds is outranked by any Regular, of whatever length of service or rank. This means that the Thames Valley Special Constabulary Chief Commandant of 25 years volunteer policing would, in any incident have to give right of veto to a 19 year old Regular just out of Basic Training. After I joined the Regulars one of our lecturers at uni, a grizzled Old School cop of 30 years named Bartholomew said he was on duty one night years ago when he passed a Special Divisional Officer in the corridor of the Nick. After he didn't acknowledge the DO they had the following tete a tete:

DO: "EXCUSE ME!"
Bartholomew: "Yes?"
DO: "Haven't you forgotten something?"
Bartholomew: "What might that be?"

DO: "Don't you salute a senior officer?"

Bartholomew: "Well, show me a senior officer and I'll salute him. Now fuck off".

He walked away while the furious DO hurtled into the Section skipper's officer to remonstrate about this insubordination. The Sergeant backed Bartholomew and told the DO to get a grip saying "he's perfectly correct. You had no right to speak to him like that, you are NOT his senior officer".

Another fairly strange point was that you could be promoted to any rank within the Specials, leapfrogging over former Sirs and Ma'ams. When I joined, the office of Commandant was vacant as the last one had retired months ago and a new one had yet to be appointed. Three ranks went for it, a DO (next one down), a Section Officer (at that time two down) and a Special Police Constable. The interviewing board was apparently most impressed with the SPC, mainly because he had over 20 years experience in Scotland as a Hobby Bobby and was the first Special in history to be allowed to serve in two Forces simultaneously as he worked in London Monday to Friday and was at home over the border at the weekend. In the space of a week he went from wearing a tit helmet and having to answer to an SO to wearing an almost identical uniform to the Commissioner and being able to call him by his first name (while on the weekends working as an SPC again, partly because the Scottish Special Constabulary have no rank structure).

He was one of the most genuine people I met during that time and the only Special that had my complete respect. He got stuck in to duties with the rest of us, frequently driving the van and going out on foot patrol, particularly in the aftermath of July 2005's terrorist attacks. He was always patient, never raised his voice but was a natural leader and always had time for people.

As the City of London has sooo many cops on duty at any one time it was very difficult to get the meaty Shouts. With one square mile of turf, and only half of it under your remit depending on which station you work out of, the exciting jobs will be snapped up like bargains in the Harrods sale on January 1st.

One day near Christmas I was put with a couple of other Specials in the Rowdy Van. One hand on our batons, growling with anticipation we were put onto the streets with about six Regulars to respond to the expected call outs for drunks fighting or being silly in the pre holiday merriment.

After about half an hour of driving around with nothing to do the radio went off:

"kkk...Control to all Units. Anyone who can attend the Old Vicar pub on West Avenue. Drunken male refusing to leave the premises, over".

The driver snatched up the radio mic, confirmed we could attend, switched on the Blues and Twos and then blatted it round there in double quick time with us lot getting thrown about in the back. We got to the boozer just as an ERV pulled up next to us on the kerb. Five of us ran into the pub to find one slightly built Polish male who was clearly drunk but not even remotely aggressive, trying to coax the barmaid into giving him another beer. We asked him to step outside where he sobered up rapidly at the sight of another five coppers glaring at him next to a Rowdy Van and a patrol car.

Overkill it would seem and I later found out that every year they put the Rowdy Van on the streets and hardly anything ever happens to justify doing it. Still, better safe than sorry.

The City of London has around 100 cameras in its square mile of space, all of which can be seen by the operators in the Police Control Room. This means that despite there being virtually nowhere you can hide, its officers can be seen and therefore given backup even if they are unable to ask for it. Conversely it means that Control knows exactly where officers are at any given time.

One day while filling out our Pocket Note Books (PNBs) in the Writing Room a Shout came in over the radio.

"kkk..Control to all units, anyone who can assist at a fight at the Jockstrap and Filofax pub in Umgowa Street. Multiple assailants. Immediate assistance required, over".

I pointed to the radio on the table and went "wait for it".

Sure enough, one second later:

"kkk...four three can attend"

"kkk...five seven"

"kkk...Dog Van on route"

"kkk...Firearms making our way"

"kkk...nine eight"

"kkk...eight one"

etc, etc.

When Control could finally get a word in edgeways the operator said:

"Last seven units are not needed. I repeat NOT needed. If not already on scene do NOT attend, over".

There was a short pause then someone tried their luck.

"kkk...five six just arriving on scene, over".

Another pause then the operator said flatly:

"Control to five six, don't tell fibs. I can see you on camera seventeen, nowhere near the scene, over".

UK LICENSING LAWS

Licensing Laws in the UK needed an overhaul long before they actually got one.

In 1914 we had the 1st World War. Most fit and able bodied men from England were fighting in it, so everyone left in the factories was needed to build "essential products". Problem was, back then alcohol was cheap and pubs were not restricted as to when they plied their trade. It was not uncommon for people, particularly on a Friday to go to the pub at lunchtime and not go back to work, preferring to drink themselves into an alcoholic stupor and fall asleep across the coal scuttle after nipping out into the garden at the back of the terrace to use the communal privvy.

So...to prevent such lax behaviour amongst the working population the British Government imposed the dreaded and much hated Licensing Laws. From 1915 pubs HAD to open no earlier than 11am. They would close at 3pm and open again at 7pm. They would then serve the last drink at 11pm and everyone would have to leave no later than 11.30pm. On Sunday the only difference was that the drinking up time was 10.30pm.

While common sense when you are fighting the wretched Hun for dear old Blighty no one bothered to repeal the laws once we'd won in 1918.

Instead we had these appalling restrictions on liberty for the next 90 years. Like having a TV licence, this time limit on having a bevvy didn't seem to be fair, have any logic or common sense and it was bizarre that unlike almost every other country in Europe we had to neck the last dregs at half before midnight, or the bouncer would take it off us.

This utterly atrocious and condescending Nanny state approach to civil liberties meant that people drank far too much far too quickly and would get into trouble for Drunk and Disorderly, drink driving, fighting or simply falling over and injuring themselves. An American tourist once remarked to me "you Brits drink like you're afraid someone's about to take it off you".

Treat people like children and they will oblige by acting just like them. If you put a box in a room with "DO NOT OPEN EVER" on it, you can guarantee that nearly everyone will take a peek. It's human nature.

In 1989 the laws were modified so that public houses no longer had to close from 3 till 7. The build up to this was lots of middle class morons being interviewed on the local news, while walking their Golden Retrievers near their detached country houses, in villages with names like Ruttingbuck-on-Weir. They would wax lyrical about the time some local yobs threw an empty beer bottle into their garden on the way home from the Queen's Legs and they were anticipating more of the same along with sexual assaults, cannibalism and possibly World War III once these same ruffians could drink for an extra four hours a day.

Against popular expectation, within six months it was proven that crime had in fact gone DOWN by 25% nationally. Simple reason being that if you allow people to drink all day they will relax and take their time because they know you are not going to shut the pub on them and send them out into the rain.

In 2005, NINETY years after their inception the old Licensing Laws were finally scrapped completely and people could drink all day. Pubs would be able to serve alcohol 24 hours if they wished, provided they got a license from the local council, approved by the Police.

So...while working as a Special we were asked if anyone wanted to help out the Regulars with the historical Night Shift where, for the first time in nearly four generations people would be able to drink as long as they liked. I volunteered and was put in a car with two Regulars and we hung about waiting to see what happened. There were an extra two cars on duty plus a van on standby for the rowdy drunks COLP fully expected to have to bang up once "TIME GENTLEMEN PLEASE" became nothing more than a bad memory.

Hanging around Bank station in the freezing cold at 1am and nothing was happening. The entire area was dark. Only taxis on the road apart from us.

Most pubs in the square mile hadn't even bothered to apply for a late license and the one or two that had seemed quiet with no trouble.

Finally at 3am we got a Body.

"kkk... five-seven to control. Can anyone assist us with a Drunk and Incapable on Little Britain. Male, IC1".

The driver of our car snapped "we'll have that!", reaching for the radio, but he was a nano second too slow as someone piped up.

"Nine-two, we'll take that. Can you confirm D&I and not D&D? Is Suspect violent?"

The patrol that are with the drunk then chip in. "No, he's D&I. Found him asleep on the pavement. He'll freeze to death if we leave him there".

"Shit!" our driver seethes. "Oh well. Let's go and see if they need our help". He turns the key in the ignition and we go back to Snow Hill.

In Custody is the most pissed person I think I've ever seen. He can barely stand up and is burbling incoherently at the Custody skipper. He is clearly fairly well to do, as are most drunks we nick in the City.

The Custody skipper is smiling as are the two officers holding him up so he doesn't collapse on the floor.

"Whazafuggintime?" he mumbles.

"It's about three in the morning mate" the skipper replies "are you ok?"

"YeahI'mfugginalright.Watyouarrestinmefor?" the drunk burbles, wiping spittle away from his chin onto his sleeve.

"You're not under arrest" the skipper says, clearly finding this highly amusing "we're going to let you sleep it off and you can go in the morning ok?"

"Soyourfugginarrestinmethen?" he says attempting to stand up straight and swaying violently before being stabilised by the palm of one of his supporting officers.

"YOU'RE NOT UNDER ARREST" the skipper replies slowly and loudly, beaming from ear to ear. "You can sleep it off and go in the morning ok?"

"Ah ok" the drunk says, waving an index finger at where he thinks the skipper is standing, but is about two feet off centre. He nods slowly, thinks for a second and then says "so...yourgonnafugginarrestmeinduhmorningyeah?"

"No you are not under arrest...lads cell 4 please" the skipper gestures to the cell wing and the two officers make to escort him. He starts to wriggle a bit so I join in, holding his shoulders and the three of us bumble him along to his room for the night.

"whatyoufugginholdinmefor?"

"Just making sure you don't fall over" the officer on his right says, grinning. He looks over at his colleague and then me "Jesus! I can't believe he's this pissed"

"It'smyfugginbirthday" the drunk offers in explanation. "Youdiddunsayhappybirthday".

We all laugh at this "Many happy returns mate, hope it was worth the hangover you're gonna have tomorrow" the same officer says.

"Yeah, happy birthday" I congratulate him "get any good presents?"

"Diddungetanyfugginpresents...'BELCH!'...no!" he replies looking annoyed.

We are now at his cell and I bend down to take off his shoes while the officer on his left removes his belt.

"whatyoutakinmyfugginclothesofffor?" the drunk mumbles.

"Just belt and shoes mate, it's for your own protection"

We lay him down on his plastic, easy-wipe mattress in the recovery position and he's asleep before we've shut the cell door.

We look at each other in the corridor.

"Fuckin' 'ell!" one of the Regulars says "he's really going to regret that in the morning".

We go back to the Writing Room to catch up on paperwork and get a brew.

Once the Duty Inspector got wind of this guy's presence in the Custody Suite he put him on 15 minute cell visits due to the state he was in. This meant someone had to enter his cell, wake him up and then leave again, marking on his Custody Record that he had "responded to oral stimulus" or some such gumph. This basically meant it wasn't enough for us to check he was still breathing, you had to rouse him from his sodden slumber.

I thankfully only had the pleasure of doing this once. It took about five minutes.

"Hey, hey, wake up!" I shake him gently and he is snoring but doesn't respond.

"HEY WAKE UP!!!" I shout at him, shaking him a bit harder. He mumbles but still doesn't wake up. I try this for a few minutes until the Custody Sergeant appears in the doorway, looks at me, looks at our prisoner and bellows

"OI! YOU! WAKE UP NOW!"

The drunk snaps awake, looks around in panicky disorientation and shouts "WHAT? WHAT? MUM, SORRY MUM! WHAT? SORRY MUM!" and then goes back to sleep.

"That's the way you do it mate" the skipper says, winking at me and turning on his heel.

The whole of this historic night did not result in even one arrest due to the extended drinking hours for either of the two COLP Nicks. Our only Body was given a bed for the night and released without charge at 9am to make his groggy way to the chemist for some elephant strength Nurofen. He wasn't even drinking due to the change in the Law but to celebrate his birthday.

PISSED SUITS

City of London drunks are usually rich, well dressed and arrogant. Hence their nickname Pissed Suits.

If stopped by Police they tend to be larey and try to talk their way out of it. If nicked they get self righteous and threaten you with a lawyer or mention that they know 'Someone'. Further they will usually be Non Compliant for the simple reason that Arrest only happens to Horrid Common Poor People and not someone who closes deals worth millions of pounds over lunch and has a villa in the south of France.

We once had a bloke in a Saville Row suit taken struggling into Custody by two officers. After a lot of swearing and grunting he exclaimed loudly "LET ME GO! LET ME GO! I'VE GOT A YACHT".

One of the escorting officers replied "good for you but you're still under arrest".

He then tried "STOP HITTING ME! OW! OW!"

The same officer then said wearily "we're on camera mate so you might as well stop telling lies".

Another time I was about to issue a Stop form to a woman who had a dodgy headlight when the driver of the Response car I was crewed in blared the horn and motioned me to get back in. I shouted over my shoulder "get that fixed ok" and clambered into the rear seats as he blatted it to where an officer had triggered his Panic Alarm.

We arrived to find a Regular Constable retching by the side of the road, his CS spray swinging lazily from its lanyard. Ten yards behind him was a screaming Pissed Suit with three officers sat on his back and one trying to handcuff him. He had snot and tears streaming down his cheeks and had clearly just been been sprayed in the face.

"YOU BASTARDS!" he shrieked at the top of his lungs "THIS IS THE WORST FUCKING DAY OF MY LIFE!"

They managed to lock the cuffs and then pulled him upright and sat him in the Rowdy Van with the window open to negate the effects of the CS spray.

An old man with a dog on a lead is standing by the side of the road watching this. The officer is still retching into the gutter. I approach him "you ok mate? What happened?"

He coughs a bit, holds up his hand and after a few more splutters tells me that he found the guy taking a piss up a wall. He gestures to the office building nearby and sure enough there's the requisite stream running across the pavement and into the gutter.

He told him to stop. The Pissed Suit told him to fuck off. He then told him he was under arrest and locked one cuff on his arm. The guy tried to pull away. He then tried the Take Down he'd learned in Officer Safety Training (twisting the cuff against the wrist and shouting "DOWN! DOWN! DOWN!") to which the bloke just took a swing at him with his fist. After a brief tussle he deployed his CS spray in the lad's face but got a back splash right in his own open mouth, hence the heaving and hawking as we'd arrived.

The bloke with the dog then pipes up. "I saw that. That was excessive force".

The choking officer then snaps "oh fuck off! What do you know?" and tries to walk towards him. I grab him by the arm and lead him away.

"Come on calm down" I tell him quietly "you'll only make it worse. He's just a nosey old bastard".

"Fucking idiot" he seethes angrily, glaring at the guy.

The dog walker then turns to the driver of the car I was in. "That was excessive force. I know you guys have a difficult job to do but that was too much".

The driver glares at him then says icily "did you see the Arrest Sir?"

"Yes"

"Did you see what led to the Arrest Sir?"

"Err...no"

"Then what gives you the right to have an opinion?"

"That was excessive. You didn't need that many people to arrest him I'm sure" he says defiantly. "I will be making a complaint tomorrow morning".

"That's up to you" the driver snaps back and walks off.

Anyone not used to seeing people get nicked will sometimes assume that things should be 'fair'. If there's only one Suspect then surely Marquess of Queensbury rules should apply and one or maybe two officers should be used to subdue them. What people don't seem to get is that violent or Non Compliant Suspects need to detained with the minimum amount of struggling and the maximum level of safety to the officers making the Arrest, the public and also the Arrestee. The idea is to have many cops as possible sitting on you until you are no longer able to fight or run away. The only physical injury the bloke suffered was from the CS, the effects of which are temporary.

Violence is ugly, no matter why it's being done.

JULY 7th 2005

I never used to 'get' the people in New York who, after the World Trade Centre attacks on September 11th 2001, came out and worked as volunteers in hastily assembled kitchens making soup for firemen. I couldn't perceive how this kind of thing would make a difference in the grand scheme of things. My perspective was forever changed in the summer of 2005.

On the morning of 7th July 2005 a series of coordinated suicide bomb blasts hit London's public transport system during rush hour. Carried out by British Islamist extremists, these atrocities were revenge for Britain's involvement in (amongst other things) the Iraq War.

Three Underground trains and one double decker bus were hit by the explosions in which 52 people were murdered and a further 700 injured. The first explosion was at 8.50am. By 9.20am London Underground declared a Code Amber Alert and suspended the entire network. Later the entire public transport system for central London was shut down. Mobile phone networks became inaccessible for about four hours. Hundreds of thousands of people spent the day frightened and confused, scared for relatives or friends they knew to be in London but could not contact. The news reports were vague and it was 24 hours before any kind of accurate report was given to the world.

In the summer of 2005 I was running an educational summer camp in London for foreign teenagers aged between 12 and 16. The centre had about 130 kids from around seven different nations and fourteen staff, ranging from English teachers to activity leaders. I was in overall control as Centre Manager with a Director of Studies and an Activity Manager below me and the others working for either of their departments. The company had around 20 centres in the UK and in October when the stats came back, mine was the only one not to have been billed for damage and to have come in under budget. Simple reason, I was strict but fair and didn't tolerate any nonsense from the kids. While they were there to have a good time it was made clear that rule breaking would result in punishment and Head Office eventually started sending me horrible kids from other centres on 'Thin Ice' agreements.

At about 10am on July 7th I was pottering about in the office when we got news that there had been some kind of explosion on the Underground in London. The kids were in lessons and the remaining staff plus those who worked in the kitchen sat or stood round the canteen TV to see what BBC News 24 had to say about the subject. As time moved on it became clear that this was not just an accident as more than one place had been hit and the footage showed wounded people being taken out of Kings Cross station. By the time we had a clearer idea of what had happened I called an emergency meeting of all the students and staff and stated that all excursions were cancelled and none of the kids were to go off site until further notice.

While landlines were still working, mobiles could not be reached. Initially we thought this was an Op COBRA measure to free up the network for essential calls but it later transpired that it was simply the amount of traffic, with people frantically phoning each other in the aftermath. I called Head Office and asked my boss if it was ok to go in to the Nick if COLP needed me.

He replied "go where you're most needed".

I warned the other two managers they might need to take control of the camp if I went in for duty but that seemed more and more unlikely as I was unable to reach my Section Officer Godfrey on his mobile.

We had been explicitly told that in the event of an emergency or serious incident we were absolutely NOT to simply turn up at the

Nick. We had to wait to be called and asked to come in. This was to ensure that the Force knew exactly what resources they had at what time and was pretty much common sense. It did not however, help my frustrations at not knowing if I was needed or not.

Finally at about 1pm I managed to get through.

"Hi it's Lance"

"I know it's you, I saw your number come up". There was a pause. "How do you feel right now?"

"Like I want to put my fucking fist through the window" I replied.

Another pause.

"Maybe you shouldn't come in then".

"Figure of speech, I'm fine. I just want to help out".

A longer pause.

"Get in as soon as you can. We need everyone who can make it. Muster is at 1500".

One of the few train lines still functioning went from half a mile from the holiday camp to Waterloo station, a mile from Snow Hill Nick. I gave the other two managers the master keys and company mobile and cycled down there. The train was visibly less populated than normal but the few people still using it appeared oblivious to what had happened four hours ago and had the usual posture of London Transport users of complete boredom.

Arriving at Snow Hill and there were Specials and Regular officers all over the place. I pegged it up the stairs to the locker room and found it packed with other Specials and even a few PCSOs. Just as I'd stripped down to my undies a head appeared round the corner of the row of lockers and said "guys. Muster is now 2.45 ok?" That left about five minutes to get all my gear on. I didn't have time to pull on my Stabby or Load Belt and was dragging them along behind me as I approached a congested Briefing Room full of Regulars, Specials, two Sergeants and an Inspector. The Commandant was standing next to the open doorway as we walked in.

"Hello Lance"

"Hello Sir"

He taps his right ear. "Still got your earring in" he says smiling.

I blush. "Sorry".

"Och, don't be silly, just take it out, no problem".

We sit or stand. There are about 40 of us in a room that usually has a maximum of 10 people in it. A female Sergeant addresses us.

"Right. At this time all we know is one confirmed dead and officially the cause of the explosion is still an electrical power surge. We are however pretty sure it was bombs but are waiting for official confirmation. Public are NOT to be given any information apart from the official version until such a time as it changes. Is that clear?"

We murmur our understanding.

"All those present not assigned specific duties are on foot patrol". She glances across the room "I'm sure the Commandant will brief the Specials on what he needs them to do."

She then adds the clincher that makes it clear just how serious all this is. "All shifts are now 12 hours instead of 8 and all Rest Days are cancelled".

An officer at the back stands up "err...Sarge I'm on Annual Leave tomorrow".

She glances up at him and says "I'll see what I can do. Right that's it. Let's get out there".

We meet in a corner of the writing room and I'm partnered with my SO. The short walk from Snow Hill down to Old Bailey reveals a scene like something from Dawn of the Dead. Hundreds of people are milling about on the streets and as the pavements are full a lot of them are also walking in the road. Nearly all of the few vehicles still moving are Hackney Cabs and the closure of the transport network has left many people without a clue as to where they are. When you walk from your job to the bus or Tube stop and from there are carried all the way to your destination you don't actually know what roads the bus takes or what locations the Tube stations between your departure and destination are in.

I was in the privileged position of knowing more or less what was going on and how serious it was, yet none of this information had at this point been given to the public. This made for a frustrating experience of people being mainly concerned with how to get home.

A woman approaches us "excuse me where's Threadneedle Street?"

"You're standing on it" Godfrey replies, looking visibly annoyed.

"Oh, thanks"

A few seconds later "excuse me, where's Waterloo Bridge?"

"Down there, turn right, five minute walk"

Then "excuse me, where's St Paul's Cathedral?"

"See that big thing behind you?"

"Oh, sorry"

About an hour later the buses were up and running again meaning the population thinned out slightly. We moved on to Aldgate station, one of the bomb sites. By this time we had had it confirmed that it was now being recognised as a bomb that had caused this and probably all the explosions. Two Cycle Response Regulars were at the Cordon tape, looking visibly bored. They'd been there since around 9am and it was now about 4.30pm. Five trays of curled up sandwiches wrapped in cling film were next to their stunt hopper mountain bikes along with some disposable plastic cups that had presumably held tea or coffee and bottles of mineral water. Turned out these were gifts from the people in the adjoining office blocks who had come out to feed them every few hours and offer them drinks. No one loves the Police more than when they feel threatened by forces they cannot control or understand.

"We're your Relief" Godfrey tells them. They chat briefly, thank us for relieving them and cycle back to the Nick for some Refs and a break.

We stand at the tape for a while. A Swedish camera crew and journalist approach me, show me Swedish TV ID and ask if they can interview me. Godfrey says no so they move off. Then a bendy bus rounds the corner and sees us in the way. The driver looks surprised and slides his window across as he gets near to me.

"I was told this road was open again".

"Nope, it's still closed. Hang on". I check with Control via the radio that it is still meant to be closed off and they confirm it is.

"Sorry mate you'll need to go back".

He isn't happy, mainly because bendy buses weren't built with reversing in mind and it takes about ten minutes for him to back up the street and round the corner.

Then we are approached by a bloke who lives on the other side of the cordon.

"How am I supposed to get home?" he enquires angrily.

I initially try to be nice about it and give him alternative directions but he clearly thinks he should be allowed to get past and suddenly says "YOU DON'T HAVE TO KEEP SAYING 'OK' ALL THE TIME TO ME!"

One of my 'ticks'. Oh well, don't like it, don't talk to me.

"I'm trying to help you, if you don't like the way I talk it's not my fault".

"Yeah, but you don't have to keep saying 'OK' all the time" he repeats, glaring at me.

"Just go ok. I've got more important things to deal with" I snap and he chunters off in the direction I pointed to.

Then a car pulls up on the other side of the road about twenty yards from the cordon tape. The driver glances across at us, switches on his hazards and then buggers off into an office block next to his motor.

I walk over to the car, take a look at it and then radio Control.

"Can I have a vehicle check please? Accompanied, Carunder Street?"

"One moment". Control come back one minute later to say it's registered to a male, at the address the driver went into.

Fifteen minutes later he comes out again and is embarrassed and surprised when I tear him a new arsehole for leaving the car there.

"I'm sorry officer I thought you saw me".

"I did, but you didn't check that. Do you REALLY think it's appropriate to leave your car right next to cordon tape with the hazards on right next to where a bomb probably went off a few hours ago?"

"Well...err...no, I s'pose not".

"I would be well within my rights to have had it towed away and destroyed. Be more careful next time. Other people CANNOT read your mind".

He apologises, gets in and drives off.

A short time later I am chatting to Godfrey when a bloke using a mobile approaches the cordon tape, nods acknowledgment at me then lifts the tape up and walks under it.

"OI!!!"

He jumps about three feet in the air and drops his phone.

After I beckon him over he starts moaning.

"How am I supposed to get home?"

"I don't care, you don't walk under a Police cordon"

"But how am I supposed to get home?"

"It says 'POLICE DO NOT CROSS' in massive letters".

"But how am I going to get home then?" he wails.

"Put your right hand out and touch the tape, then walk along the road the tape is on. It's in a big circle, eventually you'll come around the other side".

He shrugs and stomps off.

About eight o'clock and a car pulls up with three passengers, all wearing Police High Viz winter jackets. I assume it's more cops to help us at the cordon but then the front passenger gets out and says.

"Hello, I'm the Chief Constable of the British Transport Police", smiling broadly.

He has two layers of scrambled egg on his cap and bling on his shoulder epaulettes that I don't recognise. The other two get out as well. One has three pips per shoulder and is obviously a Chief Inspector. The third is similarly blinged up like the CC with insignia I can't identify off the top of my head but later found out was the Deputy Chief Constable. Caught off guard I simply stammer

"Oh...hello Sir".

Ian Johnston CBE QPM walks over and extends his hand and I shake it. "You been here a while?" he enquires.

"No Sir, about a couple of hours, we relieved two Regulars"

"Good show. We're just going to take a look at the station" he tells me.

I lift the tape up and the three of them step under it and walk off in the direction of Gold Cordon, about 800 yards away.

I walk over to Godfrey and say enthusiastically "That was the Chief Constable of the British Transport Police!"

"Good for him" he replies, glaring at me and then turning away.

Unaware of protocols for this type of thing I radio Control and tell them that the BTP CC has just entered Bronze Cordon with two other officers and is heading to Gold Cordon.

A short time later the CC and his companions return. I raise the tape again.

"Are you going to make us jump over?" he jests, chortling at his own joke. The other two chuckle as well.

As Headmaster-ish as the gag was, he's clearly being friendly so I laugh and reply "no Sir, I'm not that cruel".

He expresses his thanks, gets back in the car and the three of them leave.

Another hour later and there's virtually no one approaching us. Then a huge articulated lorry appears and trundles towards me. With a hiss of hydraulics the driver stops and winds down his window. "Alright mate, I'm delivering the generators to get Aldgate station up and running again".

No one had told us he was coming and we have been explicitly told to let no one except other cops through.

"No one told us, hang on".

A check with Control comes back ten minutes later to say that he can't go through as they have no record of him being asked to come here.

He protests "but I've got the delivery to make, it's the generators for the station, there's no power there".

"Look I'm sorry you'll have to wait. They've said no".

Finally at about 10pm our Relief arrived, we were stood down and headed back to the Nick, got changed and went home.

I still feel immensely proud to have been part of the official effort to deal with this monstrous attack on innocent civilians perpetrated by psychotic wankers. The fact that nearly all the COLP Specials downed tools from their day jobs and came in at such short notice, by whatever means they could to man the pumps made having joined completely worthwhile and negated all the boring shifts I had 90% of the time where the highlight would be issuing a cyclist with an FPN for not having lights.

Friends and acquaintances that teased me about joining the Police as a Hobby Bobby would often ask why I did it. After this I used to reply:

"How did you feel on July 7th 2005?"

(Cue rant about bloody terrorists and how they should be hanged etc).

"Well that's more or less how I felt. Difference was I was able to put on my uniform and do something about it".

A few months later I went on a blind date in London with a girl I'd met on the Internet via a dating website. During a Thai meal she asked me what I did for fun. I told her I was a Special and had been on duty on July 7th. She stared at me for about a minute, then carefully put down her chopsticks.

"Really?"

"Yes, of course. Why?"

"I was on the bus".

"Which one?"

"The one that was blown up, in Tavistock Square".

She told me later that night as we sat on a park bench near Camden Town hugging and kissing, that she has always been phobic of sitting at the back of buses which is what saved her life that day. She was about four seats from the front on the top deck and remembers being thrown violently into the seat in front of her, busting her nose and breaking her glasses. She staggered downstairs and met a cop trying to deal with it who shepherded her to the side of the road and wouldn't let her back on board to try and find her spectacles. She said she was still having rage counselling (reason being that she is unable to focus her anger as the person that did this is dead) and has permanent hearing loss as a result of the explosion. She later showed me the front pages of two tabloid newspapers with the famous shot of the mangled bus with its roof off and people milling about on the shattered top deck. She is centre stage in both photos. When they took her to Casualty she was covered in other people's blood and after checking that she was ok, the medical staff discharged her and sent her home, spattered with gore and unable to see due to losing her glasses. She still has the clothes she was wearing that day in a zip-lock plastic bag under her bed. Every ten days or so, her and some other Survivors of the attack meet as a group to support and help each other.

We are still friends now and she has told me many times how pleased she is to have met a Police officer who was there that day and helped her and people like her.

The Ferrers Trophy was initiated by former Home Office Minister Lord Ferrers. The awards have been presented annually since 1993 for outstanding achievement and commitment shown by members of the Special Constabulary. The COLP Special Constabulary won the Ferrers Cup the following year for our efforts on July 7th. It was the first time in history that we'd got to the final list and the first time an entire Special Constabulary won the award. The Commandant was justifiably proud both when he put us forward to receive it and when he went to collect the trophy (but not as proud as we were).

In September 2005 the Commandant, the Chief Super and the Chief Inspector took us all out for a drink to say thanks.

In early 2006 the new Chief Superintendent of Snow Hill station sent letters to all of his Specials, thanking us profusely for our attendance for duty on July 7th and stating that our "unselfish gesture" was much appreciated.

This one day was 100% what inspired me to join as a Regular. To have been a part of something so monumentally important and, even in a small way, to have made a difference was what made me realise I wanted to be a cop full time. I had to leave COLP as they weren't recruiting and by the time they were I was ineligible to join as my application was still being processed for the other Force and you can only apply to one at a time.

JULY 21st 2005

Two weeks after the July 7th attacks, the fuckers tried again.

Four bomb attacks were attempted and a fifth device abandoned.

Three Tube stations and a bus in Shoreditch were hit but fortunately the bomb maker was on vacation meaning his understudy cocked up the ratios in the chemical mix and all that went off were the detonator charges.

The following day a manhunt was launched by the Met, described by Commissioner Ian Blair as "the largest ever investigation that the Met has ever mounted".

Caught soon after the four would-be martyrs were found guilty of conspiracy to murder and each sentenced to a minimum of 40 years in prison.

The only casualty of July 21st was a passenger who suffered an asthma attack. Unlike July 7th the Undergound networks remained partially open.

As Thursday was my Specials shift anyway I was already down to come in when, at around 12pm an Italian girl from one of the groups at my summer camp walked over and asked me if there had been more terrorist attacks. She was holding her mobile phone and had just been speaking to her father in Florence who had seen the news on CNN. I ran into the canteen again and waited until the news channel got round to mentioning that there had indeed been more explosions on the London public transport system, in a repeat of what had happened two weeks ago.

Some of our kids had already left for a trip to London with an

Activity Leader. I called him up on his mobile and told him to get everybody back and again held a meeting to say everyone was grounded until further notice.

Some Underground lines were still running but falling like dominoes as various Station Control rooms pulled the plug until they could get a clearer picture of what was going on. I managed to get on the Circle Line just in time as the guard on the gate said that the train 3 minutes away was the last one they were going to allow in until further notice. Very few people onboard, but again those that were, were reading newspapers or looking like they hadn't got a clue what was going on or didn't give a shit.

By the time I arrived at Snow Hill Nick the excitement wasn't as high as the last time but there was still a buzz of conversation as we got changed and made our way to the Writing Room. No massive meeting of all available manpower and suspension of Leave, this time we had our own huddle and partnered off with either a Regular or each other to take foot patrol.

When we got outside the streets were packed with cops all the way up to St Paul's and the Chief Super', Super' and a couple of Chief Inspectors were all spotted doing foot patrol. This had happened since July 7th with all ranks up to ACPO pounding the Beat and the Commandant stepping out with his DO's on several occasions.

People stopped us to ask what was going on and this time it was less of "how do I get home" and more of a worried desire to know what was happening and why. We reassured them that as far as we knew no one was hurt and the transport had been suspended purely as a security measure.

After a couple of hours we headed back for Refs and then the duty Inspector asked to see us in the Sergeant's office. About fifteen of us were crammed in there when he told the following tale of caution:

"Please be aware all of you that any and all suspicious packages you see are to be reported to Control. No matter what you see, if you think it's out of place, then call it in. However, please do not do what one probationary Constable did earlier today. We had a package at

Liverpool Street station with the area cordoned off. I arrived and asked him to describe the item and he replied it was a blue shoe box, about two feet by one foot and it was heavy".

There's a pause while he looks around the room then continues "I asked him how he knew it was heavy and....he had kicked it".

Murmur of shock and amusement from the rest of us.

"Please be careful out there. Obviously this is the second time this has happened and we are taking no chances with safety. It is however considered that this may be a hoax. Please continue to reassure the Public that everything is being done that can be done. Right, thank you".

We leave and I see Godfrey standing by the door as I walk out.

"Alright?" he says cheerfully "didn't think you'd get in as they'd shut most of the lines near your place."

"Just about made it" I reply "think I got the last train in by all accounts".

We are partnered up again and while I wait for him I talk to the Section skipper.

"What happened to the probationer after kicking the package Sarge?"

"Oh, he's still with us. He's not feeling too clever right now though. The Guv tore the arse out of him for that."

Walking about the Public seem pleased to see us, many ask what's going on and we reassure them that we think it's nothing too serious. I'm asked for a photo opportunity by two Japanese tourists near St Paul's cathedral and we oblige by posing with serious faces next to the woman who grins happily with her rucksack at her feet, stood in between us. I then get them to take a photo of me and Godfrey as my own memento of duty in the face of history unfolding.

Later on we take a stroll near some of the pubs and suited City brokers are burbling with enthusiasm as we pass. Throughout July and August 2005, everybody loved cops in central London. We pass a group of guys at a table sipping pints. One of them struggles to his feet as we approach.

"You guys are the best" he says reaching his arm out to shake our hands. We oblige and while still pumping my hand vigorously he turns to his mates and says "don't care what anyone says these guys do a fantastic job". He turns back to us and swaying on his feet puts his arms out to give what appears to be both of us at the same time a hug. "God bless you officers", he burbles looking like he's about to shed a tear, then trying to embrace me.

"Please stand back" I ask him and he looks embarrassed like a kid who's just been told off and replies:

"Sorry, sorry, just... people say you guys are fascists but I know you have a hard job to do".

I shake his hand again, express my gratitude for his sentiments and then we move on. I got this type of thing at least three times that night and once or twice in the subsequent weeks. People who have just been through two terrorist attacks will love their Boys in Blue for as long as they have ceased to feel comfortable in their worlds. When they are happy and content and everything's just peachy they prefer a Police Service. When their lives are threatened and they feel scared they want a Police Force.

JULY 22nd 2005

JEAN CHARLES DE MENEZES

Two weeks after the terrorist suicide bombings that cost so many people their lives and the day after the failed attempt to detonate more bombs and do it all over again, armed Police officers chased, cornered and shot dead Jean Charles de Menezes, an innocent man.

On the morning of the 22nd, Jean Charles set off from home on his way to Stockwell Underground station. Believing he matched the description of a suspected terrorist, Police followed him from his apartment, on to a bus, and into the Tube station. Armed Police officers were then dispatched and shot him shortly after he boarded a train, mistakenly believing he was a suicide bomber.

In the aftermath of this tragedy the Metropolitan Commissioner Sir Ian Blair refused to give any further information than had already been released, stating quite rightly that "at this moment everything is subordinate to the terrorist investigations".

It transpired in the subsequent days that Charles was not a suicide bomber, nor a Muslim or an Iraqi. Through mishandling of the situation he had been killed by Police officers who fundamentally believed he was a suicide bomber, about to kill himself and innocent people on a busy Underground train.

In the wake of this event the English Police were vilified in the media. The victim's parents were flown over as guests of the British Government and could be seen on the News, wailing in misery and grief at Stockwell Tube station, at the spot where their son had been killed. Initial reports that he had run when challenged by the armed Police officers were later shown to be false and for the next two and a half years there was a massive independent enquiry which found all officers involved, including the one that fired the fatal shots, the two that held Charles down as he was killed and the Gold Commander in charge of the Op', all blameless of any wrongdoing. The Met Police as an organisation however, were held responsible for what had happened.

People to this day think this shooting was disgusting. That the Police overreacted and were sloppy in their approach to the situation. That the officer who killed Charles was trigger happy and he had effectively been murdered.

As someone who was on duty on both 7/7 and 21/7 and knows a blast survivor I saw just how scared and angry the public were in the days, weeks and even months that followed. Had those bombs detonated on the 21st we would have had the capital or maybe even the country at a standstill. Once and you can wonder why, dust yourself off and carry on. Twice will bring you to your knees. We had been granted a reprieve, solely because of the shoddy handiwork on the second set of bombs.

Not knowing what we were dealing with or where the next attack might come from it was reasonable to believe that we were now under attack from Al Qaeda and anywhere could be next. The ease with which these people could carry out these atrocities was terrifying and a third attack would leave the transport system indefinitely suspended, put the country in the grip of a financial crisis and have the entire population scared out of their minds.

When those Police officers grabbed Charles, threw him down and then shot him, they fundamentally, 100% believed they were killing a suicide bomber. They put their own lives at risk in order to save other people's. Had he been what they believed he was he could have detonated his bombs at any point and may well have done. Hey, if you intend to kill yourself anyway why let yourself get captured?

Instead of running from perceived danger, they ran towards it with the sole intention of saving innocent people's lives. They did this knowing that they could have been killed at any moment and at the point where they were in physical contact with him probably believed they might die.

Much store has been placed on the fact that the officer who killed Charles fired eight times, seven in the back of the head and one in the back. This was used as evidence of 'panic firing' and an almost sadistic attitude to the execution. What some people don't seem to realise or won't accept is that bombs can be detonated by a 'dead man's switch' meaning that the trigger could have been activated by letting go of anything he might have been holding on to. Eight shots were fired for the simple reason that if you separate the medulla in the spinal cortex the body remains in the same position it was in just before it died. The nerves are severed and the corpse cannot spasm, triggering the bombs by reflex.

If de Menezes HAD been a suicide bomber then this would have been hailed as a victory in the war on terrorism. If he had been a suicide bomber and had detonated the bombs then the armed Police chasing him would have been loathed by the public and investigated for having FAILED to shoot him.

As tragic as all this was people yet again have decided to simply hate the Police and blame them for what happened that day.

No one ever seems to blame Al Qaeda.

We are the only country in the world that want the Police to protect us but at the same time feel we have a right to despise their very existence.

The officers who chased, captured and killed de Menezes should not be despised or hated. On the contrary they should have been given gallantry medals for how they conducted themselves. No one seems to care that their motives for doing what they did were not to kill an innocent man, but purely and simply to save the lives of the public they had taken an oath to protect.

OFF DUTY INTERVENTIONS.

We were told when we joined, both as Specials and as Regulars that if we had our warrant cards on us and witnessed something then we had a "duty to act" and HAD to intervene. This could be as dramatic as performing an Arrest right down to simply taking stock of what was going on and making a Statement later.

Throughout Training and beyond I seemed to attract off duty Interventions like flies to fly paper. Several times I saw violent or aggressive incidents and in all of them did something. All incidents ended without injury, with the people involved leaving peacefully and with no repercussions.

On a train on the way to my Thursday duty a group of school kids aged about 13 or 14 were in the same carriage. They were swearing loudly (I ignored it), dropping litter (I ignored that) and climbing on the seats and luggage racks (I ignored that too). I was getting more and more pissed off at their obnoxious behaviour and the final straw was when one of them gobbed on the floor (a big, juicy greeny with what looked like a whole packet of Walker's Cheese and Onion in its midst).

"Did you just spit on the floor?"

He looks up and smirks "No!"

"Right!" I pull the emergency handle (if you ever do this it's a nice solid feeling and makes a lovely 'chunk' noise. Very satisfying).

I get my badge out and show it to him. "Right, Police. Do you think it's OK to gob on the floor?"

He blanches and begins frantically trying to wipe the greeny away with his shoe, only succeeding in spreading it about more.

"Well do you?"

"Err....no"

"So why do it then? I put up with your swearing and general stupidity but this is ridiculous".

All his mates sit there watching me and saying nothing. A group of kids farther back has taken interest, one of them stands up "what's going on?"

I walk towards him and show him the badge. "Sit down, it's nothing to do with you...I SAID SIT DOWN".

He does so, glaring at me.

After about five minutes a bored looking guard wanders up the carriage, as if he's got all the time in the world and asks "who pulled the handle?".

"I did, this lad spat on the floor. I've already given him a Police bollocking. Would you like to give him a British Rail one?"

He turns to the lad and mumbles "don't spit on the floor again OK", without much enthusiasm and then resets the handle with a key.

He radios the driver to move on and we lurch off again. "Thanks" he says "I've been spat on before and no one did anything".

The lads are still quiet and at the next stop they all get up to leave. I say to the spitter as they get off "count yourself lucky you weren't nicked. I see you do it again you will be".

Cycling back from Tesco one rainy, miserable day I heard some blokes from the local timber merchant shouting through the gate at two motorists across the road. I turned round in time to see one push the other in the chest in what was a quite impressive "double palm heel strike" and send him tottering backwards. I yelled at them to break it up, propped the bike against the wall and ran over, standing in between them and showing the badge. The driver who'd assaulted the other man was Spanish and was indignant that the other lad had bumped his car and then simply driven off, the other claimed he didn't know he'd done it. The affronted Spaniard had then chased him and forced him off the road. I got them to exchange insurance details, told the gobby Spanish bloke he was lucky he wasn't getting nicked for Assault and sent them on their separate ways.

Cycling home from an especially boring shift with the Specials where absolutely nothing had happened, I was confronted by the sight of a rather fat guy on a folding green Brompton bicycle arguing with two young lads who appeared completely drunk one of which was holding a bottle of Becks. The other lad was holding a large bag of shredded paper that he'd clearly found by the side of the road. In response to the cyclist's words he snarled and twatted him over the head with the bag, which burst sending confetti everywhere and ran off. The cyclist then dropped his bike and piled after him, grabbing him by the back of the head and thumping with his other fist twice in the face, bursting his nose open. I ran after them, pulled the fat guy away and got in between them.

"RIGHT POLICE. KNOCK IT OFF!"

The lad is looking confused and is dripping blood from his nostrils. His mate is hovering, still holding the beer bottle. I grab it off him "PUT THAT DOWN".

"Wasn't my fault. He hit me" the wounded one protests holding his bleeding schnozz and pointing at the other guy as I hide the bottle in some scaffolding. It's chaotic and I don't know how this is going to go. The fat guy is seething with rage but obeys my instruction to keep his distance.

"Are you really Police?" the mate asks.

"Yes"

"Right, leg it!" he grabs the nosebleeder and they run off.

I wear a headset for my mobile when cycling. I have the COLP switchboard on voice activated dialling. I key the button and say the phrase "the boys" and it starts to ring. I turn to the fat bloke. "Stay there ok". He is calmer now and looks embarrassed.

"Haven't hit anyone in 20 years" he says in mitigation "I just lost my temper, he was so rude".

"I saw what happened but that's no excuse for what you....Hello? Yes, switchboard. Off duty officer. I'm at...." I glance at the nearest road sign and give them the location "violent assault, one wounded. Two have run off, I've got the third person with me. Can you send uniform here please?" I give my name, number and location again and they say people are on their way. The fat guy again attempts to explain that he was merely defending himself.

"You chased him and punched him in the face" I tell him "I appreciate you were assaulted but it didn't warrant that".

He is calm now and looks upset and ashamed of himself. Truth be told I don't think I would have reacted any differently but at this time I'm trying to react as an officer and that is to apply the Law that self defence has to be proportionate AND at the time.

I see a big group of lads walking towards us from the direction the other two ran off into. I call Control back. "It's me again" I give the location and my name and Force number. "I'm still with the Suspect but haven't arrested him I need people here now to back me up". The group of lads get closer and I lose my demeanour "shit...there's a big group of lads walking up the hill. I need backup now. I think they may be with the other two!" I ring off as the group approaches. They do nothing except walk past, not even sparing us a look. Later on I saw the printout of the Shout which had my swearing and pleas for assistance printed on it in glorious black and white.

After a couple of minutes a van turns up with about six officers in it. They are responding not to the initial call but to my second one requesting backup as Control thought I was about to get a pasting and made it a Priority One: Officer in Distress. One of them takes my details in his PNB while another two talk to the fat guy who gets off with Words Of Advice and a pink slip from the Stop Form. The officers leave.

"Haven't hit anyone in 20 years" he says again. I extend my hand and he shakes it.

"I understand you were upset but you can't react like that ok?"

He nods and leaves and I finally get to cycle home.

Getting off the Tube at St.Paul's I walk down the stairs to find a black woman sitting on the middle step holding a baby and crying. I initially think that she's begging until I see a white teenage girl trying to console her. I ask her what's wrong and in between sobs it turns out that she was being helped with her pushchair down the steps by another woman and as the baby girl wasn't strapped in she fell out and landed on her head on the concrete step with a thud. The other woman has oh so sympathetically done a bunk and left the poor mother in shock cradling her baby. I identify myself and ask the woman to come with me to the station supervisor's office. I also ask the teenage girl if she'd mind coming with us to console the woman while I manoeuvre the pushchair and the mother carries her baby. The mother gives me the kid to hold while she sorts out her things, still crying. The kid is oblivious and just stares at me with big brown eyes, sucking her thumb.

"Do you think she has brain damage?" the mother wails.

Jesus! What do you say to that?

"No, I'm sure she'll be ok. Babies are quite resilient". I smile to try to boost her confidence but she is still sobbing. We walk to the office and credit to the guy in there, as soon as he finds out what happened he calls an ambulance and sits the mother down near the electric fire in the corner and offers her a cup of tea, reassuring her that her baby will almost certainly be fine but a visit to the hospital would be best, just to be on the safe side.

I thank him, say goodbye to her and make my way to the Nick for my shift.

For all of these incidents except the 'Dropped Baby' one, I was criticised officially by COLP. Official policy is that you have to phone the Control Room Inspector as soon as you can and make a PNB entry about off duty Interventions, mainly because your warrant number is visible under the badge and if anyone complains about you, you are able to say "well here's my version of events, recorded at the time or as near as possible".

For the 'Spitting on a Train' incident I was told that I could have been stabbed. That there were ten of them. That it wasn't that big a deal and I had put myself at unnecessary risk just to prove a point. My response that I wasn't stabbed, that even though there were ten of them they'd all done what they were told AND that the train guard was appreciative I'd done it, fell on deaf ears.

For the 'Irate Spanish Motorist' incident I was told that I should have left them to it and couldn't the other motorist have looked after himself? My retort that they were squabbling next to a busy road was not acknowledged.

For the 'Fat Fellow on Folding Bicycle' incident I was NOT criticised for intervening but instead for not having physically detained the lad with the nosebleed when he ran off. My argument that he was with a mate and that I was trying to defuse the situation while getting the cyclist to keep his distance AND take a potentially lethal weapon (the beer bottle) off one of them was again ignored.

It all added up to become fuel to the fire that eventually led to the suspension of free travel on my Warrant Card on London public transport. The final incident was this:

A week or so before Christmas 2005 and me and some pals were on the Piccadilly Line heading out of London at about 11pm. It was busy and standing room only, being a Saturday night and a lot of people were coming back from the pub and some appeared drunk. A middle aged, rather shy looking, bespectacled woman was sitting in the same carriage and a group of about six people got on the train and stood near to her and they were laughing and talking loudly. After a few minutes I heard one of them say "come on leave this poor woman alone" and was attempting to pull one of the group, a blonde female away from the seated woman. The blonde was holding onto the horizontal bar above the seats with both hands and trying to talk with the woman who looked visibly scared and started to cry.

The blonde wouldn't budge so I walked over.

"Excuse me you need to move away".

The blonde and her friend both rounded on me.

"Who the fuck are you?" the friend said. Well dressed, apparently in her 30s she appeared to be drunk as did the blonde.

"Police".

"Let's see your badge then" she challenges.

"Sure" I get the badge out and show her.

"That's not real".

"Yes it is"

"It's not Met" she observantly points out.

"I know it's not Met, it's City of London"

"That's not real"

"Yes it is. At the moment there's no problem here, but I don't think this lady wants to talk to you" I glance down at the woman who is now holding her face and is still crying. The blonde continues to glare at me but says nothing. The one man in their group then realises what's going on and moves towards me.

"Are you causing trouble?" he snarls "what are you interfering for?"

"He's trying to pretend he's a copper" the woman who asked me for the ID tells him.

"I am a Police officer and like I said at the moment there's no problem but it you don't back off and look after your friend I'll pull the handle and you can be escorted off by Police at the next station". In my best Betari's Box mode, as per Training, I am standing facing them with both arms raised and my palms up, the thumb of my right hand holding the wallet open to reveal the warrant card. One of the other women in the group reaches over to take the badge, I move my hand away.

"That's not a real badge" the woman insists again.

"If you want to think that that's up to you" I reply "but like I said I can have you arrested at the next station. No problem at this time but just back off ok"

"What's he so fucking nervous for?" another asks nastily, looking at the blonde.

I think 'because I'm fucking shitting myself facing six pissheads on a Saturday night with only my badge on me' but reply "like I said just leave her alone ok?"

They swear and mutter a bit more and finally get bored of me and move away slightly, turning around and talking amongst themselves, the conversation forgotten. I turn to the seated woman, still blubbing but now into a crumpled handkerchief. "You alright luv?" I ask her.

"Yes, she didn't say anything horrible she just really frightened me" she replies sniffing.

"Do you want me to get off at the same station as you? I can walk you off the train if you want".

"No I'll be fine, thank you" she smiles and puts her tissue back in her handbag.

"Ok, but do me a favour, get off at the door near me and not this one, because if you do you'll have to walk through them".

She nods and I move back to my friends.

Weeks later at my quarterly review my supervisor stated that in light of my gung ho attitude to off duty Interventions and lack of common sense he was going to suspend my free travel until the next quarterly review. I sat there gobsmacked and asked why.

"That incident with the woman on the train last Christmas. There was no serious risk to life or property" he tells me.

"That woman was crying" I state, not believing he's doing this.

"Doesn't matter" he says curtly "no serious risk to life or property, you put yourself at unnecessary risk". There's a pause and he then adds "and off the record Lance I think you enjoy the warm, fuzzy feeling of being a hero just a little too much".

"That woman was visibly terrified, there were six of them" I try to protest.

He holds up the relevant part of the Force policy on off duty Interventions to prove he's telling the truth and not making it up.

"It's here in black and white"

"So what was I supposed to have done?" I ask angrily.

"You should have stood there and let it happen" he replies "I don't think at this stage of your career you have enough common sense to justify using your Warrant Card to travel".

I am monumentally annoyed with this decision. Just fucking stand there for Chrissakes! That poor cow was shitting herself.

"If the price of free travel is having to stand there and watch people being treated like that then I'd rather not have it at all".

He writes down what I just said and replies without looking up "that's up to you".

A few weeks later we attended our monthly Training club and were met by the sight of fellow Special Stewart wearing his full dress uniform and tunic. Unsure as to why we were then introduced to the new Chief Superintendent who told us the following story.

"While travelling on the train home from work six months ago

Stewart was sitting in the carriage when he heard what sounded like an Asp opening and being closed again. He approached a gentleman in the same carriage and identified himself as a Police officer off duty and asked the man why he had the Asp. The man did not have a lawful excuse for having the weapon. Even though the gentleman was totally compliant, he was with another man when Stewart arrested him, cautioned him and called for the Police to meet them at the next stop where the man was taken to the nearest Police Station for questioning. I would like to thank Stewart for his courage in dealing with this situation and remaining calm while arresting the man even though he did not have his PPE or any Appointments with him. I would also like to thank him for taking a dangerous offensive weapon out of public circulation. It is my great pleasure to award Stewart with this certificate to recognise his bravery".

Stewart then walked to the front, shook the Chief Super's hand and a photo was taken of him accepting his certificate in its wooden frame. We all clapped politely and I silently bit my lip so hard it bled.

PUBLIC DISPLAY OF AFFECTION

While in the Writing Room on a particularly dull and rainy Thursday evening I checked my Force e-mail to find one from Snow Hill's Chief Inspector.

"Lance, please make an appointment to see me. Call my secretary and she will arrange"

I'm a volunteer, probationary Special. He's the CI. What does he want with me? No one else is CC'd into this e-mail so it's doubtful that other people even know that he wants to see me.

Shit!

Oh well, bite the rubber bullet.

I call his secretary the next day and luckily he has a vacant slot at 3pm that afternoon. I grab it and travel from Wimbledon to St Paul's by train and Tube wondering just what the hell he wants to see me about that would not need the involvement of my own line managers or even the Commandant.

At about 2.55pm I approach his office. The door is propped open with a wedge and he's tapping away on his PC. I'm working up the bottle to cough to get his attention when he looks up, smiles and says "hello mate, come in. Take a seat".

Something's odd. He's very friendly and appears uncomfortable.

"Do you want me to shut the door Sir?"

"Yeah", he says as I struggle to prise the wedge free with my foot.

The door slides into place with a thunk and he walks around the desk, holding two pieces of A4 paper in his hand.

Looking visibly embarrassed he asks "do you know Jennifer Wigam?"

"Yes sir, she's a friend of mine".

"Humph! Yes I thought she probably was" he replies, raising his eyes heavenwards and still not looking at me in the face.

"She hasn't got a problem with you, I'd like to make that quite clear. However a senior officer says you walked up to her in front of everybody and gave her a kiss, is that true?"

"Yes sir, I hadn't seen her for a while and was pleased to see her. In fact when I did it I remember her response was to say 'I hear you've got a new job my lovely'".

"Like I said, she hasn't got a problem with you. But this senior officer thought that she didn't appreciate the attention and he says here that at 6.30pm on the 27th January you walked up to her in the Writing Room, said 'give us a kiss' and kissed her on her left cheek". He is now reading directly from the papers in his hand.

"He approached her and asked her if she minded you doing that and she replied 'no, they do it in the pub all the time".

He then tells me who the senior officer was. I am more annoyed than surprised, mainly because I saw him that night and several times since and he'd said absolutely nothing to me about this.

"Sir, if Jennifer hasn't got a problem with this then why am I here?"

"I know. I even had to go and see the Superintendent to ask whether or not I needed to see you because as I said to him, there's no complaint here". He sits on the edge of his desk. "This is going straight in the confidential waste when you've gone" he tells me, looking at the papers in distaste.

I am now more relaxed, realising that the CI is simply offering advice.

"All I'm saying is for fuck's sake be careful. The same thing happened to me. I was in the canteen and a friend of mine, woman I've known for 20 years came up to me and said 'Hi! How are you?' and put her arm around my shoulder and I put my arm round hers. Next thing I know someone from the Home Office who was in that day came up to me privately and said that it was the most disgusting and inappropriate display they'd ever seen".

"Sir, why didn't he talk to me about this himself? I mean I saw him after I kissed Jennifer just before I left to go home and his parting words were 'are you off now? Right, bye' ".

"I don't know and I'm sorry to have to bring you in for this and away from your day job, but all I'm saying is for fuck's sake be careful. I'll be talking to him about this as soon as possible because THIS" he says raising the papers and pointing with the index finger of his right hand "is a load of bollocks". With that he tears it in two and ceremoniously throws it in the huge confidential waste bin to the right of his desk.

He picks up his desk phone and begins making a call, looking up at me and nodding, signalling the meeting is over.

At the next quarterly review my supervisor stated that he'd heard all about how rude I'd been to two female Specials, ignoring them completely in order to single Jennifer out for affection. He added that the senior officer who had reported me had done it for my lack of good manners and had told him this personally.

He then demanded to know what I was laughing at and became quite angry when I explained the truth. Only after I stated four times that I wanted it put to bed did he agree not to take the matter up further to find out why he'd been lied to.

Months later Jennifer called me out of the blue to say she had only just found out that I had been to see the CI and she was really sorry.

Apparently the senior officer had taken her into a room and asked her to raise a grievance against me but she'd told him to get lost, adding "whatever issues you have, don't make me part of them". She then informed him she would be making a PNB entry about the conversation and walked out of the room.

Why the hell he insisted on pursuing this even after Jennifer told him to shove off is anyone's guess. The back pedalling in changing his story only goes to show he was clearly aware that he'd made a right tit of himself.

TAZERS

Something our colonial cousins in America have been using for yonks are Tazers or Stun Guns.

A Tazer is a CED or Conducted Energy Device that is usually yellow and blue and has two barbs in a detachable case that locks onto the front. It kind of resembles a water pistol and has the lovely deterrent factor of a red laser dot to put off troublemakers before they start. It's a piece of piss to use, you just point and pull the trigger and has no recoil as it's compressed gas that fires the barbs out the front and into your Suspect.

They apparently make no noise when fired, beyond the snap of the casing release, and it's only if you miss with one barb that you get the movie effect of "crackling" as the charge arcs while 10,000 volts give the bad person a severe case of the tickles.

They are more effective than spray. Less dangerous than batons and unless you're wearing a pacemaker are not going to cause lasting trauma. They incapacitate a victim completely during the time the 10,000 volts are being released into their twitching body but have no lasting side effects. Former Chief Constable of Greater Manchester Mike Todd even let himself be filmed getting shot with one (would have loved to know how they chose who fired it) just to prove how safe they are (this has since turned up on YouTube if anyone fancies a giggle). Despite all these positive aspects though, in all but a select handful of Forces, they are only carried by Firearms officers.

Just how scared English cops are to use force and how far up its own arse The Human Rights Act is, can be illustrated by the following tale, reported in the UK press a couple of years ago.

Avon and Somerset Police were trialling these things with regular Beat officers when a prisoner went berserk in his cell and wrenched the toilet free of its moorings, smashing it to pieces. He then wrenched the exposed water pipe free and proceeded to knock holes in the wall plaster. Not content with this he then took a dump on the cell floor and wiped it on the walls and the CCTV camera.

This is where it gets silly.

Picture the scene of this immensely strong creature wielding an iron bar and strutting like some feral warthog round the cell, which is a mixture of broken furniture, flooding water and his own faeces.

Common sense would dictate getting five of the biggest blokes you could find and running in there with a riot shield, tazering the little bastard and leaving him in an ERB suit, trussed up like a chicken (with half hourly release and tightening of the Velcro straps for blood flow purposes) until he goes to see the Beak in the morning.

However...

For "Health and Safety" reasons they had to move the gentleman to another cell. An officer is quoted as having said "we told him that we needed to put him in another cell and that he would be handcuffed and asked him if he was happy for us to do that. He said that we could come and try which didn't fill us with much confidence that he was going to comply".

I am still trying to picture the Bobby using his best Betari's Box training to spark up a rapport with a shit stained, psychotic and obviously immensely strong prisoner who has just ripped the carzy off the wall. I try not to wince when further imagining the same Bobby saying "err, excuse me. Would you be happier in another, less faeces- covered cell? I believe number 11 is free".

When the reply was the expected Neanderthal grunts and verbal abuse (and one would imagine, the cop dodging handfuls of shit flying out of the hatch and the pipe banging off the door), they finally went in, tazered him and got him out.

The fact that someone holding a Stun Gun was merely trying to reason with a prisoner behaving like this only goes to show just how arse over tit the whole thing is.

While US documentary TV cop shows have names like "Scum on the Run" or "The Graveyard Shift" we have well intentioned but ineffectual bullshit like "PCSOs in Action" (oxymoron if there ever was one) and possibly in the future "Let's All Have a Nice Cuppa and Talk About It".

Trying to only reason with animals like this is unfortunately what The Job has become over the years.

THE LONDON MARATHON

There are two compulsory duties per year that Specials in the City of London are required to attend. One is the Lord Mayor's show as they are needed to line the square mile in red and white checks and form an impressive wall for the entourage to gently coast by in their limos. The other is the London Marathon as hundreds of cops from both Met and COLP are used for Public Order.

Muster for the Marathon was 6am in Snow Hill writing room, to be taken en masse to Bishopsgate for a breakfast and allocated a group. When we get there the tables are packed with bleary-eyed Specials and Regulars and the CI is knocking about as he's the highest rank on duty and is personally commandeering the whole thing for the square mile. After I get a brew and a plate of subsidised cholesterol and wait for the caffeine to kick in I spy the CI, huge shoulders swinging, making a path through the black and white scrum of shirts and clip-on ties to the food hatches.

I nudge Jason, who's sitting next to me, thinking what I'm about to say will be a revelation. "That CI. I had to go and see him recently. I got reported for kissing Jennifer".

"I know" he says matter of factly, glugging his tea. "She told the officer to fuck off when he asked her".

"You know?" I ask, surprised.

"Yes, I was in the room when you kissed her remember? He took her into a room and asked her to make a complaint against you but she told him to fuck off".

"Shit! I thought no one but me and those three knew".

"No, she told me straight after. She wasn't happy about it. Wasting time as per usual".

At 7.30 we make our way out to the mini buses and are taken out to watch over a designated spot for the next few hours. It's already tiddling with rain and cold, but I'm assured that this will make the whole thing easier to bear as I'm in winter issue uniform and therefore won't collapse from heat stroke.

I get a nice dual carriageway bit facing the entrance/ exit to a large tunnel. For the first hour or two nothing happens and I'm bored and wet. The cordons are designated and pre-arranged to be "activated" (i.e. the tape strung across the road) at 9am. This results in myself and the other two (and probably most other people manning the route) getting hungover late stayers from Saturday night's revelry approaching us, startled that they will effectively have their car trapped within the cordon for the next eight to ten hours unless they move it sharpish. Even though the signs have been up warning about this for about two months, the selective blindness of Joe and Josephine Public prevails yet again and we patiently explain that unless they move it now they are stranded till about 4pm. I get a cup of well intentioned but particularly horrid coffee off one grateful bloke and then someone comes by with squidgy cartons of Lucozade to perk up our flagging energy.

At 10am the junior marathoners hurtle through and like a cowboy finding refuge from the buffalo stampede behind a rock, I'm obliged to stand behind the "keep right" bollard in the central reservation in order to avoid being trampled by 200 teenagers in singlets and Nikes. Ten minutes later the slobs of this particular lot limp through, puffing and panting and obviously not fit enough to do anything with the Marathon except watch it on telly. I give one my Lucozade as he's clearly in some distress, red faced and clinging on to the nearest lamp post, struggling for breath.

By about 11 the crowds begin to gather and I realise the stupidity of having a long, Christmas ribbon-esque "Do Not Cross" tape, extending 25 metres and expecting dozens of people on my section to obediently stand behind it. While there's clearly no deliberate desire to pull it down or wreck it, by about 3pm I'll have adjusted, extended and tied the bloody thing back more times than I'll have shouted "GET OFF THAT WALL!" to people dangling their legs over the edge of a 20 foot drop on the other side of the road.

I am facing mile marker 24, two miles from the end which I don't actually attach any importance to initially, not realising the human misery I'm going to be witnessing in about four hours.

First of all the shiny, sinewy, not-panting-at-all runners come through after a ridiculously short time. Something like an hour and a half after the race began. Waving at anyone who hoots or cheers as they gently hurtle past at a furious pace, like it's no bother. I am supremely jealous.

Around half an hour later a call comes through on the Airwave to say that the Gold Commander (a Met Superintendent) is watching the Marathon on BBC1 and has noticed that we are facing the race instead of the crowd like we are supposed to. Could ALL officers on crowd control now turn and face the public. I am amused at the thought of the Gold Commander for the whole op (our CI presumably being Silver) watching the race on a telly in his office with his feet up, dunking digestives into his tea.

It's still relatively clear at this point on the route and when people start taking the piss I leap into action, glad for the respite from standing still for hours and occasionally adjusting the tape that yet again has been pulled down by the weight of various spectators and the inquisitive fingers of their knee-high offspring. Four times I'm obliged to "word" people that walk directly across the runners' path in order to make it to my side of the road, including one daft cow who wanted to ask me directions.

By about 12.30pm the route is now a constant, fast flowing river of shorts and thudding trainers. No way to get across unless you want a bony pile-up and a lot of cursing.

About 1.25pm my Airwave squawks telling me to take refs in the mini bus, meaning a 400 yard stroll to where Daniel (formidable Advanced driver, built like an ox) and William are milling about handing out the lunch bags to those who wander up, piss-wet through from nearly six hours of drizzle. The lunches are their usual standard of school-packed lunch, pre-Jamie Oliver sugar and fat and

I'm surprised to find mineral water as opposed to blue Panda Pops amongst the Mars, Walker's Cheese & Onion and Custard Creams. The only lavvy we can use is within a council building to the left of the convoy and we conspicuously slip in there for a waz before rejoining the gently heaving mass of humanity that's come to cheer on the runners.

The significance of being on Mile Marker 24 didn't sink in until about three to four hours after the Marathon started. I naively believed that all people attempting this would attain a basic level of fitness before running what is a far from easy race.

Around four hours into this and what looks like the wounded from the D-Day Landing first aid tent come limping and hobbling out of the tunnel, dragging bits of their bodies behind them, wincing and groaning in what is clearly a lot of pain. The tunnel is dark and we are in the grey but still fairly bright daylight. The whole thing resembles some biblical scene of the damned being evicted from Hell. In one case a woman is hopping on one leg, another stopping every 50 yards, hands on hips puffing red-faced and then closing her eyes before continuing. I'm only human and after about half an hour of having to witness all this abject suffering I happen to make eye contact with one poor woman who's clearly in agony and limping along at a snail's pace, her right foot scraping along next to her.

"Please!" I say looking at her. "St John's Ambulance are just behind you. Please get some medical attention".

She manages to half-smile, "thank you, but I'm going to finish" she replies, raising herself up straight and setting her eyes on Mile Marker 25.

We have a lot of cops using bikes to patrol the Beat in the City, mainly because it's easier to squeeze through the shitty London traffic on a Specialized than in a Skoda. An officer on a bicycle riding alongside the runners and through the crowd approaches me. He has three pips on each shoulder so I stand by to let him pass, nod as he approaches and say "Sir". It's only after he's gone past that I see on his back "St John's Ambulance", who have a similar rank structure. He got larey with Daniel further up who tore him a new arsehole and ordered him off.

Finally, like a tap slowly being turned off, the runners fade out to a slow trickle of the very unfit, the very fancy-dressed or the very don't-care and the crowds drift away.

Before long the sight of the massive cleaning up job that some poor sod will have to do becomes apparent as the road is littered for miles in either direction with hundreds of discarded Lucozade squidgy packs. Boredom being the herald of temptation I stamp on a few, taking delight in watching sometimes full packs arc their contents into the air. This is all fun until I stomp on one that is pointing at me and the contents shoot up my right leg, bypassing my Magnum boots and drenching me all the way up to my undies.

Yuck!

Standing still to attempt to dry off I am approached by an Inspector who asks me how the day has gone and then says just how much fun it is to stamp on the empty Lucozade packets.

Finally at 5.30pm we sit in the mini bus waiting for Gold to tell Silver that we are free to bugger off. Daniel looks at us thoughtfully and then says:

"I get paid for standing in the rain for hours. What's your motivation?"

EXIT INTERVIEW

An Exit Interview is a right that all Specials and Regulars have on either retirement or resignation. The DO offered to do it and stated that the Commandant was also willing to see me but I wrote back saying that I would like to see the Chief Inspector, the same one who had dealt with the 'Kissing on the Left Cheek' fiasco.

An appointment was arranged for a week after I quit and when I got there was told by Front Desk to go and sit in his office as he was running late.

Half an hour after the scheduled time he walks in and sees me sitting in the comfy chair near the door reading Empire magazine.

"Sorry I'm late" he says looking embarrassed "former Chief Super' wanted to see me then the current one".

I stand up and shake his hand "it's ok. Thanks for agreeing to see me".

He sits down, opens a large, A4 sized notebook and begins with "so did you enjoy your time with the Specials and are there any improvements you think we can make?"

As I start talking he writes down what I say. As I have a lot of things I want to say I notice after about two minutes that he is frantically scribbling away in an effort to keep up. These Interviews are clearly formalities and I don't think he expected to have me go off on one with a long speech.

I get around to mentioning other officers and say that I have nothing but respect for my former SO Godfrey and the

Commandant. I also name an Inspector I think is very good and a couple of other cops. The CI looks up from writing.

"As you've said how good you think they are....I take it you're not too enamoured with the officer who reported you for kissing Jennifer then?"

I smile and realise he must have spotted that I left this bloke out completely. Oh well, you don't get to CI by not being observant and ignoring what was deliberately NOT said.

"Call it a Significant Silence" I reply and he smiles. "Whatever his motivation was for reporting me for doing that it's never been divulged. Jennifer didn't even know I'd been to see you until months later and as soon as she found out she rang to say she was sorry. I had to explain you'd made it clear at the time that it wasn't her fault I was in front of you. I mean...I saw him on the stairs, twenty minutes after I'd kissed her. He must have just spoken to her or knew he was about to and he didn't say a dicky bird to me".

"If you join the Regulars you will meet people like him, difference is there will be other people around to support you" the CI tells me.

"Hmmm...it was just pointless. She even said that she'd told him to shove off when he asked her to make a complaint. Every time me and Jennifer meet now we always kiss on the left cheek because of that. You seemed embarrassed to even SEE me that day when I came up here. My biggest problem with the Specials is not the people or the Force. I'm proud to have served and been a part of this. Did you know Operation Stage was my idea?"

He nods.

"I mean, how proud do you think I was? An idea adopted as an official Force policy! Thing is there is a supreme lack of communication".

He smiles and says "I am having a meeting about the Specials in half an hour. I was going to raise some of the points you've mentioned anyway but thanks for telling me this. It's different if it comes from one of the ground troops". He looks at me quizzically, then says "when's your Assessment Centre for the other Force?"

"Next Wednesday".

He writes the date down in his book then says "let us know how you get on yeah".

I'm surprised at that but promise to let him know then say "one final thing. I've also noticed there's a lot of whispering behind people's backs".

"Go on..."

"At the Specials Annual Dinner the Commissioner walked past my table. I stood up and asked him 'excuse me Sir, can I have my photograph taken with you? My mother was very proud of me on July 7th'. He was nice as pie about it, even suggested we stand in front of the coat of arms, shook my hand and thanked me for July 7th. Later on I found out from a senior officer that that 'generated feedback' from other people who were there. I mean what's that all about?"

The CI shakes his head and smiles, "it's not a problem".

"Exactly, I mean if he had a problem with it, surely he'd have told me himself or I would have been spoken to by someone else later. What it probably was was people who wanted their pictures taken with him but didn't have the bottle to ask him".

He smiles and nods again, then closes his book. "Thanks for coming in. It's good to hear things from a fresh perspective and good luck with the future".

We shake hands and I leave.

The City of London Special Constabulary is well funded, well stocked, well respected by the COLP Regulars and a Force I'm proud to have served with. Unlike a lot of Special Constabularies, the COLP is in such a small area that they mingle all the time with their paid counterparts and often there is no visible division between the two. The Commandant of my time is still there at time of writing this book and just after I left they achieved their target of Specials for the first time ever. Now there are about 90 of them.

I like to think of the COLP as the Spartan Army. A tiny Force of loyal warriors, bound together by an unswerving sense of duty, but surrounded by much larger Forces that are constantly trying to conquer and engulf them.

ASSESSMENT DAY

The assessment process to join the Police is now a national standard, run by a company called Centrex. That way all the questions are the same, every Force is "playing on an even field" with regard to standards and if one Force changes stuff then the others do too.

When I filled out my application it was online. The form consisted of 25 pages and most was the common sense stuff like previous addresses, medical history, next of kin and qualifications before you got to the meat and gravy of what it takes to be a 21st century Police officer, COMPETENCIES. There were four BIG questions that had to be answered in depth. You were graded accordingly on them, with regard to prioritising, common sense and that old chestnut Race & Diversity.

The first question started with the line "It is very important that Police officers deliver an excellent service and develop good working relationships with members of the public" and went on to ask you to recall an occasion where someone was upset with service they'd been given or how they'd been treated. You were told to try and use an example where you'd done more than simply listen to them moaning.

I mentioned how a staff member at a summer camp I'd run had approached me to say he was pissed off with me insisting the kids say 'please' and 'thank you' when I was not saying them myself. I apologised, stated that my lapse was not intentional and that I would remedy the situation by talking to the other staff at the weekly meeting and invite people to pick me up if it happened again.

Question two was a right beauty and began: "It is vitally important that Police officers respect the lifestyle, culture or beliefs of others even if these differ significantly from the officer's own views". It then went on to ask you to give an example of where you'd shown respect for someone with a deep-rooted belief and how you adapted what you said or did to show sensitivity to the difference between you and the other person.

A college in London I worked at had a high Muslim population of both students and staff. Without telling anyone they commandeered the library for the Friday prayer meeting. The first I knew of this was when I stepped out of the internal fire escape at the back of the library, after having changed out of my cycling gear to find myself face down on the floor after tripping over a kneeling worshipper who had come in and knelt down on his prayer mat while I was switching clothes. Also their shoes were left in the corridor causing a health and safety and evacuation risk. I raised it with the college President and stated that while I respected Muslims' desire to pray there needed to be more communication with the rest of the faculty so anyone not involved would know what was going on and why the library was out of use. Further, we arranged to put the shoes in an empty classroom.

Question 3 was "It is vital that Police officers take personal responsibility for getting things done without having to be told. Tell us about an occasion when you have taken the initiative and gone beyond what others would have done".

I cited an Off Duty Intervention as a Special.

And finally was the wonderful no. 4. "Police officers' time is valuable and they need to manage their own time and work load effectively. Think of a day when you were under a lot of pressure to do a number of things at the same time. You will be assessed in this question on the way you decided the order that things should be done".

This was my juggling of responsibilities on July 7th 2005 between running the summer camp and wanting to attend duty in the aftermath of the terrorist attacks. I simply listed the sequence in which I'd done things.

At no point on the form did it ask the question "Why exactly do you want to be a copper?"

I got the form back a couple of months later to find I'd got high grades, had made it through Paper Sift and would be contacted in the future for an Assessment Centre.

Once a fortnight I would ring the Force Recruitment department to ask if they had a place and was always politely told 'no' and told just as politely that they would call me when a place DID become available.

When the Assessment Centre day rolled around six weeks later it was seven hours of Diversity-based interviews, Diversity-based role plays and a bit of maths and English to pad it out.

This was again held at the Police College where the accommodation block was turned over to Recruitment for the role plays and interviews while the exams took place in the main block's classrooms.

In groups of 10 or so, candidates were shepherded around the college in order to keep us away from other groups who were also under guard. The whole thing was run with military precision and we had to avoid the others, avoid talking to the others and avoid discussing what we'd done with each other on pain of instant expulsion.

My group got Interviews first. This should have been a one-to-one chat on our motivation for wanting to join The Job and what qualities you felt you could bring to the modern Police force. Predictably the first question I was asked was again "when did you last hear a sexist, racist or homophobic comment and what did you do about it?"

If I'd been honest I would have replied "like most people I want a quiet life and try not to get involved in things that might get my head kicked in or, at the lower end of the scale, make me unpopular with my peers. But hey, if you give me a chance and give me the assertiveness training needed to deal with this type of thing then I'll be out there fighting homophobia, racism and sexism with the best of them".

However.

I told him about challenging an irate train passenger for calling the revenue inspector "baboo" while working as a Special Constable (all I did was say "don't say that again").

It got me a B grade.

After the maths test (clearly aimed at GCSE level) there were the Big Brother-esque delights of Role Plays.

Four separate scenarios. Groups of four. We were sat at a table outside a door with a number on it. Inside was another candidate doing the same scenario. A buzzer sounded. We were then given five minutes to read a scenario from an A4 laminate. They all said at the top in bold type and underlined:

"YOU ARE NOT A POLICE OFFICER. YOU ARE A CUSTOMER SERVICES MANAGER OF A FICTIONAL SHOPPING CENTRE".

Five minutes later a second buzzer sounded and I walked into a room to find an actor sitting there. Further back is an assessor, pen poised over a fresh marking form with many tick boxes. As soon as I walked in the actor looked up and said "I'm Mr Jones, I understand you wanted to see me". This one had been receiving homophobic abuse from a colleague. I ask him what he'd like me to do about it. He says he wants it to stop. I suggest that the other person might not realise the effect his actions are having. The actor concedes this point. I try to gain brownie points by offering him a copy of the equality policy. He replied that he hasn't brought his reading glasses (evil bastard). I countered by offering a large print version sent via his place of work.

My second attempt was a woman who'd had a row with a car park attendant at the shopping mall as her and another customer squabbled over the same parking space. Both the attendant and the other driver spoke Urdu and she felt she was the victim of racism, particularly as the other bloke got given the space.

The third was an elderly lady whose granddaughter had been pushed over by "young hooligans" and a security guard she tried to flag down had simply walked away. I had to explain that he was on his way to deal with a heart attack on the 3rd floor and was not ignoring her and had in fact got on his radio to call for someone else to deal with her.

The Recruitment personnel that babysat us throughout the day had forewarned us that if we ticked all the required boxes for having dealt with the role play satisfactorily then the actor facing us would stop talking, lower their head and look away, remaining like this until the final buzzer sounded.

I had the luxury of this reaction from actor no.3 and it's quite unsettling to witness as one moment they are chatting and the next they are slumped motionless, head drooped like a marionette with the strings severed.

Scenario 4 was a woman who wanted me to ban the gypsies from the centre who'd set up camp nearby, claiming they were stealing from her shop even though she couldn't prove it. I had a laminate of crime statistics to prove that the shoplifting had in fact decreased since they arrived.

Finally we got to push off home, and were politely told to wait at least 28 days before ringing to check the results because if we rang before that they would politely tell us to push off.

None of this touched upon policing or being a Police officer. It evaluated your ability to sell yourself, your ability to placate those with something to get off their chests and your ability to solve basic problems of logic and mathematics.

Four weeks later and the form arrived to say I'd passed. I'd got 100% in both written and verbal communication but only 62% in Race and Diversity, giving me an overall grade of 65%. You are not allowed to get ANY low grades below a 'C' in R&D. If you do your application will fail, no matter how well you do in the other areas. The minimum pass was 60%.

The accompanying letter stated that I was now being offered a conditional place with the Police and would be contacted to attend Training in the near future.

Once a week I rang Recruitment to ask if they knew when I would be called up. They said they didn't know. After a couple of months of this I'd just finished a chat with someone who had said "you can stop calling us. When we have a place we WILL contact you" when the phone rang and it was someone else from the same department, oblivious of the conversation their colleague on the other side of the room had just had with me.

"Someone's just dropped out of next month's Intake. Can you take it?"

After I climbed off the ceiling I excitedly said that of course I could take it and was silently grateful that I'd written "willing to relocate anywhere at one week's notice" on my application form. They booked me in for a fitness test and a medical the following week.

THE FITNESS TEST

The Fitness Test was originally a baptism by fire for anyone who hadn't kept themselves in above reasonable shape and would separate the wheat from the chaff in no time at all. The Couch Potato eliminator was the infamous and hugely unpopular (with the unfit at least) Bleep Test.

You start at one side of the gym. A CD is played. A countdown begins. At zero a double bleep is heard and you have to run to the other side of the room and back before the next double bleep. Fairly easy, the only spittle on the stay-pressed is that the bleeps keep getting closer together. You are allowed two consecutive failures to reach the other side in time and on your third failure you will be sent off and will have failed your Fitness Test if you hadn't made it to the required minimum level before crashing out.

Now...

Firearms have a pass mark of 8.1 which is reasonably hard but not impossible unless you are the kind of slob who gets joggers' high from going up a flight of stairs due to drinking and smoking too much. This will test you, isn't too unpleasant BUT will weed out those too soggy around the midsection to cut the mustard.

All officers used to have this pass mark.

Then one day someone thought "hey there's all these recruits who aren't getting in due to failing the bleep test. Is it not discriminatory to restrict access to people just because they're unfit? Surely that's Unfitist. In fact, while we're on the subject, a lot of women aren't getting in due to 8.1 which means the whole system is institutionally sexist"

So...they changed it.

The pass mark was lowered to 5.4 which means tall, skinny people picked on for looking like a Daddy Long Legs at school will be able to lope across the hall without breaking sweat and only the most slothful will fail to achieve the grade.

The other part of the basic Fitness Test is push/ pull which is meant to help you to:

a). Push Harry Hooligan away from you to create our friend The Reactionary Gap.

b). Enable you to hang on to Billy Burglar if he won't come quietly, while you fumble for your Compliant Cuffs.

Pass marks for these two (on the same machine, you just change seats) are again at a low level which means nearly everyone makes it.

A guy I worked with was clinically obese and sweated if the window was closed in the car. He lived on Guinness and pies and is the last person on Earth I'd want to have my back in a violent arrest at whichever pub travellers have temporarily made their local.

The rationale for reducing the level to 5.4 was explained as to enable more women to get into the Force.

Thing is, the only people to get to level 18....were two women.

EQUIPMENT

Upon joining the Police, a couple of weeks before you start Training, you attend the Procurement office to be fitted for a uniform. In both the Specials and the Regulars this is a fairly lengthy process, almost as complex as being fitted for a Saville Row suit at a bespoke tailors.

Your waist and inside leg are measured (but they don't ask which side you dress on), your shoe size taken, your chest and neck measured and also your head to ensure the tit helmet fits correctly and doesn't either give you a migraine or slip down to your nose.

Then you try on gloves, overcoats, Traffic jackets, Hi Viz jackets, winter jackets, a patrol cap or two and a Load Belt. After all this is done you are then fitted for a tunic (for the Specials Annual Dinner, going to see The Old Man or Passing Out) and nip into a changing room to bung on some shirts and trousers, a Hot Fuzz sweater and a winter fleece.

After all this they will finally take your measurements for a Stab Proof Vest.

A Stabby is a useful tool for the modern Bobby to have, especially with the proliferation of blades on the streets. Bullet Proof vests are only worn by the Firearms Unit. This is NOT a psychological statement to the Public that the UK doesn't have a gun problem as even Beat cops aren't afraid of getting shot at, it's because the thinner the Kevlar the cheaper the vest.

It's a big, bulky thing that fits snugly against your chest and is secured by Velcro and a zip. It will stop all blades swung by a human hand (or a pissed off gorilla) and is in theory able to resist low velocity bullets (presumably those with the same force as a party popper). All of the ones I saw, including the two I was issued with, looked like a Spice Girls crop top as they ended around the belly button meaning anyone who wanted to examine a cop's intestinal tract had only to aim just above their belt buckle.

The bloody thing was immensely hot in summer and the cheap cotton shirts don't wick away the sweat. This meant your shirt stuck to your back even in mild sunshine and you would just have to put up with it. On Refs you would see most Stabbies left to one side while the officers they belonged to tried to dry out.

The ties are clip-on for the common sense reason that in a ruck a Suspect who tugs on it will simply end up holding it and not you as well, blue in the face and choking.

The shirts are white, with both short and long sleeves and have loops for the cables on the now defunct Police radios, used in the days before Airwave.

You get three pairs of trousers. Two for Patrol which can be machine washed and one 'dry clean only' pair for posh events.

Your Load Belt will hold a torch, holsters for your pepper spray and your ASP plus another for your handcuffs. It will also have a small pouch with a mouth guard in it for giving the kiss of life to some festering old tramp without catching the lurgy.

You aren't issued with boots or shoes and have to buy your own (although in the Specials they did issue us with steel toe capped Public Order boots). As these are one of the most important items of kit it's ludicrous that they make officers cough up for them but again it's all down to saving money.

The biggest problem with all of this was that the tit helmet, smart tie, shirt and trousers didn't gel with the bovver boots, Load Belt and Stabby.

Imagine wearing a denim jacket and suit trousers. Kind of sucks right? Well now imagine wearing most of a suit with military equipment on top. Sucks big time.

The old Dixon of Dock Green image of tunic and cape, with a smart shirt and trousers looks wonderful if that's what you stick with. A traditional authority figure. Mixing that with SWAT team get-up looks plain daft and does nothing to gain respect from the local wrong 'uns.

The Police baton is not given to you until you have been signed off as capable of using it. The original Police truncheon was worn down the trouser leg and not popular with Bobbies on the Beat due to its cumbersome design and bad grip. The replacement was a side handled baton like US cops have that looks great, makes a meaty 'chunka!' noise as you flick it open and will prevent you getting a broken arm if utilised correctly as a defensive weapon against attack with a blunt object.

The modern Police baton is a 21 inch, telescopic, steel stick called an Asp that flicks open with a movement of the wrist. Button-activated ones are illegal to own in the UK, even for Police Forces so we have these instead. They have a rubber grip on the handle and a knobbly bit on the end which you are taught focus the energy of your swing into when taking aim at a Suspect.

Problem with these things is that while incredibly useful if you are taught to utilise them properly (i.e. quickly and at whatever bit you can get access to on the other person's body) they are no use at all if your assailant is drugged up, drunk or even just immensely strong for the simple fact that English cops are told to aim only for the flesh of the upper thighs and the upper arms. Aiming for a bony bit is considered Excessive and we were specifically told NOT to do it in Officer Safety Training. A strike to the head with the rubber baton during role plays would result in the whistle being blown and you having to do it all again. Two strikes and you would fail your OST.

The reason for this instruction is that the upper thighs and arms 'redistribute' the force of the blows and are therefore much less likely to cause severe lasting or even temporary trauma. While wonderful if you are the Suspect, it's a choker for the cop as he or she will be in serious trouble for twatting a Non Compliant Suspect with their Asp and breaking their arm unless they are absolutely able to justify serious risk to their own or another's safety or successfully prove that they were in fact aiming for a safe zone but the person dodged at the last moment.

Another problem is that as they are activated through flicking the wrist out, it's quite easy to let go and have it end up in the middle of the road, under someone's car or over a hedge. Motion away from the body is required to extend them, meaning you have to remember to keep a tight grip on the handle as you open it.

Incapacitant Spray is another issue. A lot of Forces use CS which is a proverbial pig in blender as it cross contaminates everyone in the immediate area of spraying. Once with COLP as a Special I did an undercover Op in a pub, checking for handbag snatchers. We had radios, Asps and cuffs but had been told to leave the CS at the Nick as, due to Health and Safety rules the pub would have to be cleared if CS was 'deployed' in the bar while arresting someone. We were also told not to trigger it in a Public Order situation because if it affected the Dog Handler, then the dog would bite us.

Understandably we were reluctant to use the horrid stuff, as we would probably end up affected as well. It was not even a last resort and more of a "Where the Fuck is the Back Up?" resort.

Pepper Spray is less nasty. It will only affect the person it's sprayed on as it's basically the equivalent of liquefied chillies. That is unless you get the back splash from a burst. A few times officers were seen retching and choking after their partner had squirted someone. Another factor is the weather as it is no good at all if it's windy. One time a van pulled up outside a pub where six lads were having a dust up. The back doors opened, a female PC leapt out, dropped to one knee and dramatically triggered her Pepper Spray at the ne'er do wells. A strong gust of wind caught the jet and redirected it right in the faces of the officers coming out behind her. Cue all six lads stopping fighting, pointing and laughing at the embarrassed WPC and her writhing, screaming colleagues and then running off.

It also only affects the eyes, so if you want to resist arrest remember to wear welder's goggles just before you face off to the Fuzz.

The cuffs were the only 100% useful item in the toolkit. Changed years ago from the chain model they are now a rigid unit with a hand grip in the middle. The metal of the actual cuffs is thin steel and they are called Compliant Cuffs for the simple reason that if you twist them on a Suspect who won't come quietly then they hurt like a bastard as they dig right into the bone of the wrists. They are also useful as their design means that the Suspect, if cuffed to the front, has his hands one over the top of the other, negating any possible attempt to throttle the driver of the Police car driving the Suspect to the Nick.

With all of this you have the tools to pound the Beat in England BUT when you pile out of the Rowdy Van on a Friday night to break up a pub fight remember this...

Everything you are wearing was made by the lowest bidder.

MODERN POLICE TRAINING

Discipline: 'The training of the mind and character to produce self control'.

In the Police, until as recently as 2005 this was given centre stage during the training of recruits. People came into the Force bewildered and wide-eyed and were shaped and moulded into warranted officers.

Basic Training consisted of instruction at a residential centre. You got 15 to 17 weeks of hard, disciplined lessons in the hows, whens and wherefores of being an officer in her Majesty's modern Police (or the Corporation of London's if you were COLP).

You had to "bull" your boots every day, got paraded every morning, marched regularly and were subject to random room inspections where even leaving your shoes out of their designated spot under the sink would result in being docked points.

You stood up for everyone who entered a room. Once, the first time you saw them per day if they were the same rank as you (i.e. a constable) and every time they walked in if they were a skipper or above.

You addressed training instructors as "Staff" and skippers as "Sergeant" (and woe betide anyone who abbreviated that to "Sarge". They would usually be told, at a volume to rival a Motorhead concert "DON'T ABBREVIATE MY SOBRIQUET AND I WON'T ABBREVIATE YOURS. CUNT STUBBLE!!!".

Inspectors and above were "Sir" or "Ma'am" and you had to be back in bed by 11.50pm. You only got to go home on weekends and if you were late back on the Monday morning, you again got docked points and faced the wrath of whoever spotted you sneaking back like a naughty school kid.

Uniforms had to be pristine. You had razor creases on shirts and trousers, the aforementioned mirror shine on boots and shoes and a helmet that was not only on straight but was free from fluff and had its badge symmetrical and gleaming.

Shaving (at least for the men) was compulsory unless you already had a full beard and complaining that there was no hot water would get filthy looks and a seething rant from whichever skipper or Guv'nor had had to brave the icy chill of the cold tap that morning in order to lead by example.

Your marching was practiced and drilled. You had a Passing Out Parade, so were expected to be the business by the time your relatives came to watch you pounding around the skid pan.

You put your helmet/ cap on if outside on campus and had to march between the buildings, even if on your own (which looks daft but hey, it's a rule and ours is not to wonder why).

The whole thing was geared towards professionalism, discipline and respect for the chain of command.

In a nutshell. You KNEW where you were.

It was hard but it made it clear to you and to the world that you were training to be a POLICE OFFICER.

Then....some committee got together and had a meeting and thrashed out a few ideas. Then the Government of the day had a look at the results. Then the overriding factor came into place. It was costing M.O.N.E.Y to train recruits in this manner. A residential place for one officer ran into thousands and it was decided that a radical change was needed. Out would be the bulling, marching and discipline. In would come the world of university based training and going home in the evenings (in theory to enable more diverse elements to join the Force i.e. people who didn't want to leave their families for five days at a time).

They told the recruitment departments to tell the public that this was to enable the officers to be part of the Local Community and to allow a less rigid and more "thinking" Force to emerge.

In reality it was simply to save a few bob and slowly…like the Christmas lights going out on 13th day morning, English and Welsh Forces began to switch to a new and very different scheme.

The first week of Training we were living in the Force Training College near HQ, wearing our uniforms and had discipline. We were inspected, we had to have our caps on between buildings and we had to have our uniforms looking sharp.

But some things had gone. We no longer stood up in class as Staff entered the room for the first time and we didn't stand up at all for Sergeants, only Inspectors and above. We were inspected only once. We didn't march at all.

At uni for the second week of Basic Training we were in civvies. Accommodation was no longer provided and neither was grub. Uniforms had been tried out but it was felt to "intimidate" the general public so they scrapped that idea and allowed jeans and t-shirts, trainers and hoodies. One time I approached the campus Sergeant for a chat and after we'd finished he added "you haven't shaved today".

I rubbed my chin, blushed and said "sorry Sergeant. I shaved last night before I went to bed".

"Well in future shave in the mornings"

"Sorry Sergeant it won't happen again".

As I left his office I caught sight of my reflection in the window opposite and was reminded that I was wearing a 28 Days Later t-shirt, faded blue jeans and a pair of Converse All Star baseball shoes.

One girl on my Intake wore ripped jeans to class. Another lad wore a Scarface t-shirt.

We sat and ate cheese on toast in the canteen and sipped teas or coffees. We called instructors by their first names and only stood up for Inspectors or above (who came in only 6 or 7 times in nine months). We had long lunch breaks and knocked off at 3.30pm (3 o'clock if lucky, 4pm if the Training Inspector was in). We only wore uniform on Special Days involving role plays. We never marched. We were inspected twice in the entire initial 36 weeks.

We were encouraged to ask questions in class because this is, after all, uni based training. They told us they want a 'Thinking

Force'. Having been to uni and achieved a Bachelor's degree I slipped right into this. I think that they want what they say they want. I ask lots of questions. I refuse to give in if I believe I'm right until we've debated the point fully. I like a reasoned argument.

I later found out that I was marked from very early on as an annoying little tit who kept putting his hand up.

The only semblance of discipline we had was when the Training Inspector, Ma'am Postlethwaite was in town but she herself was in civvies when she came to visit.

She would routinely collect our PNBs and write biting comments after the most recent entry. She took no shit off anyone and was the only reminder we had of what our chosen careers really were.

This lack of any routine or organised working life meant that when we were required to be in uniform on campus (for role play days only) it took some getting used to.

Occasionally we had to visit the Police college for Training and this was where the new, slovenly world of uni clashed with the pristine order of HQ and its 90% Old School officers.

Trying to suddenly become disciplined and used to a world of protocol and etiquette is like trying to run the a Marathon after spending nine months slobbing in front of the telly. With no malice or deliberate insubordination, several trainees ended up in front of a ferocious, zero tolerance Acting Inspector who tore them a new arsehole for transgressions that at uni wouldn't have warranted more than a raised eyebrow, if that.

We came down one morning to find four names written on the wipe board near reception. After breakfast the four slightly nervous students made their way up to the Admin floor.

Acting Inspector: (after seeing them waiting) "Are you the people whose names were on the board? YES? RIGHT! IT'S ME YOU'RE HERE TO SEE. (He points at the nearest one) YOU, IN MY OFFICE. THE REST OF YOU WAIT THERE!"

The first two were torn to shreds for the heinous crime of giggling during a visiting RSPCA lecture the day before. One female recruit had hiccups which had made her neighbour laugh. She had then giggled out of embarrassment. The lecturer clocked their Force numbers and reported them.

The second one was asked "do you know what this is about?" and admitted that he'd fallen asleep in class (and said to us all after that he was glad this was why he was there, as he had half expected the Inspector to say "OH! You did THAT as well did you?")

All of these were screamed at, threatened with dismissal and told "REMEMBER MY NAME BECAUSE I CAN MAKE YOUR LIVES ABSOLUTELY MISERABLE! NOW GET OUT!"

The fourth was initially treated with the same barking tones until she started to cry. The AI apparently softened slightly at this point and asked her in a more subdued voice to explain why she'd found it appropriate to stick her fingers in her ears and look at the floor during the RSPCA's showing of a dog fight video.

This was a particularly unpleasant piece of hidden camera footage of two Pit Bulls going at it. One got its jaw round the other dog's back leg and bit down hard, making its opponent squeal and the winning dog's owner say enthusiastically in an Irish accent "go on boy! Good boy!" over and over again.

The trainee explained that she'd found the footage utterly repellent and had gone to bed that night unable to sleep due to the voice in her head saying "go on boy! Good boy" and the sound of the dog whining in pain.

The AI asked her if she had the necessary Resilience to deal with this in real life and she replied "with respect Sir. When will I EVER have to sit and watch a dog fight for five minutes? I would enter the dog fight to stop it".

Of the four she got off without being bawled out, proving that the Acting Inspector was a disciplinarian but not a bully.

Discipline needs to be in place. Set in stone and not up for debate. A fad that had thankfully died out by the time I joined up was for officers to be encouraged in Training to ask for clarification and to know "why?" they were being told to do a certain thing.

During a day with the Traffic Police a Sergeant got in the front passenger seat, looked over his shoulder, saw me in the back and snapped.

"IF I TELL YOU TO DO SOMETHING AND YOU ASK 'WHY?' I WILL FUCKING LEAVE YOU ON THE MOTORWAY DO YOU UNDERSTAND?".

Somewhat confused I replied "with respect Sarge. If you told me to do something, why would I question it?".

He relaxed slightly and then added "Sorry mate. It's just that we've had a lot of toe rags who think it's trendy to question what they're told because they've been advised to do it in Training. Suffice it to say I've got 12 years in The Job, you're a probationer. I know more than you".

The fact that this was ever considered is beyond belief. The fact that it was taught to Probies further illustrates the asinine cretinousness of trying to please everyone all the time.

The regimes and rules mutate every few years. Old School is now anyone who's been in for more than six years. We went through nine months at university believing that this sorry state of affairs, the non-existent discipline and the most begrudging nod to tradition were what the Force wanted. I later discovered that everyone up to the rank of Chief Inspector finally relaxed and breathed a sigh of relief when, two and a half years later they abandoned this weird attempt to treat us like ordinary students and brought back the discipline.

About bloody time.

MA'AM POSTLETHWAITE

The only time any real discipline even dared to show its face throughout Training was when Ma'am was on campus.

We met her on the first day, starting as she clearly meant to go on.

Any female officer over the rank of Sergeant is referred to as Ma'am. You stand up as they enter a room and in the old days you'd also salute.

Maybe it's the memories of a strict, Catholic education and only one male teacher in the school, where even dinner ladies had the power to smack unruly children. Maybe it's the Freudian thing of having to humble yourself to a (usually) middle aged woman but Ma'ams gave me the willies more than Sirs ever did.

On day one of our Training, at about 9am we were taken into the main lecture theatre of the Police Training college and told to sit down.

A female Staff Constable from the Training department told us we were soon to meet the Acting Chief Inspector. She asked us to stand up when the ACI entered, not to sit down again until given permission and to address her as 'Ma'am'. She tells us we should take what the ACI says very seriously. The cue for standing up is to be the word "parade".

She then sticks her head out the door and is clearly talking to someone who wishes their entrance to be a big event. After a couple of minutes the door opens fully and Staff barks "PARADE!". We all stand up as an incredibly stern looking woman in her late 40s enters.

Immaculate, white, Police-issue shirt, gleaming pips on each shoulder and a somehow scary black, knee-length skirt. She took up her place behind the podium and after glaring at us for a few seconds said "Intake, you may sit down".

A speech on the world we had entered was then given where she told us we were here to act as Police officers and whatever we thought we knew, to just forget it. The whole time she's talking she never smiles and retains a facial expression suggesting she would quite like to drown each one of us in our own blood. She came out with the wonderful line "if you're the kind of person that wants to cause trouble then bring it on" and the immortal "if you find yourself sitting opposite me then you've gone too far". She then, without warning, made to leave and there was a frantic scrambling of well polished and/ or brand new shoes as she swept from the room. A few bolts of lightning plus a long black cape and whip would have really put the icing on the cake.

For all of this though, I was glad that they'd made the effort. At least we were being told, despite the Widow Twanky style, that our job had responsibility and power and that we needed to adhere to a strict routine of conduct and behaviour. That was the benchmark and, as the second most powerful force next to the army, we had to toe the line.

Inspector Postlethwaite was responsible for all officers throughout Initial Training and laid it on with a trowel.

The lack of discipline at campus meant that, in the best pantomime tradition we only ever cacked ourselves when Ma'am showed up. Early releases were out, you just sat around and chatted until the unlock time and woe betide anyone who was acting like a tit when she loomed up behind them to whisper "Constable, can I see you in my office please?".

Our first real experience of her rather off kilter personality was during a Human Rights lecture where she was talking about excessive force.

"Who used to be a Special?"

Mine and about three other hands went up.

"Lance, come to the front please". She surveyed the remaining 39 and thinking out loud said "now, who's bigger than you? Most people actually but…ah, Martin can you come to the front please too?".

She passed me her handcuffs from her utility belt and said "Lance, arrest Martin for ABH".

I paused "err…do you have the handcuff key Ma'am?".

"Thank you PC Manley, good question well asked. Yes I do".

I 'arrested', the compliant and smiling Martin with his hands to the rear and Ma'am then said to everyone while taking hold of the bar between the cuff rings "is this excessive force everyone?".

There were murmurs to agree it was not.

"How about this?" she asks beginning to shove Martin in the chest with her hands. I am unsure if I am being tested, so step in between them. She glances at me and says "it's ok, just go with it".

"Martin, please lie on the floor face down". He obediently does so. "Don't worry" she exclaims matter-of-factly "my shoes are clean. Now, is THIS excessive force?" and places her right foot on the back of his neck and shoves repeatedly to which there is a slight pause followed by much laughing from everyone except me who's still unsure if I'm being tested.

At break time 25 minutes later, discussions amongst the men over a coffee were nearly all along the lines of "oh my God, I'm in love" and "phwoooar! I bet she's well dirty in bed".

Beyond all of this, most of it was for show. Many of her put downs and pithy one liners were so outrageous as to be beyond belief. One day an officer wore shorts to campus and, not knowing she was visiting until it was too late, tried to hide at the back of class. She spotted him about 15 minutes before the lesson ended and much to our very restrained glee said in a loud voice "Officer, in my opinion only good looking Italian men should wear shorts. You are neither good looking nor Italian".

In a moment of classic timing that Fawlty Towers couldn't have matched, Nigel wolf whistled at Harriet just as Ma'am came round the corner behind him. It was only when a voice like a saw blade cutting through bone whispered over his shoulder "officer, was that directed at me?" that realisation dawned and he slowly turned round.

Wincing in fear he stammered "err...n, no Ma'am", to which she snapped:

"Why? What's wrong with me?"

Another time she was hovering next to the till at the Police college canteen and scrutinising everyone's choice of lunchtime repast. Upon being confronted with a female officer with a 36 inch waist and a plate of pie and chips Ma'am enquired casually "shouldn't you be having a salad?"

During our final stage of Training, we were all in a large classroom debating the nuances and minutiae of the Dining In Night when someone barked "PARADE!" Ma'am opened the door to find most of us scrambling to our feet, frantically trying to clip our ties back on, it being a hot day in August and there being no air con. Craig, sat near the window, made no attempt to put his tie back on and sat straight back down again without being given permission. Ma'am glared at him across the room from the open doorway and, almost whispering seethed "PC Fox, are you trying my patience?"

He looked away embarrassed "No Ma'am".

"Are you testing me?"

"No Ma'am"

"Good". She looked round the room, snapped "carry on" and walked out.

We were told that on our Dining In Night when we were staying at the Police college, Ma'am would be sleeping in an unspecified room within the block and would, if woken by drunken shenanigans at 3am emerge in her nighty and make those responsible wish their parents had taken a vow of celibacy.

She had her lighter moments though. Once at a later Intake's Dining In Night she was sat next to Connor who had one too many glasses of wine and was telling everyone to "leave my Ma'am alone". He then asked her what room she was in and she replied "you couldn't afford me officer".

Then, after a short pause. "Room 101".

At the same function the charity pot was raking in money for misdemeanours such as elbows on the table, using your mobile, or for the lads taking off their jackets. Samson grassed on his female neighbour for spilling soup all down her posh dress and suggested a fiver as penance. Ma'am thought about this and said to the gathered multitude "I agree. A £5 fine. BUT as a gentleman never tells on a lady, YOU can pay it for her".

Considering some of the wurzels that hold rank within the Police Force it's just a shame that not everyone had a bit of what she did. It's sadder still that many trainees saw her as a boo hiss baddy and not as someone to look up to as a role model.

THE CLASSROOM CONTRACT.

In an attempt to foster an environment of free speech and open debate you are told on day one of Induction Week and will be reminded intermittently throughout Training, in whichever Force you choose to sign up to that whatever you say in class will remain in there and not be used against you or spoken about beyond the four walls UNLESS....

1. You admit to a previously undisclosed offence.
2. You threaten self harm or harm to another.
3. You swear.
4. You actually break the Law.

Point one is fairly useful for people to be reminded of as there is at least one story in every Force of some berk who blurted out a particularly unsavoury bit of history after getting too comfortable talking about their personal life.

A Sergeant told a tale of when he was training Regulars in another Force and five weeks into it the following occurred in class in front of about 40 recruits:

Twat: "I was really badly beaten up one night in my old job as a bouncer about 3 years ago"

Sergeant: "Oh dear, hope you weren't too badly hurt"

Twat: "Yes but it's ok because three weeks later I went round his house when I knew he was alone and broke in and beat him up. He can't walk now"

(A few moments of horrified silence followed by)

Sergeant: "You'd better come with me".

He was arrested outside the room and taken in tears to the nearest Nick. Several of his former colleagues were apparently laughing as they thought it was a joke and any attempt by him to state he was in fact making it up would have possibly prevented him getting prosecuted but would not save his job as merely saying it was "bringing the Force into disrepute".

His dorm room was cleared the same day.

Another less serious remark that still got its owner deprived of their liberty and a P45 in the mail was "oh, I once said I was the driver and took the points on my licence so my husband wouldn't lose his".

You have to wonder how these people get through the IQ test in the first place.

While this has a genuinely valid place in the structure of ethics and integrity that the Police uphold there will always be someone who takes things to extremes.

In one Police Force it involved a tangerine and a mischievous 7 year old.

One weekend during Special Constabulary training the Trainer teaching the class was lecturing on the subtle nuances of the Theft Act 1968 and elaborating on the need to have a Mens Rea in conjunction with an Actus Reus. He stated that if for example, you accidentally picked something up in a shop and forgot to pay for it but realised later then that WASN'T Theft under the definition of the Act. It would only become Theft if you then decided to keep it without paying for it as your Mens Rea would at that moment be holding hands and skipping down the street with your Actus Reus.

The following fairly surreal drama was then played out.

Female Recruit: "Oh that's a funny thing. The other day I went to Tesco and I bought a basket of flowers. I got home and thought 'hang on that's a bit heavy' and there was a tangerine in there. My little boy, he's only 7. He'd thrown it in when I wasn't looking".

Trainer: (putting marker pen down and glaring at student): "You are going to go back and pay for that though aren't you?"

Female Recruit: "Oh no, I mean it's only a tangerine".

Trainer: (walking towards student and speaking slowly but

loudly): "NO. YOU. ARE. GOING. TO. GO. BACK. AND. PAY. FOR. THAT. AREN'T. YOU?"

Female Recruit (oblivious, waving her hand dismissively while laughing): "No. I mean it's only worth a few pence".

Trainer:(walking back to the wipe board, head butting it and shouting "FUCK!!!" before turning to the two Section Officers sitting in the corner): "Right! Can you three please leave the room and deal with this?"

One of the SO's then arrested the poor cow and took her to the Custody Suite four floors below.

She was presented to the Custody Sergeant who looked at them in disbelief and said "are you taking the piss?" before doing what all good skippers do in a situation like this and phoning the Inspector.

A short time passed during which time the embarrassed and humiliated recruit was treated with embarrassed politeness by the Custody skipper and offered a cigarette, which she was allowed to smoke in the open doorway leading to the car park. After 20 minutes the phone rang and it was the Chief Superintendent, disturbed during a round of golf at his Gentlemen's club, who screeched down the blower:

"DON'T BE SO BLOODY RIDICULOUS! GET HER OUT OF THERE NOW!!!"

The aftermath of this ludicrous piece of fascist pantomime was that:

1. The Recruit was apologised to by the Assistant Chief Constable and asked to withdraw her resignation (she refused).

2. The Trainer couldn't actually be disciplined as he technically hadn't done anything wrong but was removed from teaching completely and put back on the Beat.

3. The now former Recruit went back to Tesco to get a receipt and it took her 45 minutes to convince the store manager to let her pay for the tangerine.

4. The SO who made the Arrest will even now occasionally get drunk and tell people about how embarrassed he was to have to nick her.

A year later the Deputy Chief Constable wrote letters to all the Recruits who were in the room at the time apologising for "the crassness of what you had the misfortune to have to witness".

My own experience of the Classroom Contract was as a Regular and was a retroactively applied piece of bullying that landed me with an Action Plan and two hours doing E-training for Race and Diversity.

While in Basic Training we were discussing Missing Persons reports in class. I told a story of how, while working on a summer camp in Reading in 2003, five of our Albanian teenage students had jumped ship and disappeared. It became obvious after number 2 that this was deliberate, as number 3 was seen on the CCTV tapes leaving smiling with her bags packed and their accompanying adults couldn't have cared less and acted each time a kid flew the coop like they'd just lost a mobile phone.

We got numbers 2 and 5 back. Number 2 willingly, number 5 because he got nicked on suspicion of being illegally in the country after being found blubbing over his suitcase at Leicester bus station. The little turd told the following pack of lies through a translator in front of two Police officers, me and my boss after being returned to the holiday camp.

Police Constable "Why did you run away?"

Translator "His father murdered someone in the mafia in Albania and told him he had to run away because if they couldn't find his father they would kill him"

Me (trying to keep my temper) "Err....sorry! What Mob in the world, particularly from the poorest country in Eastern Europe, are going to fly an assassin over to whack a 14 year old kid? And for that matter, if you're so scared why were you laughing and joking at the disco last night, three hours after being brought back here?"

Translator (after much muttering and glaring at me during consultation with lying little git) "he was forgetting his problems for a moment by enjoying himself at your disco".

82

I said in class that in my opinion, as we had seen a total of 18 different Police officers during these disgusting attempts to bypass immigration laws and a MisPer form had to be filled out for each one which took about 2 hours each time, surely it was a job for Immigration to deal with and these people should NOT have been recorded as Missing Persons. It was also incredibly embarrassing to be associated with people behaving like this and to be wasting so much valuable Police time.

This was my opinion. Voiced in a classroom debate. Protected in theory by the Classroom Contract.

Four or five months after this discussion it came to light that I'd said it and my PDU Sergeant used it as evidence that I was lacking in the area of Race and Diversity. The 120 minute E-package I was forced to undertake had no content whatsoever on Illegal Immigrants but was chock full of stuff on Sikhs, Hindus, Muslims, Gypsies, Gays, Lesbians, Bi's, Transsexuals, the Disabled and anyone who wasn't white. It was patronising cobblers that gave you facts about each demographic group and then asked you multiple choice questions (e.g. "Is their holy book a). The Koran b). The Bible or c). Lord of the Rings?")

I also got landed with an Action Plan for not making inappropriate remarks even though it had been noted by two other Sergeants at the time that I'd said it and no one had said anything whatsoever to me.

The Classroom Contract exists only if they feel it should.

DIVERSITY PLACEMENT NO.1

Part of the modern Police Force's attempt to be liked by Society like a new kid in class trying to ingratiate himself with the other kids at playtime, is Diversity Placements.

Given in my old Force on the second week of Basic Training these were done before any legal training beyond Race and Diversity or The Human Rights Act.

Diversity is an area that the Police do not as an organisation fully or even partially understand yet they are obliged to behave as if they do. Like a dutiful mother pinning her four year old's latest drawing to the kitchen door, even though she hasn't a clue what it's of, the Police do this because they feel they SHOULD.

It has been decreed that the Police should get to know their Community better. While at one time this would have meant getting to know where people lived on your Beat and popping into the corner shop to check they weren't having any further trouble with school kids nicking Panini football stickers, it now means finding out about all walks of life and being put in with an organisation deemed "Diverse".

This is supposed to help you enrich your understanding of the community you serve and the Area in which you will pound your Beat. You have two placements during the course of your Basic Training and are expected to make notes and submit an essay from the first about what the experience was like, what it meant to you and what you learned while there. The second will involve a Presentation on the Friday with guests from your Placement plus your PDU staff, your fellow trainees and possibly the PDU Inspector in attendance.

In theory the Force will scour the length and breadth of your county to find suitable places to really "push you beyond your comfort zones" (a phrase used several times) and get you stuck into a really challenging role, shadowing a representative of an organisation you probably never even knew existed even though it was a mile from your house.

The reality is that they will take anything that they can to bump up the numbers and stick people with organisations as radically diverse as Help the Aged and Autism Awareness but scrape underneath the barrel by filling up the slots with crap like Fly Tipper Enforcers, Traffic Wardens or Car Clampers.

Our Force PC, Jemima Hambleworth who dealt with this was one of the most patronising and condescending officers that ever swore the oath and would talk to us as if we were six years old. We all assembled in one of the lecture rooms at the university to be given the following load of claptrap the Thursday before the first placement began:

"I'm really going to push you all. If you've been working with children you'll be working with the elderly. If you're a keen sportsman you'll be working with the disabled. I'm really going to take you and make you uncomfortable. I'm going to push you beyond your comfort zones. You're going to hate it when you get there but by the end you won't want to leave. I have people ring me up all the time and ask 'oh please can I stay just one more week' and I have to laugh and say 'now come on you know they need you back at The Job'. I know one female officer who cried because she didn't want to leave".

Her tone doesn't help the anger that most of us feel at being addressed like we're infants about to be taken to the zoo for the first time.

"Now please be very careful about letting the placement providers decide whether or not they let the clients know that you are a Police officer. It's very important that in these placements the decision is left up to them".

This seems reasonable, particularly as a couple of us are in the local prison but then...

"One male officer was working at a women's refuge and it was the first time they'd allowed a male officer to attend that placement. One of the women's husbands turned up drunk at the refuge and in front of the officer he screamed and shouted at the woman and threatened to kill her. The officer DID NOT let on that he was a Policeman because he rationalised that if he did her husband would know she had been talking to the Police and might kill her".

Jesus! More likely the officer pooed his pants upon being faced with a wife beating, estranged, pissed up hubby who should have been nicked and chucked in the back of the van within five minutes of showing up. Still, fair play to him for inventing a cover story so convincing that it was used to confuse the rest of us. We take an oath when we join to uphold the Law and Off duty but with your Warrant Card in your pocket you are supposed to intervene in any and all illegal acts that you are witness to, even if this only amounts to making a statement to other officers about what you saw. We are now being told to ignore that sacred oath taken in front of the local Magistrate and act nonchalant.

She then puts the icing on the cake with this little beauty...

"And if you're asked to go out for a drink with your placement providers on the last day, don't be impolite, go. But don't drink alcohol and only have a soft drink AND whatever you do don't sleep with anyone off the placements".

The guy sitting next to me is 46. Three seats down is a bloke who joined the Force straight from the army and has a gallantry medal for courage under fire (friendly of course) from the 2nd Gulf War. The youngest of us is 20. This "keep your primal desires in your pants" lecture would probably wind up 15 year old school kids about to be taken on a trip to France, let alone trainees for the Thin Blue Line .

She then hands out welcome packs and reads out the list of placements, When it comes to me I get the name of a road. She looks up and adds "it's a school".

Retrospectively I should have challenged this in front of everyone else as it would have meant she would have had to change it then and there but I didn't and this is The Job and no one will ever admit they're wrong.

After we're told we can leave I approach her and ask "it's a school?"

"Yes" she smiles beatifically, adding "you're go-ing to loo-ove it" in a singsong voice.

"Err...you said the idea was to push us beyond our comfort zones?"

"Yes that's right" still grinning.

"I've been a teacher for the last 11 years"

The smile is wiped away by a look of astonished embarrassment and she quickly fumbles for a fat folder in her bag. "Err..." she flicks through it until she gets to my name. "I've got you down as last employment being unemployed and having a Law degree".

"That's right, but before that I was a teacher. It's on my CV. What kind of school is it?"

"Teenagers, who've been expelled from other schools"

"I've mainly worked with teenagers. I've even run summer camps for teenagers"

She looks visibly uncomfortable but the sense of self-preservation quickly overrides all the other twaddle she spouted during the speeches that ended only five minutes ago. "Well it can't be changed now" she says, putting the folder back in her bag, "but next time I'll give you something different".

So, no mass destruction of my comfort zone for the time being. In fact I'll be doing more or less exactly what I've done since 1995. Still, it's not only me. One girl was given a placement in the same company she'd worked at before joining and had the common sense that I lacked and put her hand up straight away. She was awarded something different after amused giggling from most of the rest of us. Two officers got to play football all week with local kids and one girl got to work in a local horse riding school.

I was given no information on what to expect from the placement beyond what we'd already been told and the welcome pack contained a brief description of the school and a phone number to contact the Head.

I called up and was told to turn up in smart casuals on the Monday morning at about 8.45am.

Monday morning and during a brief chat with the Head and the teachers over a cup of tea we decided that my Spooks cover story would be that I was a teacher trying the school out for a week to see if I wanted to work there. 9am and we met the kids who had been slouching in since about five to. One was pulled aside as soon as he walked in and told by the Carpentry/English teacher that he was on thin ice with regard to his behaviour and any further repetitions of the foul language from last Friday would get him excluded. He apologised and mumbled something and then sulked off in the direction of the classes. Throughout the week I did very little with regard to interaction apart from in the Metalwork and Art classes, both of which were used as rewards dangled in front of the students due to their usually vile and obnoxious behaviour in the academic lessons. The teachers suggested I sit and observe and take notes which I did, interjecting in what was going on when I felt it was appropriate.

When I was at Primary School dinner ladies could smack children. Now there is no physical contact allowed beyond self defence or preventing violence to another and even yelling can be considered too aggressive for the little poppets to have to put up with.

One lad was suspended for a week on the Wednesday I was there for saying to a 63 year old female teacher "go and lick your mother's cunt you fucking old cunt" and behaviour from the others ranged from insolence to the teachers to a kid actually walking out of the class and going home. The staff were nearly all retired, former state school teachers who had come back due to the higher salary working with these herberts paid. The only back up they had in case of mischief in class they couldn't cope with was a two way radio linking them to the Head. They were all looked weary and appeared to be bearing their daily chores with dignity yet resignation and knew that the most they could do was attempt to get some education into these kids, who simply didn't want to be educated.

The kids' reasons for being there varied from repeated and prolonged truancy to one kid who'd belted a teacher at his previous school and had been selling drugs. Not all were poor. One or two were middle class while one was homeless and either slept in his mate's car or on friends' sofas.

I got on well with all of them simply because I didn't patronise them, try to be friends or pretend I understood them. I spoke to them the way I expected to be spoken to. I only used authority if it was necessary and I made it clear that while I was happy to talk to them there were boundaries. By the time I left I made a point of saying to each one of them "do you want me to come and work here full time?" and all but one said yes with answers ranging from "yeah, you're pretty cool" to "yeah, why not". The only 'no' was conditional with "no....well yeah, but only if Mr Smith retires. He's too fucking old" from one of only three girls at the school (who was 15 and thought she might be pregnant).

On the Wednesday of the placement I got off at the train station and while mooching up the steps to the exit was confronted by the sight of one of the students having a heated ding dong with a revenue inspector at the turnstile while two of his mates loitered on the other side.

"You've fucking took my ticket you cunt. How am I supposed to get to fucking school now?"

I walked over. Time to intervene. But NOT as a cop. "John calm down, what's happened?"

"He's fucking took my ticket, stupid cunt. How am I supposed to get to fucking school now?" He looks visibly angry and is facing a ticket inspector who isn't helping matters with the smug look on his chops like nearly all of them have with fare dodgers who are easy to bully as they're not usually expelled kids with bad tempers.

"Calm down ok?" I turn to the ticket inspector "I'm a teacher at this boy's school, what happened?"

"He passed his ticket back over the barrier" he indicates the other two who are attempting to pretend they are not involved by staring into space and looking as if they have no clue what's happening. "I saw it and took it off him"

"You fucking liar!" John snaps "how am I supposed to get to school now you cunt?" he seethes.

"John calm down" I tell him again "now I'm not saying you did it and I'm not saying you didn't do it. Let's take your name and this gentleman's name and we'll speak to the Head at the school, ok?"

He shrugs but calms down and stands there while I write his name down and get the inspector's name to add to it. In a moment of extreme crassness the inspector then says "here you can have the ticket back but I know it's not yours" and hands it to John who grunts and then leaves.

At the school I tell the Head who summons John and stands him between both of us.

"What's this about you fare dodging?" he snaps.

"Sorry, I won't do it again" he mumbles looking at the floor.

"You'd better not" the Head barks at him

"To be fair John, you calmed down when I told you to and although you denied it at the time you've admitted it now so fair play. Let's put it behind us ok?" I tell him.

"Thanks" he says, still looking at the floor.

"Right you can go. Don't let it happen again" the Head tells him and he slouches off.

Jemima had given us her personal number during her sales pitch the previous week with the words "call me any time as often as you want with anything to do with your placements". My problem is that I always take people at their word and later that day rang her up to tell her about what had happened. She told me "well done" and added that she was pleased and impressed with how I'd handled the situation.

The following day I called her again to ask if it was ok to tell the students on the final day, that being tomorrow, that I was really a Police officer as the kids had got to know me and I was getting on well with all of them. She said this was a great idea and would mean they had got to relate to me as a person without having their opinions clouded by knowing what I really did for a living. Later that day I got cold feet as it occurred to me that they might not like the fact that they'd been lied to so I called her back and she agreed that maybe it wasn't such a good idea and to abandon it.

The PDU (Professional Development Unit) are usually a Constable, Sergeant and Inspector who oversee the probationary period of all trainees for their area. Ours was run by a female constable of over 20 years service called Daryl Esobé who still liked to be called WPC and her skipper was Sergeant Kerwan. The Inspector was female too and rarely seen by us.

At 2.20pm, twenty minutes after the school had closed, my mobile rang with a request from PC Esobé that I come for a meeting on the way to the placement at 8am the following morning.

When I turned up it wasn't Constable Esobé (who was off Sick more times than she appeared to be on duty) but Sergeant Kerwan.

This was the first time I'd ever met him and at first he was quite polite and seemed friendly enough but something I couldn't quite put my finger on just didn't feel right. Later on, after I resigned due to bullying and disability discrimination from this guy it all boiled down to one fact.

He was an idiot.

An ignorant little man who would come to make my life utterly miserable over the subsequent months until I quit.

He told me that PC Hambleworth had called him to say that I had been "bothering" her a lot this week and she is very busy, has hundreds of people to look after, almost as many placements and I should not call her any more. Retrospectively I should have pointed out straight away that she'd said we could call her as often as we liked but I bit my tongue. He then stated that under no circumstances was I to tell the kids at the school that I was really a Police officer because if I did it would "jeopardise the placement for years to come".

I pointed out that the kids were all local and sooner or later would see me on duty anyway.

"Oh they won't recognise you in uniform, especially if you've got your cap on"

I tried to keep a straight face at this, but doubt I succeeded.

"Have you been mingling with the students?" he asks.

"Well there isn't really time. The kids come into school at the last minute and leave as soon as the last bell rings. We only get 15 minute breaks and I use that time to debrief from the previous lesson and prepare for the next one".

"Yes but you should be using that time to mingle with them, get to know them"

I can see where this is going and throw up what I feel is a checkmate. If I'd been facing someone more intelligent than Kerwan it probably would have been.

"I was introduced to them at 9am on Monday morning as a teacher trying the school out for a week to see if I want to work there. None of the other teachers do that, it wouldn't be appropriate"

He isn't listening, just waiting for me to finish speaking.

"No, you should be talking to them in that time, playing a game of Pool with them, or asking them about themselves"

"It would undermine the authority of the other teachers if I did that. They believe I'm a member of staff." I try to reason with him.

"No no, you should be getting to know them and having a chat. What happened with the boy at the train station?"

I proudly relate the story of the boy's misbehaviour and how I'd stuck to my cover story while managing to defuse the situation as a teacher and had not let on I was a Policeman.

Eyes gleaming he then comes out with a line that blew away any further doubts in my mind that the person in charge of my continued professional development throughout probation was a complete and utter moron.

"No no that's wrong. What you should have done was said 'look John, you really should pay for a ticket but hey, I won't tell the Head if you won't". He nods enthusiastically at this as if it's the wisdom of Solomon he's imparting to me.

I say nothing and do my best to avoid looking annoyed while he rabbits on. If I had done this it would have probably made John think I was a complete arsehole. Having been a kid myself and having worked with them for years I know that children loathe and despise teachers who try and act "cool". No one will be more vilified than the one berk who comes into class and says "hey guys who saw Top of the Pops last night, wasn't it fab?" before attempting to maintain discipline and impart knowledge of the Battle of Hastings to his now contemptuous pupils. Further, this act would have been a huge breach of ethics for a Police officer and possibly justification for discipline over lack of Integrity. Thirdly it would have put any professional contact I had with John while on duty as a cop in jeopardy as he may have tried to relate to me as a "mate" and assume I would collude with him a second time.

Throughout my contact with this Sergeant he spouted crap that he clearly believed whole heartedly was sound advice but was basing it solely on the fact he wore chevrons on his shoulders and not on any practical knowledge or life experience. In his mind, telling a qualified teacher of 11 years experience of working with teenagers the best way to interact with kids was better knowledge than the teacher himself could possibly have.

Two other officers that I spoke to about this (one of which was another Sergeant) were both gobsmacked when I mentioned what he'd said. The female Sergeant told me "you couldn't have colluded with him. At the end of the day you're still a Police officer".

I saw John several times after that incident in the months following. He was always pleased to see me, smiled and said hello. By the third time we met he'd found out I was a cop as he had seen me in uniform at a spot frequented by the local chavs when we were moving people on after a disturbance. He saw me, did a double take and then went "no way!" and held his arms out to give me a hug. A couple of weeks later I saw John again and he said "if that had been any other copper I would have told you to fuck off but as it was you we did what you said".

As it was 10.30pm, dark, three months after the placement and he'd been drinking heavily this kind of puts paid to "they won't recognise you with your hat on".

One of the students was from Bangladesh and turned out to be in a notorious street gang in the neighbouring town who were constantly being shown on briefings and modelled themselves on American gangs while only managing to step up to the level of replica firearms. However, they made our lives difficult with their stealing and generally loutish behaviour and were known to frequent the park at night and had mugged one or two dog walkers, stolen their wallets and put them in hospital. There was also the odd burglary and sometimes meetings with other gangs for a punch up. A constant fly in the ointment of a well ordered, law abiding town.

Several months later I was walking through town on a night off. My mate Christian was with me who was another probationer and we were off for a pint. I saw this lad sitting on a bench near the local newspaper office with another guy and two skinny girls. As I approached I smiled and said "hello mate"

He stood up and shouted "I'm not speaking to you. You lied to me"

I replied "well that's OK then" and walked on.

He walks a few paces after me "I'm not speaking to you, you lied to me!".

I turn around, Christian too "so what are you following me for then?"

"I'm not speaking to you, you lied to me!"

"For someone who's not speaking to me you're doing a lot of talking" I walk back, Christian follows me. I stand in front of him, glance at the other kids he's with and then say "would you have wanted to speak to me if you'd known I was a Gavver?"

"No" he snaps.

"Do you think I wanted to work at a school for expelled kids?"

"Probably not".

"That's why we didn't tell you. It gave you a chance to know me. I really liked you, I thought you were a really nice lad"

He relaxes slightly. "You lied to me" he says, but less aggressively.

"No I didn't I just didn't tell you the truth. Every time I've seen you since then you've always been pleased to see me, well apart from now coz you're with your mates. Got a fag?"

He reaches into his pocket and offers me a cigarette.

"Got a light?"

"Fuckin' hell you don't want much" he says lighting the fag for me.

"I'm sorry you were lied to but we believed it was the only way for you to get on with me"

"Why are you two dressed like that anyway, you CID or something?" he asks pointing at my jeans.

"No, we're off for a pint"

"Can I come?" he asks looking hopeful

"Give it a couple of years mate"

"Would you arrest me?"

"If you were doing something you shouldn't be doing, yes."

"Oh, that's not fair"

His mate who'd sat there just watching us then looks at me and asks "do you know who I am?"

"What's your name?" He tells me and I know immediately who he is, the leader of the local gang of scrotes the student belongs to. He's on Briefings every week, has been arrested loads of times and banged up at least once. "No, sorry mate never heard of you". He looks slightly disappointed.

I turn back to the student. "I'm sorry you were lied to but like I said I really liked you, I thought you were a really nice lad". I hold out my hand. "You take care". He shakes it and me and Christian walk on.

Before I resigned the Force in 2008 the placement in 2006 was brought up more than once as an example of my "inability to communicate" due to reacting like a teacher to events I was involved in while "undercover" as a Police officer pretending to be a teacher.

The facts that:

1. All the students bar one said they wanted me to work permanently at the school;

2. John had gone to give me a hug the first time he saw me in uniform (which was the first time he realised I was a cop);

3. The lad in the street gang asked in front of his gang leader if he could come and drink a beer with me (after acknowledging in front of his gang leader that he knew me and Christian were Police); were dismissed by Kerwan as the kids "just telling you what you want to hear".

WOUNDED PRIDE AND PREJUDICE

Proud of their reputation as movers in the world of Race and Diversity. Able to communicate with all walks (not to mention all other methods of movement including those of the physically challenged) of life in a way that is clear, unambiguous and free from oppression.

Six weeks minimum in every modern Force (or Service) will be spent learning the minutiae of race, ethnicity, gender, transgender, sexuality and anything else that comes under the all embracing arms (or surgical replacements) of the world of Diversity.

Gone are the days of canteen banter where coarse humour would alienate those too shy or afraid of repercussions to voice their disdain. Now the modern Police is a world of equality and fairness where everyone can blend into a happy euphoric world of bliss and harmony.

What a load of cobblers.

The huuuge emphasis on being nice to all and sundry has had many aftershocks. The most basically obvious of all is the fact that individual officers are now held to be at fault for complaints made against the Force they work for, regardless of the nature of the complaint, IF it can be manipulated into fitting into the world of Race and Diversity. On day one of joining you will be subjected to an entire day of Diversity Training. Forget exploring why you wanted to join, the Law or what it means to have the power to deprive people of their liberty. You will be taught in the most patronising way possible about what the finer points of

Ethnocentrism, Prejudiced Non-Discriminators and Ableism are.

E.g. (In a classroom, 40 trainees, one hour into their contracts, sitting in a horse shoe of chairs around the Staff).

Staff- "John, do you have a prejudice?"

John - (squirming at being singled out and wondering what NOT to say) "Errr...no, not really"

Staff- (Smirking coz everyone says that) "Come on you do REALLY don't you?"

John- (Now wondering what the four role plays on Assessment Day were for if he's got to go through it all again) "Err...no, I don't at all"

Staff- (Smirking coz this was and always is an easy checkmate) "We ALL have prejudices. I have them. THAT'S not wrong. It's if you let them become a DIS-CRIM-IN-A-TION that it becomes wrong".

The reason for shoving this pap down your throat right at the beginning of Training, before you've even been issued with a uniform is to 'Cover The Arse' of the Force that employs you so that if a disabled, French, Atheist lesbian utilizing a wheelchair complains that you stopped them under s.44 of the Terrorism Act solely because they were black then hey, YOU WERE TOLD!

In April 2008 a detective Sergeant enlightened the CID puppies with the news that the rules on inappropriate behaviour and reporting of such were about to be modified. In a few short months it would be a disciplinary matter for you to fail to report someone for making an inappropriate remark about someone else IF you were present even IF it wasn't directed at you.

Basically this means that anything you overhear could potentially land you in trouble if you fail to challenge the remark at the time or don't slink off to the Inspector's office at the earliest opportunity.

Why the hell they have done this is anyone's guess because it doesn't take a genius to work out that this will inevitably lead to an atmosphere in the Nick of 1960s Communist Russia of everyone telling the blandest of jokes, keeping their opinions to themselves and shopping their mates just in case they are reported by someone else and end up in trouble.

Stories that are all true but beggar (sorry, ask for fiscal assistance) belief (sorry, fundamentally held view) are:

1. An officer I used to work with who proudly told me of the day that she'd ratted on two other officers to the Sergeant for saying that they thought a convicted nonce should be killed. Noone else was present when they said this...except her.

2. A lesbian officer who initiated a conversation in the canteen about gay rights with two officers she thought were homophobic. She secretly recorded the conversation and then took the tape to the Professional Standards department.

3. A white officer fired for making a racist joke to an Asian officer he was friends with. The only other person to overhear the remark was their white Sergeant. The Asian officer's insistence that he wasn't even remotely arsed and had in fact found the joke funny made no difference.

4. A white officer of 3 years unblemished service, fired for saying "watch out for the Macaroon, we nearly potted the black" as a black bloke stepped in front of the squad car he was sitting in. The black guy never heard the remark. The three other white officers in the car (including a Sergeant) all laughed. The Sergeant then reported him. Letters from black colleagues and friends insisting he wasn't racist and a public apology from the officer himself made no difference and his appeal was dismissed. Quote "it was a stupid thing to say, but do I really deserve to lose my job over it?"

5. A white officer asked by his black senior officer "do you think I'm

being promoted quickly because of my colour?" The guy who told me this said he believed his boss was genuinely up for an honest answer and they had worked together for over a year. He unsurprisingly replied "Sorry Sir. I'm not touching that with a bargepole".

6. A black very senior officer saying to his support staff "I'm frustrated. Most of the people committing crimes in this area are the same colour as me but I'm not allowed to officially acknowledge that fact" while heading up an Area operation designed to combat racism.

7. An officer who replied "you're a good egg" to a black canteen assistant who stayed open five minutes late to serve him lunch. Someone sitting nearby thought it was rhyming slang as in "egg and spoon = coon". This was stamped on by the investigating Inspector almost immediately and went no further.

8. A white female officer at her Pre-Assessment Briefing (with her proud mum) chatting to the Race and Diversity Sergeant over a cup of coffee. He said suddenly "excuse me I just need to talk to this black recruit" and left them open mouthed while he was overheard saying "just call me and I'll help you with any of the questions on your form. I'll make certain you get through".

The Law should be above everything else. The glue that holds polite society together and means little old ladies can collect their pensions without wondering if the local chavs are going to steal it in order to buy cider. Putting a wall of fear and mistrust in officer's minds that can be manipulated by those cunning enough to see a window of opportunity and even by Senior Management in order to blame the plebs for whatever toxic waste may fall on the Nick does nothing but batter morale and place an already pissed off and weary set of street soldiers further on the track to jacking it and taking up a less stressful career, like a stockbroker.

Next to R&D is the pants-wetting fear that Use of Force inspires in anyone over the rank of Inspector, not to mention the Training Staff.

In America the cops carry guns. In the UK even applying handcuffs is a Use of Force and you are supposed to fill a form out for this, but when I was serving no one did, proving common sense was still holding on by at least one of it's battered and broken fingernails.

If an Authorised Firearms Officer raises his gun and points it at someone that in itself is a UF and needs to be justified. Everything has to be JAPAN'd. While convalescing at Flint House an AFO from SO13 stated that he was on duty the day that Fathers 4 Justice scaled the walls of Buckingham Palace dressed as Batman and Robin. Only Batman made it as Robin was detained on the ground. This officer saw the man start to climb the walls of the Royal Family's abode, raised his gun and at that point the protestor dropped his overcoat revealing the costume. The rationale behind the Caped Crusader getup was to ensure he didn't catch a bullet as the armed officers would know it wasn't a suicide bomber or other nefarious terrorist as Al Qaeda don't wear superhero costumes.

The officer said he knew as soon as he saw the Batman outfit that he couldn't fire as this clearly wasn't a terrorist, only a protestor.

Ahem...!

If I was going to think outside the box for a moment and die in the name of my cause I'd possibly surmise that "hey, the English Police hate lifting their guns let alone firing them. They don't shoot comic book characters so why don't I dress up as Wolverine from the X-Men and put some spandex over the 20 pounds of semtex strapped to my pecs before I ascend in a blaze of glory to Paradise".

Most of the trainers at the Police college are ex-army (including the one, very attractive, female trainer) and have a calm, almost surgical approach to the violence that they are certificated to teach. One used to run at least 10 and sometimes 15 miles before breakfast EVERY day while another was an ex army boxer who'd served in both Iraq and Northern Ireland. They ran us ragged (and rightly so) during the warm ups and then tried to teach us the moves and holds of an English Bobby subduing a recalcitrant suspect.

The locks, pin downs and holds were sufficient to lead us along the path of confidence in our abilities and give us a secure head start when dealing with people on the street. The knife training was something else though as we sparred with partners (other trainees) for about 10 or 15 minutes trying to stab each other with rubber knives and simultaneously attempting to disarm our adversary. I managed to grab my partner's knife and was well chuffed until I realized he'd jabbed me four times during the melee and in real life I would have been dribbling claret and impersonating a colander. The cell exit and entrance techniques were useful and I've used the former in real life on two occasions. Both times the technique potentially spared me and the other officers involved from serious harm from the wriggling, swearing, uncooperative "Suspect" on the cell floor.

However....

Correct use of PAVA pepper spray (a class 5 firearm) took about an hour and consisted of spraying each other with fake canisters filled with water (urban myth of one dozy bastard who left it in his body armour for a year and only found out he had been carrying H20 instead of the real stuff at the annual refresher) and dodging about like a kid playing Army spraying cardboard cut outs of bad people.

Asp baton training lasted half a day and was lots of work with foam rubber sticks and whacking the hell out of the karate pad our partner was holding. Correct ways to open the piddly little things were demonstrated, as were the "Open" and "Closed" modes. We were told that the appropriate areas of striking were the upper outer thighs and the upper outer arms. Woe betide any wretch that aimed to the face or head or even to a breakable part of the body. Only in instances of Absolute Necessity would a blow to a Red Zone be justified.

The Chest Strike was shown as an effective way of dealing with invasion of personal space. This boiled down to a flat palm strike on the chest area of whichever scrote is trying to maul you, with one or both hands, depending on how many you had free at the time. This was meant to clear space for you to draw your spray or baton or even clear a gap to enable you to do a runner.

While in Training this was all fine (the Trainer or your partner would obligingly stagger back a few feet like something from a Benny Hill sketch and totter on their heels before lurching towards you again) in real life it has no effect at all on anyone who's drunk, angry, drugged up or bigger than you. It will ONLY work if the person you do it to is caught off guard.

When sparring with a partner the techniques are fine but we knew we would have to face The Red Man or Angry Man training.

Two of the trainers dressed up in big bulky padded suits (bright red fabric, apparently to increase the anger level of the scenario) and we formed two groups. One of us took a foam baton and faced the bulky, faux-aggressive trainer while those waiting/ just had their turn held karate pads in order to push the combatants back into the middle of the mat should the scrapping result in them moving out of the designated area. A whistle would blow and you had a one minute rehearsal each, then the Trainer who had been observing would take you behind the curtain for a debrief. Once everyone had had a practice, you had two minutes for the actual test.

Scary stuff when you're faced with people that are super fit and will pummel you if you don't do what you're supposed to. There were two mirror groups and the trainers would switch between them so we had the rehearsal with one and the actual test with another. My turn, whistle blows. One minute of getting a boxed ear, a jab on the nose and flung bodily into the pads being held by my colleagues. On the debrief the Trainer said the following.

"Good effort, you didn't back off. Good use of voice. But when he was on his knees for the second time you gave him a couple of extra bangs with the baton".

"Err...he'd just got up again after being told not to move AND he'd punched me in the face".

"Doesn't matter, at that point he wasn't a threat. Also when he had you against the pads you really battered the shit out of him but I guess that was panic. Apart from that well done".

So, calm and controlled all the time.

A mate of mine who's 6' 2" and has hands the size of toasters took a good twenty seconds to actually use the baton (and only then after getting cuffed in the ear) after walking backwards around the mat, repeatedly telling the Red Man to "back off" and when asked why replied "because you're invading my personal space".

A girl of 5'4" giggled when the guy stomped towards her which resulted in the Red Man locking her head under his arm and punching her repeatedly in the face while shouting "DO YA THINK THIS IS FUNNY BITCH?" while her little legs kicked in the air.

So, a good way to get over any fear of confrontation and in a controlled, laboratory environment get used to aggression.

Problem was that when we had the Arrest role plays (which are as close to real life as you will ever get in Training) you don't have pads and soft mats to fall on to or an adversary impersonating the Michelin Man with sunburn.

The first two weeks at uni they drummed it into us unremittingly about just how much shit we would land ourselves in for using force or our equipment (one Trainer even said while shaking his finger "if you have to draw your baton then you've lost the argument"). We were repeatedly told that reasoning with people, Betari's Box and treating people 'decently' would get everyone up to and including Osama Bin Laden to cooperate. In the first week at uni a lad on my Intake asked when we were going to do the arrest training and was met with the icy reply "why are you so keen to do that?". They harped on incessantly that physical force was the absolute last resort and through implication made us believe that it would not need to be used if we were doing our jobs properly. It was also mentioned on more than one occasion that if we crossed the line and used excessive force we could be disciplined, sacked or even imprisoned. This obviously had a clear effect on how we were going to approach the physical side of training and made us more than a smidgen hesitant to do something that might result in dismissal or a spell in Porridge. Everything had to be JAPAN'd mentally before you did it (Justified, Authorised, Proportionate, Auditable and Necessary).

One frosty morning in January we queued up, tense and nervous to face "the Aggressive Arrest Scenario". We were in groups of two with a radio each to wait for "Control" (a Trainer behind a portakabin with another radio) to call in a violent incident that needed Police attendance. We weren't allowed to watch the other pairs during their attempts and did not know what to expect. Upon getting the call we ran outside to find two "Suspects" shouting at each other and one holding two huge branches off a tree, brandishing them threateningly at another actor.

Mine went thus:

Me: "Look just calm down OK" (standing in his way so he can't get to the other actor he wants to thump)

Trainer: "Fuck off! Who are you telling me what to do? And...GET TO FUCK!" (with that he slaps me in the face)

Short interlude including calling for non-existent back up and following him as he walks away making death threats to the other actor.

Me: "You're under arrest (grab his arm, he snatches it back) you do not have to say anything but it may...FUCKING HELL!!! (he is now taking swings at me so I belt him with the rubber baton, it has no effect and he simply punches me on the left ear and Judo throws me into the mud on my back. My colleague attempts to spray him in the face but he looks away and gives her the finger before running off laughing. My cap, baton and spectacles are in the mud alongside me).

Whistle blows to signal role play over.

Trainer: (As I limp past spattered with brown and my ear on fire) "Hurr, hurr! There's nasty people about ain't there? You alright?"

At the debrief he gets to me while the crust is still drying on my stay pressed Force issue trousers and you could toast crumpets on the left side of my face.

"Right Lance. You were totally lacking in confidence, mumbling and not making eye contact AND you stood well within the Reactionary Gap which is why you got a slap"

I wince and nod, while my peers all watch me in silence.

"AND why did you not, when I slapped you in the face, NOT do anything about it?"

"Well, it didn't hurt."

"PARDON?!!!"

"Well I err..."

"IT DIDN'T HURT?!!! I'd just assaulted a Police officer in the execution of his duty. You had every right to spray me in the face, throw me on the floor and handcuff me."

"Errr...well I was trying to JAPAN it."

"WHAT? Oh for fuxake (he moves to the front of the class facing all of us) DO NOT, I repeat DO NOT any of you worry about using force in a situation like this. I don't know what your Trainers at uni have been telling you but you do NOT need to think at the time whether or not your actions can be retrospectively justified or worry about JAPAN. If it feels right it probably is. Justify it after."

He moves on to another officer from a later scenario.

"And YOU. Why did you stand back when I walked towards you and let me stab the other person to death?"

"Well, Lance got a smack, I didn't want one."

He stares in disgust at the officer, then out the window, then at his colleagues who shrug and then says "we are going to be talking to your Trainers at uni about this. I don't know what crap they've been telling you but this is pathetic".

TUTORS

In the old days of ooh...about five years ago, you would do your Basic Training, come out on to a Section and be assigned to a tutor Constable. He or she would observe and monitor you throughout the remainder of your probation and would act as your mentor and guide, steering you in the right direction if you needed help and be there to watch you grow into a Confirmed and fully fledged Police Constable.

Through this system you had consistency and solid foundations to work with plus knowing where the goal posts were with regard to correct procedure, protocol and etiquette. You would be able to observe your tutor in action and follow their example of how to be a professional, competent Constable.

By the time I joined the system was completely different.

We had four active phases during the first year of Basic Training. These were three months, five months, seven months and nine months after joining. The rest of the time we were in class or the Training college. The first phase would hopefully put you with a tutor Constable who worked directly under the supervision of the PDU (although as there was only three of them on my Area and seven of us that was impossible). You would not be expected to do much except follow the tutor's lead and only get involved in things you had actually studied at University with regard to nicking, as technically it might not stand up in Court if you arrested someone for Going Equipped when you hadn't been given the legal knowledge to back this up. You didn't work Nights, only Earlys or Lates to "ease you in". This phase lasted about two weeks and was meant as a taster of what to expect later on.

The second phase got us with other tutors from other Sections. This time we had three weeks in the field and were still expected to follow the tutor and their examples but to take the initiative by about halfway through the second week and try to "lead" now and then. You would also work Nights.

By phase three which was six weeks you had yet another tutor and were now meant to be confident enough to act on your own initiative. You would be on Nights again and considered an integral part of the Section for the time you were with them.

Phase four was only a week and was simply to get you out on the streets for some more hands on experience before you went into the college for the final six weeks of live in Training before Passing Out. You were expected to "lead" nearly all the time.

After Passing Out you went straight to a CID attachment of between three and five months. Then you would then be assigned to a permanent Section and placed with another tutor until the end of probation.

These staggered phases were meant to enrich your understanding of the local Area in which you worked, get you involved with more than one Nick (I worked at three) and let you have a wider experience of the world of Policing than if you were with just one person all the time.

It was sold to us as a gradual and gentle way of getting us up to speed on having the confidence to use our new powers and interact with the General Public as well as seeing different parts of our Area.

Ahem...!

NOS's or National Occupational Standards were about 60 in number and touched on all the areas needed to be a competent Bobby. They ranged from ability to arrest and search a Suspect to First Aid and Respect for Race and Diversity. You had to write out an incident on a Word.doc template and justify why you felt the tutor should sign it off. These were difficult to write effectively, particularly as you had to be succinct due to the template only allowing a finite amount of words to be used.

The main problem is that every copper who's been in long enough will have their own way of doing things. Some would sign off NOS's with only a basic appraisal. Some would sign them off without saying anything. Others would refuse to do so unless you sent them photocopied PNB notes to back up what you were claiming as a competency.

This all added up to become a fairly depressing experience of being criticised for not doing something properly, when it might only be because that's what you were used to doing or had done on your last active phase. You are not given consistency or ground rules as people will do things the way they see them as needing to be done. Changes in Training protocols will leave tutors giving differing instructions to their fledglings and the trainees getting into trouble for not doing something the way their current overseer believes it should be done, regardless of whether they were told to do it that way by a predecessor.

PHASE 1 TUTOR

AUBREY

Aubrey was my first tutor and was a jolly, chubby faced lad in his late 20s. He had been in the job about eight years and worked directly for the PDU.

He was stickler for "doing it by the book" and would refuse to sign off any NOS's without having photocopied PNB notes to back them up. He would also insist the wording of the NOS box be accurate and would return unsigned, anything that didn't explain exactly what you'd done and how that justified claiming a competency. I eventually stopped sending him any and sent them instead to his counterparts from later phases, who would still want the NOS to be written correctly but weren't as pedantic on supporting evidence.

He was pleasant, friendly and supportive during the time I was with him and he would sometimes take up to three of us out if other tutors were away for any reason. As we were working weekends it meant we had the more exciting stuff to deal with such as Public Order, Drunk and Disorderlies and the odd Affray to sort out.

Second evening out and we were doing a Public Reassurance exercise down the local 15 to 18 disco. The night before there had been a hideous rape in a disused car park in town, from a guy who had been released from gaol only the day before after serving a prison sentence for a previous rape. The victim was coherent and lucid and after it was over had calmly attended the Nick to give a Statement and they caught the bloke within about three days. In light of the fact that 24 hours after the event, he was still uncaught and the Public were aware of what had happened via local press, we all put on our High Viz and marched about the grounds near the disco as various teenagers milled around outside.

The disco is at the bottom of a hilly area that leads to woods that continue back for about half a mile before meeting a main road further up. It is almost pitch black in there at night and 25 yards from the disco you cannot see your hand in front of your face without a torch or clear moonlight. As drinking alcohol in public is illegal if under 18 the kids would usually sneak off to the trees further back and sup their booze on the rocks facing the disco and the main road. Then, if we walked up they could either quickly hide or throw away the evidence and casually chat (while reeking of ale) with whichever officer had strolled up to check what they were doing.

Despite our presence the kids were still nonchalantly behaving like nothing was amiss and one or two, either through genuine interest or because they were pissed and thought it was amusing to talk to the Fuzz, asked us why there was so many Police knocking about.

"A rape in town last night" we told them "just here to make sure everyone's ok".

"Oooh...God! Did you catch him?"

"Not yet, but we will".

Within half an hour the buzz around the woods was that the Police wanted to arrest an escaped convict who had raped and murdered four women last night.

Didn't dampen their ardour for getting drunk though.

There were about 20 of us and while me, Aubrey and a couple of other officers were chatting to the Sergeant in charge of this Public Reassurance, a car pulled up and a middle aged woman dropped four girls off and then drove away.

They walked past us and joined the queue for the disco. It was February and I was only sufficiently warm as I had all my winter clobber on including the Traffic jacket, a scarf and my leather gloves. All four girls, who looked about 14 to 15 were wearing crop tops, miniskirts and high heels.

"What would you do if your daughter went out looking like that?" Aubrey asked the Sergeant when they were out of earshot.

"Bloody kill her" he replied looking annoyed.

Later as my mate Samson is walking past the queue someone deliberately knocks his cap off from behind. He didn't tell me and Aubrey until about five minutes later and was clearly embarrassed. Aubrey told him to forget about it and mark it down to experience. What would have been nice was to have guessed roughly where the little scrote that did it was standing and put your arm out in front of the person nearest to you and say "RIGHT! Until the person that did that is identified, NONE of you are coming in". You can guarantee that within a minute someone would have been pushed out mumbling furious denials where we could have leisurely told him or her off and sent them home, or if feeling especially judicious, nicked them for Assault on Police. Still, live and learn.

While walking around near the trees at the rear I see a girl with her back to a tree, clearly ratarsed and swaying like the bubble in a spirit level, even though she's sitting down.

"Are you OK?" I ask her.

"Yesh, I'm fine cunt stubble" she mumbles, then hawks up a big pile of phlegm and gobs it out on the ground next to her.

Like most of them she looks about 15 and is on her own, pissed up in a dark wood, 24 hours after a vicious sexual assault in town.

"What's your name".

"Shamanthur" she slurs

"Well Samantha, I think you're drunk. Do you have any friends here".

"I'm not drunk, I've jusht got my period" she mumbles, almost falling asleep while talking to me.

Aubrey walks up, stands next to me and says quietly "Lance, get her family's phone number and call them to come and pick her up".

I crouch down in front of her. "Do you have a mobile phone on you?"

"I'm not drunk, I've jusht got my period" she mumbles again looking at where she thinks I am but is clearly seeing twins as she's off centre by about three feet.

"So, that makes you burble, spit and act like this does it? You can either give me your mobile, tell me your family's phone number or you can come with us".

Just then about three girls appear from behind me and one says "Samantha! We were looking for you. It's OK officer, we'll look after her". I glance at Aubrey who nods silently and the three girls pick up the intoxicated kid and shepherd her away, back to the main group near the disco.

I see a group of kids in the shadows near a rock pile further up the hill in the last place you can sit comfortably without being in total darkness. I stroll up to chat with them and predictably my arrival is announced by the sound of tins and bottles clattering off the trees further up. They try to adopt innocent expressions as I walk up.

"Alright guys, everything ok?"

"Yes thanks officer, we're fine" says one lad.

"Not been drinking have you?" I ask casually.

"What? Us? No way!"

"Hmm...word of advice. Next time you see a cop walking up, just hide it quietly. You kicked up such a din getting rid of the evidence just then that I know exactly where to look for it".

They laugh and relax a little and ask why there's so many of us about. I tell them and there's shrieks from the girls and one guy puts his arm heroically around his girlfriend's shoulders and says "I'll protect her officer, no one will do anything while I'm about".

Another girl says she wants to go and her boyfriend says "you go, I'm gonna stay here". She starts to walk away, into the dark recesses of a wood that may have been the inspiration for the Blair Witch Project.

I call her back and turn to her boyfriend. "I just TOLD you that last night there was a rape in town. Now be a gentleman and go with her and BOTH of you take the long way round".

She smiles at this while he grizzles and moans but fair play to him, gets up and takes her arm and they walk down to the main road. I hear her say "that taught you a lesson didn't it?" as they stroll off.

I head back to the disco and the doorman announces that the

club is full and no one else can come in. He's not prepared to do "one in one out" so we tell the kids to disperse and go home. Cue much griping and complaining and the odd "fascist wankers" being overheard as they mill about, trying to delay the moment.

I walk over to a group of three lads standing on the left hand side of the building having a fag. "Excuse me lads, it's time to...oh hello John".

It's one of the lads from the school I worked at the previous November, the same one I caught at the train station fare dodging.

He does a double take, looks startled and then goes "NO WAY!" and extends his arms to give me a hug.

"Jesus! You're a fucking copper? Never guessed. Why didn't you tell us?"

I am embarrassed by this question and ashamed that I was forced to lie to him and his mates, but toe the party line and reply:

"We didn't think it was wise to let you know what I really did. Sorry you were deceived but it was thought it was for the best".

We chat for a while and his mates watch in silence, occasionally toking on their cigarettes. "Listen mate" I tell him "we're busy so I need to go. Can you three get going now. We need to clear the area".

"Sure, come on" he motions to the other two and turns back to me "a fucking copper. Never would have guessed" shaking his head and laughing and they walk off.

After we've managed to get the assembled underage revellers moved on we are driving up the road and see a group of about five lads drinking openly from wine bottles and beer cans. We do an about turn at the end of the road and when we get back the alcohol has magically vanished but the kids are still there, loitering outside someone's house, trying to act innocent.

We pull up. "Alright lads?" Aubrey says as he gets out. "Not drinking alcohol are you?". Cue the usual vehement denials and shaking of heads. Aubrey stops to chat to them, telling them about the rape last night. One of them is separate from the main bunch and loitering on the driveway of the house they are outside of, leaning on the wall and casting occasional rapid glances under the car parked on the drive.

I walk up to him. "What are you doing?"

"Nothing" he snaps, looking worried.

"Go and stand with the others".

"Why, I'm not doing anything?" he protests.

"Just do as you're told".

He stomps over to the main pack of kids and predictably the booze is under the car. As the wine has already been opened I simply pour it down the drain in the road in front of them, to much wailing and screams of "that cost three quid a bottle!".

Unfortunately for us not all the beer had been opened so we cannot dispose of it, even though they're under 18. While I would later see other tutors and officers ask the underage drinker offhandedly if he or she wouldn't mind opening the booze and pouring it away, we cannot force them to do it due to the rules on property and the fact that it is still sealed. Aubrey confiscates it all and we tell the kids to get someone over 18 to pick it up at the Station tomorrow. Cue a drive back to the Nick and 15 minutes booking it in to the Property Store.

INTEGRITY SWEETIES

In the Nick front office, like many businesses that have offices is a box. In it are a selection of sweeties. They range from loathed Liquorice Allsorts to yummy Éclairs and they cost a pound each. The box is made of cardboard as is the smaller box with a slit in it, at the front of the other box, where you put your £1, the cost of a bag. The box is owned by the RSPCA who come by every now and then to collect the "donations".

Nice and simple.

It's based on trust.

One day I was feeling peckish and asked the bored PSE receptionist in her heavy blue, v-neck sweater "can I take a bag and pay tomorrow?".

She replied "leave an IOU. Most people take them without paying for them".

So I dutifully filled out a piece of paper with my full name, Force number, amount owing and the date. I folded it up and put it in the slot and helped myself to a bag of toffees.

Nice and simple.

About a month later I got an email from Sergeant Kerwan. In it he stated that he was not impressed to have discovered that I had left an IOU in a charity sweet box. I called him up immediately and explained that I'd simply forgotten to clear it and would be round the Nick tonight to pay the outstanding 100 pence.

He replied "it's not as simple as that. This is an Integrity issue".

"Err... the receptionist suggested it. I told her I hadn't got any money"

"That's not the point" he seethes

"Am I in trouble for this?" I ask him.

"It depends if the Inspector wants to take it any further".

So, a genuine mistake and why Integrity? What kind of twat would leave their name and force number at the scene of a crime? Call me unworldly wise and lacking in knowledge of the subtle nuances of an officer's code of ethics but surely this is "being forgetful" as opposed to trying to deprive abandoned puppies of a kennel on Boxing Day.

The second stage exam is 10 days away. This has to be passed or those that fail both the first sitting and the resit will be backcoursed. Fail the third attempt and you will be forced to resign. Worrying about a bag of toffees and if they are going to get you disciplined or booted out of The Job is not conducive to sturdy revision of PACE and whatever they have dragged up from the depths of the omnipresent ocean that is Race and Diversity.

Next day my Personal Tutor suggests a call to the PDU to emphasise the pressure that "not knowing the consequences" are having and being brought up to speed would be a stress buster.

So another phone call to Kerwan who has covered the bases by nipping downstairs at some point between this and the last conversation and has spoken to the receptionist. Her story is now slightly modified and he states flatly that she said at the time "the least you can do is leave an IOU" and was NOT happy about me taking the sweets without paying for them. He clearly believes this is the Gospel according to St. Luke and is adamant permission was not given or suggestion made.

"That's not true" I protest "she was the one who suggested it"

"STOP ARGUING WITH ME!" he shrieks down the phone.

A short pause.

He then says "we have scheduled a meeting with you and the PDU Inspector at 4pm next Wednesday about this".

This means leaving studies two hours early for the 20 mile journey through heavy traffic to the Nick. My addendum that this is causing me worry before an important exam is simply met with him telling me "you need to balance the stresses of your job".

The next week was far from pleasant. Revision, worry and also getting ready for a Race and Diversity presentation on Hindu, Sikh, Muslim or Gypsy that some genius had stuck the day before the exam.

Crunch time and the new campus Sarge at Uni was more sympathetic and as I was about to set off whispered "don't worry it'll be alright" which buoyed my spirits somewhat.

Upon arrival Kerwan was there as was the PDU Inspector plus Aubrey, the tutor from my last active phase. Ma'am wanted to know about me and asked about what I'd done before joining, which turned out to be an attempt to see if I'd wax lyrical about being a Special Constable as Aubrey had noted on two pages of A4, amongst other observations, that I tended to talk about this a lot which he felt "undermined" other officers.

They also picked up on my "obsession with rank" and getting promoted when I was only a newby of 12 weeks service. "You want to be a Chief Inspector no less" PDU Ma'am tutted (I had mentioned this ONCE in the car to Aubrey while driving around bored waiting for calls). I mentioned July 7th 2005's terrorist attacks and how being on duty that day as a Special was something I was proud of and that event had inspired me to join full time.

We then moved on to the nasty, heinous crime of the bag of toffees and she read from two sheets of typed paper written by Kerwan where he mentioned shrieking at me down the phone not to argue with him and how he had consulted many other officers to ask their opinion on the matter (but didn't name any) and they had all agreed it was a huge breach of Integrity for a cop. He also mentioned the single fact that was, when you boil it down to its basic elements, the real reason they got the arsehole over this. The fact that the Force was embarrassed by the Charity rep finding the IOU in the box on collection day.

She asked if I had anything to say and instead of sticking up for myself and boldly stating that Kerwan had not handled this fairly and that the receptionist was lying I simply mumbled my apologies and said that I was really embarrassed.

Kerwan then told me I would have a File Note for six months for Integrity, plus an Action Plan for the same and any further issues over this area would result in him approaching the Superintendent to ask for Regulation 13- dismissal of probationer.

I was then excused and told I could go, only to find I had a flat battery on the car and the AA had to come to the Nick and tow me home.

PHASE 2 TUTOR

SONJA

My second phase tutor was a bad tempered female.

She had joined three years previously, was in her early twenties and permanently looked like she'd just drunk a bottle of vinegar. First couple of shifts she was on Annual Leave meaning I was partnered with other officers off her Section. When she made it in a few days later we were introduced and began what would be an utterly unfulfilling and professionally pointless partnership in the name of probationary development.

For textbook examples she was fine. She'd done the tutor training course and was good enough at The Job to be able to demonstrate how to arrest, the correct use of Betari's Box, conflict resolution and application of the Law. However when it came to life experience she had hardly any and was one of the most ignorant officers I ever worked with.

What I didn't know at the time was that she was mentally making notes (that she would later write down) on absolutely everything I said and did, regardless of whether it was Job related or not.

One of the things she noted was my walk. It was in her tutorly opinion a "cocky strut" which she felt might be off putting to the public. I've always walked like that and still do. It's my natural gait and other than taking up Tai Chi there's nothing I can do about it. In hindsight it was inappropriate for her to even raise this, what with the rules on Diversity but hindsight is as hindsight does.

Then it was that I used "complicated language". Having been an English teacher for over a decade I am comfortable using words of more than two syllables. I also naively assumed that a fellow officer, especially one tutoring me would be at least as intelligent as me and probably more so. I never used difficult words with the public and certainly not with Suspects, but felt relaxed enough with Sonja to 'be myself' and speak how I've always been comfortable speaking. On a couple of occasions she said she didn't understand what I meant and the crunch came one night in the Writing Room when we were filling out our PNB's mid shift after arresting a couple of drunken louts.

"Hey Lance, what's another word for stubborn?" she asked, chewing the end of her pen.

"Recalcitrant"

(She pulls a face as if I've just farted and throws the pen across the table) "WHAT!...What does THAT mean? I've told you about this before!"

"You asked me for a syno...for another word for stubborn" I plead in mitigation.

"I didn't mean a word like THAT!"

She reported me in writing to the PDU for using "complicated language" and at our post phase meeting told Sergeant Kerwan and PC Esobé about this conversation. Kerwan took her side, ignored my pleas that I was only responding to a direct question and gave me an Action Plan for "moderating my language to suit the target audience".

Then she picked me up on the fact that, while telling stories I would make funny faces and do voices. This was solely during non Job related conversations, such as in the car or while having Refs. She'd said nothing to me at the time during our little chats but again wrote it all down. One time in the Nick kitchen with an officer named Tabitha she said cheerfully "hey Lance, do that face you said your girlfriend says you do when you're angry to show Tabitha". I complied with the request, Tabitha giggled and at the post phase meeting Sonja brought it up.

"I only did that because you asked me to" I said, astounded that she had the cheek to raise this as a development point.

"I only wanted to see if it freaked Tabitha out as much as it did me" she replied.

Kerwan duly compiled an Action Plan for "paying attention to my own body language and NVCs" based on both this report and the one about my 'strut'.

Other times she just gave poxy, ill informed advice that I was supposed to take as Gospel truth.

We were driving near a school one quiet, autumn morning about nine o'clock. The streets were chocca with cars parked either side from one end to the other. Kids were milling about, as were many grown ups, trying to shepherd their energetic offspring through the gates or returning home after having just dropped them off. Driving just ahead of us was a woman in a car, using her mobile phone. I spotted her and nudged Sonja who then followed her. Oblivious to the fact she had a Police car on her tail the woman continued merrily on for another 200 yards until we flashed her to pull over.

I approach the car. It contains a big, fat woman, still holding her mobile and two little kids I hadn't noticed before. One is in a baby seat in the front and looks about six months old. The rear passenger is a four year old girl. The woman winds down the window.

"Do you know why I've stopped you?", the classic opener.

"Err..no not really"

"You're using your mobile phone. Do you realise that's an offence?"

"Oh, no I didn't"

There's no way she couldn't have known as it's been illegal for around three years and two months ago became more serious.

" Do you realise how dangerous it is to drive while holding your mobile phone? It's now a £60 fine and three points on your licence. Do you want to receive a fine? "

"No, not really", looking at me with complete disinterest.

I tell her how I can, if I wish, take her to Court for this and she might be given a £1000 fine and as many points on her licence as they see fit to award her. It doesn't appear to be sinking in and she either couldn't give a toss or is too stupid to realise the gravity of what she's done. I am right on the very edge of reaching for the EFPN book when she finally shows some emotion.

"I'm sorry. I really am. I was in a hurry I won't do it again".

I relax slightly. "OK, this time I will simply give you words of advice but I have your registration number. If I see you again I WILL fine you. Do you understand?"

"Yes, thank you".

"God forbid you should have an accident and one of your children was to go through the windscreen".

She thanks me, winds up the window and drives off slowly.

I turn to Sonja who'd been standing behind me the whole time.

"What did you think?" I ask her.

"Not bad, the way you dealt with it was ok. Just one thing though. Don't say 'God forbid'. She may not have any religion and you may have offended her".

I try to ignore this but it burns its way in.

It's not like I specified a sodding deity. I didn't' say "Jehovah protect you" or "Allah save us". We're now supposed to be sensitive to offending hypothetical Atheists by not mentioning the name of something they don't think exists, as if the mention of this non-thing will drive them to the Professional Standards unit in tears of righteous indignation.

The best advice Sonja gave though, was when I told her I was taking Ginseng capsules for energy during Night duty.

"What's Ginseng?" Sonja asked, with the same face as when I'd said 'recalcitrant'.

"A herbal remedy, you can buy it anywhere".

"Do you need to go to the chemist's to buy it? Is it a prescription drug?"

"Err...no. It's a herbal remedy, anyone can buy it, they sell it in Sainsbury's".

She ponders for a minute and then says "don't take it any more. If you have an accident on duty while driving and they check your stomach they might find it and you won't be insured because they'll think it's an illegal stimulant. Drink coffee if you need to stay awake".

The fact that coffee is less effective than pure Ginseng and has adverse side effects would be beyond Sonja's ability to understand so I didn't argue. I didn't stop taking them however and wondered quietly how such a gormless individual ever got to take responsibility for Probies.

Months later I sent her a NOS to be signed off. It came back a week later with a note attached:

"I have amended your abrevasions as this is a university degree and needs to be written as such".

Oh sweet joy!

The Federation thought it was hilarious and the Inspector I took it to agreed that if someone is going to pick you up on using complicated language they should at least use words that actually exist.

YOUTH HOSTEL ANCIENT WILLIAM

Booking In to Custody nowadays is a very civilised, nae pleasant affair.

The American routine of getting locked in a big tank and names being called out as prisoners are ready to be processed is not for the English Police.

Oh no!

The entrance from the car park is an enclosed garage with a roll gate that can be sealed in the event of a Suspect being so incompliant that officers need to forestall him or her getting away before opening the rear doors of the van. You enter the back of the Custody area into the Holding Cell where, if you are a Compliant Suspect, you sit on a wooden bench and your pockets are emptied. The arresting officer then puts the contents in a large, transparent plastic bag and fills out one form to say what's in the bag and another with your personal details and what you were nicked for.

If there is a queue of Suspects to be booked in then you wait your turn. If officers arrive with someone who is Non Compliant or needs a breath test then they will jump the queue. When the Custody skipper is ready to see you you will be let into the Booking In area (through a locked gate that the Sergeant or his PSE assistant will open for you) to Be Presented.

This is a formality on a par with joining the Cub Scouts.

The skipper will ask for handcuffs to be removed if you are wearing them (provided you are Compliant) and after checking for abrasions (and provided you are STILL Compliant) ask you to remain silent and then ask the arresting officer "can you give me the grounds for the arrest please?" and the officer whose Body you are will say:

"Well Sergeant, at 8.05pm tonight in Tongue Street I was on routine patrol in a marked Police vehicle when I saw this male waving his penis at passers by in the vicinity of Luigi's Pizza House. I stopped my vehicle, parking without causing unnecessary obstruction to other road users, exited the vehicle and asked this male to put his penis back in his trousers to which he refused. I then arrested him, cautioned him (to which he gave no reply) and applied handcuffs (for reasons of officer safety) in the front stack position and in the Home Office approved manner. I then conveyed him here for further questioning".

Hopefully by this point the Suspect has long since been persuaded to put his knob away.

The Sergeant will then Make A Decision about whether or not to detain you further questioning (i.e. give you a cell) and if he does it will go like this:

"Do you have anything you wish to say at this point? No? Well, I'm authorising your detention for further questioning".

You will then be asked questions as if you are booking in to a fairly reasonable hostel from a Lonely Planet guide. The Sergeant is legally obliged to ask:

"Do you have any religious needs that I should know about? Have you ever tried to harm yourself? Are you currently on medication? Are you currently taking illegal drugs? Are you an alcoholic? Do you wish to talk to anyone about drugs or alcohol misuse? Are you nut allergic? Do you require any special dietary requirements such as Halal meat, vegetarian or gluten free food? Do you want anyone informed you are here? Do you require a solicitor?"

It goes on.

If you say no to each of the above you will be processed in about 15 minutes. You will then be scanned with a portable metal detector like they use in airports and anything you could hang yourself with you will be asked politely to hand over (belts, necklaces, tracksuit bottom cords etc) and your property will be placed in the clear plastic bag and then sealed in front of you with a unique identity tag that cannot be removed without being cut off. Your photo will then be taken against a white backboard. You will be handed a copy of your Rights While In Custody and led to a cell where you will be asked to remove your shoes and if you're really good you will be offered a cup of tea, coffee, hot chocolate or mineral water by either the officer putting you in the cell or the Support Staff helping out behind the desk. You are entitled to eight hours uninterrupted sleep (not our fault if the guy in cell 7 keeps kicking the door) and if you are considered a risk you will be on Constant. At some point your fingerprints will be taken plus DNA via an oral swab if you haven't had DNA taken before (and if you are still Compliant)

It doesn't matter what you are in for, provided you toe the line and behave you will be treated well. While most agree with the humane treatment of prisoners I have seen more than one repeat offender being fetched out of his cell on his way to either be issued with a PND or to see the Magistrates who will greet the Custody Staff by name and act like he's been staying at a mate's house.

If you are released for whatever reason but cannot afford the bus or train fare home then the Custody skipper will provide you with a voucher good for one journey on public transport to your place of domicile. If you live locally you will probably get a lift home off a double crewed car (I had the latter pleasure after interviewing a particularly loathsome 15 year old female repeat offender who acted like she was doing us a favour by even getting in the car).

The taxpayer picks up the tab for ALL of this.

The above can be summed up by the fact that someone had printed a sign and stuck it above the hot drinks machine, designated for those in Custody. It read:

"Do NOT take these drinks just because you cannot afford one from the staff canteen".

Scribbled underneath in biro was "Only prisoners get free drinks" to which someone else had added in red felt tip "Yeah, too fucking right".

OPEN DAY

Open Day is where the doors to the local Police Station are thrown open to the General Public to have a poke about the building. All areas except those classified as containing sensitive material are available for a good nose around, including the Custody Suite and the CID offices. While CID is just lots of In trays and computer terminals Custody is exciting for most people as it is a strange world to behold if you haven't been in there before as either a cop, an official visitor or an unwilling guest

The public get to see all this, the Breathalyser, the DNA kits, the LiveScan machine, the old fashioned ink method for taking fingerprints and the cells for drunks (the mattress is on the floor so they can't roll off the bed) and for Minors (a separate wing).

The car park is open (with appropriate supervision) for people to have a sit in a Police car, fiddle with the controls and giggle as the demonstrating officer activates the siren (very briefly) and the blue lights.

The event was heavily advertised in the local press, the internal briefings, on the local radio stations and via posters outside the Nick. Also word of mouth from cops and PCSOs. This was a chance to let the Public see exactly what their local Bobbies got up to and how they worked. A glorious, friendly, well-intentioned bit of positive press for the local Area and the Force in general as they strove to bring themselves closer to their Local Community and its residents.

Sounds like a wonderful idea.

Ahem...!

Due to the "confrontational" nature of an active Custody Suite it was not possible to have people traipsing about in it if there were Bodies in the Bin. The risk assessment stated that due to Health and Safety the public absolutely could NOT enter the cell area unless it was not in use.

So the Chief Super' sent out a missive stating that, the day before the Open Day, arrestees would only be admitted to the Nick up to midnight and only then for offences that would not result in the Suspect having to stay overnight (i.e. Bailable, PNDable or Cautionable naughtiness). Anyone detained for more serious bad behaviour or ne'er do wells caught after 12am were to be taken to the Custody Suite in the neighbouring Area's Designated Station.

At 11.45pm on the Night duty before the Open Day me and Sonja were having a scoff in the Refs room when a Panic Alarm was triggered. As we all dropped our kebabs and chips on the table and the TV volume was muted the following could be heard over a background hullabaloo:

"It's pandemonium here...we're at the Duck and Anvil pub in Turnbar Street...need backup NOW!"

(Panting and gasping from the officer, plus what sounds like a violent struggle with glass breaking and loud shouting).

"Repeat, backup needed asap...FUCK OFF! PUT THAT DOWN! PUT IT DOWN YOU BASTARD!...Jesus! Get everyone here who can be. At least 10 people fighting"

He went on but by this time we'd all leapt over the back of the sofas and were piling out into the vehicles at the front of the Nick. I lost Sonja in the melee and got in the back of the Rowdy Van, realising I'd get left behind if I didn't immediately find alternative transport,

The pub was within the jurisdiction of the neighbouring town's Police station and as we got there I was shocked to see it was only 300 yards from their Nick...the one with the Open Day tomorrow.

As we pulled up with a screech of tyres outside the pub many people could be seen milling about with broken glass littering the street. The majority seemed to be observing what was going on like they were tourists at a safari park, sipping from pint glasses as they watched the show. In the middle of the road were about five or six Police officers and around seven or eight civilians. One guy was on the floor on his stomach with two officers sitting on top of him, one of whom was struggling with a pair of cuffs while the Suspect wriggled and tried to shake them off. Further back was a female officer pushing a female civilian away from the three on the tarmac. The woman was attempting to slap her in the face and the officer pushed her back against a stationery vehicle and grabbed her arm, trying to subdue her. Two other officers were trying to keep a guy out of the fighting who kept walking forward, gesturing wildly with his arms and bobbing his head aggressively. Another Red Bull Rooster. Barry and the front seat passenger Tabitha both piled out into the road. I tried the handle on the sliding door I was sitting next to. It wouldn't open. I banged on the glass before Tabitha could get away. She turned around and looked at me and I shouted "I CAN'T GET OUT, IT'S JAMMED!" She shrugged and with Barry ran to help the other officers. In frustration I clambered over the back of the seats and into the driver's seat, banging my arse hard on the gear stick, jarring my knee on the handbrake and opened the door on the driver's side. Just as I climbed out I heard the guy on the floor scream at the top of his lungs and looked over to see him pinned to the floor with four officers holding him. Tabitha was laying on top of his legs (approved OST technique), two officers were holding an arm each and Barry was sitting on his back. In front of all of them holding a can of Pava, still pointed at the screaming Suspect, was Sergeant Hershey.

Sergeant Hershey was a GIANT of a man. About 6' 4" with a chest the width of an ERV's radiator grill and shoulders like that American Colonel off the Kenny Everett Television Show. He had hands like shovels and boots that looked like they were about size 14½. His load vest and Stabby had to be seen to be believed as they were at least twice size of mine and the Force almost certainly had to have had them specially made for him. He had been doing Custody skipper duty one night when I turned up with a drunk, gobby prisoner who winged, grizzled and complained while being searched and processed in the Holding Cell. When he wouldn't shut up the Sergeant walked slowly forward, nodded acknowledgment to me and then glared at the bloke through the bars of the locked gate to the Booking In area.

"OI! YOU!" he says loudly but not shouting.

The Suspect turns to him and continues moaning and swearing loudly.

"SHUT UP!" Hershey says loudly but still not shouting, standing there impassively with his hands tucked inside his Stabby. His chevrons are pinned to the front of his load vest and look tiny amongst all that webbing. "THIS IS MY CUSTODY SUITE AND IF YOU DON'T CALM DOWN YOU CAN GO IN A CELL NOW OK?"

The lad looks at him. Hershey stares back. The lad clams up and is good as gold for the rest of the Booking In right up until he went in the cell.

Tabitha and Barry are coughing and spluttering and the screaming guy underneath has tears running down his face and snot dribbling from his nose. Hershey has just sprayed him in the face. I found out later that my not being able to get out of the van saved me from Tabitha and Barry's fate as they caught the splash back from the Suspect's faceful and although luckily they didn't get it in their eyes, Tabitha got a shot down her throat (imagine eating a raw red chilli pepper) and Barry got it on his neck, causing his skin to redden.

Chaos and pandemonium. People still milling about. The woman who was scrapping with the female officer has now been handcuffed and is standing quietly. Turns out her husband is the bloke on the floor. Another woman is also in handcuffs as is a second man. Myself and other officers not being used in the actual nicking are keeping the rubber neckers back.

"Lance stick her in the back of yours will you, we'll put her other half in another van" the female officer says to me, gesturing to the sullen woman she's arrested.

I escort her to the van. "Mind your head" I tell her as she climbs in, grabbing her arm to help her up. She sits down on the wooden seat and doesn't say anything. I shut the cage door but leave the rear door ajar, as per Force policy in case the poor little waif suffocates.

I walk back to the scrum pile in the road. Hershey is in a heated discussion with another officer. There are now about 10 cops on the scene and two Rowdy vans plus about four squad cars.

"I don't give a shit!" Hershey snaps.

"But they've told us not to" the other officer tells him.

"FUCK Senior Management!" Hershey barks at him, while double locking the cuffs on the bloke on the ground. "I'm taking them to the Nick"

"They won't admit them, it's after 12" the officer persists.

"They will if I tell them to. This is fucking ridiculous, a Nick 300 yards away or one twenty miles away. What the fuck do they think they're playing at?"

He reaches for his radio, "Nine-twelve to Control".

"kkkk...go ahead"

"Message for Custody at Charlie One. Four coming in. Assault on Police, Affray and Breach of the Peace. I don't care about the Open Day, we are bringing them in. Too many people for mass transportation to alternative Area, over".

The operator begins repeating the message over the air.

The other prisoners are loaded into the van and the cars and we make the two minute journey to the station.

Upon hearing the vehicles pulling in the Custody skipper runs out looking visibly nervous and immediately takes Hershey to one side.

I stand next to the open rear door of one of the squad cars containing the second arrested female. She is the other one's mother and apparently got nicked for BoP for hurling abuse at the female officer arresting her daughter. Hershey made an example of her and had her nicked. She is calm but evidently miserable and a little embarrassed. I kill time by getting her to give me her details which I put in my PNB to speed up the Booking In process.

I get another officer to stand with her while I take details from the other male who was arrested. He is calm too and is the brother of the guy on the ground. He's been nicked for Affray due to him and his brother scrapping in whatever incident first warranted a Police response. The other parties involved either scarpered or had the common sense to stand still and act like innocent onlookers upon hearing the sirens.

After about ten minutes Hershey walks back over and says to the driver of the car the woman is in "right, they are going to book them in here but then we have to take them to the alternative Nick. This has come from the Guv'nor". He looks visibly annoyed but there's no more he can do as someone of senior rank has overridden him.

As neither me nor Sonja had nicked anyone we hooked up again and headed back to our Station.

About a week later we found out that the Open Day was a great success with a couple of journalists writing favourable praise about how professional and modern the Nick was and how fascinating it was to see the functionings of a fully active Police Station, in particular the Custody Suite. One of the journos waxed lyrical about how interesting it was to step inside a cell, even for a few moments.

Twenty miles away there were four arrestees, caught for very serious offences at an incident within shouting distance of the Nick who were, as the Open Day was in full swing, still being processed by a different Area. The journey there and back took a cage van, three cars, about six constables and a Sergeant out of the Area and out of active duty for about four hours.

In their desire to impress the locals, SMT had trodden over any sense of safety or correct utilisation of resources. They didn't care where Suspects went, they just didn't want them in their nice, smart Police Station on Open Day.

PHASE 3 TUTOR

JACOB

Old school attitude and then some, Jacob was the same age as me, had been in The Job for six years and like a few officers I knew, had been in the Army before joining up.

He stated on Day One that he wanted me to deal with three things during our time together. A Road Traffic Collision (fatal if possible), a Sudden Death and a Fight.

I was partnered with him on day one on a Morning Shift and at 5.30am a big bloke with glasses came out of the Briefing Room and went "Mulligan?"

I turned around "no, Manley".

"Oh, sorry. Do you want to come in we're about to start".

We had the initial Briefing where I was introduced to the Section skipper, Sergeant Kershaw who was ten years younger than me but super confident and reminded me of Chachi from Happy Days with his wide boy demeanour. After, me and Jacob got in the Emergency Response Vehicle after doing the requisite pre-Shift safety check (all lights, equipment, siren and radio) and then trundled along the bypass to a hot food stall used by lorry drivers and the odd early bird office worker.

First day out and we got a call to assist with a suspected Theft at a firm in the outer limits of our Area's jurisdiction. They worked installing and maintaining cash point machines for various banks and all employees were strictly forbidden to have more than £10 in cash on them during working hours. A driver had been found with a large wad of notes in a false heel of his boot and we were despatched to nick him and bring him in. His crew mate was also under suspicion and while Jacob went to arrest the detained shoe thief, I went to witness a search of the other bloke being conducted by the firm's own internal security manager.

I introduced myself and told the guy that at this moment I was just there to observe. The man was clearly uneasy and nervous and as soon as he took off his jacket I spotted a large wodge of £20 notes on the floor.

"Whose is that?" I asked them both.

"Mine" the driver says.

"Right" I pick them up and count them, there's £220 there. I put them in an evidence bag from my load vest pocket and motion to the security manager to continue. He searches the bloke but finds nothing more. Making sure I am standing in the only available exit, between the van and the wall I then arrest the guy.

"You are under arrest on Suspicion of Theft. You do not have to say anything but it may harm your defence if you do not mention when questioned something which you later rely on in court. Anything you do say may be given in evidence. Do you understand?"

He is visibly agitated, red in the face and I tense up and assume a posture more able to deal with him if he decides to get rowdy (i.e. hands on my load vest like I'm holding a pair of braces so all that lovely equipment is accessible with my body sideways on to him so I am less of a target. I also check again that he can't get past me without using force). He starts remonstrating:

"Fucking hell what's going on? That's not fair" but doesn't deny what he's been nicked for.

"I'm going to search you again. Turn around please."

"I've just been searched once" he protests.

"That was NOT a Police search. You are now under arrest and I am searching you under Section 32 of the Police and Criminal Evidence Act. Please turn around."

He does so with lots of huffing and puffing while the security guard looks on. I thankfully remember my OST and say "please put your arms out by your sides...thank you...now look to your left". I search his right side and then switch "please look to your right, keep your arms up. Thank you". I frisk his left upper half and then "please put your hands behind your back with the backs of your palms together". He complies and I grasp his thumbs firmly during a frisk of his lower half, in case he decides to move suddenly I'll know about it the same time he does it.

After finding nothing more I say "fine. You can turn around now". He is less agitated now, but still looks pissed off and upset. "If you remain calm I will handcuff you with your hands to the front. Are you calm?"

"Yeah" he replies, almost as a grunt. I mime the position I want him to adopt with his arms (think 'One Potato, Two Potato' but with each fist next to the other forearm) and then cuff him. As we walk out the yard, Jacob already has the other Suspect in the car and looks up in surprise as he sees me leading the accomplice out by the arm. He radios through to Control requesting another vehicle for my detainee as they have to be separated.

About an hour later we get them to Custody and book them in. When we are finished after about another two hours we go upstairs for Refs and over a cuppa Jacob says "that Security guard rang me about ten minutes ago. Said he was very impressed with how you dealt with that. Said he could tell you were new. I said I agreed with him and he wanted to write a letter congratulating you. I told him to address it to the Chief Super".

I am bowled over by this. First day of the third phase. An arrest AND what SMT like to call a 'Gong of Praise' from the Public. Things are looking up.

Unfortunately he never wrote the letter, or if he did I was never told but it's nice to know the thought was there, for however long it lasted.

Throughout my time with Jacob he was straight as an arrow and true as the bow that fired it. He expected me to get stuck in to everything we did but would not embarrass me like a later tutor did by watching me deal with something even if he could tell I didn't know how to. On a 6am drugs raid where Rapid Entry officers boshed the door down with the Red Key and we found heroin on the premises Jacob insisted we were at the vanguard of the entry team and later said this was because he wanted to see how I would deal with the situation.

Later we dealt with what could euphemistically be called a "Non Compliant Suspect" who was pissed and aggressive, resisted arrest and had to be Cell Exited. Jacob got me to actually nick him, while he hovered with his pepper spray, again just to see how I'd handle it.

He had zero tolerance to cell phone use while driving and would frequently park up at specific spots in the Area and wait for people to trundle past in their motor, yapping away on a mobile. It never took longer than 15 minutes to catch someone doing this. Cue sirens and blue lights and embarrassed mumbling from whoever we'd caught. On one occasion the bloke we stopped completely denied using the phone even though we had both seen him. Jacob looked at him affronted and went:

"Oh! Oh! You are lying to me Sir. I am a Police officer and my Integrity is beyond question". The guy then realised the mistake he'd made trying to deny it and after he'd been cautioned looked like he wanted to jump off the bridge we were standing next to. Jacob asked him if he would prefer the option of an FPN rather than going to Court which he gratefully accepted.

Lesson to be learned: Don't try and deny it if you know we've seen you do it.

Jacob was exactly the kind of officer you wanted next to you in a fight as he was big, not afraid of confrontation and took no nonsense. One time we were driving around near the Nick in the early hours when I spotted two lads having what was clearly a row outside a closed kebab shop. As soon as they spotted the Patrol car they immediately pretended to be pals by putting their arms around each other and grinning inanely at us. Jacob simply drove the 400 yards to the mini roundabout and did a 360, driving back in time to see them punching hell out of each other. We piled out, arrested them both for Affray and threatened to nick the girlfriend of my Suspect for Obstruction if she didn't push off and stop trying to pull her boyfriend away.

When I got my lad to the Custody Suite for Booking In, Jacob's Inspector, Mr Harwood was behind the desk filling out some paperwork. The lad had tried to talk his way out of both getting nicked and being brought to the Station and now that he realised he'd passed the point of no return he was kicking up a din to the skipper, crying about how unfair it was and waving his hands about aggressively. His cuffs had been removed and the skipper was making no attempt to stop his behaviour. Inspector Harwood stood there watching me and the Arrestee in silence.

After a couple of minutes I took the initiative and said "listen, if you don't calm down and start being respectful you're going back in handcuffs". He continued to winge loudly so I got the cuffs out, slapped one on his left wrist and was about to put his hands behind his back to lock the other one when the skipper said:

"It's ok".

I removed them and put them back in the holster and the Suspect remained calm for the rest of the Booking In. After I'd put him in a cell I walked past the Inspector and nodded "Sir", fairly embarrassed that this had happened while the Guv was observing me. He smiled and replied "I think you handled that really well".

Jacob was also fair and had a lot of compassion, particularly for the elderly and children. We had to nick a guy in his 70s on Suspicion of Indecent Assault and when we arrived at the address Jacob told the man's concerned wife that we needed to chat with the gentleman in private. We took him out to the car, sat him in the back where he was arrested and cautioned but not handcuffed. Later Jacob pointed out that if the case went nowhere it wasn't fair to nick him in front of other people for something he may be innocent of.

Another time a woman approached us when we were in a public car park with her very timid 7 year old daughter hiding behind her skirt. She said the little girl really loved the Police and wanted to see a real Police car. Jacob got out straight way and let her try on his cap and sit in the driver's seat while he activated the lights and siren. Then we both posed for a photo with the still-shy kid (still wearing Jacob's cap) sat on the bonnet with us either side.

A pain in the arse of our Nick was a local homeless woman. She was constantly getting arrested for everything from Criminal Damage to Shoplifting and was cunning and crafty in her methods. Jacob said he believed she was trying to get herself committed to a mental hospital so she could have somewhere to live and so far her attempts had been in vain as she'd been assessed at least twice and they wouldn't declare her insane.

She weighed 17 stone, was about 5 feet 4" and although obese was immensely strong. One day we got a call from Control to say that Paramedics were with her near the river and were scared as she was threatening them.

Jacob warned me that she would kick off if she felt like it and might need subduing with force. When we got there there were two ambulance crew standing well away from her while she sat smoking a cigarette on a bench. She'd apparently called 999 to request their help but once they'd turned up had got aggressive and obnoxious.

"Alright there, what's going on then?" Jacob said cheerfully.

She looked up under her baseball cap brim at him, shrugged and then went "oh just fuck off all of you, you're no fucking use to me".

The ambulance crew drove away and when we were content she was simply going to sit there we left too.

Three minutes down the road and CCTV radioed us directly:

"kkk...Yankee-Nine from Cameras over?"

"Go ahead".

"She's just thrown one of the life rings into the river".

We head back and she's standing there looking smug. About 50 metres away and heading out on the current is the aforementioned life ring, no use to anyone now.

Jacob walks towards her "what did you do that for?"

She says nothing but stands there smirking.

"That could have saved a kiddy's life" Jacob tells her looking pissed off.

"I've killed 74 people you know" she proudly states "I buried their bodies under the river". There is no trace of anger, shame, nervousness or even agitation about her and she's clearly saying this in order to get nicked.

"Really" says Jacob with one hand on his Pava "when was that then?"

"Last year" she replies still smirking "they're buried under the riverbed".

"Well we dredged the fucker last month and we didn't find them".

"I'm very good at it" she says, not missing a beat, then adds "I'm thinking of killing more people, I really enjoy it, I just can't help it. I'm also thinking of killing myself".

The claims of genocide (and presumably a very large wet suit and scuba equipment) plus the threats of self harm mean we are now obliged to do something and can't just leave the malodorous lump like last time.

"What did you throw the life ring in for?" Jacob asks again "a little kiddy could drown because of that".

She shrugs and smiles broadly "I just love killing people. What are you going to do with me?"

"Take you into the countryside and fucking leave you there for all I care darling".

He gets on his radio and tells Control that we're taking her to a mental hospital in the adjoining Area.

She is completely compliant and sits in the back of the car quiet and docile with me next to her during the drive to the hospital.

The duty manager is immediately abrupt and doesn't want to admit her. Jacob pulls him to one side and they step into a corridor and close the door to have a chat. After ten minutes Jacob comes out and we sit and wait with her for about an hour until the manager and a nurse come out and ask to speak to us outside. Our Suspect has sat there all this time without saying a word. As we walk out the front the sliding doors dramatically close in between us and the manager. They clearly planned this because when we turn around the manager has started walking back into the building. Jacob taps on the glass and says "open the doors" and reluctantly they do. "Are you not going to admit her then?" Jacob asks.

The manager shakes his head and our homeless mass murderer then says angrily "well if I'm not crazy why do I keep killing people?".

The manager smirks at this and she lunges towards him shouting "WHAT! YOU THINK THIS IS FUNNY?" and takes a big haymaker swing at him with her fist. He steps back so it doesn't connect but me and Jacob both spotted the way he jutted his chin out as she started the punch. However, his instincts overrode his desire to force us to have to nick her and there was no physical contact due to him leaping back like a startled salmon at the last moment.

I grab hold of her and pull her to one side. As she is twice my size and about a third again of my strength it is obvious she is letting me control her.

"Calm down or I'll put the handcuffs back on".

"Think I care about your poxy handcuffs?" she sneers but remains standing still.

Jacob and the manager talk briefly and then Jacob walks over to us.

"Plan B. There's another place we can go to". He winks at me after she turns around and we get back in the car. I don't like sitting next to her as she stinks but it turns out this was to be a very brief trip.

He drives into the town centre, about three miles up the road. "Lance what we're about to do is called Positive Action if you get my meaning". I don't but guess he's got something planned that he's trying to communicate to me, even though I have no idea what it is.

We pull up outside a newsagents. Jacob unclips his seatbelt and turns to me "Lance, leave your seatbelt on". Then he looks at her and says "before we go to the next place do you want to get a chocolate bar or something". He reaches into his pocket and pulls out some change. "Here's 60p, get a Yorkie or something yeah?".

She looks suspicious but doesn't say anything. Still smiling Jacob then casually says "come on, I'll come with you. I want to get a paper anyway".

She gets out the back and Jacob the front. They walk together into the newsagents. Ten seconds later Jacob comes pegging it out of the doorway, grins broadly at me through the window then gets in and starts the car, pulling away rapidly. Within about two minutes we are half a mile away.

While astonished at this I think it's hilarious and am still giggling when Jacob says "best tell the skipper what happened" and radios in that procedurally he's done everything by the book as she's an adult, doesn't have anywhere to live and as the hospital wouldn't admit her she's therefore not a "Vulnerable Person" and is in fact legally sane. He also adds that while dumping unwanted gits on other Areas isn't the done thing, it's only because the hospital is in their jurisdiction. The skipper backs him up and it's the last we hear of it.

A week later he nicked her again while I was on a separate attachment. This time for shoplifting a rucksack in Millets. A week after that I was in Custody as another officer was booking her in for Assault. Later still she smashed up the foyer of the Youth Offending Team offices with a hammer. Each time she was arrested they simply Bailed her or Cautioned her. A probationer off my trainee intake said she had overheard her screeching "I'm carrying syringes full of HIV-infected blood every day. Do you really want me on the streets infecting everyone?".

At the end of the phase Jacob gave me constructive feedback and was fair and balanced about it. He told me that tutors are taught never to solely praise ANYONE they observe but instead to use the "Shit Sandwich" and balance good feedback with bad. This might seem fair but if you're perfect as you can be, they will STILL find something to have a go at you for even if it's to put more polish on your boots or tidy up your PNB handwriting.

Of all the tutors I had, Jacob was the fairest, most level headed, streetwise and inspirational. He didn't expect you to do anything he wouldn't do, gave the same feedback verbally at the time as he did later on in writing and didn't try to cover his own arse by blaming anyone else for his own mistakes. I learned more from him in six weeks than I ever did from any of the others and had I remained under his tutorship I may even have still been a cop today.

INSPECTOR HARWOOD

The Duty Inspector of Jacob's Section, Mr Harwood was Fast Track, six years in The Job and in his early fifties.

He'd apparently held high rank both in the British army and as a manager of some vast conglomerate after that. He joined the Police around 2002 and specifically said that provided he made the grades he wanted Fast Track as he did not wish to remain a Constable. He was a fairly imposing figure, looking like a retired rugby player with a full head of white hair and an intimidating stare.

He was Old School in his mentality and not afraid to state his opinions in front his Section, as controversial as they usually were.

He was one of the rare Inspectors that got stuck in to work with the rest of us and would routinely drive around on a Shift in uniform but in an unmarked car to see if there was anything he could deal with.

If working weekends on Earlys we would sometimes chip in for a fry up and cook it about 8am if things were quiet. One day Jacob popped his head round the kitchen door. "Guv wants in, says only one egg".

A female officer in a pinny and holding a spatula frowned and then replied "he hasn't chipped in, there won't be enough".

Jacob chuckled. "Guv wants in. Can't not give the Guv breakfast. See who doesn't want what and give him what they're not having".

He joined us for the fry up and liked to chat. That is he liked to tell stories and although he dominated the conversation, he did at least have something to say worth listening to and was refreshingly un-PC. He regaled us with one tale of while he was on Section as a Constable of two fellow officers asking the Section Sergeant for his PNB so they could photocopy the relevant pages for an Arrest they'd made that the skipper had been involved with. He gave it to them but had apparently forgotten that he'd spent the last few months noting down everything any other officer said that was even remotely controversial with dates, times, what they'd said and who was present. His rationale for doing this was clearly ammunition to use against them if necessary at a later date. The two officers told everyone on the Section but managed to keep it quiet from the Sergeant who from that day on was noted as a sneaky, underhanded, little tit.

The Guv stated that now he was an Inspector and this bloke was still a skipper he would love to meet him again so he could tell him that he knew what he'd written in his PNB and further more just what he thought of him for having done it.

He had the habit of filming Suspects at the Nick with a digital camera, well aware of false claims about Police brutality. A local Nominal was notorious for not only making false allegations against officers but in pursuing them as well. One night when he was brought in to Custody the Guv went to a first floor window and surreptitiously filmed what was going on. Sure enough, fifteen minutes later the prisoner demanded to see the Duty Inspector, claiming the escorting officer had punched him in the face as he was taken to the Holding Cell. The Guv played him the footage and asked "still feel the same way?" to which the prisoner apparently mumbled something about rotten, crafty coppers.

He also told us that he fully expected to be getting a call from the Chief Inspector any day now about an incident two days previously.

A Shout had gone out that officers were required to attend to help an off duty officer from another Force who had been involved in a road rage incident. Apparently a car full of chavs had cut up the officer's vehicle, (which also had his wife and infant son in it) and he'd had the immense cheek to blare his horn at them. They slowed down in front of him until he had to stop completely and the driver and passengers then got out. The driver was brandishing a gun.

The driver spent a couple of minutes swearing at and threatening the off duty cop, enjoying his moment of power, until the officer identified himself and realised the gun was a replica whereby he snatched it off the kid.

He nicked the lad, called the incident in and officers from our Section but from another Nick were despatched to assist in detaining the now deflated aggressive little shit and his mates.

All fine and dandy.

Then the Control Room Inspector piped up over the air that the officers were to back off until Firearms Officers (that he was at this moment despatching) arrived on scene.

This could take at least an extra twenty minutes as the Firearms unit was in another Area.

This in turn could mean that the outnumbered Off duty officer would lose the edge he had over the Suspects who may kick his head in in front of his wife and child or simply drive off.

It was also worth noting that people who threaten complete strangers with guns (albeit fake ones) after forcing them off the road probably aren't going to show much compassion to a woman and a toddler.

The Guv was listening to the situation on his radio as it happened and intervened, telling his officers to ignore the last order and to continue to the scene. A few moments later his Job mobile rang and it was his counterpart in Control Room, demanding to know what the hell he was playing at.

The Guv told him to shove it.

He also told him that the incident did NOT warrant Firearms' attendance as the gun was a fake AND the officer had control of it. Further the woman and child were at risk the longer it took officers to arrive. He added to his opposite number that he felt he was being overcautious and putting civilians, not to mention a very brave off duty officer in jeopardy.

He then hung up and repeated his original order over the radio.

He told us that he had technically been in the wrong as the Control Room Inspector had veto in the situation but he wasn't prepared to sit back on such a stupid principle of etiquette and put people at risk. He was fully expecting a bollocking due to having stepped outside his remit.

It was nice to know that there was someone of rank who was willing to put their neck on the line to do the right thing. Even more so that he was prepared to be honest with his Section about his motives and just what he believed in.

Sadly, he is in a very small minority.

PCSOs

POLICE COMMUNITY SUPPORT OFFICERS

Introduced by then-Home Secretary David Blunkett in the Police Reform Act 2002 these were spun to the public as a subsidiary arm of the Police, assisting them in the community and supporting Police officers in their duties.

Someone realised long ago that Police have loads and loads of powers, but only really use about 50% of them. The same person thought "why not give those additional powers to other people, leaving the Police free to deal with more serious crimes". So we had the birth of the PCSO. Problem was and still is...people know that coppers can escalate the powers they are using so, if you tell a Police Constable to go and fuck himself after he tells you off for dropping litter he can then warn you under s.5 of the Public Order Act and if you do it again he can nick you. A PCSO cannot do anything except utilise the basic powers that they are given by their Force. The Catch 22 is that more money is spent on training PCSOs, which reduces the number of Police trained which means that we have tons of PCSOs that are given some of the powers of cops but don't have the extra ammunition to back themselves up if need be and less cops to be there for them when they need help.

The recruitment ad blurb states:

"In your distinctive uniform you will soon make a familiar face in the local community, providing reassurance to members of the public worried about crime. You are a highly visible point of contact and help to deter anti-social behaviour and nuisance crime".

Their "distinctive uniform" is meant to be "similar but markedly different" (it looks the same except the tie and epaulettes are a different colour). They are the "eyes and ears on the streets" but that's all they are as they cannot nick anyone. Eyes and ears are fine for observation, but you needs hands and feet to act. The reassurance they provide is solely to little old ladies who belong to the lace curtain twitching brigade. Lots of people in High Viz who look 80% like Policemen walking about the cul-de-sacs will have the old dears sipping their tea with a more relaxed air because these days there seem to be Bobbies everywhere. The only crime they deter is the stuff they can see, committed by 10 year old kids who run at the sight of a uniform.

They have a training period of around four to seven weeks depending on which Constabulary they work for, are classed as Civilian Employees (and are therefore allowed to join a trade union which cops can't) and while they take the same fitness test as Police officers (and on my test five of them failed it) their OST is limited to anything that can help them do a bunk quickly (such as the palm heel strike but followed up by legging it as opposed to reaching for pepper spray) due to the 'Non Confrontational' role they assume.

This basically means that a PCSO absolutely CANNOT get involved in anything involving violence or even getting shouted at. They are not trained in confrontation, are not insured for it and are not expected to deal with it. They can issue tickets such as Fixed Penalty Notices but if the person they are attempting to issue it to gets aggressive they have to back away and call the real Police. They have the power to detain someone suspected of a crime for up to 30 minutes until Police officers arrive on scene. However this power of 'Detention' is limited in all but a handful of Forces to simply telling the person to wait and if they walk away, having to follow them UNTIL they become "confrontational" where they then have to back off.

Initial reaction to this major change was mixed.

Kent's Chief Constable of the time stated "over my dead body" and only took them when his annual budget was threatened. The City of London Police refused to take any at all until the Home

Office forced them to which meant that in 2005 fifteen joined the ranks of a Force patrolling a community of one square mile that has only 7000 residents and a transient working population that goes home by 9pm.

Powers range wildly between Forces. COLP gave them the most basic powers possible from the menu available. The Met on the other hand gave theirs slightly beefier powers including the right to physically restrain a suspect during the 30 minute detention window. The BTP gave theirs handcuffs and told them they could use them on anyone who needed detaining while they wait for proper Police to arrive.

The Home Office had NOT given PCSOs nationally accepted, uniform powers. Instead of a coherent structure and the public knowing exactly what PCSOs could or couldn't do the Chief Constables and Commissioners were given the right to decide themselves. As each CC is a god in his or her kingdom then each would do whatever they damn well liked and thought appropriate. While this may not seem such a big deal things can be brought into perspective by July 7th 2005's terrorist attacks.

Liverpool Street Train & Underground station is almost directly opposite Bishopsgate Police station. One of the two active COLP Nicks. The BTP have an office in Bishopsgate station and have PCSOs patrolling in Liverpool Street. The Met's jurisdiction starts just down the road. Liverpool Street was one of the targets of the bombers on July 7th. In the ensuing chaos you had THREE Police Force's PCSOs in Liverpool Street station trying to deal with what was going on. Three sets of PCSOs with different powers, around five weeks training and a non-confrontational job description dealing with hundreds of angry, frightened, confused people. All it would have taken was one crafty scrote to realise that the COLP PCSO that physically prevented him crossing the cordon didn't actually have the right to do that and the Force could have been hit with a lawsuit. I seriously doubt that in the initial chaos anyone noticed the difference between a PCSO and a cop or even cared but had anyone taken an interest you had three Force's PCSOs in one train station, only one of which was on its own turf and only two of which had physical detainment powers. Unlike cops, PCSOs have no jurisdiction outside their own territory.

I had a case dropped by the Crown Prosecution Service solely due to the piss poor Statement made by the only real witness to a motorcycle theft...a PCSO. While working for CID I saw the Pocket Note Book photocopy in the case file of a PCSO who had seen a lad trying to kick start a stolen motorcycle and shouted at him to leave it alone. The lad dropped the bike and ran off and the gung ho PCSO gave chase (which should have been a disciplinary issue due to his non-confrontational role but we'll let that slide). He gave the most dire Statement I have ever seen. Lack of continuity, a clear description of the Suspect, the motorbike or what the Suspect was doing to it. He'd clearly forgotten all about ADVOKATE and the most depressing thing about it was that as they have a more reduced role and are meant to be the "eyes and ears on the street" this is one area they are supposed to be good at.

I asked him to do it again, being nice and "suggesting" a few things that he might like to include, such as a full description of the Suspect and what time of day it was. He was so keen that it seemed cruel to burst his bubble and it was unfair to assume he couldn't get it right with some guidance. The second attempt was just as bad with the extra information simply tacked on the bottom. Realising that to ask officially for another one would be noted on the case papers and possibly picked up on by the defence brief I simply handed it back and again "suggested" that there were just a smidgen more things he might like to add.

Through all of this he remained buoyant and keen as a yappy terrier and while his final attempt was better it still wasn't up to it. Asking again would have to be marked on the file so I accepted it. Making sure not to burn any bridges I told his supervisor just how impressed I was with his enthusiasm (well, it wasn't a lie) and submitted the completed file to CPS. They dropped the case a week later with a note that the PCSO's Statement was the key evidence and did not make it clear that the Suspect was actually doing anything wrong.

Once as a Special with COLP I had to babysit a couple of

revenue inspectors on British Rail. One bloke who didn't have a ticket was drunk and was gobbing off to the inspector in front of me and a female Special. Choice snippets of dialogue included calling the revenue inspector "Baboo" (he was Indian) and asking my female colleague if she wanted to go to bed with him. Three BTP PCSOs were next to us through the entire thing and simply stood there saying nothing unless the bloke swore when one of them would waggle his finger in the guy's face and shout "I'M WARNING YOU UNDER SECTION FIVE!" without actually specifying what Act section five was in or what he was warning him for doing. I found out later that they had been told to "get a lot of section fives in tonight" by whichever twat of a Sergeant had pushed them out onto the streets.

An off duty Special with their warrant card would have more authority in any given situation than any PCSO of any length of service.

PCSOs in London in 2006 were being offered a starting salary (with overtime) of 24,000 pounds. Three grand less than the starting pay of a London Police officer.

No matter how the Forces and the Home Office try to sell this about "eyes and ears" and "getting in touch with the community" it is simply policing on the cheap and a shallow and dangerous attempt to fool everyone into believing their are more cops out there than there actually are.

THE DOG SECTION

One day in Training at Uni' we were visited by the Dog Section. Two rugged, stocky chaps with years of experience between them. They had buzz cuts, wore blue polo shirts, Cargo pants and big boots and looked like the kind of blokes you'd want to have your back on Fight Night.

They told us all about working with the mutts they train, having to take them home and how being on Dog Section is a huge commitment due to the wrenching changes it inflicts upon your social life. They talked about a grim shift pattern of 7 days on, 2 off and then brought out the dogs.

Drugs dogs are Springer Spaniels due to their acute sense of smell and a puppy was let out the back of the van, yipping and wanting to be fussed. Adorable, with little stubby ears and too-short fur it was still being trained up so wasn't on Active duty but all the women and most of the blokes wanted a stroke and a fuss of the slobbering pile of affection. These things are "passive" meaning that it is not trained to act aggressively but will instead simply sit down next to someone and wag its tail while gazing up at them. This means that heroin mules at airports will hopefully be unaware of why the nice doggy is being so attentive until four burly cops are standing around him and one says "excuse me Sir, this dog has identified you as being in possession of an illegal substance".

Next was the German Shepherd. Lively, friendly and super smart the trainer explained that this was the 'finding things' dog and that the dog thinks it's all a game so when it locates someone or something it is given its ball to play with as a reward. He then asked us to offer up personal items. A ring, scarf and mobile phone were handed over and placed around the grassy area at the back of the Uni canteen. The dog was let off the lead and went snuffling around for a couple of minutes before yipping excitedly and sitting down next to the phone. The Trainer patted it, gave it its ball to play with and then let it go to find the other two items.

This dog can be used to trace lost items or people who are hiding, either in the open or in buildings. It is not taught to bite but will go berserk if it finds someone as it's trained to bark furiously as a pre-emptive measure against the person kicking off.

At the back of the Dog van was a cage with a dark sheet covering it. Every time anyone got near to the van the cage would growl menacingly and then go quiet again.

"What's in there Sergeant?"

"Ah, can't show you that one I'm afraid. Only person it won't bite is me. That's the NCS dog".

Non Compliant Suspect dog. A Malanoir, otherwise known as a Belgian Shepherd. A bad tempered, muscley, lean streak of a hound that is one step down from the Armed Response Unit in terms of Use of Force. At time of writing only a handful of English & Welsh Forces still use them. All others have washed their hands of a canine that is such a potential risk to a career ladder or a successful portfolio (i.e. it gets stuck in and bites horrible people to make them "comply"). It is only used on Suspects who are violent to the point of being a danger to the Public or the Police and deemed unable to be subdued by normal force. Every time a Police dog bites someone it is a potential GBH so the decision to unleash this thing is not taken lightly. It is a "line of sight" dog in that it has to be able to see you in order to go for you. During the 2007 Police shooting of a woman armed with a pistol in (the first time in UK history that a woman was shot dead by the Police) the NCS dog was on standby but couldn't be deployed as she was behind a wall.

The other legend about this frenzy of fur was during a hostage situation where a man was holding a young child in a locked bathroom with a knife. He agreed via negotiation to let the kid go but wouldn't come out himself. As he still had the knife the cops on the landing did a Dynamic Risk Assessment and then kicked the bottom panel of the door out and pushed the Malanoir through the gap. The gentleman is now living his life bereft of one testicle.

While recuperating in the Force convalescent centre with a bad back I met a Dog Section constable from another Force. He said that due to the controversy of having dogs trained to bite plus the difficulties of justifying the Use of Force AND The Human Rights Act, his Constabulary were now considering muzzling all their dogs and training them to headbutt.

He wasn't joking.

KIDDY SWEARING

During Training at Uni one of the lecturers named Bazzer, 29 years in The Job and about to retire stated about how much he missed the Good Old Days and how some people could be taught to behave just by being shoved in a cell for a short while.

He said that on a few occasions many years ago he'd had irate housewives turn up at the Nick front desk with their 10 year old sons to say "officer, I've just caught him stealing from my purse. Can you teach him a lesson and lock him up for a couple of hours?"

The overly nonchalant child would then be taken to the Custody Suite, busily chewing gum or picking their nose and shown an empty cell. Bazzer said that once they saw it they would lose the cockiness and once inside would look visibly frightened. The officer would then step back outside and shut the door with an extra hard push so it made a loud clang and the mechanism clicked in the lock.

He would then stand and look at his watch and no more than ten seconds later you would hear:

"AAAAWWWWAAAAAAAA! MUMMYYYYYY!!!!"

They usually gave it ten minutes and then opened the door again to find the kid curled up on the bed blubbing hysterically and would say "right! Job done. Out you come you little bastard, DON'T do it again".

Nowadays no Custody skipper in the land would ever authorise this due to the field day the newspapers would have (HEADLINE: "Unable to catch terrorists or rapists, cops now lock up pre-teens for stealing 50p"), the bad reputation it might give the Police and the bloody Human Rights Act.

One day I was on Front Desk at the Nick with a seasoned cop named Rossana. She was six feet tall, had short blonde hair and could outstare a gargoyle. While we were chatting at the desk a middle aged man in a Barbour jacket with designer spectacles came in, holding a squirming 6 year old by the hand.

The kid looked visibly terrified and was struggling to get free, gazing at us in mute horror and then at what presumably was his dad in a silent plea for mercy.

We stood up looking puzzled and the guy approached the counter:

"Officers, sorry to bother you. He's just used a VERY naughty word to his mummy. I want you to do something about that".

Trying to keep a straight face was hard, particularly as the little kid is now chalk white with fear and is in danger of pulling his own arm out of the socket to get away. Rossana walks around the desk and crouches in front of the boy, who squeaks as she gets down to eye level with him.

"Listen to me young man" she says quietly "you mustn't swear at your mummy. We've got the power to lock you up".

The kid stares at her while the father looks on. "Do you understand me?" she asks him, still quietly.

He nods rapidly and then looks up at his Dad again hopefully.

Rossana stands up and the father expresses his thanks. "Thank you officer, we couldn't believe it when he said that, don't know where he heard the word. Usually such a good boy, aren't you Rupert?"

The kid nods his head furiously again, clearly beyond fear by this point and coming out the other side.

They make their way out of the Station and we can hear the father gently ticking off his son as they walk down the steps.

I manage to hold it until they are out of sight but then look at Rossana and we both burst out laughing.

I always imagined the family were sitting having dinner, with the Evian water in a glass jug and a wooden salad bowl in the centre of the table. After finishing their organic quiche the mother turned to Rupert and said:

"Darling, would you like to pass mummy one of the loganberry and guava yogurts from the refrigerator?" and Rupert in a moment of uncharacteristic spontaneity had gone:

"Fuck off you cunt!"

Cue the wooden salad bowl going up in the air, the mother shrieking hysterically and needing a lie down to recover and the father saying to Rupert "right you naughty boy, put your coat on, I'm taking you to the Police Station".

In years to come Rupert might well be a Chief Constable and will, as he makes his inauguration speech, say "many years ago when I was six my father took me to the Police for swearing at my mother. This zero tolerance approach to discipline made me realise what I wanted to do with my life".

BANK HOLIDAY DRINKING

Jacob and me had just set off from the Nick to trundle about the Area when a call was received to attend a drunken argument between two of the requisite bank holiday revellers,

It's a sunny Friday afternoon and apart from being a three day weekend it's also the end of the month meaning pay day for the majority of people.

Instead of just enjoying the sunshine and an extra day off work, some cretins have to get tanked up on cheap cider and walk around with their shirts off

When we get to the park an ambulance crew are still there. They tell us that our chap got aggressive when they approached him, was bleeding superficially and had staggered off over the bridge in the direction of the public toilets after mumbling abuse at them. Apparently there were two, but they have no idea where the second bloke has gone.

We get back in the motor and pootle off to the other side of the park to see a swaying, young white male standing outside the locked public toilets. Jacob saunters over, one hand on his Pava and says casually "alright fella?".

The drunk turns round, tottering on his feet but managing to retain his balance. He is clearly shitfaced and has blood on his ear. He simply stares at us both through bleary, crossed, bloodshot eyes. He mumbles something incoherent and continues gently swaying on his filthy, once white trainers. "Listen fella, you need to move on. You've clearly had a lot to drink" Jacob tells him. I'm trying to remember all the things I've been taught like Reactionary Gap, non-threatening stances and how my tone and body language may affect his reaction.

"YouthinkImfuckingmad?" he mutters glaring first at Jacob and then at me.

"You're drunk in a public place fella, it's an offence. You need to move on".

"YouthinkImfuckingmad?" he mutters again, still swaying and looking and smelling like he's imbued the entire contents of the local brewery.

I join in. "Look mate, you need to move away, you're drunk in public, just move on we don't want to arrest you".

Pause.

"YouthinkImfuckingmad?"

This goes on for a couple more attempts while Jacob casually unclips his Pava and grips it in his fist, I follow suit and the passive stance and tone we were trying to use starts to change to a more combat ready one. I finally realise that his reluctance to take the hint and just piss off is because he is assuming, in his own drunken, mentally retarded way that we are going to grab him as soon as he turns around. "Look, we're not trying to fool you" I venture as an option "just walk away". I look at Jacob and take three steps backwards. Jacob nods, then follows suit.

Pregnant pause.

"YouthinkImfuckingmad?".

Jacob then snaps. "Lance I'm bored of this. Arrest him".

I get out the handcuffs." Right turn around face the wall". Unbelievably he actually does and lets me lock and double lock both cuffs before he then starts squirming and trying to pull his hands free. I later found out that this is a common phenomenon and known as a Handcuff Hero. We force his head down so we can march him along and when we get his wriggling body onto a grassy bit, take him to the floor. Our Arrestee starts squirming and I tighten my grip on the cuffs.

"Once he stops resisting, take the pressure off Lance, remember 'Pain and Reward' " Jacob advises me.

Once our Suspect stops fighting against the pressure I relax my grip which immediately results in him kicking to get free again. Jacob makes the call for a caged van to come and get our prisoner.

While sitting on top of him, a family of mum, dad, seven year old son and a dog walk past. The father nods at us and says "good afternoon" as if the sight of two cops sitting on a half naked drunk who is wriggling furiously is an everyday occurrence.

"Hello there" I reply "everything's under control".

A few minutes later the van arrives, driven by our hands-on, fast track Guv'nor, Inspector Harwood. "Afternoon Sir" I nod as he gets out of the van and approaches us, still trying to retain my grip on the rapidly sweating upper torso squirming beneath me.

"Good afternoon lads" he says, clapping his hands together and rubbing them briskly. He glances at the Red Bull Rooster we're sitting on and gets out his PNB. "What's your name then young man?" he asks our boy.

"COULDN'T GIVE A FUCK!"

"That's a long name" the Inspector replies, writing it down. "Can we get Mr Fuck in the back of the van please lads? Or can I call you Couldn't?".

We pull him to his feet as the Inspector opens first the van and then the cage and we, as gently as possible, shove him in the back and slam the door hard.

A leisurely five minute drive to the Nick and we arrive at the back doors and the entrance to Custody. Jacob goes to tip off the Custody skipper that this will probably be a Cell Exit.

While we wait the Inspector chats to me.

"So young man, how long have you been in The Job now?"

"About seven months Sir".

"Really? Enjoying it? Hang on..." he reaches for the back door handle of the van.

"Alright in there are we?"

"COULDN'T GIVE A FUCK!"

"Really? Well we'll just leave you in there a bit longer then".

He shuts the door and we chat about The Job. He starts to talk against the party line and then pauses, glancing across at Jacob who's just got back from talking to the skipper and back at me.

Jacob nods and says "it's ok Sir, he's one of us" and the Guv continues, coming out with quite delightful un-PC opinions including some about our friends in the travelling fraternity.

"Best open the door, let him get some air" he muses after about 10 minutes, releasing the handle again and revealing the slumped, glowering figure with his hands cuffed behind his back glaring at us, his jeans covered in grass stains and dirt.

"We'll get you out in a minute ok?"

"COULDN'T GIVE...."

The door is slammed again before he can finish.

When Custody decide that they're ready Jacob tells me to get him out the back of the van personally.

"Watch his feet" he warns. Like the last time, our boy waits until both me and Jacob have hands on him and THEN starts to kick off. Once again he's marched with his head near to his navel and as we get into Custody about four other officers emerge and get every door open for us. The Custody skipper stands there overseeing it while the Guv'nor starts filming the incident on his digital camera.

We get him in the cell and by now he's going berserk. Another officer thoughtfully plonks the wipe-clean mattress on the floor and we force him down onto it, again conscious of the fact that we are required to be as gentle as possible with the little bastard. As he's so violent he might Self Harm so all his clothes have to be removed bar his undies. His trainers, stinking socks and tracky bottoms are pulled off. While his trousers are being pulled down his boxers begin to follow. The Guv'nor lowers his camera slightly. "Don't pull his pants down, remember his Human Rights".

I gingerly grip the elastic and hoik them back up again while another officer pulls the stained trousers off. Why the hell we couldn't just strip the silly sod naked and then push his undies back through the hatch is beyond me.

Finally we're ready to leave and one at a time the officers peel off like dive bombers after dropping their payload. I am momentarily in the belief that it's me that's going to be leaving backwards, but I'm third to last and while our boy still wriggles and kicks the rest of us look on from the door as the penultimate Bobby walks up behind the cop sitting on the Suspect's back, grabs his belt with one hand and taps him twice on the right shoulder. He then yanks him backwards, but unfortunately he gets his elbow caught on the doorframe and like a ferret the Suspect jumps to his feet and runs at the door, just as the visibly shit scared cop manages to stand back and slam it in his face.

Cue two hours of door kicking and swearing before he collapses in exhaustion on his cot.

The following morning the lad woke up, not knowing where he was or why he'd been nicked. He apologised profusely and shook every officer's hand that he could reach, clearly embarrassed and ashamed. He got a PND which was £80 and a Sanctioned Detection (gold dust) but about as much of a deterrent to his behaviour as giving an ASBO to the average chav. The following week he did the same thing again. Turned out his mother runs a pub about half a mile from the Nick. In future at least they won't have to go far to arrest him.

SIGNAL FAILURE

Moving out of London was a bit of a shock when it came to public transport, in particular the trains. London Underground has trains on the major lines running once every minute at peak weekday hours. My new abode, while only 20 miles from the university I would be training in, had a five minute bike ride to the train station. From there it was 30 minutes to the next station where if I was lucky it was five minutes until my next train arrived and if unlucky an hour. I would then cycle the ten minutes from the station to the uni. Fun it was not, especially as Training began in November.

I was sitting on the train home in sweat dampened winter sports clothes reading a book while waiting for it to move off when about ten teenage school kids got on the same carriage. They looked reasonably normal, didn't look like they had gang affiliations and didn't look even remotely intimidating. They did in fact look very normal. Kind of like most kids looked when I was at school. They were quite loud but not overly so and I carried on reading while they took up positions further along the carriage.

About five minutes after the train pulled out of the station they began acting up.

First of all it was increased volume. Well, that's up to them, not hurting anyone.

Then it was leaping about and shoving each other into things. Well, that's their choice as long as they keep it amongst themselves.

Then it was foul language at the same volume as the previous shouting and I could feel my temper fraying. Cycling in the freezing cold to complete a journey of over two hours that in London would take about an hour if that, can make you a bit crabby particularly if it's pissing with rain.

One or two of them are eating and dropping litter on the floor. I still ignore them and try to focus on the delights of Nanny Ogg's cat Grebo in Terry Pratchett's 'Witches Abroad'.

They are spilling into the area I'm in which contains three other people.

Two of them, while laughing then try prising the doors of the train open. We are still moving at what feels to be about 50mph.

I snap.

"ENOUGH! THAT'S ENOUGH!"

They freeze. The one with his fingers still in the crack in the door slowly turns to look at me. They all turn to look at me. They are all quiet.

"THAT IS ENOUGH!"

They say nothing. They look scared. They are clearly not used to grown ups making it clear that they've even seen them, let alone taking offence at their tribal stupidity.

One of them then starts grinning and looks right at me. He chuckles.

I glare at him.

"DON'T YOU SMILE AT ME YOU LITTLE WRETCH!"

He blanches and goes white in the face. His bravado slips and he looks away. They all go quieter still and simply stand there. When I'm certain they are going to remain like that I ignore them once more and go back to the book.

Two minutes later we pull into a station. As they are still gathered near the doors the chuckler who tried laughing at me is bumped into by a lad holding a bicycle. He turns round and catches him a left hook across the face. The lad retaliates. The chuckler then grabs the kid's head under his arm and begins punching him in the face repeatedly. The bicycle goes crashing to the floor of the train. I get up, throwing my book on the seat and grab the chuckler round the waist and yank him free of the other boy. The freed kid tries to go at the other lad so I swing him away and stick my right leg out, shoving the other kid back with my foot.

"BACK OFF! POLICE!"

The kid freezes. The rest of them are watching on in silence.

Still holding the lad round the waist I turn to a guy sitting on the other side of the carriage to where I was, who is watching this. "Do me a favour mate and pull the handle will you?"

"Sorry?"

"Pull the handle. I'm a Police officer. Warrant Card's in my pocket. Don't worry I'll take responsibility".

He gets up and yanks the handle. The doors are still open as we have yet to pull away from the station. A few seconds after he's pulled the handle the warning alarm for 'doors closing' bleeps. The doors try to shut. Still holding the lad I stick my foot out prevent them from closing. They open and try to close again. I stick my foot in them a second time. They open and this time remain that way.

I let the kid go. "Right" I tell all of them "you and you are in serious trouble" indicating the two scrappers.

About a minute later a very annoyed-looking train guard appears from outside, obviously having left his cabin to walk along the platform to get to our carriage.

He stands in the doorway and glares at me then asks "what happened?"

"Police. These two were fighting. I broke it up. Pulled the handle but the doors tried to close. I had to stab my foot in them to prevent them shutting".

He glares at me and sneers "I know". He glances around the carriage and then looks back at me. The driver has now come out of his cabin through the door behind us and is watching what's going on. The guard continues "thanks a lot mate we're already late because of signal failure".

I am completely astounded by this as I have just broken up an Affray on his train.

I decide to remain professional even if all I want to do is knee this jobsworth in the bollocks. "I was defusing a violent situation, I'm sure you'd have done the same" I tell him.

164

"No, I'd have just let them get on with it. We're going to be really late now"

I can feel my temper getting worn down again. This stupid bastard is undermining my authority and making it clear to a Police officer and everyone else present that he couldn't give a shit if people get hurt on his train.

He then asks "so what do you want to do now?"

"I'm happy to do whatever you want to do" I reply, expecting him to realise that that means he can simply ignore everything like he clearly wants to.

"No, no" he says smirking "I mean do you want to use your authority to make certain they're separated by making one get off here for example? Do you wish to have other officers attend to arrest them?"

"Like I said I'm happy for whatever you want to do"

"No, no it's your decision" he says "you pulled the handle".

I wish I'd realised at the time I could have simply threatened to nick him for Obstruction. I just glare at him until he sighs heavily and then resets the handle. He stalks out the carriage and I turn to the driver who smiles and says "Don't worry mate, you did the right thing, he's just having a bad day" and goes back into his cabin.

"Do either of you get off here?" I ask the two fighters.

"I do" the chuckler says.

"Right, off! And don't let me see you again". He slopes off.

The doors close the train begins to move again and after about five minutes the other lad walks up to me. "Can I make a complaint about him at school tomorrow?"

I am still fucked off. Both with them and that stupid, lazy guard. I reply "up to you, but it's nothing to do with me if you do it at school".

"But I can make a complaint against him?"

"Yes, if you want to".

He ponders on this and then moves back to the rest of the group.

After being stung so many times with COLP over this type of thing, I didn't declare it. Unlike COLP my new Force's warrant card didn't have the warrant number under the badge so there was no way they could prove who I was if someone reported it. I believed I'd acted appropriately and defused two situations.

The next day I was sat on the same train. The same group of kids went to get on, saw me sitting there and moved to the next carriage. For one day at least, the 1630 Local had some semblance of calm.

TRUCE IN THE AFTERMATH

Phase two of our rather relaxed and bizarre university-based Training culminated in an exam.

Not just any exam. This was the mother and father of all exams.

We were clearly told that if we failed this exam then we would be entitled to a resit. If we failed that then we would be back coursed to a later Training group. We would then have a final attempt to pass, which if we failed would result in being forced to resign.

We had a lot to learn for this one. Cramming on coffee breaks and lunch was common place, as was staying in the library for a couple of hours after lessons ended. The week before the exam we were all getting agitated and edgy and everyone was spending as much time as they could swotting up.

The day arrived and everybody was in an hour early, chatting for about 45 minutes until we ventured into the upstairs corridor where three sandwich boards proclaimed "Exam in Progress: Silence Please". We then hung around nervously and tried not to stand too close to Jeremy, who when stressed would lick his index finger and insert it into your ear in a hilarious diversion called The Wet Willy.

At five to nine we were allowed in by a tutor who was a bit too flippant about the sodding thing for his own good. Richenda had warned me just before we entered "if you sit there chewing tooth picks again like last time I'm going to ram one down your throat". Unfortunately for her we were sat at designated desks and fate had placed us next to each other. She was going to have to tolerate me munching my way through a large pack of menthol wood densticks before three hours was up.

The tutor wrote the starting time on the board and wished us luck. We turned over our papers and plowed into the horrible thing.

Multiple choice, short answers, medium answers and long answers.

I quoted anything that appeared even remotely relevant to what was on the page, was there for almost the full three hours, was one of the last to leave and walked out with wanker's cramp in my writing hand, a pile of wood shavings on the desk from repeatedly sharpening my pencil and about thirty five chewed toothpicks littering the desk. The room was spinning and everything appeared a little too vivid colour wise, due to a lack of oxygen from holding my breath for too long.

We waited all day for the results.

Non-specific deity bless the trainers and tutors as they blitzed the marking just so we could have our grades before we went home. Home time was usually about 3.30pm but we hung on till ten past five before the Staff came down and approached the canteen area where we were all huddled chatting and feeling sick. They beckoned us into the main lecture theatre and Bartholomew, the most grizzled looking and Old School of the Staff said "we have both your last assignment results and your exam results. The exam results are on these pieces of paper" he said, waving a big bunch of what looked like raffle tickets in the air. "When your name is called out, please put your hand up". He starts reading names and the slips of paper are passed directly to the wide eyed, shaking person they belong to. After what seems like about 20 minutes (in reality my name was the 8th or 9th read out) he calls me and hands over the paper. I immediately shove it under the desk in front of me so noone else can see it and then, taking a breath, slowly edge it out of hiding. 66%. Pass is 65%. I mentally triple check both the pass mark and that it definitely says 66% and then breathe out.

I spot the slip of paper of the girl in front of me. 82%. Christ! Further down the seats I hear Deidre start blubbing loudly. Wailing, wracking sobs and glance across to see Kerry with her arm round her shoulders. Samson is sitting behind me and looks visibly pale and sick. I try to make eye contact but he looks past me. I then get my assignment. 70%. Pass is 45%. Starting to feel better now.

After a few minutes a Sergeant we don't know enters the room and asks for silence. "For those of you, who have passed, thank you. You all worked hard. Please leave the room." We stagger out and I notice nothing except the vending machine facing the door and the table next to it. It's a couple of minutes of sitting down before I realise who I'm next to. Noone is really talking.

Then the mood magically lifts and people start asking each other what result they got. There seem to be a lot of 66%-ers knocking about. After a couple more minutes a small group emerges, about three people. Those that got between 60 and 64%. They were apparently told "no hard feelings, you obviously worked hard. Better luck next time." Rose starts crying even though she was in my group of 65+.

People begin to stand up, moving around and chatting. Like any big group of people we have cliques. These are a fact of human nature. No malice. No pretence. No reason. They just ARE. But for 15 minutes they don't exist. It's one of those rare, Breakfast Club moments where we are all just human beings, relieved to have made it through one of the most difficult tests of our new careers so far. It's like when the German and English soldiers came out of their trenches in the First World War to play football on Christmas Day.

Craig, someone I never got on with before today, and never got on with after, walks up. "What did you get Lance?" he asks smiling.

"66%".

"Me too, there's a lot of us I think" he says extending his hand, which I shake.

Rose is still crying. "What's wrong with you? YOU passed!" I ask her.

"I'm upset for Georgy" she says, a friend of hers who is looking down in the dumps and being hugged and clapped on the back by a group of about five people. I walk over to shake his hand.

"I'm just pissed off it was 64%" he says. "If it was a bad fail I'd think fair enough, but one fucking percent!".

Everyone is smiling and being nice. Those that only just failed are being consoled. Then the larger remaining group emerges. Dolly heads straight for the exit and is gone in about 30 seconds. The squeal of her tyres loud enough to be heard throughout the campus. Samson is in this group. 59% and below. Everyone closes around them like concerned mother hens.

"Alright mate" he says as I tap his arm.

"What did they say?"

"He was a right arsehole to us that prick Sergeant" he replies angrily. Samson is 6 feet 2 inches tall and never loses his rag but looks visibly annoyed and upset. Their speech from the Sergeant was far from friendly and he basically told them (as if they didn't have enough shame, embarrassment and disappointment to deal with) that if they weren't going to try then The Job didn't want them and that there were plenty of people waiting to join that would love to take their places.

This stressful, difficult, heart-breaking, barrier-melting, lets-all-have-a-hug exam ended up with seven people resitting and five of those getting back coursed including Samson, when they again failed to achieve 65%. Of those five, Dolly failed the 3rd attempt and resigned rather than be forced out.

It cost five good people their place in our Training group, put them back six months and cost the Force (and therefore the taxpayer) a not insignificant sum in funding for the extra class time. Dolly despite being moody, was by all accounts a decent Police officer.

You'd think that the day before such a crucial, lifestyle affecting, career changing assessment of our abilities as trainee officers, time would have been given over to final, hard studying and dedicated revision.

You'd think that lessons and activities would be cancelled to allow us to focus on what we knew may end up costing us our places in The Job.

You'd think that common sense would prevail and those in power, responsible for our Training would appreciate just how stressed and unhappy we all were and allow us to channel all our energies into this evil bastard of an exam.

Ahem...!

The day before we were obliged to present (in groups of five) a presentation to the other 15 in our squad on the cultures of Hindu, Gypsy, Muslim or Sikh.

We had known for four weeks that we had to do this.

It had to be researched, presented with respect, with an eye for detail and for unusual facts that we thought would be a revelation for not only us but to the other 15 watching us, plus our tutors. This took all morning and left us with only the afternoon to revise. The presentation itself took a good couple of days to put together, each of us knowing that while the exam could be career halting, a Race and Diversity presentation was something that, in this mutated world of modern policing, we could not afford to mess up or be perceived as having gone into half heartedly.

The only nod to our stress levels over this exam (that they'd repeatedly told us we HAD to pass) was that they cancelled a proposed invitation to representatives of each of the cultures we were dealing with, who were originally to come in, watch and listen and give feedback on what we'd said. Craig apparently had to write a 200 word essay as a punishment for saying "pikey" during his Gypsy presentation.

The fact that doing a Show & Tell about minorities was considered more important than studying for such a crucial exam is yet more proof of just how far off the scale this job's priorities have become.

FORCE SECURITY

Security: "Something that provides safety, freedom from danger or anxiety".

Every Police Force has a Chief Constable (except COLP and Met who have a Commissioner). In total there are 43 Home Office Forces in England and Wales with a high profile leader in each one. Chief Constables in nearly every Force will nowadays try to be as public orientated as possible and my old CC would occasionally go out on the Beat to prove he was "one of the troops" (and one time nicked someone for Assault. Would have loved to have seen the Custody Sergeant's face during that Booking In).

They have an office at HQ, as does every rank from ACC upwards as well as whichever not-quite ACPO staff plus PSEs are required for steering the ship in the right direction.

Chiefs and Commissioners have complete control over their Forces and have from around 850 officers (Warwickshire) to over 8000 (Met). They are in the local papers at least every other week and on TV or the national press if something serious (usually bad) happens in their Constabulary area.

Security, you would imagine would be shit hot and high budget with ID cards, metal detectors, frisking and the like for anyone entering the realm of the Top Brass. You would like to believe that there would be security guards, or even Police officers rotad on to keep the ACPO corridor protected and that when the CC was out and about there would be a bodyguard with him or her to prevent any attempts to harm the capo di tutti capi.

Ahem...!

My old Force had HQ next to the Training college. The Top Brass would flit between the two, mainly as the canteen was in the college. There was no gate leading to HQ and you could walk from the road the fifty yards to reception. Once, when I visited reception there was noone there and I waited five minutes for the middle aged, female receptionist who didn't look like she was a black belt in Kung Fu to come back behind the counter and ask what I wanted.

You need a passcard, or someone to let you in, for the buildings further in past reception. These are for Procurements, the shop which sells Force memorabilia and patrol boots and the admin wing, NOT anything top level.

The doors that are security enabled are all opened with a swipe card, given to you by reception. The doors are magnetic but if you push or pull them hard enough they will open anyway, without triggering any kind of alarm.

During my Passing Out parade preparations at the college we were told to meet our invited guests at the gate, escort them to reception and NOT let them wander about without us with them due to the "security issues" of an unidentified civilian mooching about unaccompanied.

The main gate of the College slides back when opened and can only be accessed by a card or by the receptionist buzzing you in. There is a camera above the intercom button and another on a pole further back to clock the vehicle you are in. Twenty yards to the right is the pedestrian gate which is opened the same way and again has a camera on the intercom. Once you arrive in reception you speak to the receptionist who will mark down your details and issue you with a pass to enable you to open the magnetic swipe doors. If you are an officer in uniform you will still need the pass. If you are a civilian you will get the pass, plus a Visitor card and if you are an officer but NOT in uniform you will have to carry either a pre-issued ID card on a chain around your neck or wear the Warrant Card holder with the shield visible (e.g. from a top pocket of your suit jacket).

Sounds good eh?

The main gate was always left open between 8am and 10am

from Monday to Friday as that is when most of the people arrived at work who were at the college full time or attending courses. This was to spare the poor receptionist the stress of having to constantly buzz people in for two hours and have a queue of vehicles blocking up the housing estate the college was on. The camera on the driver gate intercom was permanently up the swanny and never worked the entire time I was employed. This meant you could see the vehicle from the pole camera but not the driver. Once through the gate (that it is possible to climb over if you are even superficially fit) you make your way (unaccompanied) to reception and introduce yourself. Along the way you pass the OST department, the Firearms training unit and the accommodation blocks. All have those lovely magnetically sealed doors that you can shove open and OST will sometimes have the door held open with a traffic cone or table or even just left ajar as it wouldn't self seal without assistance.

Once at reception you say who you are and they don't usually ask you for ID to prove it. You are invited to sit and wait if you are a visiting civilian and to give your Force number if you are a cop. Out of dozens of visits to the College I was only asked for accompanying ID while an officer, not as a civilian and then only TWICE. I flashed the badge in the wallet and was NOT asked to show the actual Warrant Card underneath.

If you face the College entrance from the road, turn right and walk for 500 yards you come to a turn on the left. Take that and walk straight for 200 yards and follow the road as it curves to the left. Keep following it and you will come to another gate that is left open all day long and is the back entrance to the Police college. It is only closed at night. One time I was sitting in my car in the car park at 6pm chatting on my mobile phone and the caretaker came out to ask if I wanted to leave as he was about to close the gate for the night.

A Chief Constable does not have a bodyguard he has a driver. The driver picks him up at home and drives him to work, waits for him to finish work and drives him home again. The driver is not armed. The driver does not have to be a cop.

At the Police station I worked in, you have a reception that is closed after 5pm. It is manned by civilians and next to it is another magnetic door. The back entrance has a high wall and four gates. Two together for vehicles entering and pedestrians, two on the opposite side for vehicles leaving and pedestrians.

One day an angry email was sent out from a Section skipper who had had the pleasure of a civilian putting her head round his office door and saying "Hi my boyfriend's been arrested can I see him please?" When the furious Sergeant asked how she'd got in she replied that she'd followed an officer in through the gate (who held it open for her) and while trying to get her bearings in the courtyard (right next to the open rear gate to the Custody Suite) she asked another officer where to go and he directed her to go (unaccompanied) to the skippers' office.

The email had the Super and Chief Super Cc'd on it and requested that in future challenges be made of anyone seen on or attempting to enter Police premises who was unknown/ not in uniform/ not wearing ID.

A week later I was driving in to the Nick and saw in my rear view mirror a Kenco van attempting to tailgate. I got out to speak to the driver.

"Hello mate, have you got any ID on you?"

"What, no understand?"

"Do you have any identification?"

"I no speak English well"

For God's sake. He's working fixing the coffee machines in the Nick and he can't even speak the Queen's!

"Don't follow me in OK, push the intercom"

"What? No understand"

"DON'T FOLLOW ME IN. Push the intercom...you know, the button" I mime what I want him to do.

"Ahhh...err ok. Is first time they ask this"

I don't know what was worse. The fact that neither he nor his company had been told to always buzz the intercom, the fact that he couldn't speak English well enough for basic communication or the fact that nobody had challenged him before.

When you are assigned to a Nick you get a swipe card. This enables you to enter the station without being buzzed in by reception and means you can use either the car gate or the side gate simply by pressing your warrant card holder, with the card in it, against the card reader. The light changes from red to green, the mechanism clicks and in or out you go.

Simple.

One shift I entered the Custody Suite through the internal entrance (i.e from within the Nick) and found an irate Chief Inspector stuck in the no man's land of the second corridor.

To exit or enter the Custody area you have to go through three security doors, all of which only open with a pass card no matter whether you are coming or going. This is simply to prevent our honoured guests from scarpering if they manage to make it out of the Booking In area or the Cell wing. The CI had left the main part of the Suite as someone else was coming in, without using his pass and had then got stuck.

He glared at me in anger through the safety glass window in the door as I held my card to the reader and the door clicked open.

"Sir", I said nodding.

"Bloody things. My pass isn't working" he said looking both embarrassed and angry. I guess when you get to six pips you assume the least you will be given is unrestricted acess in your own Nick.

"Mine's working Sir, would you like me to let you through the other door?"

"Yes, you'd better had" he harrumphed. I let him through and then went to speak to the Custody Sergeant and forgot all about the incident for a full five minutes until the skipper's phone rang.

"Custody. Sergeant Tob speaking. What? What do you mean you can't get in? Hang on". He turns to me and cradles the phone between his shoulder and chin. "Nip outside and let DC Spurlingham in will you, he appears to have forgotten his pass again". I can hear the receiver squwarking with what sound like furious denials as I put my pen down and retrieve an annoyed CID detective.

Later on, calls over the radio make it clear this isn't just a coincidence involving Sir and the DC.

"kkk...Four-seven to control we have a prisoner in the back of the van and he's Non-Compliant" (background babble of what sounds like someone shouting and swearing incoherently while repeatedly kicking the van's interior). "Can someone open the gate for us we can't get in?".

Later still.

"kkk...Four-nine. We're trying to get in for Refs but the gate won't open. Is there anyone at Delta-Yankee to let us in?"

And so on.

This phenomenon was unexplained and at the moment unexplainable. As my pass still functioned the word was put out amongst my Section that if they needed to come in and we were either near the station or on Refs they could come and liaise with us. Others had to find out who was in the Nick at any given time and call them on the Job mobile to door or gate from the inside.

It turned out it wasn't the Designated Nick either, all Nicks in the Area were now inaccessible.

Next day it was the same, except this time the duty Inspector had the foresight to actually find out whose passes were still up and running and distribute the few that were amongst the Section and told everyone to keep in contact so we'd know who was able to let who in at any given time during the 11 hours we were on duty.

As it was the weekend and the Admin department wouldn't be open till Monday we just had to put up with it.

On the Tuesday it transpired that the passes had all expired on midnight the day that I found the CI trapped like a parrot in a pet shop cage. All passes issued the year previously (they all got renewed at the same time) had a time limit and at 12am became good for nothing except scraping mud off the soles of your Magnums. Mine had been issued only a month before due to me joining Section out of sync.

It was a week after the cards expired that they actually issued everyone with new ones again. Noone had realised the cards would become null and void, including the PSE responsible for issuing them to the entire Area.

Similarly, another fiasco occurred at one of the Nicks I worked out of.

Some genius in SMT had had installed what were described fairly accurately as "nuclear sub doors that they probably got for a fiver each off the navy after the Cold War". They were the front and back doors of the Nick and were intended to make trespassing and burglary things that could never happen.

They were at least five inches thick and ideal for a modern Police station. Robust, intimidating and solid. You needed a key or swipe card to get in to the station and a key or swipe card to get out.

Fine.

Then the flaw in the scheme occurred and the proof that, as ever, SMT do not think of a Plan B.

One day the front door lock got stuck. It turned out that as these things were so heavy and unyielding there was no way of manually overriding the locking mechanism OR of forcing the door. This effectively meant that officers were trapped in the Station with no way to get out and had to call for a locksmith to extract them.

After the lock was "reassessed", SMT had a push button release installed next to the swipe card box on the inside.

A similar travesty of common sense was when they decided to fit the vehicle fleet with smart cards.

Police vehicles were fitted with card readers. Drivers were fitted with cards. These had the officers' details, a photo and a micro chip. When inserted in the reader it knew who the officer was, what time of day it was and could monitor speed, fuel consumption and knew exactly when you'd stopped and for how long.

This was meant to be able to be accessed in the event of a POLAC or to verify what an officer said in Court. In reality it was a tachograph from hell and simply a way of keeping tabs on what we were doing.

The car absolutely would NOT start until it had read and verified the card. It was wired to the ignition mechanism, meaning you had to have the light turn green before you could twist the key and hear the reassuring splutter of the engine turning over.

Problem was that the readers sometimes threw their teddies out the pram and refused to read the cards.

There was no backup for this and you had to either sit there continually trying the reader until it stopped sulking or get someone out to fix it. While this may not sound like more than an annoyance it can be brought into perspective by the fact that if you are trying to leave a situation or your car stalls you will be unable to move. On two occasions while I was employed we heard frantic calls for assistance from officers who had attempted an arrest of some chavvy Asbo in one of the more undesirable housing estates and had been attacked with fists, feet and blunt heavy things by the arrestee's family and friends. Only by piling into to the car while spraying Pava out the windows and screeching off down the road had they escaped getting a right good kicking.

Now imagine if they'd been in the smart cars. The car might not have started. The officers' only hope of escape would be to lock themselves in the vehicle and trigger their panic alarms. Then to sit tight and wait until back up arrived, which in my old Force might have taken up to 20 minutes if they were in one of the outlaying villages.

They still hadn't remedied this issue by the time I left even though various drivers from Basic to Advanced had stated in writing to SMT the safety issues prevalent in such a stupid system.

Four miles from my station was the neighbouring Nick. It had the same basic measures for security but shared its rear car park with the theatre next door. This was due to an agreement between the Police and the local council. I vividly recall that during a production of Scooby Doo we piled into the vehicles to attend a flash call for Officer in Distress after someone's panic alarm was triggered. Attempting a three point turn next to the open backstage entrance and in our way was The Mystery Machine which we had to manoeuvre past to get out.

BASIC TO ADVANCED

Up until about six years ago, once you passed your Police Driving Test, you were then allowed to do what every 10 year old boy dreams of and drive like Lewis Hamilton on the final lap of the Grand Prix. Through red lights, up one way streets the wrong way, roundabouts anti-clockwise and 70mph in a 30. All with your Blues and Twos on as you careened round corners and the siren blared its tune to herald your arrival at whatever Priority One had warranted you flaunting the Highway Code.

Then the Forces and Services realised that they were getting too many accidents and vehicles damaged, not to mention the much more important "complaints from the general public". So they changed the rules.

Now you have three levels of Police driver.

There is Basic who has basically done his or her DVLA test over again in a squad car under the supervision of a Police driving examiner and answered some questions on a written Highway Code test. Takes less than a day.

There is Standard, who has spent three weeks learning the subtleties of exceeding the speed limit, assessing the road ahead for hazards, blatting it around the Skid Pan and being bored out of their head in a classroom most of the time.

Then there is Advanced who has spent another 3 weeks in a classroom and is empowered to pursue the kind of criminals seen on TV shows like 'Police, Camera, Action', can drive at over 110 mph and is authorised for the almighty T-PAC manoeuvre.

This sounds reasonable as it means in theory you will get a higher quality of driver and officers will now be much more well trained and aware of the road, its hazards as well as fully understanding the vehicle they are driving.

Ahem....!

The reality is thoroughly depressing.

All officers on a Section will be Basic at a minimum. As this test is usually done during initial Training before you are assigned to a permanent squad then everyone can drive a normal Police car and pootle about the town. They cannot however under ANY circumstances flaunt the Highway Code and during the Basic Highway Code Test will be told in writing (capital letters, bold, larger font, italicised AND underlined) and verbally by the examiner that "NOBLE CAUSE IS NO EXCUSE" and running a red light or exceeding the speed limit to assist an officer who's just pushed their panic button because 10 pissed up football hooligans are giving them a shoeing will only get you into trouble and your Force will NOT waive any penalty points you accrue through getting flashed by a speed camera doing this. Nor will they help you if you cause or are even involved in an accident. It also means that any and all calls, no matter how urgent, will have all Basic trained officers attending at the appropriate speed limit, stopping for Zebras and red lights and not using their sirens or lights (which for Basic can only be used to control traffic if the vehicle is stationery e.g. at an RTC to block other vehicles from passing at night).

So next time the Police take 30 minutes to turn up after you call to say your neighbour is murdering her husband with the rotary hedge trimmer, don't wonder why. It's because the driver was Basic.

Standard drivers are like gold dust and there are meant to be several on any given Section. They can flaunt the Highway Code if circumstances permit and are able to drive up to 110mph. They cannot pursue beyond this speed though and have to break off from a chase and let an Advanced driver take over if the Suspect is caning it along the M6. Reality is that you will get one or two at the most, particularly in rural forces and they will be given the ERV for the duration of the shift.

That's if you have one.

If the ERV has been commandeered by the governor of another shift or is in the garage for servicing or repair you will have a Standard driver without a Standard vehicle. You will also have the Magnum-tarnishing frustration of the Standard driver then having to drive Basic. Any vehicle not authorised for Standard use cannot be driven as such, even by a Standard or Advanced driver. So next time you wonder why the guy you saw blatting it through the town centre in a squad car at 80mph last Saturday took 45 minutes to arrive when you called to say your shed was being set on fire by the local chavs, it's coz he was a Standard driver in a Basic car.

Advanced are rarer than Venus's arms or comfortable body armour. They are mythical creatures that can occasionally be found in the canteen or heard over the radio pleading for T-PAC authorisation during a pursuit. Basically to Police driving what 1st Class flying is to Business Class they are allowed to chase people for miles and can, in theory use T-PAC to force a vehicle to slow down by more than one of them boxing the vehicle in and forcing it to a halt or even ramming it off the road. This sexy little bonus to the menu of an Advanced's abilities is meaningless most of the time as they cannot self-authorise for T-PAC and have to get a Control Room Inspector's authority over the radio in order to use it. This is rarely given as:

a). The Police car will almost certainly suffer at least minor damage, even in the "boxing in" manoeuvre.

b). The Inspector will have to bear the brunt of it if anything goes wrong.

A pursuit I overheard on the radio had two officers repeatedly requesting authorisation for T-PAC and stressed it needed to be quickly given as the person they were chasing was driving a 4x4 and they knew that sooner or later he would go off road where they would not be able to pursue him any more. Sure enough, no response from the Inspector (who I've always imagined was sitting six feet from the operator and mouthing "tell them I'm not here!" with frantic hand motions). The 'Suspect' went off road, which meant the pursuit had to be abandoned.

Which brings us to the subject of vehicle classification.

All drivers can drive Basic cars if they pass Basic. Standard can drive Basic and Standard cars and Advanced drivers can do all three. If you want to drive the mini-bus (or Rowdy or Pub van as it's also known) then you have to be tested for it. If you want to drive the Cage van you have to be tested for it. If you want to drive the Police Landrover you have to be tested for that too. BUT there are two tests for it. One for on road and one for off road.

In the end you can take a dozen tests if you want to drive every vehicle the Police Force you work for owns.

The reason for the lack of Standard drivers (and subsequently of Advanced) is simply MONEY.

The budget has to be watched like an old crone guarding her silver by whichever senior officer controls the purse strings. A nice bit of publicity on a Saturday night by having officers patrol en mass in High Viz while chatting to the public will be a priority as will anything suggested by the Race and Diversity department. Posters advertising who your local contacts are within your local area (mainly PCSOs) will be a priority. Paying everyone overtime to do a shift at the Lord Mayor's inauguration will be a priority as will having an open day at the Nick so the general public can see just how their local Bobbies operate.

Standard drivers were trained at a rate of about 10 per year per Area in the Force I worked with.

The Superintendent in charge of budget allocation announced at an annual general meeting that he was generously increasing the number to 12 for each Area this year. Noone dared say at the time that this was unfair as the largest Area was three times larger than the smallest and Sir clearly hadn't thought this through very well.

The magnificent ineptitude of this embarrassing display of stupidity can be summed up in its entirety by the following instruction issued to Police officers a few years ago:

"Drivers in pursuit of suspects on a motorcycle are to abandon the pursuit if the rider or passenger are not wearing helmets or remove them during the pursuit in case the rider or passenger suffers injury as a result of being pursued".

THE RHINO AND THE P WORD

My mate Kev owns a small pub called in a medium sized town in Warwickshire.

It's a decent pub and unlike a lot of the posh, wanky places in town has mainly decent people drinking in there on the weekend who will either talk to you or ignore you and only give you trouble if you start it. He serves four types of lager, usually a guest bitter and all three types of Guinness, including that nasty red thing that noone seems to buy. He has three happy hours per day, cheapest at about 7pm when beer is £1.80 a pint.

The pub is fairly basic and the decor good but nothing flash. One big room with an area up the back where the DJ puts his stuff and a small dance area in front of that where the drunks get up and have a boogie. It's got a kitchen and serves hot food until 3pm or maybe not if the girl serving has decided to knock off early.

Most of the staff in there are female and about 90% are well fit. It's always busy as people know each other in there and there is very rarely any violence or trouble as Kev gets on well with nearly everyone and is one of the rare landlords that if he bars you will not automatically stick you on PubWatch. He knows most people will come back and say sorry once they're sober.

The posh pub across the road and the one a two minute walk away have much more trouble than he does and have two bouncers from Thursday to Sunday on the doors.

The most violent incident in there in recent years was the St George's Day massacre of 2003. I was at the boozer down the road and had stayed for one last Cherry Veeba before heading back. Turned out to be the wisest investment of £2.50 I'd ever made as, upon arriving in the pub, there was blood and glass over most of the floor, two lads with busted noses and tables and chairs thrown around like something from a Western. 30 guys from Birmingham had come in and suddenly kicked off for no reason, trashing other blokes, each other and the pub before running away down the street. The Police caught 18 of them and noone could understand why they'd only Booked In nine. A couple of years later I met a cop in COLP who had transferred from Warwickshire and who told the following, fairly unsettling story:

"We only had nine cells at the Nick and as you can't double up any more due to Health and Safety we had to let half of them go. Guv'nor hit the roof when he found out".

How they chose who left and who was deprived of their liberty remains a mystery. Maybe it was like that scene in James Clavell's Shogun and they made them choose amongst themselves.

When the licensing laws changed in 2005 Kevin wanted a late license. He applied for it and the Police decided to pull his chain. First of all he had to have at least three trained door staff for all the extra trouble that they were positive he was going to have if his pub opened later than 11.30pm. Simple solution to that, he just got himself, the DJ and one of the barmaids trained up and problem solved.

Then it was that he had to have CCTV installed. The public area of the bar is the same size as my step-father's lock-up and while four cameras might have seemed excessive they insisted he did it and later made him increase it to ten. Ten cameras in a pub that is just one big room. Every time he calls for Police assistance or they come to deal with something they blame him for whatever it is. Hence the fact that he is loathe to call them in.

One night a couple of women came hurtling down the three steps that led from the dance floor grappling madly with each other in that hair pulling, scratching, pulling-each-other's-clothes way that drunk birds do when they're having a barney. The DJ yelled over the mic for Kev and they managed to get them separated and took the perceived wrongdoer outside. She was twice as aggressive as a wounded rhinoceros and was flailing punches everywhere, most connecting on Kevin or the DJ. We watched them both manage to wrestle her to the pavement where she continued to flounder and thrash about, ripping Kevin's gold necklace off and kicking passers by and any onlookers who were near enough to her.

I stood in the closed doorway of the pub and tried to keep everyone from going out. This worked for a few minutes until the woman got up again and belted Kev who went flying back into a parked car.

Kev's daughter was watching this through the window and screamed "THAT'S MY DAD!" and tried to get past me.

"Leave it, let him deal with it, you'll just make it worse".

"THAT'S MY FUCKING DAD! GET OUT OF THE WAY!"

I stood back, knowing that physically preventing her would either result in her giving me a slap or other people misunderstanding why I'd done it and thumping me. Afterwards I spoke to Kev who said that he never wants her to get involved because as calm as he usually is he knows that if someone belts his daughter he will then lose it and end up getting arrested.

This was like opening the floodgates and everyone who wanted to then followed her out. The woman was punching anyone who came near and kicking hard at some poor old bloke walking his dog, catching him a right beauty right up the arse. Kev and the DJ had now managed to get her on the floor again but she was struggling to get up and quite clearly would not calm down without the aid of an elephant tranquiliser.

I shouted over "Kev, you've done what you can, it's not your fault. Take it to the next level". He reluctantly then used the headset he was wearing and asked for Police assistance.

She got up again so I walked behind her and got her in a Full Nelson, putting my hands up under her shoulder blades and then linking my fingers behind her neck. As strong as she was she was now unable to lash out except backwards and was frantically trying to punch me over the top of her own head. I just put my face into her back and when she finally paused, shouted "STOP IT! YOU'RE GOING TO GET NICKED. DO YOU WANT TO GET NICKED?"

She starts trying to back punch me again, screeching "FUCK OFF YA CUNT! LET ME GO OR I'LL FUCKIN' KILL YA!".

Other people trying to separate us then use too much momentum the wrong way and we end up going backwards on to the bonnet of a car. I am now pinned underneath a strong, drunken, violent woman who is trying to stand up again, but unable to as I am underneath her. Some bloke pulls my arm and yanks hard, clearly thinking it's hers.

"That's my arm!" I yell as he almost breaks the grip I have on her.

"Oh sorry" he says, clearly drunk himself and looks puzzled at the various appendages, before choosing one that belongs to her and giving it a cautious tug.

Just then we hear the sirens and I let her go as a Police car pulls up. "Calm down or they will nick you" I say quietly. An Asian officer and a young female cop get out. I walk towards them but don't identify myself. "It's all blown over now" I say to the female officer.

"Can you get onto the pavement please?" she replies, clearly looking nervous at having to deal with this.

I go back in the pub and we watch them talk to the slightly calmer female for a few minutes. From their arm gestures it's clear they're telling her to push off and eventually she does, stomping away down the road.

A short time later she comes back, presumably thinking they'd be gone and they are still parked up and again tell her to sling her hook.

She slopes off but comes back AGAIN and this time they finally nick her. Took long enough but at least they did it in the end. I went back to having a quiet beer and forgot all about it (apart from the piss taking from my mates about using arrest restraints) until three weeks later when I came back into town again.

The second time she came back the only reason they arrested her was because she called the Asian officer a "paki bastard". As Racially Aggravated Section 4a of the Public Order Act is an area that the Police don't have any discretion in any more and she had now crossed the line they had to nick her. All the Criminal Damage, Public Order, Breach of the Peace, Assaults and Affray meant nothing next to her using racist language to the cop. They were quite prepared to let her walk away in light of all the other stuff she'd done and gave her two opportunities to do so. Core Section for this town and its two neighbours on the weekend is 8, yes that's right 8 officers for all three, so the last thing they wanted to do was nick her and take themselves off active patrol. Once she uttered the 'P' word though, it was no longer up for debate.

The stupidity of allowing discretion for all the other stuff but not for this can be summed up by an addendum to this story I heard about six months later.

Apparently the Asian officer she insulted (remembering that this is a man who at some point in his career may have to deal with a messy car crash, deliver a death message at 3am to a dead teenage girl's parents and be involved in a fight to save himself or a colleague from serious harm) was so distraught and upset to have been insulted in this way that he had to take three days off to recover. This fact was used in the evidence when the woman appeared in Court.

THE MACC LADS vs
THE BRONX WARRIORS

In 1982 Enzo G Castellari, an Italian exploitation film director made a movie based loosely on both Walter Hill's The Warriors and John Carpenter's Escape From New York. The title of the movie was 1990: The Bronx Warriors.

The movie's plot is that it is the future. New York's Bronx district has become so crime ridden that it has been officially declared "No Man's Land" and the Police no longer exist there.

Starring Vic Morrow and Fred Williamson the movie topped the American Billboard charts for three weeks in 1983 and spawned a sequel in 1985 named Escape From the Bronx.

At the age of 13 there was virtually shite all to do in my home town. It was and still is a monotonous dump with no night life beyond the pubs. The Youth Club had a film night on Mondays (remember this was 1984 and a VCR was still an expensive luxury). We would pack the TV room in our sweaty hordes to watch whatever they'd got for us out of petty cash. Usually it would be crap like "Splash" or "Flashdance" but once this film got rolling we were presented with a synthesised music score showing a montage of weapons the various gangs in the movie use. Then the opening five minutes had me and everyone else hooked as the Riders despatched the Zombies in some atrocious martial arts choreography.

I was completely blown away by this film and had never seen anything like it before. Decades later when DVD was born the movies came out but alas and foresooth only in German. I bought them anyway and when they were finally released in English I put the two German versions on Ebay.

The winning bidder was the director Enzo G Castellari.

After some email exchanges where I ascertained this was really him and not a fan taking the piss he endorsed a website I set up for the movies at www.bronxwarriors.com and in 2004 I flew out to Rome to meet him where he autographed all my memorabilia, posed for photos and let me interview him for the site. A year later I met him again and Enzo's son Andrea has told me that his father now considers me a friend and was very flattered to have the website set up in his honour.

In 1988 I was sitting in a mate's bedroom reading comics and he asked if I wanted to listen to a new punk band he'd recently been introduced to. He put on a cassette of a song called "Sweaty Betty" by The Macc Lads and I had never heard anything like it in my life. Before the term politically correct had reached my ears the best way to describe this band would be "very rude" as the song was about an enormously obese woman that the singer had apparently shagged (think AC/DC's 'Whole Lotta Rosie' but funny). It was as if Bernard Manning or Chubby Brown had picked up a Gibson guitar and hired a drummer.

I immediately burned my Climie Fisher collection and for the next six years was a massive fan of the band, following them on tour and eventually getting to know one of their roadies who got me into gigs for free where I would help out or even do security in the pit occasionally to prevent the fans climbing on stage.

Formed in 1981 and hailing from Macclesfield in the north of England they were completely offensive to all and sundry. The subjects of their songs being alcohol and sex in the mainstay (first album was called Beer and Sex and Chips 'n' Gravy), fighting, football and even sheep shagging. The lead singer/ songwriter/ bass player and manager was Muttley McLad, on guitar was The Beater and drums was Stez Styx. They packed out mid-size venues all over the country in the late 80s and early 90s, despite getting no radio play due to the profanity and vulgarity in the songs and being banned from ever appearing in any college or university affiliated to the National Union of Students.

In 1998 I found a website set up by a 19 year old fan who had never seen the band perform but loved their stuff and had put the word out for info on them. I emailed him with my involvement, we renamed the site The Bear's Head (The Macc Lads' local pub) and over the next two years succeeded in getting various ex band members, roadies, support acts and associates to do interviews. In 2001 Muttley McLad, created his own Macc Lads website where The Bear's Head now resides as a tribute to our efforts.

Muttley to this day insists that most of the fans 'got the joke'. My argument that they wouldn't have turned up to gigs in their hundreds, got completely drunk and moshed their heads off if they thought he was insincere, is something we still have to agree to disagree on.

Fast forward to 2007 and a former Macc Lads roadie and Bronx Warriors fan is now PC Manley.

One morning me and Jacob were out in the ERV and had set up by the side of the road to see if we could catch anyone using a mobile phone while driving. Jacob's Job mobile was in the hands-free cradle and at about 10am we got an unexpected call.

"Hello this is Chief Inspector Nutall are you 10/8?"

"Hello Sir, yes I am" Jacob replies.

"Is Lance with you Jacob?"

"Yes Sir, he's next to me, do you want to speak to him?"

"No, it's ok. Can you get him to come and see me at 12pm please in my office".

"No problem, will do Sir".

The CI rings off and I look at Jacob. "What's that about?" feeling a little nervous.

"It's OK, he probably wants to just meet you to say hi. They do that sometimes with probationers. It's probably just a 'handshake' to welcome you to the Nick".

I think on this. Doesn't quite gel. "But we've already had that with the Super' a few months ago. Who is he anyway?"

"Joined same intake as me. SUPER Fast Track that one. He's OK...look don't worry. If it was important they'd have requested it in writing".

Half an hour later and we both end up nicking two blokes on suspicion of Theft after one was caught with money hidden in his shoe and the other dropped £200 in twenties on the floor during a search by his firm's security guard which I was overseeing. Jacob calls the CI back who tells me to come tomorrow instead at 11am.

At this point in my career I was not yet used to the underhanded ways of my PDU Sergeant, Kerwan and his deputy PC Esobé and of being lied to or deceived about what to expect. This time I trusted Jacob's reassurance that it was probably only a chat and although nervous to be heading up to the SMT floor, was confident it wasn't anything to get worked up about. As I left the Writing Room Jacob called after me "don't worry it'll be fine. Meet you back here later".

I approached the SMT secretary, a serious woman who told me that they were all in their daily meeting and to take a seat. After about 20 minutes an Indian CI entered the room. He looked about late 20s early 30s and was tall and thin. I got to my feet as he entered, as per etiquette and he smiled and then said "hello Lance, I've just got some things to take care of and then I'll be with you OK?".

Friendly and no trace of any annoyance so maybe this is just a chat. Jacob had told me to carry my cap under my arm as I entered the office and wait to be offered a seat before sitting down, just to give a good impression. The brim had practically worn a groove in my the soft skin of my upper arm when he returned a few minutes later and told me to follow him.

As we entered his office I was surprised to find PDU Ma'am sitting on the other side of the desk.

"Ma'am" I nod to her and she nods back.

"PC Manley".

The CI takes his seat and motions me to sit. I put the cap on my lap and they both look at me.

He begins. "Now Lance the reason we've brought you in here today is that we understand that you're involved in a couple of websites. The Macc Lads and the Bronx Warriors".

"Yes Sir, that's right" I answer nodding. Jesus! Why the hell are Senior Management bothered about this?

"We're not sure what they are, we wondered if you could explain it".

"Well they're just a couple of fan sites. They've been on the Net for years".

After a pause he opens a cardboard folder and takes out two photocopied sheets of A4. I've always believed since then that he wanted to see if I'd deny involvement so he could pull them out and go "WELL, WHAT'S THIS THEN?".

One is the main page of the Bronx Warriors website, with the ad line from the first film about the Bronx being No Man's Land, below are two images from the German DVD covers that I sold to Enzo and at the bottom is a photo of me and Enzo outside his office in Rome plus a counter to monitor how many people have visited the site.

The other is a page from the The Bear's Head and is a list of contributors to the site with photos.

"Can you explain your involvement in The Macc Lads please?"

"Well the Macc Lads are a band I used to work for when I was younger. I haven't been involved with them for about seven years".

PDU Ma'am who until that point had simply sat there looking at me, reaches across the table and without saying a word takes the piece of paper from the ACI's hand in her bony fingers and glares at me malevolently. She then coughs slightly and with a voice that could fossilise dogshit says:

"But PC Manley if I could just read you what's written about Rachel, one of the contributors to the site who's listed two below you". She puts on her glasses and squints at the page. "Apparently, according to this 'Rachel is our own Miss Macclesfield. She has taken a break from giving blow jobs and doing the washing up to help us with the website. She has real big tits and lovely slappable arse which are yours to do what you want with for the price of a Dry Martini'."

She then slaps the paper down hard on the table and glares at me. "PC MANLEY do you REALLY think that's appropriate for a Police officer to be associated with?"

I am currently writhing in embarrassment and wishing the floor would swallow me. Making this worse is the fact that PDU Ma'am looks at least 55, is female, of senior rank and talks like she went to Debutante School and attends Ladies Day at Ascot. I know blokes who would pay good money to have that kind of prurient filth read to them by a posh, late middle-aged woman that has to be addressed with an honorific and stood up for.

"I didn't write that" I manage to stammer.

She continues to glare at me and replies "I know you didn't", practically hissing the words. "If you had we wouldn't be talking like this. However you are associated with it. What if Rachel finds out what you do for a living now?"

"It's been seven years since I've been involved with them at all" I protest.

"Yes, I do grant you that that photo was probably taken a long time ago" she concedes, pointing to the black and white photo of me taken in 1991 and about two stone heavier, mainly around my face.

"Yes, Ma'am when I was 20"

"You student days are over. Get your photo off there immediately". She sits back and glances over at the ACI.

The CI then picks up the other piece of A4. "Now the Bronx Warriors, what's that about?"

"It's a film Sir, I saw it when I was about 13, I've set up the website as a tribute".

"A film?" the CI says looking surprised.

"Yes Sir. Have you seen The Warriors?"

He shakes his head.

"Escape From New York?"

He looks blank.

"Err...ok well it's a bit like both of them. It's about the Bronx being lawless and the gangs controlling it. It's a sci-fi film". I decide not to go into plot details but instead say "I know the director, I've met him twice and he gave me permission to set up the website in his honour. He's a cited influence on Quentin Tarantino and Tarantino's about to remake one of his films".

I'm glad they didn't ask me which one as it's called The

Inglorious Bastards but I suppose I could have translated the original Italian title of 'Questo Maladetto Treno Blindato' which means 'This Goddamn Bulletproof Train' in English.

CI Nuttall and PDU Ma'am glance at each other quickly.

"From what we're aware of it's a website about a gang called The Riffs who live in the Bronx".

"No Sir, Riffs is German for Riders, the name of the gang in the film. Those two photos are of the two German DVD covers for the film and the sequel".

There is a pause. They glance at each other again and he again asks "it's a film?"

"Yes Sir. You can buy it for a tenner in HMV. It came out in the budget range about four years ago".

Reading this back now, I can see the ammunition I was providing them with through mentioning lawlessness, gangs and Police in one sentence.

"We understand there's also film content on the website but we are unable to access it to see if it's inappropriate due to our firewall".

Jesus! How detailed was this investigation I wasn't even aware of?

"Sir that's the trailer for the film".

I have by now realised what they thought the site was about, but am avoiding focussing on that thought for fear of bursting out laughing and not being able to stop.

"It's not copyrighted which means I didn't need permission to use it. If you take off the firewall I'll access it now on your computer". I point to his PC in the corner.

"No, if you promise me it's not inappropriate then we'll believe you" he assures me.

They then start to wind up the cogs in hastily re-edited "advice" around an officer of Her Majesty's Police being involved in such a website.

PDU Ma'am then enquires "what does 'Die Gewalt Sind Wir' mean?" pointing to the picture of the German DVD cover for the first movie. This is the caption below the words 'The Riffs'.

"Ah, that means roughly 'We Are Scary' in German" I tell her.

Rallying magnificently in the face of their concealed embarrassment she comes back with a superb flanking manoeuvre.

"Ah, but PC Manley, what if you arrest someone who speaks German and they know you run this site and they think 'is this officer going to be scary with me?"

The ACI then says "can you see it from our point of view? How do you think it would reflect on the Force if someone knew you were involved in this site about gangs and there being no law and order?"

"Sir, it's only a film. It was number one at the American box office for three weeks".

There's a pause then he adds "well maybe you could stay in overall control of the site but not run it on a daily basis. Obviously a lot of people have visited it, you've had errm..." He consults the photocopy "1734 visitors since 2005".

Ma'am then says "if a journalist puts your name in Google then they'll find out that you run these sites".

"Someone's obviously already done that" I reply

The ACI glances at the sheet again and says "I'm not prepared to go into that now".

PDU Ma'am then adds "yes, if a journalist knows you run this site and decides to put it in the papers you will, without having meant to, have brought the Force into disrepute and you'll be suspended", still glaring at me with a stare that would make Medusa seriously consider retirement.

We wrap things up with the ACI changing the subject completely and telling me to remain focussed throughout probation. I tell him about yesterday's arrest of the thief and that the security guard had told Jacob that he was well impressed with how I'd handled it and had said he was going to write saying so to the Chief Super'.

"Good, good that's excellent, that's what we want, you're a young officer who's just come to us, you need to work hard and get some good work reports and then think about moving on"" the CI replies, smiling while shoving the photocopies back in the folder.

"Yes" the Inspector snaps "focus on what you're doing now, before you think about promotion".

None of this last bit had any bearing on Rachel's slappable arse or The Riffs and was basically a distraction technique.

Ma'am repeats that it's time to leave my student days behind and we conclude.

Jacob is smiling when I see him but his jaw drops with an audible thud when I tell him what happened.

"What? Seriously? How the hell did they find out? It's not like you've done anything illegal. That's stupid" he gasps. "What's it got to do with them what you're involved with outside work?"

I then ring Muttley McLad and ask him to remove my name and photo from the site. He listens to my reasons and then replies "they're angry with you because of something someone else wrote about you? That's just SAD".

The fact that the ACI had a page of A4 with detailed (but highly inaccurate) synopses made it clear to me that someone in a damp, darkened basement office somewhere in the vaults of the Professional Standards Department had typed my name into a search engine and found me in all my chubby, punkified, early 90s glory.

The content on The Macc Lads site was clearly offensive and I understand completely why they didn't want one of their cops to be associated with it.

The saddest and funniest thing though was that they clearly believed bronxwarriors.com was a site set up to glorify a real street gang, with me as an affiliate.

Enzo G Castellari is now lecturing in film studies at Cinecitta Film Studios in Rome. Whenever he gets a new class he tells the students this story and they apparently always piss themselves laughing.

A REAL MAN

Jacob was on Leave one day when I got partnered with a different lad named Aldrin, called in from another Section when ours was so under staffed that the skipper was having to tutor me in the absence of any other officers.

A petrol station in our Area would give coppers free coffees. That is to say we would always offer to pay for them and they would then say "no it's ok". This meant your precious Integrity was still unbreached as you had offered payment but had had it refused.

After a fairly piss poor shift where we couldn't even catch someone using their mobile phone while driving, me and Aldrin were stirring our frothy mochas when the cashier called us over and whispered that the large, red van filling up outside was constantly involved in either bilking or not having any money after filling the tank. The drivers were always bereft of ID, gave false addresses and never returned to cough up. He produced a sheaf of papers all with different names and addresses and said the van belonged to a building firm local to the area. He added that the firm was known to be run by local 'settled' travellers.

A morose looking woman that you could take a guess was not having the best of days (i.e. slightly unkempt, denim mini skirt, pink crop top and a black eye the size of a cricket ball) was filling a plastic petrol container with diesel while three kids aged from about two to six were clambering about in the cab.

Outside we asked her to replace the hose and put the container in the back of the van. She looks surprised but then shrugs and after she's done both I explain that the vehicle has been identified as being involved in making off without payment and she needs to make certain she can pay for the fuel.

Aldrin then gestures to the vehicle with a fairly unnecessary set of hand movements, as if he's talking to a deaf person. It's only the third time he does it I notice the large, rusty kitchen knife jammed in between the rubber seal of the windscreen and the glass on the driver's side. She clearly didn't know it was there and says the van belongs to her husband.

We do a section 1 PACE search of the vehicle. The children have to get out for this and begin milling around on the forecourt. The youngest, snot and marmite covering his upper lip and chin starts to move too far near the other pumps and I run over and grab him, picking him up and putting him down at his mother's feet. After a perusal of the van's cockpit we find another rusty blade in the glove box. Both knives are confiscated.

Just then Seb and Katrina turn up for their free coffees which means I don't have to call a female officer to do a physical search. Nothing is found on the woman who asks if she can go. Aldrin points out that there are four people in the front of the cab when it can only legally take three and as the vehicle does not have rear seats if she drives off the forecourt he will arrest her.

I ask her if someone else can come and pick up one of the kids. She says her husband can. She then looks at me and begins to cry. "My husband won't like you talking to me, he can get very funny."

"Fine" I reply "we can get funny too. Did he give you that black eye?"

She nods. It's literally a quarter the size of her face, red and swollen, her eye is half closed. "He's a very possessive and violent man. He doesn't like me talking to other men. He won't like me talking to you."

"That's his problem. Do you want me to do anything about this?"

"NO!" she almost shouts, looking more worried "please don't, he'll be really angry"

"Have you tried looking for help? The Police have numbers you can call that will help you".

"I left him and went to a women's refuge but when I went to my mother's for the weekend he came and made me go back".

"Is that when he hit you?" I ask her.

She nods. "But please don't do anything" she says again, tears in her eyes.

"OK, don't get upset, but I want to help you. Do you have a phone so you can call someone to come and take one of the kids?"

"No, I'm not allowed to have a mobile phone".

Jesus! This gets worse. A possessive, controlling, jealous, bilking, wife beater.

I ask her for her husband's phone number and call him from Aldrin's job mobile.

"Hello?"

"Hello this is Police constable Manley. Nothing to worry about but I need to tell you that your wife is at the petrol station on Applewood Avenue with too many children in the vehicle. We need you or someone else to come and take one of the kids because she can't drive away at the moment"

"Oh I'm sorry Sir. She's made the decision to do that on her own. I keep telling her not to but she won't listen".

About ten seconds into this verbal diahorrea I realise I'm talking to a lying, cowardly, little cunt.

"Like I say Sir, I'll be down straight away. I'm about three miles away I'll be there as soon as I can".

I approach Aldrin. "Look, is there nothing we can do about this? He gave her that black eye and he forcibly made her go home after she left him and went to a women's refuge".

"Not if she's not willing to pursue it or make a Statement" he matter-of-factly replies.

I approach her again. "Do you absolutely not want me to do anything about what he's done?"

"Please don't" she replies, looking utterly miserable.

"Ok, don't worry" I say putting my hand gently on her arm and trying to smile "but I had to ask you."

"He's not a real man but, he gets angry if I try and leave him".

We continue to chat and about fifteen minutes later I hear a harsh, aggressive, Irish accent behind me say "what's going on here then?"

Straight away from the arrogant, overly brash tones in the slurred voice I can tell without turning around that:

a). This is the husband;

b). He's almost certainly had too much to drink and;

c). He's giving it the big 'un to see if he can intimidate me or take the dominant role in the conversation.

I turn round and glare at him. He's a short arse. About 5 feet 4 and stockily built, early 40s with a tacky white shirt open to the fourth button displaying too much chest hair. He has an Elvis style quiff with pork chop sideburns. He's glaring at me and standing too close. Booze reeks on his breath and I'm probably getting drunk just on the passives.

"Was it you I spoke to on the phone?" I ask him, staring him right in the face.

"Yes."

"Well I don't need to tell then do I because you already know".

He instantly changes. Takes one step back and moderates his tone. "Oh ok, just checking everything's ok" he says, giving a false laugh.

"Are you driving? I can smell alcohol on your breath?" I ask him as Aldrin walks up and stands next to us.

"Huh!" he tuts looking skyward, glances at his wife and tuts again. "I value my job too much Sir to do that. I've got my car at the pub, my mate's going to drive me home. I was in the pub when you called me".

It was only hours later that I remembered he'd told me he was three miles away when I'd called him.

He picks the youngest child up and swings him up on to his shoulders. He looks at his wife "I'll meet you back at the house then" and begins to walk off.

"I think you can see what kind of man he is" she whispers to me before starting the ignition.

As he walks away and she drives off I turn to Aldrin. "You know he's going to hit her when he gets her home, is there NOTHING we can do?"

"You spotted he'd had a drink so, yes. We'll go to his address and wait to see if he drives there".

We blat it round to his home. A 'settled traveller's abode' is the polite way of describing the large portakabin on low stilts that we spot as we park up at the end of his long drive and see his wife and kids get out to be greeted by another guy.

We stay out of site and after 15 minutes of sitting there decide to move off.

"He's probably not stupid and won't go straight home" Aldrin tells me.

The road is narrow and as we get near the bottom see a vehicle coming towards us. A large 4x4 with orange emergency lights on the roof. This last fact is the only reason I don't suspect it's our man. The vehicle sits there stubbornly and flashes it's headlights for us to move out the way. Aldrin winds down his window and angrily motions for the driver to move across. He slowly does and just at the precise moment that we are clear enough of the other vehicle for it to get past Aldrin shouts "THAT'S HIM. YOU, WAIT THERE!".

I look across to see the startled face of our drunken wife beater before he roars off up the lane. Aldrin does the quickest three point turn I've ever seen but we lose him down the winding country lanes almost immediately.

I turn to Aldrin when we decide to give it up. "Can't we go to the house? They might know where he is".

"Yes but remember he might take it out on the wife when he gets back."

"We should do something. I don't like the fact that he's laughing in our faces."

Aldrin nods and we drive up the lane to the house. Garden gnomes and coach wheels on the walls signify the style of décor. A big Alsatian bounds up and sits on its haunches staring at us. A young guy comes out of the house and saunters towards us with his hands in his pockets. I wind down the window.

"Can I help you officers?" he enquires in a broad Irish accent.

"First of all take your hands out of your pockets"

"Oh sure" he laughs "what's the problem?"

"Do you know where Callum is?"

"No I don't to tell you the truth" he replies smiling smugly at me "would you like me to give him a message?"

I am trying to keep my temper. "Yeah, give him my best and tell him I hope he has a brilliant weekend."

"Will do officer. Just one thing, why did I have to take my hands out of my pockets?"

"So I know you're not holding anything you can use as a weapon"

He laughs. "Oh right, so you are" and walks back inside the house.

Back at the Nick I state my concerns about the woman's safety and ask the skipper if there is anything we can do. He suggests that the only thing available would be an NIP for failing to stop when Aldrin told him to but it would be difficult to prove so it's best not to bother.

I never felt more ashamed of being a Police officer during my entire time with two Forces.

An ABH, theft of fuel, drink driving and potentially another ABH or worse (as well as arguably abduction for forcing his wife to come home) and we could do absolutely nothing to help the poor woman.

I joined to protect the weak and innocent. In this case I was able to do neither and found out to my disgust that we didn't have the powers to anyway.

THE SPOILT MISPER

A Missing Persons form is a right turd to fill out.

It takes at least a couple of hours, what with the many pages it contains plus the Inspector's authority needed for approval.

While Jacob was still on Annual Leave me and a female officer named Mary got tasked with dealing with a very worried couple whose son Tarquin hadn't been seen for 3 days. He was 16, had never run away before and wasn't replying to answer phone messages they were leaving on his mobile.

We took the parents plus two sisters aged about 10 and 12 into a private room near reception at the Nick and took PNB entries to get as much information as possible on the lad. This took about an hour as the details had to be exact. Physical description, clothing, identifying features, friends, acquaintances, enemies. We had to ask if he had met anyone on the Internet, if he had been having problems at school. Had he tried to commit suicide? Had he talked about it? Was he depressed? Was he taking drugs? Did he have friends who were? The list went on and on.

The two girls sat in the back of the room playing games on handheld computer consoles and would occasionally chip in with snippets of information the parents had forgotten or didn't know (such as one of their brother's nicknames being Conan).

The mum and dad looked visibly worried and were obviously holding it back and trying to keep their chins up in what was probably an incredibly stressful time for them. The mother looked close to cracking up while the father seemed weary but would crack a smile occasionally and squeeze his wife's hand when we reassured them we would do everything we could to help find their son.

After we had what we needed they left and we promised we would be round in a couple of hours to check his bedroom as per normal routine, to see if there was any clue as to where he'd gone.

In the Writing Room we started on the laborious task of filling out the MisPer form. Pages and pages of it which after about another 90 minutes we reckoned we had it down pat. The Inspector was approached for his signature, gave it and off we went to Tarquin's house for the mandatory check.

The father answered the door and immediately said "have you found him?" looking hopeful as we stood on the doorstep.

"No Sir, I'm afraid not. Can we come in and check his room?"

He let us in and we saw a typical middle-class, sixteen year old's room, with clothing, magazines, old socks and food wrappers strewn about the place, the duvet buried under the garbage. Nothing leapt out as being untoward. No suicide note placed next on his desk, no discarded syringe under the bed.

We went back downstairs and entered the lounge. His wife is sat in an armchair, a big Golden Retriever at her feet. It got up as we walked in and the father shooed it out the room. "We can't see any clues in his room as to where he's gone so we'll check out the addresses you gave of his friends ok?".

"Bring him back with you will you please?" the father asks.

"Of course. If we find him we'll bring him straight back. He's a minor so it's not his decision".

We check out the first address about half a mile away from their house.

"Is Tarquin here?" I ask, not expecting them to have any clue where he's gone.

"Oh yeah" the girl astonishingly replies "at least he was, he's gone round to Judy's house. What's he done?"

We go in the house to get Judy's address and then head off, finding that it's only three streets away from Tarquin's house where his anxious parents await his return, clearly expecting us to come back looking solemn with our caps under our arms to say "can we come in? I'm afraid it's bad news".

A woman answers the door. "Hello" I say cheerfully "are you Judy?"

"No I'm her mother. What's the problem?"

"Nothing to worry yourself about. Have you seen Tarquin? He's one of Judy's friends".

She opens the door fully and says "oh yes, he's in here. Is he in trouble?" motioning for me to follow her into the house. She clearly doesn't even know that Tarquin is missing from home, let alone that his parents are more wired than caffeine addicts due to his unplanned absence.

We enter the lounge and see a scrawny, white kid in a pair of baggy jeans and a Marilyn Manson t-shirt. He had floppy brown hair over his eyes and looks like he weighs ten stone piss-wet through. He certainly doesn't look like someone who's nickname is Conan.

"Tarquin?"

"Yesss" he sighs, looking bored. "I knew it was too good to last".

While elated to have found him so quickly I am annoyed at his flippant attitude.

"You need to come with us. We're going to take you home. Your parents have filed a Missing Person report on you. They're very worried".

"Typical" he shrugs. "Ok" and moves to follow us back out.

"Do you need to collect any stuff?" I ask him.

"Nope".

I thank Judy's mother who says "I thought you told me your parents knew where you were" to Tarquin as he mooches unconcernedly past her.

"Sorry" he mumbles.

We get out onto the drive and he starts mimicking The Last Post theme in a falsetto. I turn round and glare at him. He looks up past his fringe, catches my expression and stops it.

We get him in the car. "Right put your seat belt on mate" I tell him.

Mary then asks "before we get back is there anything you want to tell us?" turning the key in the ignition and pulling out onto the road. We are literally a five minute walk from his house and therefore a two minute drive.

"What about?" he says disinterestedly, looking out the window. I can feel my patience getting even thinner with the little prick.

"Is there any reason that you ran away? Do you want to tell us anything that you might not be comfortable saying once you're back home".

"No, not really" he says, shrugging again "just fancied a break".

I glare at the little bastard. His parents have been having sleepless nights, we've spent around three hours looking for the silly sod and he couldn't give a toss. He's clearly educated by his accent, demeanour and deliberately scruffy attire and is also evidently middle class judging by his parents' large detached house and the Golden Retriever (not to mention the 4x4 in the driveway).

We get back to the house and I knock on the door. His father answers it.

"I've got something that belongs to you" I say smiling and gesture behind me to the sullen oaf now sloping up the gravel driveway. We enter the lounge and I can see how angry his father is. His mother looks relieved but incredibly upset and his sisters look relieved to see him as well. The father asks the two girls to leave the room and with me and Mary present turns on his son. I was expecting a righteous smiting in the name of parental discipline but instead it went like this:

DAD: "Do you have anything to say for yourself Tarquin?"

TARQUIN: (slouching against the chest of drawers near the window, arms folded and gazing at the floor) "No".

DAD: (In a forced, controlled tone) "For three days we have been worried sick about you. Your mother has cried herself to sleep every night. Why didn't you answer your phone or return our calls"

TARQUIN: "Because I was bored. You guys are just so boring. I needed a fucking break".

He says "fucking" like Prince Charles would i.e. without any aggression or fervour and in a posh voice which makes it more annoying than it would be anyway.

I interject. "Don't swear Tarquin, not with US here".

DAD: "You have everything you could want here. You could have called us to say where you were".

TARQUIN: "Yeah, well I needed a break. You're always going on about teenage angst".

DAD: "I am VERY disappointed in you. You have got us worried sick".

MOTHER: (finally losing it and crying) "What if I'd got a phone call to say you were in the morgue?".

I've finally had enough of this little turd and decide it's our turn.

What I want to say is the following:

"Right you. Stand up straight and look at me, unfold your arms. My go. You are a spoilt, ungrateful, arrogant little twerp. I would have thought that after hearing 'your mother has cried herself to sleep every night' you would be on your knees begging for forgiveness or at the very least saying sorry. But oh no. Not you. You seem to think you're hard done by. Well I tell you what. Your father has....DON'T INTERRUPT!....your father has told me where you hang out on the weekends. Well I'm sometimes on duty down there and if I see you drop litter, spit or even swear I'm gonna be all over you like a rash. You'll wish your mother had had a headache the night you were conceived. Now say sorry to your mother. Now your father. Now me and my colleague. We are NOT a taxi service for spoiled little brats".

However...what I actually said was the following.

"Tarquin we have spent a total of three hours looking for you. My Sergeant and my Inspector have both been involved in this. I don't like your attitude. Now say sorry to your mother".

TARQUIN: "Sorry mummy"

Mummy?! Jesus! That about sums it up.

"Now say sorry to your father and finally me and Mary".

We walked out into the corridor to be greeted by the dog. I patted it while the father apologised for wasting our time.

"Don't be silly, we're here to help. I'm just glad he's OK" I replied, secretly wishing they still had National Service for wankers like Tarquin.

We go on our way.

When Jacob got back I told him what had happened and what I'd wanted to say but had bit my tongue for fear of getting into trouble for being too aggressive.

Jacob simply replied "No, that would have been right. That's exactly what I would have done. Next time we get a MisPer like that I'll show you how I do it. Puts the fear of God into them".

THE SOUL SINGER vs
THE RED BULL ROOSTER

One Night duty in the Rowdy Van with Sergeant Kershaw and a couple of female PCs was fairly unexciting until we were asked to pick up a drunk, aggressive male at 3am, arrested in one of the outlaying villages of our Area.

We got there in about twenty minutes to find Sergeant Hershey and another lad kneeling on a guy who had his shirt off and was face down on the pavement. He'd been nicked for Drunk and Disorderly and Assault on Police and was clearly furious at being deprived of his liberty as every time one of the officers moved even an inch he would wriggle and kick out, swearing his head off.

"Anyone got an ERB?" Hershey enquired.

Sergeant Kershaw replied, "there's one in the van but I ain't trained to use it. Are you?". Hershey shakes his head.

"Aw, bollocks. Just get him in the back. Enough of us holding him it won't be a problem".

The guy has Hershey's 20 stone and the other officer on his back and legs but manages to seethe through gritted teeth.

"YOU FUCKING CUNTS! LET ME GET UP AND I'M GONNA FUCKING KILL YOU! THIS IS FUCKING POLICE BRUTALITY"

Hershey unclips his spray and holds it in front of the bloke's face.

"Calm down dipstick or you're gonna get this, understand?"

"FUCK OFF PIG!"

Someone opens the back doors of the van, then me, the two

210

female officers and the skipper grab the bloke and with two of us holding his legs and two his upper body stand him up straight. Hershey stands directly in front of him, glaring the whole time and holding his Pava a foot away from the bloke's face.

We lift him up and put him upright in the back. Predictably, as we let him go to slam the doors he spins around and tries to kick out. Three of us lean on the cage door and shut it hard, then the rear door and wipe our hands on our trousers before getting back in for the journey to the Nick.

A couple of minutes later I turn around and see through the perspex screen looking into the cage that our Suspect is standing up, hands still cuffed behind his back and glaring at me.

I walk over to the screen and point to one of the two wooden benches. "SIT down!".

"YOU FUCKING CUNT! YOU FUCKING LITTLE WRETCH!" he screams, violently headbutting the screen and then gobbing on it.

"Sit down, you're gonna get hurt if we make an emergency stop".

"YOU FUCKING LITTLE WRETCHED LITTLE CUNT" he shrieks and starts repeatedly nutting the perspex, pausing occasionally to spit on it again.

"Fill your boots mate, you're the only one suffering through doing that".

"CUNT WITH A CAPITAL 'K'!" he screams, headbutting the screen. Fortunately for him it's got a lot of 'give' meaning the worst he's gonna have is a headache and not a bleeding forehead.

"Sit down you idiot!"

"BASTARD" (Bang!), "CUNT!" (Hack-Puh!), "FUCKING WRETCH!" (Bang!)

The skipper, who's driving, shouts back "Lance just leave him, you've given him ample chance to do as he's told".

I sit back while the headbutting and swearing continues in the background.

"Anyone fancy some music?" the Sergeant enquires and turns on the radio. He twists the dial until he finds an easy listening station and it's some romantic old track being played.

"Ahhhh...I love a bit of Soul don't you" the skipper says as the dulcet crooning fills the van. He turns the volume up fully and it's a competition as to who's the loudest:

"I love you more each daaayyy...FUCKING WRETCHES! (Bang!)...I miss your tenderness and IIIIII...WRETCHED LITTLE CUNTS! (Bang!)...fee-eel looo-ove I hope you understand".

When we get to the Nick we alert the Custody skipper that this is a potential Cell Exit and he tells us to round up some big lads to get the bloke out the van.

I open the rear door and the bloke is finally sitting down and glaring at me sullenly.

"Alright in there fella?"

"FUCKING CUNTY WRETCH!"

"Charming. Don't you know any nice words?"

Just then the other arresting officer who was with Sergeant Hershey walks up, stands next to me and says "is he still being a twat?".

The officer has a beard and so do I. The prisoner looks at him, then at me, than back at him again and says to me "Oh, sorry mate. I thought you were the cunt, but it's him who's the cunt. Sorry". He then screams "YOU FUCKING CUNT, YOU FUCKING LITTLE WRETCH!", then pauses again, looks at me and repeats "sorry, thought you was him....FUCKING LITTLE CUNT THAT HE IS!"

After another fifteen minutes of swearing and what looks five of the England Rugby team but in Police uniforms come and stand near the back of the van. They are clearly the 'extraction' crew.

One of them looks at the prisoner and says "you gonna behave mate?"

"Yeah."

"Good, because if you don't you're gonna be hitting the floor and we don't want that do we?"

He is good as gold and doesn't get violent or even swear from Booking In to going in a cell. I'd put this down to simple exhaustion though, as opposed to any change of heart on his behalf.

POSITIVE INTERVENTION

One of the few areas that Police have powers appropriate to their role in society is for Domestic Violence.

Nowadays you are obliged to enter the home, ascertain if anyone has been assaulted in any way or if property has been damaged and more often than not one of the people will have to leave, definitely so if there is a child present. It can be via arrest or the person deemed at fault agreeing to vacate the premises for the remainder of the day. Officially this is to prevent a Breach of the Peace. As many people as are involved will be separated into different rooms by the cops that attend so they can get stories without the parties colluding. They will then compare notes to see who, if anyone, is getting nicked or taking a walk.

The days of people getting killed due to cops not taking DVs seriously or having their hands tied over exactly what they could and couldn't do has led to much stricter rules about Positive Action and if you choose NOT to act you'd better have a bloody good reason to tell the Sergeant back at the station.

Attending a call from a concerned neighbour one night in one of the grottier parts of town resulted in a malnourished-looking woman in a nighty with a tracksuit top over it, reeking of whisky and blubbing as soon as she opened the door. The two female officers took her into the bedroom for a chat while me and the Sarge spoke to her boyfriend. He'd obviously been drinking too but was calm and relaxed, more than happy to talk with us.

Their flat was basic, mattress on the living room floor and gaps in the wallpaper but the requisite 42" TV was blaring out when we walked in and the Sarge found the remote control to mute the volume. Asleep in the corner was an adorable little baby girl whose doting dad told us "every time she smiles it makes my heart soar". He said that during a row with his missus she'd bitten him hard on his arm and showed us the bite marks. He'd slapped her to make her let go. Our two female colleagues then returned and the stories matched. Without any hesitation the Sergeant tells him that he has to come with us and that he's under arrest for Common Assault. He immediately gets agitated and angry, stating that he'd only been defending himself and the silly bitch had bitten him and wouldn't let go.

"That's as maybe" the Sergeant replies "but you've admitted that you hit her and we're not leaving you both here with a 10 week old baby in the house".

I am prepared for the worst here, particularly with the tantrum he's throwing, huffing and puffing while pulling his clothes muttering that he's clearly the more rational and was only defending himself.

He gets larey when I go to handcuff him and the Sarge nods as I look at him.

"You will be handcuffed, I'd prefer it if it was voluntarily" I tell him and he reluctantly complies after pulling on a grotty pair of trainers and his jacket.

At the Nick he was crying in the holding cell while I filled out his details, refusing to tell me his name and promising to go to the newspapers the following day as he felt the man always gets blamed even if it's not his fault.

Another incident me and Jacob attended was twenty minutes before knocking off time. Control put out a call for a DV eight miles away and noone else could take it meaning we had to go. As we pulled up at the house Jacob said with a loud sigh "let's just hope she tells us to fuck off and there's no signs of a disturbance".

The door was opened by a bawling female with blood on her the back of her right hand. Visible distress and signs of injury.

She's still holding the mobile phone she used to call us and we follow her into the lounge.

"Can I have a hug please?" she sniffs.

I freeze and stand there motionless while she puts her face on my left shoulder. I don't reciprocate or even give permission but just wait a few seconds and then say "would you like to sit down and we'll talk about this?".

Jacob asks her where the other person is and she points upstairs. He tells me to talk to her while he goes to chat to her boyfriend.

I then have to ask her the DVRAM questions, Domestic Violence Risk Assessment Model.

These are designed to give you a clearer picture of just how serious the incident is and if incidents like it have occurred before, regardless of whether they were reported to the Police or not. They are deeply personal and have content such as "have they ever tried to strangle you?", "have they ever tried to rape you?" and "have they ever tried to get you to do something sexual you were uncomfortable doing?". They are printed on a laminated card you carry in your Warrant Card holder and you have to write the answers down in your PNB and preferably get the person to sign them at the end.

I've almost finished when Jacob puts his head round the living room door and says "Lance, section 47 please".

"What's that?"

"ABH".

The woman's not stupid and despite Jacob's attempts to be subtle immediately squeaks "what ME?", begins blubbing again and stands up.

I walk back over to her. "Look, you've been calm up to now. I'm going to arrest you but I don't want to put you in cuffs ok?"

Just then her boyfriend appears and tries to get past Jacob to talk to her. He is also under arrest for ABH but doesn't seem to realise that we need to keep them separated.

"I just want to speak to her for a minute"

Jacob pulls out his Pava. "Well you can't just back off".

"Why not?" he says in exasperation, throwing his hands up in the air.

"Because I said not that's why, back off or I'll spray you in the face"

"Fuck off!" the bloke curses but backs away.

As both remain calm after this we keep them apart without incident until another patrol car arrives to escort the guy to Custody while we take the woman.

Due to the genius architectural planning at the Nick, we have to keep her in the garage next to the holding cell in the 7am chill while her other half's processed until we can book her in.

Later I found out that her boyfriend told Jacob she'd grabbed his testicles and squeezed hard which was why we nicked her as well. There were no witnesses to say who'd started it and Jacob rightly decreed that it was up to further questioning to find out who was to blame. Her, him or both of them.

Considering how lily livered most of the Laws are in the UK, it was reassuring to know that in this type of situation you could act the way a copper always should. Judiciously, quickly and with a total focus on ensuring justice is served without worrying about making the Force look good or bad.

MICHAEL

Part of the final stage of our Training was a visit from the Youth Offending Team.

This public organisation exists to try and rehabilitate young offenders under the age of 18, help them become decent, respectable citizens and find ways of channelling their energies in more productive ways than committing crime.

This lecture was at 4pm and, knowing that we usually knocked off at about 4- 4.30, the two cardigan-wearing, bespectacled YOTers cracked a couple of gags about being the least popular lesson with every group of trainees as they always got the twilight shift.

The female of the two did 99% of the talking and from her first sentence I knew this was going to make me angry.

"We're working with a young man, let's call him Michael and after an England World Cup game last year where England lost he violently beat up a man in the street. His name's not Michael, but for this story let's call him that".

She then proceeds to tell us all about this creature that the taxpayer is coughing up hard earned mullah for. She relates his story, with her hands clasped to her bosom, gazing into the middle distance, putting all the passion of an evangelical American preacher into the tale of the revolting little shit she and her colleagues are working with.

"Michael had drunk about 6 pints of Stella Ar-toys..."

(she actually pronounced it like that)

"...at a pub and he was only 16. After the game he left the pub

217

and was walking down the street attacking random strangers because he was so angry. He then targeted a poor man who was waiting for a bus and didn't even know him. We've seen the CCTV footage and what happens next is very hard to watch. He beat him up so badly that he needs five thousand pounds worth of dental treatment, he's lost his job due to so much time off sick, his marriage has been indefinitely postponed due to a personality change and he's only been out of the house for 3 days in the last year".

She pauses for breath and then says brightly "but we're making so much progress with Michael. We are trying to get him to write a letter of apology to the man he attacked and get him to face up to what he's done. That's difficult as he refuses to believe that it happened even though he's seen the CCTV footage and his mother is on his side, saying that her son wouldn't do something like that".

I can feel my fingernails making bloody crescent moons in the palms of my hands. I am fighting to keep my mouth closed during this and not because Richenda had whispered as the speakers arrived "you ask any bloody questions and I'll kill you".

"He was sentenced to 5 years for GBH but it was reduced to 3 on appeal".

At this point I actually draw blood from my left palm with two of my fingernails and have to unclench my fists, exhaling slowly and realising that I've gone dizzy from holding my breath.

"He is having Anger Management and Counselling and is making good progress. We are trying to get him to address his anger issues and hopefully we'll be able to find him a job using his hands when he gets out of gaol as he likes to make things, it's what he's good at".

She witters on for about 25 minutes in total, only 1 minute of this actually spent paying any kind of lip service to the poor bastard that this wretch assaulted due to Peter Crouch being off form on match day.

"Any questions?"

Simon, ex-army puts his hand up and from his face appears also annoyed by what he's just had to sit through. "Is Michael going to pay for his victim's dental treatment?"

She looks flustered "Ooh, err, no. I don't think so" as if this radical gesture on behalf of the increasingly sorry and 'facing up to what he's done' Michael is some new and unheard of theory. "I believe he'd have to sue privately in civil court".

I put my hand up. "Why not make him write a letter to the victim regardless of whether he means it or not?"

"Because it needs to be something he WANTS to write, we can't force him and the victim needs to know that he means it and wanted to write it".

Errr....why does the victim need to know Michael's feelings? Why would the victim give a toss how Michael feels?

Ernie, also ex-army asks a question. "Is any counselling or welfare being provided for the victim?"

"Err...I don't know, I don't believe so".

The fact that she didn't know anything about the victim other than what Michael had done to him makes it clear that her and her organisation's sole focus was Michael himself. They clearly aren't even remotely concerned with how the victim is getting along after the beating of his life.

The reason they came in to speak to us is left unexplained. They just witter on about the wonderful, publicly funded treatment worth thousands a month that Michael is receiving.

They then ask us to write down on a piece of paper what percentage of young offenders we believe reoffend after prison and what percentage after community based rehab. I write 90% for community and 20% for prison. Turns out it was the other way round. Oh well, live and learn.

To my great relief the lecture finally ends and while everyone else piles out the door, I approach them both privately.

"Thanks for coming down, but I don't agree with any of this. I want my nickname to be One Warning when I've been in a couple of years".

The woman visibly winces as I say this. The guy is clearly clocking my badge number. "I can't agree with you, but thanks for enlightening me to the fact that less people reoffend from this type of treatment than incarceration, I wouldn't have believed it before".

They smile politely but clearly don't feel comfortable talking to someone who doesn't embrace the sheer fluffy loveliness of converting a nasty, evil, selfish little cunt into a decent human being.

While people like Michael need to be rehabilitated, so do victims. It seems surreal that so much effort, compassion and money can be spent reforming criminals while leaving those they caused to suffer to find their own way.

PHASE 4 TUTOR

PERCY

Only met him once as he was off Sick or on Annual Leave the rest of the week I was with his Section. Seemed like a nice chap the one Shift we did though. Black hair as I recall.

DIVERSITY PLACEMENT NO.2

My second Diversity Placement involved drug addicts and alcoholics.

Jemima Hambleworth addressed us for the second time about what to expect, dribbling on about the spiritually uplifting experiences we were lucky enough to be being given and adding "if you think it was good last time just WAIT till you see what I've got for you now".

Ho, hum.

Me and another lad got Substance and Alcohol "misusers", him in his bit of the county, me in mine. Turns out it has the same Area Manager (who we both met) and there are two teams of people called Care Managers who look after those who have been put their way by Social Services. Both teams deal with people who have serious or chronic addictions to drugs or alcohol and try to put them on the path of recovery. We were given info packs about the placements and what to expect to be doing from Monday to Thursday. I called the number on the chart and got the Deputy Manager who said they were looking forward to my arrival.

Got there early and found it was a big office building on a vast industrial estate. I was taken upstairs and sat at a desk while the Care Managers slowly drifted in to work. After about an hour I was invited to attend the weekly meeting in the board room downstairs and got pen and paper ready, expecting this to be a full immersion in the world of substance misuse care involving discussions on how they deal with clients and what the week would involve.

As it was they spent over an hour squabbling amongst themselves about the fact that the absent Area Manager was intending to spend the annual team building day budget on a get together of all the teams under his jurisdiction. Clearly an unpopular decision they sat there hurling insults at him in his absence, venting their spleens at the stupidity of his thinking and then most of them repeating what they'd said a short while before, practically verbatim. The female care manager Glenda that I was later put to work with kept saying "he's a right idiot, but don't tell him because he'll kill me!".

Very professional.

The final five minutes of this embarrassing display of schoolchild tantrum throwing was the only part that had any relevance either to their jobs or my reasons for being there and was where the Team Manager showed up and they briefly discussed the visits to clients planned this week and we went back upstairs.

Knowing that the presentation needed to be prepared, I asked for access to a computer but was told that wasn't possible due to the IT department not being able to set me up with an account for at least a week and them not being able to let me use someone else's account due to security.

I asked for reading material and was pointed towards the stack of magazines in an in-tray that the popular AM had given to the Team to enrich their knowledge of the world they worked in. I flicked through them to find there was virtually nothing in there about the placement as the magazines were designed to cover the medical and social services professions generally.

At lunchtime Glenda came over and asked if I'd like to come to Asda with her and another CM.

We spent an hour driving to the supermarket, leisurely strolling around the aisles and then driving back. For the first of what would be many times that week Glenda said loudly upon pulling into the car park "WONDER IF THERE'S ANY SPAZ BAYS FREE" as she drove past the disabled parking spaces. This type of language would get a substantive Police officer disciplined and probably get a probationer fired. One of my best friends is permanently disabled after a hit and run that left him lying on the M55 embankment at

11pm. However I surmised that I was there to learn from the placement I should simply let this slide.

Finally in the afternoon we visited a care centre that had just been relocated to a brand, spanking new building right next door to the old one that was now boarded up. Glenda introduced me to the staff there, the manager of which then took me on a tour of the building, showing me a few inventive touches (such as clients' rooms that could, if necessary, be opened from the outside even if barricaded from within as they had a reversible hinge mechanism) and the video library.

We chatted in the kitchen for a little while and I decided to be open about my own feelings and stated that there was a decision to take "the first fix" or drink and in my opinion people who became addicted to drugs or alcohol had done so through their own choice and lack of willpower. The manager replied that not everyone in life has the same opportunities and education and may not have realised what they were doing.

Sat outside were two guys having a cup of tea and enjoying the last rays of the autumn sun. They were clearly clients so I asked if I could speak to them as I hadn't met any yet and the manager took me out, introduced me (but didn't say I was a cop) and then asked if I wanted a cup of tea. My former best friend has a huge problem with alcohol and while now living abroad in Thailand is constantly getting into fights (thankfully only with other ex-pats as the locals would probably just shoot him) and drinking to excess. He's very strong willed, determined and apart from having tattoos all down both arms, is a body builder with a bad attitude and has a black belt in Judo. He was robbed at gun point in Thailand and got away by punching the gunman in the face and legging it. We haven't spoken in about seven years and while coming to this placement I was aware that I would potentially see people that would remind me of him. However, the whole purpose (we were told) of these placements is to "go beyond your comfort zone" and I even wondered if the Force knew about my mate and had given me the placement for this reason. So, as uncomfortable as I was, like curing a fear of spiders by touching one I asked to speak to these two blokes.

We chatted for about 15 minutes about this and that and they seemed quite pleasant and not evasive, crafty or untrustworthy as I had imagined they would be. The manager returned with a cuppa in a football mug.

"Arsenal. Ugh!" I hammed it up.

The two of them laughed and after we'd finished we said goodbye and Glenda then drove me back to the office. Pleased I was, mainly due to being able to chat with people who reminded me of my estranged friend without getting agitated.

That was it for the day with regard to meeting clients or anything with purpose to do with the placement. Still, we are guests of these people so you have to go with the flow. I went home that night after having spent maybe one hour of an eight hour working day doing anything that could be called constructive.

Over the next three days I saw just how spoiled the people in this world were.

When I asked if the treatment was funded by the taxpayer or through charity donations Glenda immediately got the hump and snapped "taxpayers pay policemen's wages too you know!" to which I replied that I wasn't criticising I just wanted to know. A centre we visited on the Wednesday was a converted country house in beautiful grounds with acres of gorgeous gardens. The client we had come to see, Sebastian, was about to leave after going through the full process of "tiers" that the therapy offers. They left me alone with him for a chat and he showed me round the centre, to the kitchen where they bake their own bread and out to the garden. He asked me why I'd joined the Police and I replied it was after being on duty as a Special with COLP on July 7th 2005 as being involved that day had made me realise it was what I wanted to do with my life. He then introduced me to about five other of his fellow clients, one of which had been in London on July 7th and upon being told by him that that was why I'd joined she relaxed and we had a nice chat.

The centre they were at costs £800 per week, per person. Half of this is paid for by the taxpayer (I never found out where the other half comes from) and Sebastian had been in there twice before. It is the kind of luxury most people can only dream of and whatever therapy he was getting by being there clearly wasn't working as him and others like him said to me that they kept coming back. The round trip to the centre took six hours in Glendas' car. She cursed out other drivers as "fucking wankers" (and occasionally "cunts" as well) for using their mobile phones while driving or anything that got on her wick. We had another Care Manager with us and during a chat about the previous night's episode of Big Brother Glenda loudly announced that the camera was "so far up Charley's skirt you could see her gash". She also told a story about "fucking Pikey rogue traders" coming round her elderly neighbour's house.

She was a thoroughly obnoxious, foul mouthed old bag the entire time I was with her. The Charley remark would make you wince normally. When a 55 year old female comes out with that kind of language it makes your eyes water.

While they left me with Sebastian the two of them went to visit a female only centre down the road. I was told I couldn't attend as it was forbidden for men to go there. The women at the centre had complex emotional issues and nearly all had been abused by men in the past.

At another centre I asked to meet with the clients and was told by the practice manager that it was not appropriate due to the emotional state that her clients were in at that stage of therapy.

Another time it was not possible to meet clients as they were about to go to a monthly cookery class so I was left to chat with the secretary while Glenda went off on an errand for an hour and a half.

Most of the information that I gleaned from the placement came from staff alone. There were only two meetings with clients arranged by the placement provider themselves. The only one that was prearranged was with Sebastian. The other was when I accompanied Henry the Deputy Team Manager to visit one of his clients who he made it quite clear, might not want to see us and might not want to let us in when she found out I was a Police officer. Upon being let in I was confronted by the sight of an emaciated and pale little woman whose two concerned adult daughters (one of which was heavily pregnant) sat with us. The woman looked frail and desperate, with stick thin arms and had a swollen belly. Henry chatted to her in calm, subdued tones and she said it was fine for a cop to be there once he had introduced me. I was impressed with her courage to face her issues as she was about to enter rehab and moved by the appalling life she was living (her current boyfriend apparently rang her up three times a day to say he wished she was dead).

The point of these placements is that you learn SOMETHING. It isn't set down what that may be but you are told that you should absorb yourself in whatever it is you are doing and follow what the people you are working with show you. With no access to a computer, hardly any access to clients and having to glean information from staff and what little written material I was furnished with, I put together a presentation that detailed how I had initially had no sympathy for people who get themselves into this kind of state of addiction but had now had my eyes opened through this placement as I accepted not everyone has the same opportunities in life. I added that the most important thing I'd learned was compassion and that nothing is scarier than my own imagination as the clients were not as I expected but were simply normal people with the courage to face their issues.

The clients were not the problem. The system that supported them on the other hand is the reason they simply keep returning to it. There is no definitive end to any of this treatment. Once 'clean' they are returned to the outside world and monitored only if they choose to be. Relapses are in the majority and a guy at the country house casually mentioned that it was his 8th time in rehab.

Misgivings and my own opinions aside. The positive aspects of this experience were that I knew I would be less wary of how to deal with substance and alcohol misusers and would now be able to communicate with them or even arrest without automatically assuming they were going to try and deceive me or that I would have to be on the defensive. Through my own experiences with my friend and people I know either socially or from being on duty who drink too much I had formed opinions that were now modified through having attended this placement.

That said, the lack of any real interaction with the subjects of this treatment, the lack of background material and the atrocious behaviour of Glenda did nothing to endear the organisation to me. The meeting on the Monday morning where they'd wasted so much time ranting and raving and insulting their boss, oblivious to the fact that I was there representing the Police made me realise I wasn't dealing with professionals but at least I'd had a glimpse into a new aspect of society and had come away with a different perspective.

On the Thursday I had a forty five minute meeting with Toby, the Team Manager and he asked me if having done the placement it would change how I would arrest any of the clients. I replied no because an arrest is subjective and it depends on how someone reacts at the time and not their personal situation. I added that I would however interact with them differently as I had seen that they were normal people with issues that I was now aware I could communicate with.

The following day we had two hours to prepare for our presentations. This was the only official time allowed and in my case the only time I'd had all week due to not being able to use a computer at the placement. True to Force ineptitude we had seven officers and two computers with the hours between 8am and 10am to knock up a Powerpoint show for use on the overhead projector. We all blitzed it and were frantically flitting about. Each officer had to log off from their account before another could log on and while logging off was no more than two minutes it took about five to log on meaning time was of the essence and we did what we could as quickly as we could. With literally five minutes to go before it was my turn I had my material ready.

Sergeant Kerwan, PC Esohé and the PDU Ma'am were all present for mine, as were Toby and Henry. I gave a synopsis of what they did, gave the aforesaid facts about learning compassion and the enlightenment of finding out that the clients were at the end of the day just normal folks with problems. I put three quotes in there. "Nothing is scarier than my own imagination", "courage is not the absence of fear, it's doing what it takes despite the fear" and "when I have the courage to face what is lacking within me then I have grown" (this last one was from one of the magazines at the placement). Nervous though I was I approached Toby after who said that apart from one mistake on the facts of how they work the presentation was good and when I escorted him to the door I apologised for not covering more in the presentation but added that I'd had to fit it in a time limit and that what they did was very broad. He smiled, said "you encapsulated what it's about, thanks and good luck with your career" and shook my hand, clearly expecting to never see me again.

My presentation lasted about 20 minutes. I used Powerpoint on the projector and even a couple of props from the placement (magazines and a drug kit). I had two guests present and would have invited more if I could. One of my colleagues spoke for 10 minutes and did not invite guests from his placement. Another spoke using only hand written prompt cards and did not invite guests. The whole point of the presentation was solely to allow you to show to those present what the placement actually did and what you'd learned.

Three days later I was on an Office Day at the Nick and there was an email from Kerwan in my inbox. It stated that I would soon be receiving feedback from the placement and "some development issues have been raised from this placement". He added that he had arranged a meeting with me, Esobé and Toby to be held in four weeks at the Police college (where I would be living in, doing final stage training) at 11am and he needed me to book the room for it. The wording was vague to say the least. Development issues? With me or how to develop the placement itself? If they want me to book the room then surely this must be fairly important? But then again as it's four weeks in the future then it can't be that urgent? Esobé was sitting at her desk in the main office next door so I approached her.

"Err...I've just received an email from the Sergeant. Was my presentation ok?"

She looks up, pauses to think and then replies "it's hard to say"

"Well, it's just that I've received an email and it doesn't say why but apparently there's going to be a meeting with you and the Sergeant and Toby. What's it about?"

She pauses again, looks at me and then says "I'm not going to say now. You'll find out when you get the feedback form. The meeting would be sooner but the Sergeant's on holiday. I won't be drawn into it. All will be revealed". She says the last line while gesturing with chubby arms in a pushing gesture.

"Is there anything I need to know?" I persist.

She looks irritated but then says "Well I will say that I thought you were rather rude to poor old Nigel when he was doing the slides for you during the presentation. If we hadn't had guests I probably would have said something".

"Oh, ok". I am at a loss as to what the hell she is referring to as Nigel is sitting in the room I've just left in order to come and speak to her and is as friendly as he ever was.

She tells me not to ring Jemima Hambleworth up and pester her to find out what the feedback form says or what the meeting is to be about and repeats that all will be revealed.

I go back to the main room and approach Nigel.

"Listen mate" I get his attention. "I've just found out that apparently I was rude to you during my presentation. Sorry about that, I didn't mean to be".

"What?" he says, looking up surprised "who told you that?"

"It doesn't matter, just err...I'm sorry if I was rude to you I didn't mean to be"

He looks visibly pissed off. "No you weren't! Who told you that you were?"

"It doesn't matter, it's just been brought to my attention that's all"

"Lance you know me well enough by now to know that if you had offended me I'd have told you at the time. I didn't realise you were doing anything wrong. You didn't offend me and I'd like to know who told you that you did. If I had a problem with you I'd have told you myself".

"Look forget it ok, it's just what I was told"

He tuts and goes back to his PC. Well, that one covered. Not only is he not upset with me but he is annoyed that they have taken offence on his behalf.

Two weeks later I pass Jemima in the corridor of the Police College.

"Oh hi" I tell her nervously "errm...I have a meeting with my Sergeant Kerwan and Toby from my last placement. I haven't received the feedback form yet".

"I understand that the Sergeant's dealing with that" she replies, already moving away "just hang on and see what transpires". She winks at me just before she walks off.

So, I've now made two attempts to find out what this is about and have been told to wait and see on both occasions. It's four weeks from the placement end that we are going to do this and the wording is ambiguous enough that it could mean they want my opinion on how to develop the placement itself. Hey, maybe they were so impressed with my presentation that they want my input for future Police involvement with the provider.

I talk to a few of my fellow trainees. They all agree that if it was serious I would have been told of the content in advance and it's probably just a chat that they want. I've already booked the room for one hour, 11am to 12pm in the Driver Training wing of the college and will now just have to wait and see.

When the morning arrives we are doing Interview Training with a Detective Constable from CID. I'd already told him that the meeting was to take place which pissed him off as he had to rejig the pairings for the Interview practices but I assured him it wouldn't last more than an hour and I'd be back before lunch.

Five to eleven and I make my way to the college reception. Toby is already sitting there waiting. I smile and say hello. He stands up and shakes my hand and I take the seat next to him. "How's the team going?" I ask.

"Oh we're really busy this period. Same as ever but things are good. How are you?"

"Fine thanks just doing interview training today. Have you seen the Sergeant yet he's supposed to be meeting us here?"

He is relaxed and friendly at this point but seems slightly nervous. "They put a call out for him, I think he's on his way".

Just then Kerwan arrives from the door to our left. He doesn't spot me and speaks directly to Toby "Thanks Toby, let's get you a cup of tea".

I stand up and Kerwan does a brief double take of surprise when he sees I'm already there. I hold up the plastic bag in my hand. "I already have tea and coffee and a kettle in here".

Kerwan looks me up and down, a look of disgust on his face and then says "what room did you book? Go and wait for us there".

I mooch over in the drizzle to the driver training block and find the appropriate classroom. Try to do some revision for the exam I have in two weeks but can't focus on it. Why the hell do they need to take him away for a cup of tea if I had the provisions to make it with me? While Toby was friendly the Sergeant certainly wasn't. What the hell is this going to be about?

I sit there and wait and after 15 minutes Kerwan, Toby and Esobé enter the room.

The Sergeant hands me a form. It's feedback from Toby. It's negative and it says "He doesn't seem to be absorbing anything from the placement. He's also inviting everyone to his presentation. Is this appropriate...WE DON'T THINK SO!".

I look up. "I haven't seen this before"

Kerwan replies "They were sent out a couple of days ago"

"I checked my email at 12.30pm two days ago, it wasn't there".

"It must have arrived later on".

I am now fully aware that this is not going to be pleasant.

"I didn't know what this meeting was going to be about. In light of what we're about to discuss do I need to have someone with me?"

Kerwan smiles cheerfully and replies "that's up to you but I don't think that's necessary as this isn't a disciplinary". For a reason that to this day I don't fully understand I decide in that moment to trust the Sergeant's judgment and decline to have someone of my choice sit in on this meeting.

It was the last time I would ever again trust him.

"Are you sure that you're happy not to have anyone with you?".

"Yeah, it's ok" I reply.

"I believe Toby has some things to say to you"

Toby is now completely different. His body language is tense. His hands are clasped in front of him. He looks pissed off. He launches into what would turn out to be two and a quarter hours of humiliation and bullying with:

"So, what did you learn from the placement?"

Retrospectively I should have done many things. Not least of all was been aware that this duplicitous, hypocritical CIVILIAN was addressing a Police Constable in uniform like he was a child in front of a Sergeant and another Constable.

I stammer slightly. Caught off guard by his tone and the abrupt change in his manner. "Well, like I said at the presentation it was that the clients are just normal people with issues, nothing to be scared of"

"Really? I don't think you learned anything" he replies glaring at me "I think you've got issues and you joined the Police in order to work through them"

I am knocked for six by this. This is NOT how a civilian is meant to address an officer, regardless of their opinion of them particularly in an official meeting. I glance across at Kerwan and Esobé and catch an expression on both their faces that haunts me to this day. They both were smirking and looking impressed. They appeared to be thinking 'this is better than we thought it would be'.

Toby goes on. "I understand that when you first met our clients YOU DIDN'T EVEN TELL THEM YOU WERE A POLICE OFFICER!" The last bit is shouted, as if it is beyond comprehension in a civilised, ordered world for such a travesty of etiquette to have occurred.

I fall back on the company line. "We are told specifically to be VERY careful about letting the placement provider decide whether or not to let the people we meet know that we are really Police officers. The manager who introduced me knew and didn't tell them when he introduced me".

Kerwan interjects at this point "actually Toby he has a point. They are sort of 'undercover' on the placements".

Toby grunts "oh" and looks away.

"I'd just like to say and forgive me if I get upset talking about this that a good friend of mine has an alcohol problem and in my opinion he has a death wish. I didn't find the placement easy because the clients reminded me of him"

Toby glares at me again. "Why would our clients remind you of him?"

"Errr..because some have problems with alcohol like my mate" I reply.

"But why would they remind you of him?" he repeats, ignoring my answer completely.

He then comes out with a line of questioning that at the time I found simply rude but now cannot believe he was allowed to get away with in front of Kerwan and Esobé and left no doubt in my mind that they had asked him to come in and speak to me like this.

"I also understand that you went around telling people at the placement that you joined because of July 7th's terrorist attacks. Why say that?"

"I only mentioned it if I was specifically asked why I'd joined".

"But why SAY that?"

"Because I was a Special Constable with the City of London Police and was on duty at Aldgate station which had been bombed"

"What kind of reason is THAT?" Toby snaps, shaking his head looking angry.

"That's when I decided I wanted to join full time" I reply

"But why would THAT make you want to join?"

"It was the worst atrocity in 20 years I wanted to be able to do something"

He shakes his head, still looking like he can't grasp what I'm saying. "But you were already part of another Force"

"They weren't recruiting....look, my ex girlfriend was on the bus that was blown up!" I add this last bit expecting it to shut him up. Instead he shouts at me.

"WERE YOU ANGRY?"

"No, it's something I decided I wanted to do. It's my fundamentally held belief that I did the right thing by joining".

Esobé then interjects with a line that should have got the vindictive sow disciplined the moment I reported her for saying it. "I've said before Lance, with your Intake it's like I've got six puppies and you're the naughty one that keeps running off ahead".

I sit there confused. What sodding relevance does this have to the subjects under discussion and how dare she compare me to a dog in front of a civilian. What if I have to arrest Toby at some time in the future or even take a Statement from him. Is he ever likely to take me seriously after this? She'd used this analogy once before but it was in private as developmental advice and I had found it useful.

Toby then says "I don't think you'll make a good Police officer because on the street it's not about you it's about them. You talk about yourself too much". I am by now totally miserable, confused and upset. He has no right whatsoever to talk to me like this, especially on duty in uniform AND he's attacking my personality NOT anything I did or didn't do at the placement.

Kerwan then pulls out a piece of paper, consults it and then asks me "tell me the life story of one of the clients please Lance".

What the fuck?!!

"I don't have that information" I reply.

He feigns surprise. "Why not? You're supposed to get in there and ask them about themselves, surely you spoke with the clients?"

"Yes, but we didn't spend very long with them"

"What did you talk about?"

"Different things"

"What subjects particularly?"

"This and that, they showed me around the centres".

He looks smug. An expression that I would come to know more and more over the time I knew him. "Your presentation was shallow. You went into it half heartedly. When you mentioned that centre with the beautiful architecture and gardens, that had nothing to do with the placement. I was waiting for you to start talking about the clients and their life stories but you only knew about the actual centre. That proves you went into it half heartedly".

"Well what was I supposed to have done?" I ask, feeling utterly confused and miserable at this cowardly ambush they are subjecting me to.

"An officer from a previous placement said to one of the clients 'so tell me, what first made you take drugs?' If you'd done that then they'd have bonded with you and you'd have had this heart warming story to tell everyone".

Esobé then pipes up "that woman you told everyone has her partner call her up saying he wants her dead. You should have asked her 'so why do you keep answering the phone to him then?' That way you would have understood her".

Even at the time I knew they were talking out of their arses and I wondered then if Kerwan had found his chevrons in a packet of Frosties. The people I met have complex emotional issues. Loping up beaming and saying "hi, I'm a cop. What made you take drugs?" is the last thing I should have done. Also they may have admitted to something illegal which would have left me obliged to at least report them for it. I've no doubt that humanitarian ambassadors to the U.N would be jealous of someone who can, in a 60 minute meeting (the maximum time I spent with any client in that placement) bond with an alcoholic or drug addict to the extent that they are willing to share their life story with someone they've only just met and who they know to be a Police officer.

Toby then adds "most of them are more than happy to talk about themselves".

Great. Like I'm supposed to fucking know if you don't tell me.

Kerwan goes on. "And you didn't even remember people's names from the places you visited. Proves you weren't paying attention".

"It wasn't that. I was told specifically not to mention people's names due to confidentiality"

Toby then says "to be fair there is a confidentiality issue".

Kerwan looks annoyed for a split second but then recovers with "well you could have said 'person A or person B' or even made up names instead".

Errr....how does that change the situation you spiteful twat? Retrospectively, had I not been so upset it would have been clear that they were determined to rubbish everything I'd done and anything I said would be simply dismissed or ignored. I was facing people who had no intention of letting me disprove anything they threw at me.

After more of this Kerwan says that Toby has kindly come down to give me this feedback but is busy and now has to leave. Purely out of politeness as Toby gets up to go I stand up and extend my hand. He looks momentarily surprised but shakes it and as he does so winks at me.

I am to this day confused at this. A handshake is simply polite (the only reason I offered him my hand in the first place) whereas a wink is more intimate and potentially a conspiratorial gesture. It wasn't an involuntary facial twitch. Opinions on why he did this ranged from the Federation's view that he was simply making fun of me to the investigating Inspector (after I made a complaint against Kerwan and Esobé) that Toby was merely embarrassed over the feedback he'd given. Looking back on it I believe he was trying to communicate that he had been put up to this.

After he left I couldn't hold back any more and burst into tears while Kerwan escorted the wretched man back to reception. I have never cried like this since I broke up with my ex in 1997 and was unable to speak for several minutes I was so upset. Esobé simply sat there impassively watching me cry and said nothing as I fumbled for a tissue and dripped snot down my white shirt. Kerwan then returned, looked at the state I was in and sat down next to Esobé. He theatrically shook his head repeatedly and said as if addressing a small child "Lance....Lance, Lance" as if to say "what can we do with you eh?". I spoke about my friend and in the emotional state I was in gave more information to these two repulsive morons than I wish I had. I told them that I missed him very much and that my last attempt to contact him had resulted in him simply telling me to fuck off. I also mentioned the incident of him being robbed and thumping the gunman to escape. Esobé spoke to me like I was in Kindergarten and said that I should respect his desire to be left alone and far from being worried about him punching the guy with the gun I should be proud as he had "stood up for himself".

Just days previously to this meeting we had been shown a video in class called Red Mist about NOT giving in to anger or strong emotion when involved in confrontation or rescue. The stories included a Police constable who tried to take a loaded pistol off a drunken man who had come round to his ex-wife's house to take their infant daughter away. The gun went off. The child was killed. The now ex PC is still to this day having counselling. We were told that the PC was trying to be "Charlie Big Potato" and in a situation like that we should back off as it was clear the man only wanted to spend time with his daughter and was not going to use the gun on her. Somewhat different from what Esobé was telling me.

Kerwan then repeated that I had gone into the placement "half heartedly" and had "blown it again". When I asked what he meant by "again" he cited the previous placement in 2006 with the school.

"That incident with the boy at the train station. You just can't communicate with people. You reacted to that as a teacher instead of trying to understand him"

He isn't even looking at me while he's speaking and is smirking the entire time. I retort that "that lad I've seen several times since then and he's always pleased to see me AND he thought I was his teacher because I was introduced to him as a teacher by the Head at 9 o'clock on the first day"

Kerwan shakes his head "You reacted to it as a teacher. It's all you can do because it's what you used to do".

I am getting more frustrated by his unwillingness to accept contrary evidence than by the whole disgusting abuse of power that this vicious bully and his two faced deputy are putting me through.

"They're kids who've been expelled from other schools. They're not exactly shy about expressing their true feelings" I try to reason.

He shakes his head again. "No they're just telling you what you want to hear" he says, still not looking at me.

"One of them is in a street gang and asked me in front of his gang leader if he could come and drink a beer with me. Another went to give me a hug the first time he saw me in uniform"

"No, they're just telling you what you want to hear".

He consults his piece of paper again. "And the way you spoke to Nigel at your presentation. Just flicking your hand out, almost clicking your fingers to indicate when he should move to the next slide".

Esobé then butts in with "if you'd spoken to me like that I'd have punched you in the face".

I believe I have this one covered "I found out about this before now and approached Nigel straight away to apologise. He said he wasn't offended, hadn't noticed and was quite annoyed you'd raised this on his behalf".

Kerwan doesn't miss a beat but simply replies "that's because he knows you and he knows how you are".

He then moves back to the placement "you're the only person ever to have received negative feedback from a placement provider. You just didn't do it properly. I remember during the presentation Toby asked you a question and you didn't know the answer to....I forget what it was now. You just wasted that opportunity".

Esobé then looks at him and tuts and says in the most patronising tone I have ever heard in my life "I wish I'D had that opportunity".

I remember sitting there at the time, knowing that she rarely leaves the Nick, let alone to get involved in anything outside of her nice, warm office.

She then adds "I don't think you're ready for this"

Kerwan agrees "neither do I. You may think it's a cowardly thing to decide to leave but most people would respect you because they'd realise that you had the bollocks to make a tough decision. This job isn't for everyone and it's not just Toby, everyone feels the same way about you"

"What do you mean?!" I ask

"Colleagues, supervisors, people on placements. Nobody likes you" he says, still smirking.

"If neither of you think I'm suitable for this job then why...and I know you've been on holiday...but why have you waited four weeks to tell me this?"

They sit there looking at me. They say nothing. They don't acknowledge this question or reply. They do not speak or say anything until I then say.

"Even if you don't believe I can do it I know I can. I'm not resigning unless something bad happens"

Kerwan leans forward "what do you mean by that?" he asks

"I mean something really bad, that's the only thing that would make me quit".

"Yes but what do you mean by that?" he says, glancing sideways at Esobé.

Now, retrospectively this following line was not the most sensible thing to say but I was under duress, very upset and retracted it as soon as I said it. Kerwan however wrote it down and months later it came back to haunt me.

"Well, I mean if someone was hurt or killed"

Kerwan and Esobé both grimace like they're in a 1920s silent movie and then gasp audibly. Kerwan says "That's TERRIBLE!"

Esobé then says "you just can't communicate with people. These two placements should show you that"

"Inspector Harwood thinks I have good communication skills. He said so in an email".

After I had been congratulated by Inspector Harwood for how I dealt with a larey prisoner at Booking In Jacob had told me to write to the Guv, asking if he'd email the PDU recognising the incident. He had addressed it to Kerwan with me CC'd on to it noting it was "handled in a very professional manner and a particularly good piece of effective communication and problem solving".

There's a pause. She looks around and licks her upper teeth with her tongue. Then says "have I seen it?"

I reply "the Sergeant's seen it" pointing towards Kerwan.

"Why haven't I seen it. Why isn't it in your portfolio? What do you THINK your portfolio is for?"

"I don't think it's fair for Toby to come back and criticise me like this. I asked him for feedback after the presentation and he said it was OK".

Kerwan snorts and then says "well he's not going to say anything negative at the time is he?"

This confuses me even more so I try "but he shouldn't say anything if he had a negative opinion. He said 'you encapsulated what it's about, thanks and good luck with your career' and then shook my hand".

Esobé laughs and says "well that's hardly a compliment is it?"

I then bring up the subject of Glenda's atrocious language but don't name her. What I said was interrupted twice by Esobé making noises that I had to ask someone else's opinion on how to describe when I was compiling evidence to take to the Federation. We agreed that the best way to describe them was 'rhetorical sarcastic oohs'.

ME: "I heard inappropriate remarks from one of the care managers during that placement. I chose not to say anything because I wanted to learn from the experience...."

Esobé: "ooooOOOoooo!"

ME: (After a second's pause while I register that she did ACTUALLY just do that) "...like I said I'm not going to tell you who that was but I didn't say anything because I wanted to learn from the placement"

Esobé: "ooooOOOoooo!"

After two and a quarter hours we finally wrap this up. I feel like I've been kicked to death. I was given no warning about the meeting's content. I was not given the feedback form. I made two attempts to find out what was going on and on both occasions was told to wait and see. I have been humiliated in front of a civilian. I have been cross examined by that civilian on why I joined the Force. I have been crying in front of two people that I wouldn't give a blood transfusion to. I've also missed my lunch.

They get up to leave. I am determined to hold on to some dignity and as we leave I walk over to Reception with them, remembering to put my cap on as we leave Driver Training. Despite the fact that I look like I've just been PAVA'd and I am bunged up with snot the Sergeant has the temerity to say "how's that lovely bicycle of yours?"

I reply it was stolen months ago.

"Oh dear" he gives a false laugh "you can't trust anyone these days".

Jesus! He's made me cry and he's now indulging in light banter about my cycle.

I shake their hands at Reception, purely out of politeness, and they leave. I make my way back to the Interview training classroom. It seems a week since I was in it. Everyone looks up as I walk in. The Trainer looks visibly concerned.

"Everything alright?" he asks.

"No" I reply "do you mind if I take another few minutes to go to the Training Office to speak to Sergeant Taggart?"

"No, go right ahead" he says "come back when you're ready to".

Her office is down the corridor and I knock on the door and am told to come in. I have managed to get myself together emotionally and she is alone in the room she shares with four other Sergeants. She invites me to sit down.

"Sergeant were you aware of the content of that meeting I've just had?"

"As I understand it it was solely to discuss your Diversity placement. Why what's the matter?"

I can feel the tears coming back and fight to stay in control.

"That's not just what they discussed" I tell her "they told me to resign".

At this I start crying again and it's as bad and as snot-ridden as before. She looks at me in disbelief and embarrassment and I hold up my hand. I manage to get out "I'm sorry".

"It's OK" she says softly "what did they say to you?"

I tell her about it all and that they hadn't told me what was going to happen and that they allowed Toby to cross examine and insult me. While we're talking Ma'am Postlethwaite enters the room. You stand for an Inspector, no matter how bad you feel.

I struggle to my feet and keep my back to her so she won't see my face "Ma'am" I mumble in acknowledgment.

"Oh hello Lance, bless you. Didn't see you there". She hangs around for a couple of minutes until she's got what she wants then leaves.

"Can I make an appointment to see you please?" I ask the Sergeant.

"We can do it now, it's what I'm here for. Come on let's go to a private office"

We walk down the corridor and find an empty room. I tell her again what happened. At the end I ask her "can I change Areas?"

"Well that's what I was thinking" she says quietly. "Let me talk to the Inspector and I'll get back to you".

I go back to my bedroom in the accommodation block and as

soon as my key is in the door former Special Constable and father figure Ryan puts his head round the corner of the adjoining corridor and says "you ok?".

"Nope. You?"

"A lot of people have been asking about you you know" he says "they didn't know where you were".

"Took longer than I thought. Although I'm flattered my absence garnered interest".

"Seriously a lot of people were worried" he tells me. "Eight people have asked where you were and I think at least two of them said 'he drives me mad but I hope he's ok".

I manage to smile, "thanks" and open the door to find a note has been pushed under it. It's from Harriet, one of the trainees off my group.

It read:

"Lance,
I really hope it went ok for you today.
I know I'm a grumpy cow but if you want to sound off I will be in the common room after 8pm tonight to watch the football.

Harriet xx
P.S If you want to call me here's my number.

While I had spoken to Harriet on many occasions I never considered we were best mates and to say this letter lifted my mood would have been an understatement. Later that night she sat on her own with me for fifteen minutes on the stairwell and said amongst other things "don't resign. You're a much better person than they are" and gave me a hug. I kept her letter for months after, pinned to the notice board in my kitchen and would read it on really bad days.

I also had two ansaphone messages from concerned fellow trainees (as I'd left my phone in my room) and was approached later that afternoon by the Interview Trainer offering me contact with the Federation so I could get official support for what had happened.

The fact that so many people were so concerned kind of pisses on Kerwan's statement that "everyone feels the same way about you. Colleagues, supervisors, people on placements. Nobody likes you".

The most fitting epitaph came from Ryan and was:

"Maybe you will make a Police officer, maybe you won't make a Police officer but that's NO way to treat somebody".

MARCHING

Marching was never much fun and for students studying a Foundation Degree in Policing who wear jeans and tee-shirts 90% of the time it was nothing but a tiresome chore that pissed us all off.

The final six weeks of training we move into the Police College, adjacent to Headquarters and were marched twice a week. It looked like a pack of Cub Scouts and Brownies on Remembrance Sunday. The drill Staff was about 5 feet 2 inches of crimson rage at the progress we continually failed to achieve as the days turned to weeks and we could quite often hear her bellowing "MARCH PROPERLY OR I'M GOING TO GET ANGRY IN A MINUTE....RIGHT! YOU! COME 'ERE!" at which point some wretch would be pulled out, red faced from the ranks and giving a stern bollocking for "teddy bearing" or "tick tocking" or simply marching like a twat.

Problem is that the lack of discipline we had been indulged in since we joined meant that hardly anyone actually wanted this type of regimented routine and it was like trying to get a seven year old to eat his spinach after he's spent two weeks at nan and grandpa's getting fed sweets and spoiled rotten.

The Passing Out Parade was originally not until a year after Basic Training. This gave you time to become Independent and make it out the other side of the fragile world of probation. This all came to an end with the Intake before mine when, on the Dining In Night a love triangle of two female recruits and the bloke who'd been shagging both of them had too much wine with their dinner and began scrapping in the foyer of the College. Luckily for them

Ma'am Postlethwaite was not on duty (quote "If I'd been there they'd all have been arrested and fired").

So...with the following intake they put the Passing Out Parade the day after the Dining In Night. Official blurb read that it was to give our families and friends the chance to see us at the end of our Basic Training and to make us and them proud. Unofficial word I got from at least two senior officers plus a couple of Staff was that it was to act as a fuse so people would think twice about getting shitfaced at the dinner if they knew they would have to face their parents the following morning.

We were sternly warned of the consequences of imbuing too much sauce at Dining In Night and our Drill Staff glared at us all and said "ANYONE WHO'S PISSED ON PARADE WILL BE TAKEN OUT IN FRONT OF EVERYONE ELSE AND DISCIPLINED...WHAT ARE YOU LAUGHING AT PC JONES? RIGHT! COME 'ERE!"

While marching itself wasn't eventually THAT hard to crack, the minutiae of Left Wheel, Right Wheel, Eyes Right, Halt, At Ease and Attention proved to be the realm of the gifted. We finally got it about a week before crunch time and even devoted a couple of hours in the evening to polishing off the rust before the big day came.

Come the time, we were instructed to meet our families at the gate and escort them to Reception where they would be issued with visitors' passes and were not allowed to roam the grounds freely without us with them due to the 'security risk'. This from a Force that leaves the front gate open in the mornings because there's just TOO much traffic for the poor receptionist to keep buzzing in. Presentation as they say, is the key.

I met my folks in two trips and took them to the Parade Ground (actually the Skid Pan where the Standard and Advanced Drivers practice, sometimes with us still marching. I often expected to hear the sound of a Ten Pin bowling alley strike and see tit helmets flying up in the air).

The music for the march was originally going to be provided by a hired in brass band. This proved cost prohibitive so instead we had a big fuck-off amp and "Theme from The Great Escape".

One of the ACC's had taken time out of his hectic schedule of scouring the DCC vacancies in internal memos to inspect us and a Superintendent (albeit an Acting one) plus Ma'am were going to be there.

Two hundred or more relatives and friends from mothers to boyfriends, infants to fiances. We lined up out of sight in the staff car park near the portakabins. Issued with white gloves, boots bulled to a mirror shine, tunics ironed. Drill Staff stood before us, looked to check we were all as we should be and then barked "RIGHT! FOR THE FINAL TIME. TEN SHUN!". The music was cued and we marched out across the Skid Pan. I had one of the other two former soldiers in front of me so my nervousness was somewhat dissipated by the sight of him marching, proud and erect with his left arm swinging in unison with his right leg. In her best red sash and holding her riding crop was Drill Staff watching us intently while tapping the crop into her white gloved left hand. "LEFT WHEEL!" she bellowed and we smartly switched to a course 90 degrees different (well, it was either that or march into the fence). We approached our proud invitees. "EYES RIGHT!". Trying to march in time when you can't see the direction you're marching in is never fun. Got a quick glimpse of my mum and Ma'am and then we did another circuit of the Pan and finally came to a halt in front of the assembled mass.

"TEN...SHUN!" Everyone snapped to attention. "MIDDLE AND REAR RANKS...AT EASE!". My rank and the one behind moved to the appropriate stance while the front rank remained erect, legs together, palms down by the creases of their trousers, facing straight ahead. The ACC and the Acting Super' then came out to inspect us. The ACC had a little surprise for every 3rd or 4th person and would follow the normal pleasantries with "Officer, definition of GBH/ Theft/ Affray etc...if you please" to which he would either get a text book definition reeled off verbatim or lots of blushing, stammering and mouth being opened and closed before he magnanimously let a neighbour bail them out.

He reached the end of the front rank and like a typewriter carriage was about to move to the other end of the middle rank. Drill Staff then roared "FRONT RANK AT...EASE! MIDDLE RANK...TEN, SHUN!" The ACC started to move to inspect the person three along from me. Just as he was about to approach, my sodding mobile phone went off.

I'd had it on to arrange the 'front gate' meetings with my family and had forgotten to switch it off in all the excitement. The ring tone was an MP3 of the theme to 1980s, sword and sorcery movie 'Hawk the Slayer' and the air around me was full of the sound of pan pipes going berserk.

The guy next to me swore through gritted teeth "LANCE FOR FUCK'S SAKE!" as I scrambled frantically to retrieve the phone while the oblivious ACC walked past without even clocking my panicked struggle with the heavy fabric of my tunic , my white cotton glove snagging on the silver buttons. Drill Staff dashed up and skidded to a halt "WHAT ARE YOU FIDGETING WITH?" she snapped.

"Err...my phone went off" I stammered, wishing an earthquake would kick in about now.

She gives me a look that Barack Obama probably gave Hillary Clinton when she offered him the chance to be her Vice President and snaps "GIVE IT TO ME!" I hold it out and she snatches it, pushing various buttons until it's switched off and then thrusting it back into my hand.

She seethes "YOU BASTARD!" before stepping back.

I mumble "I'm sorry" and just manage to snap back to ten shun (with the phone still in my hand) as the ACC wanders up, totally unaware of what's going on.

"Officer, definition of Burglary if you please"

"Ah, Sir that is to enter a premises with the intention to steal or commit GBH"

"Good. Or...?"

"Or having entered to then form the intention to steal or commit GBH"

"Sections....?"

"9(1)(a) and 9(1)(b) of the Theft Act, Sir"

"You forgot the bit about being a trespasser but good working knowledge, should do you well on the street. Well done"

The Acting Super' then adds "and your helmet's on crooked".

After he's inspected all of us Drill Staff dismisses us for the final time and when we are free to mingle with our folks I approach her to apologise.

"I'm REALLY sorry".

She glares at me with an untamed stare that would probably bore holes in an iceberg. She doesn't say anything

"I feel I've let you down"

She glares at me then says "It's done now".

"I'm really sorry" I say, feeling really, really bad.

"It's done" she says again curtly, moving away.

We move back to the College reception where a buffet has been laid on. I hear my old uni Sergeant, recently promoted to Inspector chatting to my folks. "Ooh, it must be very hard with all those students to look after" my mother speculates.

"Is with him in the class" she replies, glancing over her shoulder at me. "I bet noone else even had their phone switched on." She catches the look on my face and smiles to let on that she's pulling my leg.

I stand and chat with my folks for a little while. The ACC wanders up and asks us how we enjoyed the Parade. My mother exclaims how smart everyone looked. Taking the opportunity to gain some Brownie points I ask "Sir, what's the best advice you can give me with regard to my career?"

He thinks for a few seconds then replies "Humility. I would say that's the most important thing. I learned that recently when I was in Mumbai and Madagascar".

A little later and I see Drill Staff walk past with a tray of devilled eggs. I approach her and extend my hand. "I'm off home now, take care. Thanks for all your hard work with us".

She puts down the tray and looks me up and down, then says "come here and give me a hug you silly man".

S.O.P.H.I.E LANCASTER

There were about 10 reasons for jacking The Job.

Sophie was number 8.

I never understood the kind of council estate, lard arsed, dole claiming, Jeremy Kyle viewers that would hang around the Old Bailey and throw abuse and stones at the Police van as Maxine Carr was driven into court.

If you weren't involved, didn't know anyone who was and have no connection to the events of the crime then why treat the whole thing like some interactive soap opera?

Have an opinion, voice it, write it down but why waste all that energy on something you have no personal attachment to?

Then something happens that gets right into your own sense of injustice and you can empathise just a little bit more with angry fat morons.

Sophie Lancaster was 20 years old and on August 11th 2007 at 3am was murdered by drunken, feral teenage thugs in Bacup park, Manchester. They initially attacked her boyfriend Robert Maltby simply because he and Sophie were dressed as Goths or "Moshers" and instead of running away she tried to stop them which cost her her life. After Robert was beaten unconscious she was sitting holding his head in her lap and crying hysterically. Two of the assailants then ran back and repeatedly kicked and stamped on Sophie's head until she was in a coma. Paramedics on the scene said that Sophie and Robert were so badly injured that they couldn't tell which was male and which female.

Sophie died two weeks later without regaining consciousness.

The gang responsible were caught soon after and during Police questioning of the ringleader the investigating DCI had to pause the tape, take the Brief outside and tell him to advise his client that he was being interviewed for a serious crime and it really wasn't appropriate for him to be sitting there laughing and joking with the AppAd (his mother).

Found guilty of Murder the judge laid down a minimum term of 18 years on the ringleader (a very rare thing to have happen and almost never handed down, it basically means he can't be paroled and has to serve the full whack) and described the gang as having "degraded humanity itself". The others got from 4 to 16 years each.

Robert is permanently scarred emotionally and physically from this.

Sophie's family and friends have more grief to deal with than anyone should have to shoulder in one lifetime.

My friend runs a shop. It's a nice shop selling nice things like incense, fairy statues and alternative clothing. Look up the word 'nice' in the dictionary and you'll probably find a photo of her and her husband below the definition, smiling in their nice hand-knitted lambs' wool cardigans and holding a nice jar of homemade rhubarb chutney.

The local chavs gravitate to their shop like magpies to silver and have reduced my friend and some of her 18-20 year old, female, art student staff to tears with their loutish aggression. I once threw three lads out of there for mouthing off and far from being grateful at this Off duty Intervention my friend said "please don't do that again. They'll just come back when you're not here". The poor woman would rather tred water than risk going under completely.

When I was a teenager we would give someone over 18 (or who looked it) our pocket money and get them to buy us booze. We would then slink off to the park or cemetery to drink it and would drop it and run if challenged by an adult or God forbid a copper.

Now kids drink openly on street corners because they know the only people that can take it off them are coppers and on the chavviest estates the local Police presence is some flabby PCSO with no arrest powers and less respect than the chip shop owner. If they can't afford the booze then they steal it.

I joined the Force because I wanted to help people, with high aspirations of protecting the weak and bringing justice to the world. I imagined emerging from a burning building with a puppy under one arm and a baby under the other, body armour smoking heroically. As it was I spent most of my Shifts giving motorists a hard time for a dodgy rear light just to generate paperwork. Kids like those that murdered Sophie hung around the town I patrolled like flies on a dog turd. We were not allowed to do a Rudolph Giuliani on their arses and shake them down for simply being in public in groups of more than one. No, we had to wait until they actually did something before we could act, regardless of what they had done before and how often.

Noone could protect Sophie Lancaster that night. Not because of what happened but because society has shown too much compassion for the criminal for far too long. The modern English Police puts an emphasis on trying to empathise with why people rob, fight and bully and wants their officers to be able to get inside the heads of criminals and wayward youth to find out what drives them. That's NOT a Police officer's role in society and is incalculably dangerous because it means your impartiality is permanently threatened if you are attempting to "understand" just why Jimmy feels it necessary to drink 10 pints of Wife Beater and start fights in the pub (simple answer: because he's a cunt).

We now have to "feel" the world of the wrongdoer. Try to empathise with exactly why they steal, fight, rob and hurt people and be understanding of whatever demons are perceived to have led them to commit crimes in the first place. The victim is left outside the circle of care, left to fend for themself. The gang that murdered Sophie were molly coddled by the local system. Respect for authority has waned to such a point that beating someone to death is considered a right laugh and the scum that did this to her were part of a youth project, given taxpayers' money to make a rap video indulging their violent fantasies by advocating just how "hard" they were in their gang The Bacup Crew and allowed to roam the streets preying on the weak and helpless. Their lack of any sense of shame or even awareness of the gravity of what they'd done is a damning indictment of a modern society that refuses to let teachers smack kids, but allows the kids to abuse the system and hasn't protected decent people.

Until the age of 37 I had never seen a News story in my life that made me cry.

This one did.

Garry Newlove was killed in similar circumstances but he was a man and was murdered by (although I use the word in its loosest possible sense) other "men". Sophie was a young woman. No threat to anybody and was murdered for kicks by people that I honestly hope share their cells with predatory, Viagra fuelled, life term rapists who bore them out every day that they're in prison.

But I doubt they will.

Three square meals a day and relative comfort and when they're released the ringleader will be younger than me and able to lead a normal life in the outside world.

The sense of impotent rage is still with me over Sophie's death, even though I was hundreds of miles away in another Force when it happened. She represented every person I had joined to protect and in the end my colleagues in Lancashire Police were not there to save her. What possible pleasure could anyone get out of doing this to a 20 year old girl? And why were the people who did it to her allowed to devolve so far to become worse than animals? It was another straw on the camel's back of my patience with the lack of justice and sympathy for criminals that we wallow in in the UK.

The case became worse in late 2008 when it was announced that one of the murderers had succeeded in having his sentence reduced by nine months. Appeal court judges stated that not enough consideration had been given at the original trial to the fact he'd pleaded guilty.

During initial Training we had a visit from the Youth Offending Team, raving with misty eyed passion about the latest revolting creature they were rehabilitating out of the public coffers.

We had two drug addicts come to talk to us, one of which spent an hour raving in between sniffles about how much he loved his two year old son.

We never had a visit from a victim of burglary, to tell us just how it felt to come home and find someone had robbed their grandfather's engraved watch and taken a shit on their bed.

Noone who was raped but had the courage to stand up in front of cops and tell their story.

The amount of agencies and charities that exist to help offenders is staggering. Yet you'll find a couple of little old ladies working two afternoons a week who will listen to your tales of woe over a cup of stewed tea if you are the victim of a crime.

What would be nice was if instead of all these over indulged, spoilt bastards blaming society for their lack of moral fortitude while sponging off it in a half hearted attempt to change, we had Robert Maltby walk into the lecture theatre of the nearest Police Training College and say to the new recruits "Hi everyone, you may not have heard of me but I'm one of the people your Laws failed to protect".

CID

Straight after finishing Basic Training we were put on an attachment with the Criminal Investigation Department as detectives.

This was intended to allow you hands on experience in how to build and investigate an active case file and get your paperwork and Statement taking skills up to a professional standard. The attachment length varied from five months to ten depending on Area.

On the Monday morning after our Passing Out Parade we made our way up to the top floor of the Area HQ and were greeted by our two acting skippers, Jarrod and Julian. Jarrod was a spitting image for footballer Ian Rush and Julian bore more than a passing resemblance to Barry Manilow.

After a cup of tea they informed us just what we would be doing for the next few months.

First of all we would be assigned cases to our own 'pot' that could be seen by logging on to our own bit of the Force Intranet. We would then be given a blue folder with a Suspect's name and their alleged offence written on the front plus any other relevant information. Inside would be various paperwork such as PNB photocopies, Statements and photos. We would have to investigate the offence and deal with it up to its conclusion. This could be one of several things such as prosecution, a Caution or No Further Action (NFA).

We would usually be paired off with each other in order to increase safety and so you could rely on your partner's knowledge. We were in suits for the duration of the attachment.

The files we were given were the bottom of the barrel crap that proper CID officers didn't want. While it's logical they gave probationers the low level cases some of the 'crimes' we had to deal with defied belief:

These cases all took a lot of time, energy and paperwork, not to mention diesel in the pool cars to trundle around the Area following up leads.

We worked either 8am to 6pm or 12pm to 10pm, switching shifts each week and every fortnight having Friday to Monday off, negating POETS day. The two ADS's were well aware of my action plans from Sergeant Kerwan and he held a meeting with them which I wasn't allowed to attend Two days later Jarrod said "you're not at all like he's described you". When I asked him to elaborate he replied "well for a start you seem quite humble".

Anyone who made a mistake while on the attachment had to buy doughnuts for the rest of the team. The incidents ranged from putting petrol in the diesel cars (or vice versa), taking Police car keys home with you, forgetting your Airwave when out of the Nick or leaving yourself logged on to a computer. I only fell foul of this once and while most of the incidents were minor or even amusing, mine was quite serious.

Me and another officer called Benedict had visited a gobby 16 year old female to administer a Home Caution. She had gone out for a Chinese meal on her birthday and then deliberately left the restaurant without paying. The Home Caution meant she was legally recognising she had broken the Law and was signing a piece of paper that she understood the potential consequences of doing it again. We got back to the Station and I turned around to grab my rucksack to find it wasn't on the back seat where I always left it.

"Shit! I've left my fucking bag in that girl's house!"

"What was in it?"

"Only my bloody baton".

I only carried personal items in the bag but that day had put the Asp in as well. We were told to carry our Personal Protective Equipment at all times when out of the office but as hardly anyone had invested in those covert harnesses that look cool on US cop shows it meant either carrying them in your bag or putting them in your pockets.

Benedict ran into the Nick, told Julian what had happened, grabbed his own PPE and we headed back to her house. I was pissed off at myself and shit scared that she would either deny it was there or worse still have hidden it or thrown it away. The last thing I wanted, particularly as I was under action plans from Kerwan, was equipment going missing on my first week with CID.

We got to the flat and her brother answered the door. I stated with a straight face that I'd left my bag there. He stood back to let us in and it was exactly where I'd left it, next to the armchair I'd sat in when I'd issued the Home Caution. No one had even noticed it was there.

I breathed a sigh of relief, we headed back to the Nick and after Benedict had gone me and Julian had a chat.

"I don't know what to say Lance. We said we'd give you the benefit of the doubt after having spoken with both you and Sergeant Kerwan and four days into your attachment this happens."

"I know. I am really sorry. I'm not making excuses".

"Well that's good because I wouldn't accept any. Do you realise the potential consequences of her having that baton in her possession? Do you realise what she could have done with it?"

"Worse case scenario she could have sold it on Ebay or even twatted someone over the head with it, me getting the blame as my force number is stamped inside the handle".

"Good, well at least you know the gravity of this. You have to ask yourself if the situation with your PDU and the extra pressure you're under has contributed to this".

I pause then ask "was that rhetorical or do you want me to answer it?"

"No, I want you to answer it."

"Well I don't think it's helping".

He sits back in his seat. "The team need to know they can rely on you, and after this I'm not sure they can. I'll think about this over the weekend. I'm not going to make any snap decisions but then again I'm not going to dwell on it either."

As we are on a four day weekend it will be Tuesday before I know what he's decided to do.

"Ok, I'll accept whatever you decide, but I want you to know I AM sorry I let you down."

"We'll talk about this on Tuesday".

The following week he took me to one side and said "I've decided to make a Day Book entry about this. The PDU are aware of what happened but I promise you that unless this happens again it won't go any further".

I breathe out heavily. "THANK you".

"I think you know you let the team down and I believe that in itself means it's unlikely to happen again".

I nod.

"Now, get down Sainsbury's. Doughnuts are on you I believe".

After this embarrassment I invested in some holsters for the cuffs, spray and baton and wore them on my suit belt. While this got sniggers from a few of my colleagues, particularly if I took my jacket off, I felt a lot safer with them within reach than I would have done fumbling around in my rucksack for the Pava at an inopportune moment. It also negated the possibility of losing any of it if I was wearing the items.

Around this time I also met face to face with the Federation Representative for my Area, James Wilne who was a detective Constable.

As the Police are prohibited by Law from forming or joining a Union, the Federation is the next best thing. They protect those officers that pay the membership fee each month from bullying, mistreatment and unfairness and will represent them at meetings and disciplinaries if asked to. On every Area there has to be three ranks, a Constable, a Sergeant and an Inspector representing the Federation. I had spoken to James on the phone three days after the meeting with Kerwan, Esobé and Toby and he had heard about it from his counterpart in the Police college and had also made his own enquiries. When I asked him his opinion on what had happened he said "I think what they did was absolutely outrageous". He met me in the office next to the CID block and assured me that he would look after me and further that I needed to write down any and all contact I had had with the PDU, or incidents I felt were relevant to how I'd been treated by the Force. This was a pre-emptive measure against any possible invocation of Regulation 13 by Kerwan. A couple of days later he told me that he'd spoken on the phone to Kerwan who had stated he would leave me alone in future provided I could get through the action plans he had set.

While I was supremely grateful to Julian for giving me another chance and for the Federation for taking up my case, two weeks later I was signed off sick for three months.

FURTHER BULLYING

After I complained to Sergeant Taggart about Kerwan he went up a notch or two and began bullying in earnest.

I saw him in the college smoking area with Taggart the day after the meeting and found out from her that she'd brought him back to explain himself. She was furious about what he'd done as he'd originally told her that the meeting was solely to discuss my Diversity placement. When she found out what had actually gone on she wanted to know what the hell he was playing at.

She told me later that she'd spoken to Ma'am Postlethwaite and I couldn't move Areas until I had had my Action Plans signed off.

She was responsible for all probationers during their time at the Training College and answered directly to Inspector Postlethwaite who had an office four doors down. He had effectively walked right into their turf and humiliated a trainee to the point where he was in tears, after having misled them about why he was coming and why that trainee needed to miss over two hours of Final Stage Training.

He apparently tried the excuse that he thought I'd received the feedback form from PC Hambleworth, which didn't gel as I'd told him I hadn't before we started. I later found out that of all the trainees on my Intake I was the only one to NEVER receive it. I don't believe in coincidences when it's people's arses in the fire and it was her own sense of self preservation that led her to distance herself from what he was up to. I saw the form twice, once when Kerwan showed it to me and the second time six months later in a meeting to discuss my complaints against him.

A week after the meeting where they'd torn me to shreds and made me cry Kerwan forwarded an email. It was feedback from Toby, two pages long and written the day after the meeting.

It was far from pleasant.

Complete character assassination talking about how I had wasted the opportunity to get involved with a "diverse element of society" by failing to communicate adequately with his clients but at the same time saying that he had found me "overly familiar". He again stated that he believed my "unsettling early life experiences" had affected me in adult life, something he had no right to even verbalise, let alone put in print. He was a Care Manager for druggies and alchies, NOT a psychiatrist.

He stated that I would change subjects in mid conversation to topics of my own and didn't appear interested in learning. This was inaccurate as I had made multiple attempts to glean info from his team and was given only the most basic. Further, the chats where I changed the subject were invariably involving Glenda's foul mouth and observations on Big Brother contestants' genitalia.

Of all that he wrote though, he attacked the one thing most personal and precious to me and stated:

"He placed great store by the fact that he was on duty after July 7th 2005's terrorist attacks. Staff were subsequently left with the impression that he was actually in the area of the attacks. We now believe this to be untrue".

He had no proof I was lying or any reason to believe what I'd said was made up. I had mentioned it a total of three times during the placement and only then if asked why I'd joined. I had specifically told him in that meeting that my ex-girlfriend was a survivor of the attacks. He was now spitting on my Integrity and insulting me, the City of London Police and someone I still care very deeply about.

The final exam was three days away and getting an email that effectively sent the clear message "You Are a Twat, Why Don't You Just Accept That?" didn't help my revision or concentration.

The following Monday was the first day of my CID attachment. Within an hour of arriving Kerwan emailed me, casually mentioning that my File Note for Integrity had now expired and he had removed it. He then wrote:

"I am now asking you for the second time if you told your Trainers for final stage Training that you were under Action Plans. You opened my original email asking this on August 11th 2007 at 15:18 but I have not yet received a reply".

You will know if anyone has read an email you sent them as it tells you via an automatic 'read receipt' as soon as they open it. I replied that I hadn't told my Trainers that I was under Action Plans as I had discussed them at great length prior to attending Final Stage Training with Inspector Postlethwaite who is head of the entire Training system for all probationers.

A short time later he sent a seething email, saying this was not good enough and did not help 'personal responsibility' (one area of my Action Plans). He had cut and pasted an instruction from an earlier email reminding me to tell them. He added that I had now wasted the opportunity of constructive feedback and this was not acceptable.

While his attitude was predictable I could see that he had a point, even though I had done what I'd believed was a viable alternative and hadn't simply forgotten or not done it because I couldn't be arsed. I was prepared to put it down as a learning curve until he sent another email an hour later.

It contained an attachment of even more feedback, this time from DS Tudor, one of the Training Sergeants who had lectured us on a couple of occasions and was the skipper of the two Training DC's at the College. It stated that she had been invited to attend a meeting between Inspector Postlethwaite and Kerwan and while there had been asked if I had told her or her DC's that I was under Action Plans. She stated that I had not. She was then asked to give feedback on me which she did and Kerwan was now forwarding it.

He accompanied this with a curt message that said simply "I received this from Inspector Postlethwaite. As you did not make people aware of your Plans I have had to seek feedback retrospectively".

Only problem was, it was from lessons at Uni four or five months previously and not for the period of 'missing' feedback from six weeks ago..

I was totally gobsmacked by this and felt angrier and angrier as I read what she'd put. It noted my remarks about Illegal Immigrants being recorded as Missing Persons during a class debate and how she had approached the Campus Sergeant to discuss my attitude after the lesson. It noted that I had asked a couple of seemingly irrelevant questions during lectures and how I had raised my voice to ask a question during one lesson. It went on to say that during a lecture given by her Detective Inspector I had approached the DI during any breaks and "engaged her in intense conversation". Finally it mentioned that I had an unfortunate habit of "invading personal space" when talking to people, which had been noted by both her, her DC's and the DI and 'might be off putting for a vulnerable witness'.

Nobody had said anything whatsoever to me at the time these 'incidents' occurred. The fact that a Ma'am and two skippers were discussing it but didn't feel I needed to know what they were talking about made this retroactive assessment completely nonsensical. By not addressing the issues at the time they had, in theory, let me carry on doing these things without being aware of it, unchecked for months while I was on active duty.

As angry as I was at what Kerwan had done and as frustrating as it was to have things sprung on me out of the blue like this, I then figured out what he'd really been up to.

DS Tudor's form was dated one week previously.

Sitting in his office, seething with wounded pride and embarrassment that he'd had to explain himself to another Sergeant and an Inspector, Kerwan had decided to bin me through what he believed was going to be an easy option.

If your Integrity is out of sync as a cop you will be dismissed.

Some Forces will let their officers keep their jobs if caught drink driving, provided it's the first time and provided they plead guilty. Integrity is another can of worms though and any officer found to be lying can be fired very easily if it can be proven. If cops can't tell the truth what is the world coming to?

As a probationer you will have a much rougher ride if your Integrity is flawed, as Kerwan's performance over the charity sweets had proved. He casually mentioned that this File Note had expired and then asked me if I had done something (making it clear that he knew that I knew he'd ALREADY asked me) and had DS Tudor's form locked and loaded ready to launch in my direction.

He clearly believed that I was going to lie to him whereby he could then forward the email, grinning from ear to ear as he hit the Return key with a note saying something like:

"No you didn't. I know you didn't because I have proof you didn't. This is the second time your Integrity has been in question and I will today be approaching the Superintendent for invocation of Regulation 13".

As I had a reason for not having told them, all he could do was bang his head on the keyboard in frustration, try to make out that I had still fucked up and then an hour later in a spiteful tantrum, send me DS Tudor's form anyway, not realising that a six year old would see that he'd already had it for a week.

The Federation stated flatly that "he's just being vindictive" and when I complained about Kerwan officially, the investigating Inspector stated that it was not unacceptable for him to behave like this. When I pointed out that he'd tried entrapment the subject was very quickly changed.

My Action Plans were retained and increased by about another 40% after this. He used DS Tudor's back dated comments and Toby's feedback for most of the extra points and even invented several things, such as giving me a plan for Resilience and not blaming others for my mistakes, even though no evidence, either written or verbal was presented to back this up.

A week later and he sent an email saying I would have to see the Acting Superintendent. He asked if I wanted anyone from the Federation at the meeting at which he himself would also be present. Knowing he wouldn't act up in front of the Super I declined.

The meeting lasted two minutes:

"Hello there PC…Manley isn't it?" the Super' said looking at the Action Plans on his desk. Kerwan was sitting opposite him.

"Yes Sir, we've met before".

"Oh really was that Area Familiarisation week?"

"No Sir, I was at a petrol station with Jacob from 12 Section, you were Off duty with your children".

He smiles and says "Ah yes, I remember" then gestures for me to sit.

He looks at the Action Plans and shakes his head. "Well I can't imagine any ACC NOT invoking Regulation 13 after looking at this. What you need to do now is work hard to get these Plans out the way". He looks up at me "I take it you don't have a problem with any of this Feedback?"

Jesus suffering, fuck! What the bloody HELL am I supposed to say to THAT?

"I have no problem with feedback from other Police officers Sir, no".

"Good, good. Hopefully I'll be seeing you in happier times in the very near future. Your Sergeant is going to take you into another office now to discuss the Action Plans once we've had a short discussion".

I blanch at this but keep quiet and he directs me to leave and I take a seat outside.

Ten minutes later when Kerwan comes out to get me he casually goes "right, come on" and is already heading for the open door next to the Super's office.

I stand up. "If it's all the same I'd like to have someone else present for this."

He looks genuinely surprised but then says irritably "oh, that's up to you. If you want to. Go and fetch someone".

I go up and wait in the CID office for Julian to conclude a phone call and ask him to sit in. He does and Kerwan immediately drops the bomb shell that my CID attachment has been reduced from five months to three and I will be rejoining Core Section in December. I'd heard rumours of this but nothing concrete and the Friday before had had Annual Leave approved and had paid for a ticket to Greece to visit my father at Christmas.

"We can work around that but you will lose Annual Leave later on" Kerwan tells me.

This is completely unfair as I had deliberately, with an ADS sitting next to me, booked the Leave around and over my Rest Days so as not to waste any precious Leave unnecessarily. I'm now being told that while they have to respect that previous decision I will suffer for it later on.

He then gets me to sign the Action Plans and says "this of course will all be handled fairly like it has been before", presumably for Julian's ears as there's no way even he could be stupid enough to think I'd believe that.

As we leave Julian says "noone's picking on you you know". It was a statement he would retract months later.

Three days after this and Kerwan made me do an E-Package on the Force Intranet for Race and Diversity retraining for my comments about Illegal Immigrants. It took two hours, had nothing to do with Illegal Immigrants and was utterly pointless.

The day after that and two lads from my intake on the same CID attachment were off to the PDU. I asked them to pick up my Airwave radio and then changed my mind. An hour after they'd gone my mobile rang and it was Tom, asking where I'd left it. As I was flicking through my PNB to find out the name of the officer I'd given it to, I could hear the background conversation in the PDU office:

TOM: "He told us not to bother but it's a nice day so we thought 'why not?"

PC Esobé: "What's he doing?"

TOM: "Just looking up the name of the tutor he left it with"

PC Esobé: (Assuming mimicking tone) "Oh can you pick up my Airwave for me but I don't know where the FUCK it is".

I wrote down in my PNB what she'd said and got Tom to countersign the margin. Months later I was told that she had been disciplined over this via a verbal telling off. However they'd got Kerwan to do it as he was her line manager, even though they knew my complaints were against the pair of them.

Finally I got an email from Esobé questioning a NOS I had submitted to Jacob, who had signed it off. During my arrest of the Cashpoint lorry driver I had held his hands behind his back in an OST-approved manner by gripping his thumbs while I searched him.

He had tried to dispose of evidence and was agitated and bigger than me. Esobé demanded to know why I'd found it necessary to do this and stated that it was potentially an "unlawful use of force" unless the prisoner was Non-Compliant and unless Jacob was willing to back me up. Fortunately Jacob did.

Esobé and Kerwan had earlier castigated me for not using any physical force when dealing with a gobby female who was only verbally aggressive. This led to my first Action Plan for "responding appropriately to the threat level".

I wish only the very worst for the pair of them for the rest of their lives.

OFF SICK

Around September 2007 I slipped a disc in my lower back.

I was sitting with fellow Probie and CID puppy Christian in a satellite Nick where we'd arranged to positively dispose of some shit case file by Interviewing the Suspect and giving him a Caution.

About halfway through my back started hurting. It kicked in quite quickly and I was confronted with what felt like a candle flame being held to my right buttock. I managed to keep it together for the ten minute Interview, got gitface to sign his Caution in triplicate and then sent them on their way. I asked Christian if he'd mind driving back as I wasn't feeling too good, but didn't specify why.

Back at our normal Nick and Julian was debriefing us but I was in so much pain that I couldn't concentrate on what he was saying. As standing only exacerbates the condition I sat on the edge of a desk trying to look interested and not wince at the feeling which was now not only in my arse but down my right leg all the way to the calf muscle. It felt like a flexible, red hot poker had been laid inside the flesh of my leg.

I drove home squirming and next morning it was just as bad. After calling in Sick I went to Casualty who prescribed some Diclofenac (oh nasty, alcohol unfriendly stuff) and sent me home.

For the next three months I was in almost constant pain and could barely stand for longer than a few minutes. I was told to try and get a brisk walk in each day so bought a walking stick from Millets and would hobble around town like some bent old crone, swearing at red traffic lights and becoming more like Victor Meldrew as time wore on. I visited the GP regularly and he signed me off continually as he was unable to raise my right leg to more than half the height of my left when he got me to lie down on his couch. In his opinion I had a prolapsed disc and it was probably what was causing the pain by pushing against my sciatic nerve.

Throughout this time I was absolutely miserable with pain that could only be relieved slightly by lying down either in bed or on the sofa. While sitting relieved the pain, it made it worse once you stood up again as the disc had oh so considerately used the increased gap to squeeze out a bit more, meaning that when your vertebrae realigned, the two either side of the disc would close up and squeeze the little fucker even more.

It was like having sulphuric acid down my arse and leg and the only thing I've ever experienced that was more painful was a couple of occasions when I banged my testicles.

As I was having grief with Kerwan I made certain that I kept a file on my attempts to get better, with the doctor's notes and photocopies of the prescriptions and any official diagnoses. Apart from the National Health I was also paying privately for Osteopathy which meant lots of hobbling the half mile to the clinic once a week.

About a month after I had first been signed off I got a call from Julian:

"Hi there. We need to do a Home Visit on you as part of your Return to Work plan".

"Fine by me, when do you want to do it?"

"Now, see you in half an hour".

Him and a Temporary Sergeant from the neighbouring Area named Declan turned up and declined the offer of a cup of tea. They looked at me and asked how I was feeling.

"Like shit. You?"

"Are you getting enough sleep? You look knackered."

"About 12 hours a day. It's the pain that's exhausting".

They were surprised when I asked them to sign my PNB to say they'd visited me and later on when I got to know Declan through working with him he said he couldn't understand why I'd asked him to do that. I replied that after so much backstabbing and cloak and dagger bollocks from the PDU I was taking no chances and wanted everything witnessed.

I asked them for a lift to the Osteo and they obliged, only to find that their car had a flat battery and they had to get me to sit in the driver's seat while they pushed it down the road and got me to pump the accelerator.

The whole time I was off sick at home was boring and depressing. The pain was constant and the Osteo's therapy wasn't working despite costing me around £20 a time. I was prescribed even more painkillers, including one called Tramadol, which although it sounds like a woman of easy virtue who touts for business on public transport, is a nasty piece of shit that gave me some of the most unpleasant nightmares I've ever had. This plus the Diclofenac and a constipation-inducing little bastard called Codipar (ever tried to have a shit with a slipped disc?) meant that I was also having emotional lows brought on by a cocktail that might have raised a few pennies on the streets with the local junkies.

I was off work for a full three months. During this time I didn't hear once from Kerwan or Esobé who had been only too keen to throw all manner of evidence at me that I was unsuitable material for The Job but clearly couldn't have cared less about my convalescence.

I was back on Restricted Duties before Christmas. Only four hours a day to start with, completely office based, absolutely no confrontation and visits to Force Occ Health as part of my recuperation. Occ Health were strict with exactly what I could or couldn't do and I had to visit them once a month for appraisals and see the Force Physio' once or twice a week.

Declan had decided, as the Sergeant who organised probationers for the whole Force throughout their CID attachment, to put me with the adjoining Area until I was fully fit. This meant a six mile drive to work instead of twenty and put me in a nice little village in a converted house. The Village Wardens, PCSOs and Community Police had an office next door while we used a ground floor room looking out over a fairly well kept garden. Our neighbours were in detached houses either side and a school was 200 yards down the road. Declan and an Inspector had offices on the first floor and there were up to fifteen of us in there at any one time at Shift change.

By Christmas I was more mobile and the pain was merely a dull ache. After consultation with the Federation I flew to Crete to visit my father, a trip planned and paid for before I went off Sick. While there my back went again and I flew home in a wheelchair. This time the pain was twice as bad and it didn't matter what position I sat or lay in, it was always excruciating. I got about 2 hours sleep per day and on my return to England visited Casualty. After waiting 3 ½ hours I was examined by a flippant Doctor who simply raised my right leg until I screamed loud enough to get the neighbourhood tom cats howling and prescribed some morphine to go home with.

By the time I got back home a week later the condition was the same as before Christmas and I got back into work. Gradually I got better but was still on fully Restricted Duties for the first month. This was relaxed later to allow me to drive Force vehicles (irony being that I could drive into work but couldn't then use company cars due to the Health and Safety issues and insurance) but I still couldn't enter the Custody Suite due to its inherently confrontational nature and was told to check any and all situations that might be confrontational before going into them.

In early February I finally heard from Sergeant Kerwan. He sent an offhand email asking me to let him know how my application was progressing for an MRI scan via a Force fund that pays for officers' treatment provided it's the cheapest you can get. This was the final straw and was what led to me consulting the Federation again and writing to the Superintendent asking to move Areas. This in turn led to over four hours of meetings with an Inspector and another Sergeant to investigate my claims of bullying by Kerwan and Esobé.

Through all this pain and misery, not knowing if I was going to remain like this for the rest of my life, having a urine sample probably worth £40 a pint to drug addicts and being pushed around in a wheelchair he had never once shown any interest at all. Kerwan was PDU and directly responsible for my development and should therefore have been in regular contact to see how I was doing or passed that responsibility to someone else. I actually didn't want to hear from him but he was as usual, not doing his job properly.

An attempt by the Force Physio to give me traction resulted in waking up the following morning in worse pain again and not being able to stand up straight. My GP signed me off for a week again and it turned out I was the '1 in 10'. Apparently the disc had a scab that had attached to the sciatic nerve. When he put me in the traction machine it pulled the spine and ripped the scab, causing further inflammation that took a week to go down.

Two days after being signed off again I was back in the Force Physio's office when he said "oh, I got an email about you from Sergeant Kerwan asking about how your condition was going?"

"Can I see it?"

"Sure, it's your medical records. You've every right to see them. Hang on".

He boots up his PC and opens an email, gesturing me to read it.

I read what's on the screen and feeling overly cautious ask "is it ok to scroll down and read the rest?".

He nods and I use the central wheel on the mouse to read the remainder.

Unfortunately for him it's NOT the email he intended to open but another one about me. At the bottom is an earlier email from my new Acting CID skipper Declan.

After consultation with the Federation about moving Areas and who I should address this to, I wrote a polite email to the Superintendent with Inspector Postlethwaite Cc'd into it, requesting a relocation and pointing out that the Federation and myself were able to disprove most of the PDU's criticisms and further that I had experienced a distinct lack of "objective and impartial treatment".

Fate being what it is, the day I was signed off Sick the Super despatched an Inspector named Gerva to the satellite Nick I worked at (on a Rest Day no less, which proves they were taking this seriously) who arrived to find I wasn't there. He had emailed me the day before to say he was coming but it had arrived after I had gone home meaning I had no clue he was coming in.

He then emailed me again saying he would come and see me next

Monday, but as it was a Rest Day for him again, he would appreciate it if I could let him know if I couldn't make it.

I didn't find out any of this until much later.

The morning I saw Declan's email I had called the Fed Rep at 9am who told me Inspector Gerva had phoned him to say that he would now be taking charge of my probation, moving me away from Kerwan and Esobé and would be coming to see me as soon possible.

Ten minutes later the phone rang. It was Declan who said he was doing the 'follow up' call required as I was off Sick yet again. I then mentioned that I had just heard via the Federation that an Inspector had taken up my issues with the PDU.

Declan snapped "I know, he came to see you this morning but you weren't here. He's coming back next week on his Rest Day to see you again".

"Oh, I didn't know that, that was quick. Jesus!" I then said "I won't be in Monday as it's a Rest Day but I'll see you Tuesday".

He then rang off and I thought no more of it. That is until I read the email from him to the Physio which contained the following:

"Lance refused to come in to see the Inspector on a Rest Day next week even though I told him that the Inspector had already come in on a Rest Day to see him and was prepared to give up another. I do not think this is the right attitude to have, especially as this is about something that he says he really wants. What I would have expected to hear was 'even though it's a Rest Day I'm prepared to come in'."

He had sent this to Kerwan and the Physio, clearly never expecting me to get wind of it.

I gaze at the screen, incomprehensible. Why the fuck would he lie like that?.

"I never bloody said that!" I manage to stammer as I turn round.

The Physio looks at me puzzled and then looks closer at the screen.

"Oh shit! That's the wrong one. Sorry I meant this one" and opens the email I was meant to see.

I am confused and angry and have a nasty taste in my mouth.

"Time for some acupuncture" the Physio says cheerfully as he opens a pack of needles. He catches the look on my face and asks "are you going to be able to relax for this?" looking concerned.

"Yeah, yeah" I say, lying down on the couch and positioning my face through the hole at the end.

"Now just try and relax" he says as he begins sticking me with the needles.

After about five minutes of silence I blurt out:

"BUT I NEVER BLOODY SAID THAT!"

The Physio told me a couple of weeks later that he could see from the tension in my muscles just how upset and angry I was even though he couldn't see my face and joked that he'd thought of getting a suit of armour as he was half expecting the needles to come flying out across the room at any moment.

As I lay there feeling completely miserable I heard him sigh "All right. Owning up time. It's not your fault. I should have checked what I was opening".

I heard him tapping away on his keyboard and a few minutes later when he pulled the needles out and told me to roll over he said that he'd emailed Kerwan and Declan and told them that he'd accidentally opened the email and that I'd read it.

The following week at our next appointment he told me that Kerwan had replied within five minutes saying simply "have read your email, suggest you call" and when he phoned him was met with "Lance shouldn't have been using your computer". He apparently had to tell Kerwan twice that I wasn't actually using it, I was merely reading an email off the screen that he'd opened for me and given me permission to read, while he stood directly behind me.

I immediately called the Fed Rep James Wilne for advice. He was surprised and annoyed at what Declan had done and advised me to phone him and confront him. He also suggested that as I was at the Training College maybe I should ask to speak to Inspector Postlethwaite about it.

She shared her office with another Guv'nor and after the introductions she gestured for me to sit down. I looked at the other Inspector and said "would it be possible to talk to you in private Ma'am?"

We went into a ground floor office and I told her what had happened. She suggested I email Declan to say that there had been a 'misunderstanding' and to put my side of the story to him. She also listened to me talk about what was going on with the PDU and after I'd finished said:

"Lance, I don't think you've got what it takes for this job. I never have done. I think you have certain qualities that would be useful to us, such as in forensics or as an investigator but I don't think you've got the necessary stamina".

"Fair enough Ma'am, but I can respect you for saying that now even though I don't agree with you. You are telling me with respect for my dignity and in private, not in front of a civilian after ambushing me".

She looks at me thoughtfully for a few moments and then asks "could you for example deal with a case of a 6 year old girl who was repeatedly raped? And could you bring the person responsible to court, who we all knew was guilty and then have a retrial after a hung jury. Then on the retrial for the man to be found not guilty? Could you deal with that? I don't think you could."

"Yes" I reply "if I believed 100% that I'd done everything I could".

"I don't think so Lance. I know you have no support network. You live alone. I mean, I've met your family so I know you have people in your life but they're not here with you".

"The feedback I got from my friends after that meeting with Sergeant Kerwan was 'that's NO way to treat somebody'".

"I disagree. If people need to be told they need to be told".

"I found out a couple of weeks later that you'd had a meeting with Sergeant Kerwan where I was the subject under discussion and DS Tudor was there too".

She nods.

"Now it could be that you were having a meeting where my name happened to come up, or it COULD be that you brought him back here and tore him to pieces for walking into your territory and doing that to me".

She looks at me but doesn't say anything. She doesn't

acknowledge or deny what I've just said but continues to look at me impassively.

"I'll say this now Ma'am and it's not because you're sitting in front of me or that you're my senior officer. I've always respected you and looked up to you. If everyone was the same as you then everything would be much better. Unfortunately for every one of you there's one or two who aren't quite so good".

A flicker of surprise and embarrassment crosses her features but she catches them quickly and returns to being poker faced.

"Sergeant Kerwan...well he's ok. Not like some other PDU Sergeants we've had" she tells me.

"He's done nothing but bully me since I forgot to pay for those charity sweets. He's become even worse since I complained to your Sergeant about that meeting".

Her mobile rings and it's apparently her boyfriend as she says "hello darling, yes I'll be out in five minutes". She hangs up. "Lance we need to conclude this now. Write an email to Declan with what we've said". I walk out with her and she heads to the car park while I go to an office to find an available computer.

It takes me about half an hour to compose, check and then do about 10 rechecks. I sign off with "once again, I regret that a misunderstanding has occurred and hope this email has put the record straight. Please call me if you wish to discuss this further".

I log off and put on my coat. As I reach the door my mobile rings, less than two minutes since I sent the email. I recognise the number.

"Hello Declan"

There's a very long silence and then he says "do you understand how embarrassed I was when the Inspector turned up here to see you and I didn't know anything about your PDU transfer request?"

"That wasn't my intention. I consulted the Federation about who to include on the email and you weren't one of the people they mentioned. I take it you've seen the email I just sent".

"Yes it's in front of me. Lance, in my entire ten years in this job I have NEVER heard of someone approaching the Superintendent directly without consulting their line manager".

"Neither have I. I didn't know what the protocols were. I was told to go straight to the Super with just Ma'am Postlethwaite Cc'd in. I only found out ten minutes before you rang this morning that the Inspector had been in".

"You may have noticed that I didn't chat for very long this morning. I was still pissed off".

"Do you think I wanted to upset you? I did what I thought was right".

"No, I can see that now and that you sought advice on what was appropriate. Where are you?"

"The College. I'm just getting into my car". As I get into the driver's seat the caretaker taps on the window and asks if I want to leave as he's about to shut and lock the back gate. I tell him it's ok and he walks off.

"Look I'm happy to show you the letter I sent to the Super I wasn't trying to hide this from you".

"What did it say?"

"Just that I respectfully would like to be moved to another Area as I don't feel I've been treated fairly by the PDU and respectfully request that consideration be given to this request. Signed 'respectfully yours'. As you can guess there were a lot of 'respectfuls' in it".

He chuckles, then "alright send it to me when you get back. How long are you signed off for?"

"A week, back next Tuesday. Can I self authorise return if I feel up to it?"

He chuckles again "you're a scallywag. NO".

We wish each other well and then end the call.

Declan was a good Sergeant and had arranged it so I could work the remainder of my CID attachment in the neighbouring Area, with him as my skipper as it was closer to home than my own Nick and therefore easier for someone with a bad back to commute to. He had patiently listened to me on several occasions, the first time when he checked my PNB and found backdated notes on conversations related to incidents the PDU had raised. He couldn't understand why they were there so I decided to trust him and told him what was going on. He'd also made arrangements to have me stay with them longer than the initial month he'd intended, solely because he knew I didn't want to go back to my own Area and be under the remit of Kerwan again.

He'd done all this for me and then the Inspector had turned up with the news that I'd gone over his head and approached a very senior officer without consulting him first.

After we sorted this out the incident was never discussed again and when I left he gave me the most constructive and balanced feedback I'd ever received. It was about four pages long and said that I had made dramatic improvement in all areas of my Action Plans except Resilience, which he was unable to judge due to the non-confrontational risk assessment I'd been operating under. He also noted that he wholeheartedly believed that with further time with CID I would have improved even more. He stated that my Race and Diversity Action Plan should now be completely written off and gave evidence to back this up.

I still to this day want to believe that the email I was never meant to see was merely a misunderstanding.

I had the MRI scan a couple of weeks later (which isn't an experience I recommend if you're claustrophobic) and it proved that I had a slipped LS-5 vertebrae, the prolapsed disc nuzzling up to the sciatic nerve.

I had over four hours of meetings with Inspector Gerva and a Sergeant about my complaints against Kerwan and Esobé. He pointed out that if I was unable to get better after this second trip to the rehab centre then I may be invalided out of the Force.

After another month and after a meeting with the Force GP, a pre OST Refresher meeting with the Trainer who'd belted me on the ear during my initial Training and finally the OST Refresher itself I was finally signed back on for full duties again.

FLINT HOUSE

The English Police's best kept secret that isn't a secret.

When we joined we were given a big pack of documents and advised it was in our best interests to sign all of them. One had a picture of some bloke getting physio for a bad back at a private health care centre. This was part of the Benevolent Fund's stuff and we were asked to contribute £6.90 per month to help sick officers, knowing that we too could utilise its services if injured in the line of duty. I signed the form and thought no more about it.

When the back pain became more than just a few weeks of hobbling around swearing, the Fed Rep suggested utilising my payments to the Benevolent Fund and taking a trip to the Police rehabilitation centre, Flint House in Oxfordshire. He and everyone I spoke to, raved about this place. "5 star hotel with nurses", "fuck me, they sending you there? You jammy bastard", etc etc.

It was wonderful and the only good thing to come out of my injury was that I went to the centre twice.

The centre is on the outskirts of a small village. It is set way back from the road behind a wood and as soon as you arrive you can see just how exquisite the place is. Sumptious gardens and sprawling grounds with beautiful views of the surrounding hills and fields. The architecture is that of an old country mansion (what it used to be) and the tone of the place is like some posh London hotel, all lush wood and subdued lighting, plush carpets and framed oil paintings. The recreational lounge has the biggest flat screen TV outside a council house and leather sofas and chairs. In one corner is a unit with filter coffee, hot water and about ten types of teabags, milk and biscuits. Adjoining it is a bar which sells tap ale and Guinness and runs two pub quizzes per week.

The bedrooms are ensuite with wardrobes big enough to fit a rugby team in. You have a TV, kettle, toiletries and a phone. The shower is huge with a saucer sized head and the floors are heated.

There are about four family rooms and on one occasion there were two Armed Response officers and their nine month old baby staying. The dad was built like a gladiator and his wife was like Private Vasquez from the movie Aliens. Watching them spoon feed their quite adorable little boy was highly amusing.

There is a swimming pool, sauna and gym plus an exercise room with Swiss balls and mats. There is a physio suite, massage parlour and two recreational lounges with TV's not quite as big as the one in the main lounge. There is a Snooker table and an Internet point as well as Wi-Fi in the lounge for a small fee.

While there you get spoilt rotten.

First of all you're given a physio assessment and poked and prodded into various positions by blue shirted staff who assess your condition. Then you attend a welcome meeting which lasts all of five minutes and is basically a rundown on the fire drill and how the only places you can openly get drunk are the bar or restaurant. Finally for inauguration purposes you will be seen by a Nurse and given several samples of litmus paper with essential oils sprinkled on them. The three that you like most will be mixed up and presented to you in a little bottle along with an oil burner so you can sleep more easily or just chill out to the aromas of camomile, tangerine and black amber.

The average day will be spent getting up for breakfast and then having a physio class and maybe a pool session. After several hours of relaxing over cups of herbal tea and a newspaper you go for lunch and then have a gym class to strengthen whichever malfunctioning body part brought you to the centre. Counselling is provided if you require it as is massage with whale songs played in the background and possibly acupuncture.

The rest of your time is divided between watching TV, having a sauna or just luxuriating in the utter decadence of first class private health care. Your most pressing concern throughout the fortnight will be whether or not to have a Full English breakfast again or not.

One thing that took me completely off guard was that rank is absolutely non-existent at Flint House. Normally when off duty but socialising with senior officers it is considered polite to call them 'Guv' until given permission to do otherwise. According to the nursing staff people had arrived in the past who tried to give it the big 'un and were soon put in their place. The whole purpose of convalescence is to get better and part of that is that you relax and leave your baggage at the door. I made friends with a very attractive woman from another Force who was in for a broken ankle. She was great fun to be around, liked a rum and coke or two and when drunk told some delightful stories such as having her clitoris pierced and how she likes to walk around at home completely naked. She turned out to be an Inspector.

Another time I sat opposite a guy at lunch who looked about my age and we passed the time chatting about changes in Force policy over the years and how nice the fresh strawberries tasted that we were both tucking into. He was a Superintendent from the Met.

There were three Firearms Officers from S013- Royal Protection in there, one of which said that Viscount Linley is the only Royal who refuses to carry ID, as per official policy. One day when he was on duty a new officer was heard over the radio saying "I've got some scruffy cunt here who won't show me ID but says he's Lord Linley".

The Inspector then came back with "That IS Lord Linley, let him in and then come and see me immediately".

One thing that could get even senior ranks squabbling was meals. First weekers had second sitting at all meals meaning that the yummier desserts were usually snaffled by the second weekers (which we took great delight in doing when it was our turn). Banoffee pie proved to be the one pud guaranteed to start a stampede of recuperating cops, screeching to a halt at the cake stand and lamenting the fact that there's never enough left. Squabbles between officers of all Forces and ranks broke out with salt and pepper being sprinkled on the banoffee pie or a digit being inserted in it for a japeful prank.

For a convalescent centre they had a large emphasis on socialising over a bevvy. Most nights were spent in the bar and trying to persuade the barman to stay open longer than 10.30pm.

The pub quiz is always good for proving just how much you don't know. Dingbats being the biggest bastard in this department. ("BLU E" turned out to be blue movie but absolutely nobody got it right).

The first series of Ashes to Ashes was on during my second stay, but on quiz night which meant lots of giggling as Gene Hunt's banter appeared as subtitles on the massive plasma screen TV in the bar with the volume muted. A scene of Chris and Ray giving a bloke the shoeing of his life after stabbing Shaz Granger led to a few whoops of delight, fists being punched in the air and "YEESS! THE GOOD OLD DAYS!" resounding throughout the bar from one or two Old School coppers. The popularity of this show can be illustrated by the fact that at least three quiz teams had names derived from it and the group I was with called ourselves "Wear Something Slutty In My Quattro".

The fortnight's healthcare turned out to be worth around two thousand pounds to anyone who felt like coming in off their own bat. Reasons for being there ranged from depression (hence it was deemed rude to ask "why are you here?" on first meeting someone) to injuries sustained outside of work (such as one lad who was in for the fifth time after getting injured yet again playing rugby). Frighteningly, many officers seemed to be in for back pain brought on by wearing the Stab Proof Vests. Stabbies are undoubtedly useful but are heavy, unforgiving items. Some Forces have now opted for an improved version with thinner Kevlar but it is yet another sign of the Police's incompetence that something clearly injuring its staff is allowed to continue until the budget can allow for change.

Once you have retired from the Force you can come to the Centre for free and one ex officer in his 90s was there due to having his hip replaced for the third time. He was a cop in the 1930s and told us all about cycling around on his Beat in villages straight out of Heartbeat and that back then there were absolutely no female officers on the payroll.

Another retired officer in his 70s was sitting next to me when I had a coughing fit during a pub quiz. A slipped disc is exacerbated by coughing or sneezing due to the raising and lowering of the diaphragm and each splutter brought on pain about as intense as getting kicked in the testicles. Each time I coughed I swore loudly and it went a little like this:

"COUGH! FUCKING CUNT!"

"COUGH! FUCKING BASTARD!"

"COUGH! FUCKING CUNTING BASTARD FUCK!"

etc.

When I finally managed to stop I looked across to my right and saw the retired Bobby and a female Sergeant looking at me open mouthed. I explained that the coughing had hurt my back and the Sergeant laughed so hard she had tears running down both cheeks. She told me later that both her and the old boy had thought I'd flipped out completely or had Tourrettes syndrome and it was only when I started talking normally again that they'd realised I was ok.

Everyone I met there on both visits seemed to benefit not only from the treatment and care but also the fact that for what may be the only time in their careers they could be themselves around other officers and even other ranks without worrying about someone stabbing them in the back or reporting them for their behaviour. In the Police even counsellors will specifically tell you on the first session that the oath of secrecy is null and void if you cross certain lines. Flint House counsellors made it quite clear that you could say whatever you liked in therapy sessions and it would absolutely NOT be reported back to your Force.

A Pakistani officer on my pub quiz team on my first visit came out with some outrageous, Reg-9able remarks (usually over a beer) which noone, not even the pierced, naturist Inspector took offence to as it was noted "that's just him".

Classics included "Urrgh! Who's dropped that? Smells like a white man's fart" and "I like British and US porn coz white women are dirtier than Asian women".

From Probationers to Sergeants, Inspectors to Firearms officers everyone relaxed and were able to communicate as people for once.

Initial nervousness, bred into you from Training and being on Section would dissolve within the first two days as you found everyone just wanted to relax and the normal barriers of self-preservation and mistrust had been temporarily put in storage.

I found out from the Fed Rep that Sergeant Kerwan was off sick from duty after having had an operation. Knowing that I was probably being overly cautious I checked the list, at the start of my second week, that Flint House hangs up on a Monday morning of who is staying and what Force they work for. Kerwan's name wasn't on it and I quietly berated myself for being so paranoid when I didn't even know if he'd been referred to the centre or how serious his operation was.

Turned out he was admitted the Monday after I left.

MEETING WITH INSPECTOR GERVA

After the mix up over my illness and crossed wires between me, Declan and the Inspector I finally got to see him a week later.

He was about fifty, quite short and amiable. He'd been in The Job for years and worked overseeing two or three areas including the PDU, now Ma'am was about to be put out to pasture.

With office space being at a premium he had booked the Chief Superintendent's office for our chat as Sir was away for the afternoon. It wasn't like I'd imagined it would be with plush leather seats, a library of hardback first editions and a decanter of good malt whisky in a glass cabinet, but the same as everyone else's office, right down to the PC on the desk.

I showed him the huge folder of evidence I'd put together on the Federation's advice to refute what Kerwan and Esobé had said or had got other people to say. I also handed him photocopies of the letter from the Chief Super of Snow Hill thanking me for 7/7, a letter from my friend stating she was a survivor of the terrorist attacks and a three page letter from a Drugs and Alcohol Misuse counsellor at an English prison which blew Toby's criticisms out of the water and pointed out the flaws in both his care team and my placement

He looked at it all and then said "I need time to read through all this. As I'm very busy the best thing we can do is rearrange to meet in a fortnight".

He then asked me to synopsise what I felt were the problems and we spent nearly an hour going over it. I showed him my Action Plans and drew his attention to the piece, included without any evidence or explanation by Kerwan, that I was not to 'generate justified complaints from members of the public'. This was another attempt at creating a failsafe by Kerwan as modern English cops run the gauntlet every day of receiving complaints from our Customers and getting a Reg 9 in the mail. This doesn't mean you're guilty of whatever they're moaning about, just that it's being investigated. Inspector Gerva looked at it and said "yes, I agree. We all have to adhere to that one, it shouldn't be part of an Action Plan" and drew a line through it and signed the amendment.

Two weeks later I came back in my best suit and met him outside his office.

"Hello Lance, this is Sergeant Vivanco, she deputises me. She'll be sitting in through this to chip in with anything she feels will help the discussion and to make sure I'm doing my job properly". He grins at the last bit and I shake her hand. We go again to the Chief Super's office and sit down at the oval desk.

He pulls out the pile of documents and we begin.

Retrospectively I don't think the way it went was completely his fault. He knew from reading the evidence that I'd put together that I was being treated badly and that even if not all of it was provable, there were serious issues that needed to be addressed. He was however in a difficult position and needed to balance following up my grievances against his subordinates with being loyal to his own team. Unfortunately by trying to strike a balance he effectively achieved nothing, as Kerwan didn't change his attitude for the simple reason that he wasn't punished for what he'd done.

Various points are discussed and we get to the bit about PC Esobé comparing me to a dog in front of Toby in the meeting.

"I can see where you're coming from but I think you're being oversensitive" he replies "that's a wonderful analogy, particularly for developmental advice".

"I agree Sir, it's not her saying it that's the problem, it's her saying it in front of Toby. What if I have to arrest him at some point in the future or even take a Statement from him? Is he ever likely to take me seriously after that?"

The Diversity placement itself is next on the agenda and he

states flatly that the team slagging off their boss in front of me was "terrible and inexcusable". He agrees that Glenda's appalling language was out of order and points at each word in turn saying "never used that word, never used that one either and I've certainly never used THAT one!" (respectively: pikey, spaz and gash). He states he has read my letter from an expert witness, effectively shooting holes in their whole argument and will pass it on to the relevant department.

I mention being told I'd been rude to Nigel during my presentation and the Inspector states "maybe you were just nervous". I reply that I'd already raised that and PC Esobé had simply snapped 'ha! Thinking about yourself again'.

We then get to Esobé saying I should be proud of my mate for 'sticking up for himself' and punching a guy holding a gun on him. The Inspector points to what I'd written about being disciplined (if still alive) if I'd done that. "I take it you wrote this BEFORE you were taught that you may use all necessary force to defend yourself".

I don't argue about the Red Mist video, or how we had been specifically told to back off and not be a hero when faced with a gun. Nor about 'Charlie Big Potato' who is still grief stricken after getting a little girl killed through being a twat.

He asks me if I have the required stamina for attending a Sudden Death of an alcoholic.

"Most definitely Sir, I joined expecting to deal with that. I did not expect to be kicked to death by my own PDU.

He agrees with me that Sonja should use real words if criticising me for using ones she can't understand herself and adds "not making any excuses for her BUT it was three in the morning when she sent that email".

He then gets to an off duty Intervention I had noted from about two weeks prior to our first chat.

I was driving home feeling particularly irritable after a shitty day on Restricted Duties. I joined the motorway and just off the slip road passed two kids on mountain bicycles, cycling in the slow lane, oblivious to the danger they were causing themselves and the motorists roaring past them. It was 4.30pm and very busy. Luckily there was a bridge just ahead so I pulled up on the hard shoulder, put the hazards on, got out the passenger side of the vehicle and as the kids approached, motioned for them to pull over to the embankment. I then took them and their bikes behind the concrete barrier running parallel to the hard shoulder, just past the bridge and showed them my badge.

"What on Earth do you think you're doing?" I ask them.

One of them shrugs "got lost, that's all".

I wrote down their names, addresses and DOB's in my PNB and then called it in via 999.

After the requisite transfer from a call centre in Glasgow to the local Control Room I give my name, rank and number and describe what's going on and that we are waiting behind the concrete barrier and that I have the situation under control but require Police assistance to get them off the motorway.

About five minutes later an ambulance pulls up behind my car on the hard shoulder and then reverses up to us. Two female Paramedics get out and approach. I initially think they're responding to the CAD but it turns out they just saw what was happening and decided to help out.

One of the Paramedics says to me "so pleased when I saw you were standing behind the crash barrier, most people don't and sometimes that's a big problem".

I suggest sticking the two kids and their cycles into the ambulance and using the next slip road to get off. She agrees and we shove them all in, take them to the adjacent junction and luckily we are right near the local Traffic Police depot and within about ten minutes a couple of Uniform turn up and take over. Turns out one of the lads lied about his age and both seem oblivious to the danger they were in and had put others in. They want to cycle to a relative's house about 10 miles away but as they have no lights (either on their bikes or in their brains) and it's about half an hour before darkness the female PC talking to them phones one lad's mother.

After the initial introductions it went like this:

"Well it's getting dark and they've got no lights. They clearly have no common sense and....what do you mean it's not your problem? He's YOUR son and his friend. We caught them on the motorway. Do you want them to have an accident? Can't you come and pick them up?....Well how about paying for a taxi then? What do you mean you're too busy?"

She hung up, glared at the two kids then looked at me and shook her head.

Due to the Duty of Care that the Police have in a situation like this the cops had to do something and couldn't just leave them where they were in case they went back on to the motorway. Further they were both 16 and still minors so someone had to take responsibility for them. The end result was that the two officers drove the kids to their destination 10 miles away while the Paramedics followed with the bicycles in the ambulance. The cycles couldn't be left at the roadside as the Duty of Care extended to their property.

At taxpayers' expense these two were chauffeur driven to where they wanted to go and an ambulance that could have been needed to save someone's life transported their property for them. All because their parents hadn't given them any common sense and couldn't have cared less about what happened to them.

Inspector Gerva looked at me and said "from me to you, well done. Officially however I'm obliged to tell you that you put yourself in danger and it might not have been the most appropriate measure".

I am pleased he's acknowledged that I did the right thing but am surprised this is officially 'wrong'.

"Err... Sir, we were on the hard shoulder"

"Statistically that is the most dangerous place to stop" he says with a smile.

We get to Toby's claims that he believes I'm lying about my involvement in July 7th. I point out how upsetting this still is and that it should never have been allowed to happen. The Inspector holds up the photocopy I'd given him of the letter from Snow Hill's Chief Super.

"Has anything been done about this?" he enquires.

"No, they've never apologised to me and neither has Toby. Sergeant Kerwan knew I was involved in 7/7 because I'd already told him".

He thinks for a minute and then says "well, maybe Toby thought you were saying that you were there when the bombs went off. I mean, I can see from this letter that you went in immediately after but maybe he thought you were saying you were there before".

Grasping at straws and splitting hairs. Toby had written 'in the area of the attacks' he didn't specify when.

"With respect Sir. Secondary devices? Unexploded primaries? The first wave of something MUCH worse? We didn't know what was going on. It was still officially a power surge when I went on duty. This is insulting to me, insulting to the City of London Police and insulting to a blast survivor".

I glance over at Sergeant Vivanco as I say this. She looks away quickly.

"Well, like I said" he continues "maybe that's why he said that because he thought you were claiming you were there before".

"Err...Sir, why would a Special be on duty before it happened?"

He ignores what I've just said and instead returns to the main document.

"Now, you didn't tell your Trainers for the Final Stage Training that you were under Action Plans".

I point out that Kerwan deliberately tried to get me to lie to him about this. I add that this was done, in my opinion, solely to get me fired. I also make it clear that I'd done what I believed was an acceptable alternative in discussing them with Inspector Postlethwaite and I hadn't simply forgotten.

He replies "it wasn't unreasonable for Sergeant Kerwan to do that in light of the situation".

"Sir, he tried to entrap me into lying to him". I glance over at Vivanco again and she again looks away and avoids eye contact.

He briefly becomes immersed in reading something on the page he's holding up and then changes the subject pointing out that if I don't get fully fit then Reg 13 will be invoked for medical grounds, regardless of what's gone before.

"Sir, if it can be proven to me that I'm not up to this job, objectively and impartially then I WILL happily leave. I am not prepared to put pride before anything else in a job where you have the power to deprive people of their liberty".

"Personally Lance I think you need to just forget about this and move on, you're dwelling on it too much".

"Because Sir, I've not been allowed a fair chance. I don't want privileges, I don't want special treatment. I just want to be treated like anyone else from my Intake and at the end of the day I need to have a marker in the sand to look back on and know that, whatever the outcome, I stood up for myself".

After just over three hours and three coffees (one decaf) we wrap this up. I have put my case forward and believe that I've been listened to but I'm not naive and expect very little will happen. What I want is both Kerwan and Esobé fired. What I will settle for is a reboot of my probation and all this shite forgotten. A fresh start and the switch reset so none of the bullying can be used to criticise my abilities.

Three weeks later Inspector Gerva sent an email. He stated that Esobé swearing in the background during my phone conversation with Tom had resulted in him passing this information on for 'intervention'. However he had given the job of intervening to Kerwan.

My remarks about the Diversity Placement and the expert witness statement of my friend the Drugs & Alcohol Misuse counsellor were passed on to PC Hambleworth to absorb.

Nothing else had warranted official action.

Everything else, he stated, was so far behind me that it should be left there and not dwelt on any more. He concluded by saying that I would remain on the same Area and that Kerwan and Esobé would continue to do their jobs with regard to signing off my NOS's and dealing with the machinations of my probation as before. He promised however, that he would personally oversee my remaining time under the PDU's jurisdiction.

I'd got not what I wanted but what I expected. No justice but at least a fresh start and I could now approach The Job without the constant fear that had been there for months. From now on I would be treated the way I always should have been, with objective and impartial analysis.

A couple of months later when I was declared fit for duty Inspector Gerva asked to see me. He was very pleased and happy that I would be joining Section again and when he found out that my partner was to be a veteran constable named Nathaniel he said how lucky I was to be with such a fine officer. He was grinning broadly, clearly happy that I'd made it this far and looking forward to hearing about how I did now I was back and fully fit.

What neither of us knew in that brief meeting where we shook hands and he wished me well, clapping me on the back as I left the room was that Kerwan had no intention of letting me make it through and 14 days later I was gone for good.

WRITTEN OFF

After I was put back to work on Restricted Duties I worked out of a satellite Nick in a village 12 miles from the Area HQ. Declan was my Sergeant and my acting skipper was a lad named Clive. Clive was thin and wiry and had a pencil moustache. He was mid twenties, engaged to be married and super confident. He reminded me of those kids at school who are good at football, popular with the girls and always in trouble with the teachers.

Not long after starting a Shift a body came into the bin and I was assigned by Clive to deal with it. A straight forward case. A prolific shoplifter was in Custody and needed a detective to deal with him. He had Previous up to his armpits and was probably going to cough it.

Declan phoned ahead to Dawn asking her to babysit me, as it was my first real case with CID and I would need help

I headed over to the main Station, ready for an open and shut case safe in the knowledge that my more experienced colleague was there to help me fill out the paperwork.

The guy was Polish, spoke passable but broken English and in Interview admitted the offence, said he knew it was wrong and that he had taken two packs of blank CDs to sell in order to buy food as he was homeless. He hadn't offered resistance when challenged at the door by a diminutive female Security guard and was compliant and co-operative 100% of the time. His only noticeable quirk was that he wanted extra helpings of the food prisoners are served (microwaved chips and beans, yummy!) and slurped down about six cups of hot chocolate with extra sugar.

After the Interview (clock ticking, roughly 90 minutes after we had first been given the job) I went up to see Dawn.

We had to do two files. Because of his Previous we were looking to remand him which meant a purple file for Magistrates Court and a red one for us. The contents of the red one had to be duplicated for the purple one. We had to print off six copies of his Previous, which meant murdering a couple of trees in the process. This was apparently for the Magistrates who aren't able to work a photocopier themselves and clearly don't understand the primary school concept of "one between two" let alone the expression 'carbon footprint'. We then had to obtain a Loser's Statement from the store (i.e. a statement from an employee saying what was stolen) and fill out a Remand Application detailing to the Custody skipper why we believe our lad should be detained and not released back into the community. This was evocative, emotive prose detailing all of his nefarious, scallywag deeds and the fact that he's homeless, unemployed and reportedly has a 30 per day heroin habit to fund. It contained expressions such as "danger to the public" and "serious risk of reoffence". We then had to fill in another form detailing his crime and synopsising the actions of it. We then fill out a list of evidence form. Then we consult the Crown Prosecution Service about the case but found as he'd admitted it didn't warrant their attention. We then got a PNB entry from the arresting officer photocopied and put that in duplicate into the files. Additionally, all the Custody paperwork went in as well.

I go back to visit our boy in the cells to find he's getting more agitated.

"When I be released?"

"When we're ready"

"But I've been here long time now"

"Because you've been arrested for AND admitted to a very serious offence. Just wait and be patient".

"Can I have another hot chocolate?"

"I don't see why not"

I approach the duty skipper at about 4pm and present him with the precious Remand Application. After perusing it he says it's too brief and adds that while "the nice Custody Sergeant" might let it through, it wouldn't make it past the magistrates in the morning. I go back and tell a slightly pissed off Dawn that she has to redo it. Half an hour later I go back to Custody.

At this point an Oriental gentleman of non-specific nomenclature is being booked in. Despite speaking English on arrest he has now forgotten how to. They took a guess at Vietnamese and phoned the translation line. This was set up some years ago and at any time of the day you will find nearly all languages it is possible to speak on a long list and you simply call the appropriate one up (or what you think it is, if the Suspect is unable to tell you themself) and they will explain to the person in Custody why they are there, translate the Caution and explain their Rights.

Sounds wonderful.

Only problem is that it costs between £9 and £12 per MINUTE and as Booking In takes at least fifteen minutes for a fully Compliant, Mother Tongue English speaker, you can be on there for up to an hour for a foreigner.

This thing, while guaranteed to enable a smooth Booking In is subject to the requisite hold music, long intros from robotic call centre operators and any Suspect who's upset wailing down the speakerphone in their own language and wasting time while lamenting the unfairness of being arrested when they were only selling a few pirated DVDs. After he stares blankly at the phone for a couple of minutes, while the translator bungs a few phrases at him that he clearly doesn't understand, she is thanked for her time and the skipper hangs up. This lasted about five or six minutes and will have cost between fifty four and seventy two pounds. The skipper then tries Mandarin Chinese. This turned out to be the oil strike he was looking for as the Suspect begins chatting happily to the operator.

Just then the skipper's own mobile phone rings and he says "sorry, gotta take this, important call" and steps into the back room which has no door. For the next ten minutes, presumably thinking we can't hear him, he chats loudly about a patio door he's ordered for his house while the translation line operator holds in silence, the

Suspect looks bored, the arresting officer looks at me and raises his eyebrows and I try not to show any emotion.

"Is she still there?" I ask, motioning to the phone.

"Oh yes" the arresting officer replies.

Just then the operator pipes up "sorry, what was that".

I reply loudly in the direction of the speakerphone. "Sorry, we are just dealing with a serious problem. Thank you for holding".

After about ninety to 120 pounds of taxpayers' money has been burned like charcoal briquettes while the skipper waffles on about his personal life, he returns and finalises booking in the DVD seller and getting him a cell. He checks my form again and says it's still not good enough. We approach the Duty CID Evidence Assessment officer for advice who examines it and in exasperation says it's fine and as it's not a murder does NOT need a two page explanation. We redo it yet again and finally it is deemed good enough and the Suspect is brought out. I forewarn the Custody skipper that "he might get larey" as he is clearly expecting to be released. He is walked up to the Custody desk and as the Shift has just changed another skipper tells him what's going to happen. He absently reads the pieces of paper he's just been handed while the Sergeant is talking to him.

I push them down and tap him on the arm. "Can you listen to what the Sergeant's saying, this is important".

He grunts and while leaning on the counter with his head on his forearms makes a passing attempt to take in what he's being told. Two uniformed officers who've just booked someone in have heard my warning of potential tantrum throwing and are hanging about in case he kicks off. It slowly dawns on him that he's not leaving and he tries to argue that he should go to Court next week not tomorrow morning and that he should be released. The skipper patiently explains that's not the case and remands him for the night. The Uniformed officers offer to take him back but I escort him while he grizzles and moans that "you promised me I would be released".

I point out I said no such thing and that as he's homeless he will get a warm bed for the night, a blanket, more food and as much hot chocolate as the gaoler is willing to take to him. He goes back in with a final few grumbles and throws himself down on the cot, arms folded in a bratty sulk.

Me and Dawn spent eight hours on this case. It would have taken longer if I'd been on my own but Dawn was more experienced. We used about 200 sheets of A4, two case files and a couple of cassettes for the Interview. We burned diesel both to deal with him and for the Loser's Statement which was collected after he had been nicked.

The cost of this whole thing, in my estimation, would have been in the region of £1000.

All for £14 of CDs.

Next morning he attended Magistrates' Court and was found guilty of shoplifting. He was fined £150 but as he had spent 22 hours in Police Custody they felt he had suffered enough and wrote it off meaning he paid nothing.

TEEING OFF IN THE WAKE

A PCSO sticks his head into the CID office, 20 minutes before knocking off time.

"That lad's been at it again" he says, peering round the doorframe from the kitchen.

Some local scrote had decided to take a golf club to numerous parked cars in the street adjacent to the Nick. We'd heard about this earlier but there was no sign of the perpetrator and Uniform were dealing with it. He's now come back which means that three of my colleagues have damaged vehicles due to not being able to leave their own cars at the station and having to use the surrounding streets to park up.

"Who own the blue Astra?"

Mickey puts up his hand. The PCSO winces. "Ooh dear, that's got a nasty dent in the driver's side door and the wing mirror's been knocked off".

Apparently whoever did this has now gone home and home is conveniently about 200 yards from the crime scene. The PCSO also cheerfully informs us that the Suspect has mental issues. He adds further that there's not much he or his fellow PCSOs can do as they are by the nature of their job, non-confrontational.

We start to debate what to do next. That takes 30 seconds. Declan and Clive decide we should go round there and nick him. Fine and Dandy. We then spend ten more minutes debating who should go.

This was the day after I had been officially signed back on as fully fit for duty after seven months. During that time I had avoided absolutely all confrontation as per the risk assessment. As soon as they asked for volunteers I put my hand up and Declan told me privately later that "when you offered to go I felt a warm glow inside me. Then you went and spoilt it by putting your long, black Matrix coat on".

Me and about seven others pile round to a house two streets away where a tall uniformed Bobby and a large collection of people in what are blatantly funeral clothes are gathered in front of a big, detached house. This is a wake for a dead relative, buried only a few hours before. There is also another PCSO on scene and some kid who I at first thought was connected to the Suspect by the ferrety way he kept hanging around but turned out was just some local, bored chav being nosey.

The PC asks us if we are there to help. We reply yes. He then asks if we are wearing Stabbies. We reply no. We then have to walk back to the Nick and put on our body armour. I opted for the covert option, which meant my chest looked like it was wearing a nappy. We then run back to the scene. 22 year old Adrian is practically sprinting, a big grin on his face.

"Mmm, you can smell the testosterone" I muse.

"Fuck it, this is what I joined for" he says, not taking his eyes off the destination.

"Yes I'd heard that" I reply "also heard you took a sulk and threatened to resign if you had to remain in CID longer than five months".

"Too right, I would as well. I joined to be a copper not do bloody CID" he says, his acne catching the fading sunlight in this formerly picturesque village.

Clive, Declan and Dawn then show up. Clive is dressed sensibly in body armour with his jacket zipped up over the top. Declan is driving an unmarked Police vehicle and has sunglasses on, even though it's twilight. He also has his jacket off and his shirt sleeves rolled up. Dawn is wearing a reasonably tight, size 11 black dress which comes to about 6 inches above her knees. She has her Stabby with "Police" written on it, over the top. We try not to giggle.

Everyone is in Bad Boys 2 mode.

Clive and the uniformed PC then mooch off to the Suspect's house for a recce and I chat to one or two of the people in funeral garb. One of them shows me a photo on a digital camera of a bloke with a nasty, bleeding gash above his right eye and blood on his once-white shirt. Apparently when the Suspect was cycling around teeing off with people's automobiles, two of the funeral party challenged him as he cycled past with the words "why are you doing this, we've just buried our mum?" to which he screeched to a halt, dismounted and clobbered one of them over the head with the 9 iron.

After a few more minutes Declan tells us all to go towards the scene of the potential arrest and we move as a big group to the house, three piling into the unmarked car for a journey lasting two minutes on foot.

I get there to find Clive and Dawn (who is shaking her pepper spray vigorously as per Force regulations and looking like something from a Terry Gilliam movie) outside the house with the Beat Bobby. Clive motions me to remain out of sight and all ten of us loiter, one hand on our batons, behind the hedge at the end of the cul-de-sac with our breath held ready for the sounds of a violent kafuffle or the words "FUCK FUCK HEEEELP!".

The whole thing resembles the build up to the opening ruck in The Football Factory·

Two minutes later Clive shouts "It's ok. Stand down" and I see the Beat Bobby leading a lad in a baseball cap by the arm, who is smoking a fag and swaggering arrogantly, towards the Police car.

We loiter for a bit. Dawn is tasked with taking a Statement. David is given the job of accompanying the guy to Custody. I get in the unmarked car for the journey back to the Nick. Clive sticks his head in the driver's side and says to Declan with a smile "they never fight any more".

A violent, potentially deranged thug took a golf club to seven or eight parked cars, three of which belonged to Police officers and thumped someone who challenged him, committing not only multiple criminal damage but also GBH.

A PCSO was the first to deal BUT as he is "non-confrontational" was unable to do anything other than come and get us. We spent about 15 minutes fannying about pulling on body armour and PPE and more time debating the Risk Assessment. Ten CID, one Beat Bobby and two PCSOs and, like many such situations, it ended with complete compliance and the neighbourhood getting high from inhaling the passive smell of coppers' testosterone.

The officer whose car was wrecked, Mickey, had to pay 250 excess on his insurance and lost his no claims bonus.

The man belted with the 9 iron had to go to hospital.

Thousands of pounds worth of damage and a drawn out conclusion to something that could easily have been controlled if we had any type of power to be judicious in our use of force (march round there en masse, knock once, if it's not answered kick the door in and drag him out).

He was also allowed to finish his fag before getting in the car. Lit cigarrettes burn at 300 degrees centigrade. Why on Earth the officer making the arrest felt it appropriate to let this guy smoke his tab on the way to the Police car is beyond comprehension. Presumably as he was being Compliant it was felt it would only piss him off if he was ordered to put it out. However as he was already wanted for questioning for violent behaviour committed less than an hour previously it would have been common sense to assume he could use it as a weapon. The English Police's 'softly softly' approach which makes it's officers afraid to use more than the absolute minimum force (in this case a light grip on the Suspect's upper arm) could have got this Constable invalided out of the Job and wearing an eye patch for the rest of his life.

The following day while sitting in our satellite hub doing paperwork, we get the heart warming news that the chav equivalent of Tiger Woods was bailed the same night he got arrested.

He went to the Nick and after being questioned was released into the community. He went back to the house he was arrested at, which is on the same street as the cars he vandalised and the GBH he committed. Imagine if you'd just spent four hours in Casualty getting your bonse sewn back together and the bloke you knew had done it was sauntering past your kitchen window the morning after the crime.

The only reason we could think of for why he wasn't remanded in custody was that whoever was tasked to deal with the case didn't want the arse ache of compiling a Remand file and the hours of work that would entail so took the simpler option, regardless of the potential risk to innocent people or possible revenge attacks that may be perpetrated on the Suspect by his irate victims.

Because he had "mental issues" (i.e. can't control his temper) he also got a lift home from the Police after being bailed as they have to remember that good ole Duty of Care.

COULDN'T GIVE A MONKEY'S

Luck of the draw one Wednesday afternoon got me and Samson a Theft job to handle.

The case file notes read that a black male had been arrested at a supermarket four miles from the Nick. He had tried to pinch a packet of sandwiches and was spotted and challenged at the door by shop security. He kicked off and tried to escape and was brought to the floor by the security guard and the assistant manager. It took 45 minutes for the Police to arrive, during which time the thief wriggled, kicked and swore and was far from compliant. He'd apparently started to behave once the cops turned up though and was conveyed to the Nick without further misbehaviour.

He was mine and Samson's Body and was waiting to see us in the Cells.

We went down and did the usual introductory preamble.

"Hi, I'm PC Manley, this is PC Keitel. We'll be interviewing you shortly. Is everything ok? Can we get you a drink or anything?"

"Yeah, a coffee please mate".

Me and Samson tossed a coin to see who led the Interview and he won meaning I sat there while he questioned the bloke, only chipping in if I thought it was relevant.

The guy admitted to stealing the sarnies and said it was because he had got out of prison a week ago and had to wait at least ten days to get any Benefit money off the Social Security. This was blatantly unfair as he was released from gaol without any cash or access to it. They refused to grant him a loan and he said he was starving and had no choice.

He then started to claim that the security guard had used excessive force when restraining him. Samson asked him to describe what had happened and he replied that he was held on the floor with his arm up behind his back while two blokes sat or knelt on him. Samson asked if he was resisting being detained. He begrudgingly admitted that he was. Samson asked him in light of that if he still felt that the force used was unnecessary. He replied "no, I s'pose not".

He then tried a different tack which threw the case into another light completely and ended up with a further two hours work for the pair of us.

"That manager that was kneeling on me. He called me a monkey you know".

Me and Samson look at each other and Samson then leans towards the wall mic and says loudly and clearly "do you want us to do anything about what you've just said?".

"What do you mean?"

"Do you want us to investigate what you've just told us?"

As anyone listening to the tape later would know I was in the room too from the introductions at the start I add "yes, do you want us to follow this up? Do you want to make a complaint against him for doing that?"

"Yeah, I do. He was racist".

Both me and Samson are now both covered with regard to responding 'appropriately' to what was just said, but both know it means we will have to visit the supermarket as soon as this is concluded

After the Interview is over I walk the Suspect back to his cell.

"Want something to eat?" I ask, feeling mildly sorry for him as he claims to have stolen the food solely because he was hungry and penniless.

"Is it that microwave stuff?"

"Yeah, I believe so"

"Urrgh! Fuck that, I'm not eating that shit".

I close the door to his cell and meet with Samson back on the CID floor.

We consult our skipper, Clive who says to go back to the store and get a Statement off the manager alleged to have used the racist term and after that to see if anyone else was witness to what he did or didn't say.

At the supermarket we are taken into the empty staff room and I get out a Statement form.

"Now then, we've interviewed the Suspect in this case. It's fairly straight forward. However he's made an allegation that you used racist language against him while you were detaining him before the Police arrived. Can you offer any explanation as to why he might have said that?"

"I know what he's trying to do" he replies shaking his head and smiling. "While he was trying to fight with me and the Security guard he said 'my arm's hurting' because I had him in a Half Nelson. I replied 'I couldn't give a monkey's!' " .

"Fair enough, I need to take a Statement though, mainly in case there's any further comeback about this. Did anyone else hear you say that?"

"Yeah, Don the Security guard. Do you want me to call him?"

"No, it's ok my colleague will go and find him". Samson leaves to locate the witness and I write out the Statement with the manager's version of what was said.

The guard arrives as we're finishing up and after the manager has left we ask him the same question. He corroborates that it was 'couldn't give a monkey's' and we get a Statement from him too.

We drive back to the Nick. As it's now rush hour, this takes half an hour.

We consult Clive again who reads the Statements and says "fair enough, but just to be on the safest side, go and see the Duty Guv'nor and tell her that the guy might be making a complaint against the store but not us on his way to Court tomorrow".

I go up the Section Inspectors' office. It's my old campus skipper from uni who's recently been promoted. Odd seeing her in uniform, even odder having to call her Ma'am.

"Oh, hello Lance" she says smiling "what can I do for you?"

"Sar...err, Ma'am, just so you know. The guy in cell 5 brought in for Theft. He's coughed it but may be making a complaint against the store he stole them from on his way to the magistrates tomorrow".

"And why's that?" she asks, still tapping away on her PC.

"He claimed he was called a monkey by the store manager. We got two Statements that say what was actually said was 'I couldn't give a monkeys' though".

She looks at me and tuts "rather silly thing for someone to say to a black man don't you think? Easy to be misunderstood".

I grunt and then thank her for her time and meet up with Samson again to conclude the case file.

Whether or not the Suspect genuinely believed he was called a monkey will never be known to anyone but him. What is totally beyond the pale though is that two cops investigating this guy for a Theft where he was abusive and aggressive to store staff had to involve their skipper and an Inspector and divert all their attention to checking out whether a racist word had been uttered. This was solely to cover the arse of the Force so that if his solicitor did raise the issue then the Interview tape would prove both me and Samson had offered to follow it up and there were two Witness Statements in the file to prove it hadn't happened, collected at the earliest opportunity. Furthermore, the Duty Guv'nor was in the loop to back us up if need be.

PORCOPHOBIA

As was usual for the low level CID work on the attachment, we arrived at the Nick one afternoon to be told that there were three cases and then asked 'who wants the first one?' Details were not forthcoming so I decided to jump in the plunge pool and take a chance.

A Domestic Violence. Positive Intervention Policy. Mother and Son.

While leafing through the case file I discover the following.

A 17 year old lad had turned up at his mother's flat and during an argument about his younger brother had begun chastising his mum for her lack of parenting skills to which she'd taken off her flip flop and hit him with it once on the forearm and then upside the head three or four times. He in response hurled his microwave corn beef hash on the floor, spattering peas and mashed potato on the sofa and the linoleum.

Police were called, both got nicked. Her for Common Assault, him for Criminal Damage.

While preparing the case file I see photos of the lad and his supposed injuries, which aren't there. A photo of a skinny arm and the back of his neck reveal no visible wounds or welts and appear in duplicate in the file. Accompanying these are two photos marked exhibit AA/001 and AA/002, of the dinner on the floor.

I check his Previous on the Intranet, he has lots. I check her Previous, she has even more.

Their address has a history of Domestic Violence incidents, most of which are marked "No Further Action" and the pair of them are a royal pain in the arse to the Police.

I prepare for Interview and decide to do the lad first to see what he has to say for himself and also because he was the original 'victim'.

A scruffy teenager is woken from his nap in a cell and given the requisite greeting, introductions and offer of a hot drink. He accepts a hot chocolate and during Interview is quite articulate, reasonable and calm and basically admits to hurling his nourishing meal on the floor but only after being hit several times. He also says he took a wet sponge and began to wipe up the food. However this was after the Police arrived and says he can understand now that maybe they thought he was trying to dispose of evidence.

We put him back in the cell.

I look at the notes, make a few new ones and then pull the mother out for Interview. As soon as the hatch was dropped on her cell door she began moaning about what a little git her eldest son is and how she's not sorry she hit him. This plus the other pearls of maternal wisdom she spouted after arrest are all Significant Statements and have to be written down and put to her in Interview. Before she spouts off too many I offer her a hot drink and she opts for coffee.

Myself and a female colleague called Katrina then interview her where she comes out with some right blinders of conversational joy. These include objecting to being called a "dopey old pig" by her son because she's scared of pigs and that she wants to go on Jeremy Kyle to tell the world what a horrible little bugger her boy is. She is wearing the 'weapon' from the crime scene and takes if off her foot, waving it about and slapping it against her arm to illustrate what happened. I have to say "for the benefit of the tape the Suspect is miming with her shoe". The whole time she's performing I avoid making eye contact with Katrina because I know I'll probably giggle.

As expected, we get her life story where she moans and complains about her son, his friend who was there too and how horrible her life is in general. She then gets upset and starts to cry. The Duty of Care kicks in and in a clear voice, speaking slower than normal while leaning towards the mic I say "would you like us to suspend this Interview while you take a couple of minutes to compose yourself?".

She looks at me blankly and replies "what does it mean, pose myself?"

At this I can't hold back any more and burst out laughing as does Katrina. We quickly get ourselves under control and I rephrase the question as "would you like a couple of minutes to calm down?" which she accepts.

We note the time verbally, switch off the tape and she blags another coffee. Guessing caffeine is not a good idea at this moment I get her a hot chocolate and say that we're all out of Lavazza.

We start again and after more stories of misery and woe she begins moaning that her back hurts. Again in a clear voice, speaking slower than normal while leaning towards the mic me and Katrina both say "would you like to suspend the Interview while you see the nurse?" She refuses. We offer again. She says she can hang on, it only hurts when she stands up.

We finish and put her back in the cell.

An hour and a half later we decide after consulting line managers that the best thing to do is Refuse Charge him and Caution her. The lad is brought out of his cell, given his mobile phone back and sent on his way. The mother is then brought out. The Custody skipper looks down at her from his Desk.

"We meet again" he says, looking over his spectacles.

"It's not me it's my boy, little git" she grumbles.

"Well this officer has asked me to Caution you which I'm willing to do, BUT if we keep meeting like this I WILL send you to Court".

"Oh, will you?" she says, folding her arms and looking away.

"Yes, I WILL."

She is Cautioned, signs the forms and we get her stuff together for her.

"Can I see the nurse?" she says, wincing and holding her back with her hands.

"I think she's busy now" the skipper tells her.

Just then the nurse walks up behind the Sergeant and begins filling out a Custody Record.

"Ooh nurse, could you look at me please?" she says in a whining plead

"I'm very busy now" she replies, not looking up from her writing.

"Ooh, I'm in such pain, could you massage my back for me?"

The nurse looks up at me and raises her eyes heavenwards. "I don't do massages" she snaps and walks off.

"Not even I get those" the skipper japes.

She gets back her property and walks out. Back no longer hurting it appears.

Two CID officers, their line managers, a Custody skipper, an Evidence Assessment Officer and the nurse all had to interact with this pair of idiots. Four slaps with a flip flop resulted in him hurling his food on the floor in a temper and them both getting nicked.

The Positive Intervention policy was brought in to give the Police power where they formerly didn't have it and be able to act to prevent serious assault or murder in Domestic Violence situations. Unfortunately this policy means some cops will nick anyone deemed to be involved rather than judge the situation on its merits just to prove they did something.

Common sense would have been to have simply barked at the kid, "RIGHT YOU! Clean that mess up and piss off. You come back here again and I'll nick you".

THE NEW NICK

After years of preparation, we were excited to be informed that our new Area Police Station was finally ready.

The thing had been commissioned yonks ago and, while using the ancient, pre-Life on Mars Stations throughout the Area, we sat trembling with anticipation for the day we could move into this slick, high-tec, 21st century base of operations.

Combining the current three active Stations within our Area's jurisdiction and negating any further need to use the decrepit Custody Suite at the current Area HQ, we were only awaiting the final lick of paint and fitted fuse before we could begin work in our spangly, new, dog's bollocks Nick.

Our guided tour was planned three weeks in advance and true to form was still lacking cohesion an hour before we set off to attend it. We were told to bring along 'High-Viz and a hard hat' due to the work still going on within this gargantuan monument to Law and Order. A hard hat can realistically stop your bonse from caving in (or at least reduce a fatality to a coma) but I fail to see how wearing a Teletubby coat will make a falling piece of scaffolding swerve to one side at the last second. Maybe they thought it was like The Matrix and we could do a 'Bullet Time' limbo dance, testing the limits of our lumbar vertebrae while the falling object sailed past, leaving ripples in the air in its wake.

The final decision was 'go as you are' and we arrived at a huge car park, the size of four football pitches with a steel fence around it. All intimidating-looking with grey mesh and sloping struts on the top. The whole thing was impressive, apart from the one fundamental flaw.

Its height.

At about six and a half feet at the tallest point it was likely that the local scrotes would be hoying bits of concrete and loose paving slabs over the side with joyful abandonment before the inaugural ceremony was over.

The Station was very close to a part of town known to contain numerous Nominals and other undesirable denizens who wouldn't need to go far to exact revenge for getting nicked on Sus Theft the day before. To really make it perfect, there was a large copse of trees facing the car park, at the top of a steep grassy rise. This meant you could see right into the car park from the highest point amongst the leafy glade. Ideal hiding place for anyone with the strength to pull a catapult with the added bonus of a sharp, downward angle to facilitate better aiming.

We entered the Station in a group of about 20 and stood in an area the size of a small shopping centre watching blokes in yellow waistcoats climbing ladders and waited. The sheer vastness of the thing took your breath away as it was roughly the same size as a shopping mall. The acres of unused space within it defied belief. The whole thing was geared towards astounding height, length and breadth which the architect HAD managed to achieve. Magnificent glass walls meant that everyone could be seen clearly along with whatever they were doing or not doing. The walk along the 150 metres from one side of the ground floor to the other was very impressive and awe inspiring.

After 30 minutes of waiting Declan had the initiative to phone someone who told us to go back outside. Assembling just beyond the main entrance we were approached by a bloke with a clipboard who introduced himself as a retired officer and led us around our new place of work.

Then the rot started to set in, while the final coats of paint were still drying on the walls.

We entered the new high-tech Custody Suite to be confronted with a Booking In area that has a desk about eight feet off the floor.

This is designed to create a sense of power and intimidation to those facing the quiet wrath of the Duty Sergeant(s) as they are deprived of their liberty/ given a Caution/ PND'd etc. There are touch screens for certain procedures in four separate places which means that you could potentially have four Custody skippers working simultaneously. Then it was pointed out that if a short arse or a juvenile was being booked in they would not be able to see over the edge and if the skipper was sitting down on a quiet shift there might be the comedic silent scene of him not knowing that a shy but vertically challenged colleague was waiting for his attention a few feet below behind the grey Formica.

We then entered the cell area and were initially impressed by the layout. Constant Supervision cells with unbreakable, transparent doors meaning that the officer who drew the short straw won't have to sit with the door open while playing the games on his mobile phone out of boredom watching someone they've nicked snoring through a hangover. Then a voice behind me points out that the unbreakable doors were tested at another Station and are anything but.

A huge, long, horizontal scar runs the length of the corridor wall, round the corner and along the next wall as far as Booking In. This was originally the "panic" bar, in case you needed urgent assistance while dealing with a violent detainee. Great idea until they realised that:

a). The bastard thing was activated by wayward limbs, spiteful guests or simply fat arses and;

b). The plastic strip (think of the rubber hold rail on an escalator but thinner) could be ripped out and used as a weapon.

So back to the drawing board on that one, a week or two before the Nick becomes functional.

Then we were taken to Custody's arrival area. This is similar to an airlock with enough room for two vans and concertinaed, folding doors like you get on a warehouse. The guide proudly tells us that the internal doors can't be opened until the outer doors are closed to ensure maximum security when people are brought in.

I raise my hand. "What if the outer door can't be closed, can the internal safety thing be overridden".

He looks puzzled and says he doesn't know. This undoubtedly means it can't and that if the system is up the swanny and you have a prisoner in a caged van you'll be fine but anyone who gets larey as they arrive in the car/ minibus/ on foot will have to be detained in the outer shell, while those in the warmth of the main Station can only look on helplessly through the window as you try to subdue your unwilling guest.

We go upstairs to visit the SMT level. This is CIs and above. The Area Commander will be here. His is the only office that doesn't have the full glass, goldfish bowl effect and in fact has almost complete privacy via normal non see-thru walls.

We go in to his office and take it in turns to sit in the chair. It is the size of a reasonable studio flat

"Enjoy it Lance" Mervin japes from the other side of the desk. "Last time you'll be sitting there".

"Yeah? But I imagine you'll be on THAT side of his desk a fair few times eh?"

We are then told by the guide that the whole premises are leased from a private company as they worked out it was cheaper to do that than buy it. His next nugget of information is that it costs around 15 grand per DESK (as it's a flat fee for a number of years). You have to wonder how many millions this is costing the public.

We finally get to the CID bit and like eager school kids squabbling for the back seat on the bus Declan and the two acting skippers run in and begin deciding which desk they're going to have. After this initial joy has passed the Sergeant sees the vast air conditioning unit right outside the windows, about 20 metres across, blocking two thirds of the view.

"Errr…the window's can't be opened?" he puts to the guide.

"No, safety feature, all floors".

"What if the air con packs up?"

"Oh, errr…I'm sure there's a plan B".

If it's a summer like 2006 when it was 35 degrees Celsius in July, the building will be uninhabitable. Due to the lovely Human Rights Act the pendulum will swing in the Police staff's favour and they will be entitled to leave the building until it's fixed. This would ultimately result in the entire Area grinding down until the air con's up and running again.

We are casually told that there are only 2 hot water points in this whole, cathedral-esque Nick. One in Custody for prisoners and another in the canteen, provided by the leaser. It is a condition of the contract that no kettles are to be brought in. This means yet again that the only people who can get free drinks officially are prisoners.

As we leave I glance up. On the third floor is a geezer in a yellow waistcoat. He is leaning over the balcony, cleaning the glass panel with a squeegee. He does not have anything securing the squeegee to his hand. We are directly below him.

The final thing we see is the staff gym. It is the smallest gym I've ever seen and has no showers. They are 40 metres away up the corridor meaning sweaty, cops and PSEs in shorts and vests will have to meander past visitors and SMT to get changed. One of the showers is disabled even though the gym has no disabled access.

As we leave I spy the SMT car park. Unlike the one for the plebs it has a 20 feet high steel fence, meaning the Chief Super's BMW can't be catapulted by kids hiding amongst the trees.

Gotta love it.

BACKING UP THE MINIONS

While I was filling out the Custody Record for a woman caught with Class A drugs a rather serious looking chap in a fairly horrid sports anorak walked into the Custody Suite.

I could tell this was a Guv'nor for no reason other than he didn't ask the Custody skipper's permission before walking behind the counter.

I moved the chair from between him and the shopkeeper's hatch at the side and sure enough the anorak came off to reveal three pips per shoulder. He was the Area Chief Inspector, third from top in the SMT.

A bloke in his 60s was being Booked Out after accepting a PND. The CI glared at him and, after placing his jacket over the back of the skipper's chair interrupted what was going on to identify himself.

"Mr Smith? I'm Chief Inspector Cade. I've come down here just to speak to you. I've heard a lot about you".

The old man looked a bit confused.

"I understand you shoved one of my officers. One of my PCSOs."

"Well he pushed me first...." the soon-to-be-released prisoner mumbles back.

"NO!" the CI barks at him "Don't interrupt and don't get into it. Just listen. I do NOT tolerate assaults on my officers. In future think twice before you think about assaulting one of my staff".

"Yeah but he pushed me"

"NO! DON'T get into it mate, just be quiet. If this happens

again you won't be dealt with so leniently. Just behave like a decent human being and keep your hands to yourself".

He takes his coat and walks out.

"He pushed me, he started it" the old man grumbles.

"I'm not listening and I don't want to know" the CI snaps without looking at him, swiping the door release with his card and letting himself out.

The old codger turns on the skipper. "One rule for one and one rule for another, hey?"

"Mr Smith, it's very rare that the Chief Inspector comes down here, he's clearly very angry with what you did. I would bear that in mind if I was you".

Some mumbling later, he's released into the streets.

It was good to see this and warm glow-inducing to know Senior Management were so annoyed that one of the soldier ants had been assaulted that a CI came into the basement to vent his spleen at the perpetrator. For him to be so visibly pro active in front of random officers is the way it should always be.

Maybe cops should have "Righteous Bollocking" training along with how to understand the Sikh calendar or how to be nice to the homeless.

SCREEN WASH

Sometimes a common sense reaction can still be achieved in the face of ludicrous self importance.

A highly unpopular Constable entered the station one afternoon and while parking his car in one of the few available spaces for anyone who isn't Senior Management, a visitor or a Response driver he spotted another officer with the hood of his VW Beetle up, filling the windscreen water tank with Police issue screen wash.

Crimson with rage at this abuse of privilege and the insurmountable lack of Integrity he marched straight to the Section skipper's office and demanded that someone arrest the Constable, adding "and if you don't do it then I will".

Attempts by the skipper to placate the fuming cop and find out what was going on were simply met with blustering indignation about abuse of company property and the lack of honesty in taking a product designated for Police vehicles.

Realising he was going to get nowhere, the skipper suggested that they both go and see the Chief Inspector.

In the Chief's office the righteous officer related his story again, adding "and I've got a witness Sir. PC Emblethorpe was vacuuming his car in the next bay and can confirm it".

The Sergeant then said "well in that case I want him nicked as well for abstracting electricity".

The Chief looked at them and without standing up snapped "FUCK OFF the pair of you...and get out of my office".

FINAL PHASE TUTOR

NATHANIEL

When I rejoined Core Section following the CID attachment my final tutor was an Old School perfectionist named Nathaniel.

Nathaniel had been in The Job for 22 years. Two years in the Met before transferring away to calmer climes. He was in his early fifties, very straight laced and whippet thin.

He had a civilian gallantry medal awarded by a member of Royalty for taking a gun off an armed robber he had chased and arrested while unarmed on foot,

His son was a PCSO at a neighbouring Nick who was about to apply for The Job via the shortcut system they had recently introduced for Community Support Officers to take the step up into the world of possessing a Warrant Card.

Nathaniel also Acted Up as Section skipper if our real one Sergeant Rine was off for any reason.

He was completely professional at all times while on duty and very slick. Able to issue all manner of tickets, think laterally to solve problems (such as VDRS-ing a bloke who didn't speak any English by borrowing his phone and getting the bloke's English speaking brother to translate) and always on the ball with regard to procedure, new legislation and paperwork. Watching him deal with people was like watching a robot as he was totally confident in his own abilities and knew exactly what needed to be done.

When the Federation found out I was assigned to him as my tutor I was reassured that he was a "top bloke" and would be a very good partner.

The PDU Inspector had waxed lyrical on how good Nathaniel was and mentioned the gallantry medal, adding that Nathaniel was a humble man and did not boast about it and might not even bring it up (he didn't).

Sergeant Rine also spoke very highly of Nathaniel, singing his praises and noting that he was one of the few officers that had adapted smoothly over the years to the myriad changes in Force policy.

After three months off sick at home, two on a computer and a further two on Non-Confrontational, Restricted Duties I had had only had one month of fully active service out of seven. This was in a CID attachment so my Policing had been limited to the role of a detective. I had not been with core Section since July of the previous year and only then for four days. My third and longest phase was the previous May, meaning it was one month shy of a year since I had been fully immersed in uniformed Response Team work.

Expecting to be eased back in gradually it was a complete shock to find out that while Nathaniel was indeed an exceptional officer, he was a piss poor tutor.

As a perfectionist he expected me to have the same high standards as him, which I did but was unable to match his prowess on the battlefield. He would watch me do something and then give constructive feedback. He would then demonstrate how he did it and expect me to follow his example. All fine and dandy so far. Only problem was he would expect it to be spot-on the second time and would criticise me heavily in writing if it wasn't.

As my Action Plans from Sergeant Kerwan were still in place, Nathaniel was obliged to fill out a daily feedback form to submit to the PDU.

Throughout the CID attachment we were told that when taking a witness Statement you first get them to tell the story and listen without interrupting and do not make notes. Then you ask them to repeat it and make brief notes in your Day book. Finally you get them to tell it a third time and this time you write out the Statement as they speak, pausing them if you need time. This is meant to enable consistency on their part and for you to get the statement accurate.

One Shift he watched me take a Witness Statement and afterwards pointed out that, in his opinion it would be inadmissible in Court as I had not taken it in direct speech and had in fact written it as I thought she'd said it. When I pointed out that was how we'd been trained by CID he shook his head and replied "I refuse to believe you were taught to take Statements like THAT!"

Talking later my Declan, who'd supervised me in CID he confirmed with an amused chuckle that of course that was the way that you were supposed to do it and you could even write out the Statement yourself at the Nick and get the witness to sign it later provided they agreed it was what they had seen or heard.

I watched Nathaniel take a Statement at around 4am from a very patient and public spirited witness to a violent assault. The woman had seen it from her bedroom window and called the Police. The statement took 1 ½ hours and was about seven pages long. It was the most detailed I'd ever seen and would have made Stephen King proud with its vivid narrative description.

Three days later I took a statement from the manager of a newsagent for a shoplifting. I was as attentive to detail as I had seen Nathaniel be. He sat there and watched me do it. After he said that I had wasted time and that I hadn't needed to do it like that at all. In his opinion I should have had the common sense to realise that the assault was serious and required a detailed statement whereas an attempted shoplifting only required a brief one. He again put this in writing to the PDU.

I pointed out the amount of time I'd had off sick and away from Section and Nathaniel replied "but you've just come out of CID, surely your paperwork and statement taking should be shit hot".

The following day he was on Annual Leave and I got partnered with another lad off the Section called Rodney. Half an hour before knocking off time we needed to get a Statement. Rodney wrote it out at the Nick, took it round to the witness's house and got him to read then sign it. This was not done to cut corners. Rodney believed this was acceptable as did my former CID skipper.

Another time he castigated me for spending over the allotted hour on my Refs when I could have been doing paperwork. This again was part of the daily reports to Sergeant Kerwan. The following Shift a cop off our Section spent two hours of a Night duty watching TV.

DRUNKEN CHAVS

Beloved of many Police customers is alcohol.

They don't seem to care what shape or size it is, as long as it gets them utterly steaming and unable to enunciate properly or stand up. Polite society do this in the pub or at home not in the street while burbling abuse at passers by.

Underage drinking is a problem in England like it is everywhere else. Nowadays, with the softly softly approach adopted towards these ill disciplined monsters they have evolved into a species that no longer fear or respect the Police or what they represent. The only thing they fear is being deprived of their liberty even though Arrest is meant to be the ultimate option in a Beat Bobby's repertoire.

At the end of the day they fear and respect any of their own fraternity that are able to handle themselves physically. They respect the dying breed of Old School coppers that take no nonsense and will nick immediately given justification. They do not respect PCSOs, older people, the fact that young children are present or general common values. They are semi-feral and terrifying to anyone who isn't able to stand up for themselves or adjust to this new world of a bored, aggressive, violent youth that have little to do and have grown up without any fear of authority.

My father was a child during the Second World War and would say that coppers were feared in the 1940s for the simple reason that if you were caught scrumping apples or fighting they would give you a clip round the ear and promise that next time they'd tell your dad.

A call to a small, posh village, (with requisite quaint post office and thatched cottages) reveals three teenagers standing opposite the post office leaning on a fence. A PCSO and a Village Warden are standing well away from them and tell us over the radio that the kids were with a lad who ran off when asked why he had a crate of Carlsberg Special Brew stuffed up his hoody. I get out the car and the kids react with no more interest than if someone had just changed the channel on the TV.

I tell them they've been ID'd as being seen with a suspected thief and ask their names and addresses.

"Wadyouwantmyname'n'addressfor?"

"I've just told you why"

With much mumbling and me asking them to repeat bits they give me their details which I check with Control. One comes back as having warning markers for violence and another has Previous for Theft.

While I'm asking for their details and relaying this info over the air the three of them keep shrieking, singing and generally making communication difficult. I repeatedly tell them to be quiet to which they look all sheepish and for about five seconds shut up and then they're off again. I eventually get a brainwave and point out that the longer they keep acting like idiots the longer they are going to be detained while I ascertain if they have told me the truth about their ID and addresses.

None have mobile phones so they are kept by the side of the road while Nathaniel chats to the PCSO. The lad appears about 17 and is unshaven and chewing gum while talking to me. He reeks of alcohol and when told that drinking in a public place while underage is an offence he states with a smirk that he didn't know. One of the girls keeps blubbing and it's clearly not to do with us as she is yakking to her mates every time the waterworks start. I ask her what's wrong and she claims she's "a bit emotional today". Both girls are clearly drunk and keep squealing and hugging one another. The PCSO has gone to the supermarket where the booze was stolen and hasn't returned. Then one of the girls has a brainwave. "Hey, why don't we go to the shop. They'll tell you we didn't steal nuffink".

"Ok let's go to the shop then" Nathaniel replies and we head off the 200 yards to the store, him heading them up and me at the back.

They defy all expectations of childish ignorance of the potential trouble they're in by the lad shouting loudly and laughing and one of the girls skipping along singing in a screeching wail. Nathaniel turns around. "Right, listen" he says sternly. "I know that at home you have no guidance, noone sets an example for you to follow and you can do whatever you like but when you're with me....DON'T INTERRUPT!...you behave properly, all right?". They mumble acquiescence and we continue.

Just then the second girl sees someone she knows on the other side of the road and waves, shrieking "eeeh, hello" and jaunts across to give a middle aged woman a hug who is with four or five little kids. I shout her name but she ignores or doesn't hear me so I have to go over, take her arm and escort her back.

We walk into the store and one girl runs up to the counter, butting into a conversation a customer is having with a cashier. "Tell 'em" she shouts, pointing at us. "Tell 'em we didn't steal nuffink".

The cashier looks at me. "I think she took the beer" she says, nodding towards the second girl. "Darren saw them, do you want me to call him?".

Two minutes later a nervous-looking bloke in a red polo shirt comes towards us and Nathaniel asks him what happened.

"He was rude to me when I wouldn't serve him cigarettes" he says pointing at the lad who's slouching against the tinned vegetables rack and still chewing like a cow on the cud. "She stole two cans of Special Brew" he adds gesturing at the girl nearest to me.

"Oh REALLY?" Nathaniel says.

She starts crying and tries to walk off. I take her arm, say "come with me" and lead her out of the aisle to the front of the shop near the magazines and newspapers.

Her friend flounces up next to us "You're not going to arrest her?" she exclaims. "She only took two cans of beer!"

"Go away" I say and turn to the blubbering girl. "Right, I'm arresting you for Theft" then I caution her and add "due to your emotional state and the fact that you tried to walk off I'm going to handcuff you".

She continues crying and turns around, assuming I'm going to handcuff her with her hands behind her back.

"You're going to handcuff her?" her friend protests "she's only 13 for fucksake!"

"Look I won't tell you again, go away or you're coming in as well".

My prisoner is wailing, tears and eyeliner running down her face. She then blurts out what is known in The Job as a Significant Statement. "I didn't want to steal them but he told me to".

"Listen, if you promise me you'll behave I'll handcuff you with your hands to the front, but you've got to promise me you're going to calm down".

She nods and I give her Front Stack, making extra special care to ensure that there's a thumb sized gap between the steel and her wrists and then double lock them. Nicking a shoplifter is justified, using cuffs is too but I'm well aware of the political fall out of not being super nice to a crying 13 year old, no matter how pissed or chavvy she may be. The lad goes to give her a hug, not appreciating that she's in legal custody.

"Hey, back off" I shout and separate them.

"What's your problem?" he blurts out, looking offended.

We escort her to the manager's office so my colleague can see and seize the CCTV.

She slumps down on top of the safe in the storeroom next to his office. I give her a tissue to wipe her eyes. "I just want to end it. It's all shit. ALRIGHT I ADMIT IT I STOLE TWO CANS OF SPECIAL BREW FOR FUXAKE!". Another Sig Stat, I dutifully record it in my PNB. She sniffs loudly and continues wiping her face. "I need the toilet" she looks up at me, her eyes all swollen.

"When that lady PCSO gets back from trying to stop your friends getting back into the shop, then I'll get her to take you to the Ladies ok?"

"Are my friends still here? Can I speak to them?"

"No"

She starts crying again. Moaning about how her parents kicked her out and she's been sleeping at her friend's and HER parents kicked her out too so she's got nowhere to go.

"I s'pose you're gonna just leave me after you've let me go when I've been to the Station" she states.

"No, we won't do that, if you've got somewhere to go we'll drive you there".

"But I've got nowhere to go. You're going to put me in Care aren't you?"

She starts wailing again and slides down onto the floor.

"It's filthy down there, you're going to get dirty".

"I don't care" she sniffs without looking up.

"Yes, well I do. Come on, sit on the safe again".

She struggles up and sits down hard.

Nathaniel emerges with a VHS tape under his arm and a jacket that was found, apparently abandoned by the main thief.

"Do you want to bring the car round in case her friends are outside?" I ask, aware that it's not a short walk to our Patrol car.

"No, I hope her friends are out there, we'll arrest them too" he states flatly.

As soon as we get out there her female pal is in our faces. "Tell them about that time that boy tried to rape you" she says at least four times. "Why didn't you do anything when that boy tried to rape her?"

A new, taller chav lad is with her this time, no sign of the original one. He has his shirt off and a baseball cap on back to front.

"I've got a criminal record but can I be her Appropriate Adult?"

"Up to you" I tell him. "Make you way to the Nick if you want to do that".

"CAN I SLEEP AT YOUR HOUSE?" my prisoner wails to her friend.

"Course you can" she replies, then glares at me. "Why you bein' so 'evvy 'anded?" she demands.

"Because she's just stolen something that's why".

We finally get her in the car and I stick her in the back, fasten her seat belt and ask her if it's on comfortably.

"I don't care" she sniffs.

"Yes, well I do, I'm responsible for your safety and I don't want you to get hurt. Is it comfortable and while we're on the subject are your handcuffs too tight?"

"It's ok and no they're not".

We set off. She complains she needs a wee.

"We'll be at the Station soon, you can go as soon as we arrive"

"I'll pee in your car" she threatens.

Nathaniel tells her without taking his eyes off the road "if you do that I will rearrest you for Criminal Damage".

"What for peeing in a Police car?" she giggles. "I've got a bladder infection" she states, as if that's going to swing it in her favour.

"Well, no doctor in the world would say after examining you that that justified you soiling the seat of a Police car"

She starts crying again. "You don't understand me" she moans. "You don't care"

"Did I or did I not ask you twice if your handcuffs were too tight?" I ask her.

"Well, yeah. I s'pose so, but….well…you're ok I s'pose but noone else cares".

A short pause.

"Can't we go faster I really need a wee"

"We'll be there soon" I tell her.

"Aren't Police cars supposed to go fast with the lights on and thing?" she asks.

"Not with a prisoner in the back no".

"Ah, right".

Another short pause.

"You probably won't believe me but I'm never going to do this again. I don't like being arrested".

"Glad to hear it" I reply. "Best way to stop that is don't steal".

"Yeah, I got a Reprimand before you know. I stole a pizza".

"What happened" I enquire.

"Me and my boyfriend ordered it and when the bloke handed it to my boyfriend we shut the door in his face" she giggles. "But seriously, I'm never going to do this again, you probably don't believe me".

We arrive at Custody.

We get the keys so she can go to the toilet and she is escorted by my colleague while I fill out the two initial forms for arriving in Custody. Prisoner's details and Prisoner's belongings. I then radio for a female colleague to come and search her as only in the direst of emergencies would a male cop consider searching a female Suspect (which we are trained to do but using the backs of our hands so noone can say you had a grope). However there's no way on non-specific deity's Earth that I'd even think of searching a female juvenile.

She comes back five minutes later a little more chirpy and not blubbing. All goes well until she sees a lad she knows being Booked Out of Custody. A 15 year old toe rag who has just been bailed over a charge of racially aggravated Assault.

"Cooee, 'ello" she shouts, smiling and waving at her pal through the Holding Cell bars. He is about to reply but is barked at by the skipper and I glare at him and motion for him to look at the Sergeant.

"Ok, being nice is over" I tell her. "You need to act with respect now and no shouting to people across the room, ok?"

She mumbles an apology and begins shuffling her feet. The lad is being bailed for a very serious offence and both of them act like they're in the school playground.

After a few seconds her goldfish like memory lapses again. "He's really sweet, do you know him?"

"Nope"

"He's really cute, you wouldn't believe how old he is he looks so young"

Her definition of cute isn't mine, particularly as he was in for hurling racist abuse at an Asian lad and belting him in an unprovoked assault.

She is taken in to meet the skipper. I give the grounds for the Arrest and she starts contradicting what I'm saying.

"Right, stand up straight, look at the Sergeant and stop interrupting. If you show respect and be quiet this will be over much sooner".

"I don't think it will" the Sergeant replies. "I think she's staying overnight, she's clearly been drinking".

She pouts and starts to argue but then looks at me and shuts up.

"How much have you had to drink?" the skipper asks her.

"The two cans I stole" she replies.

Another Sig Stat. I get out my PNB again and write it down.

"I'm on my period" she states flatly.

"We've got stuff we can give you for that" I tell her.

The skipper runs through the tried and tested formula. When he gets to the bit about a solicitor she immediately says yes, although she clearly doesn't actually know what one is. It is explained to her in detail. She will also need an Appropriate Adult. I ring her parents and get number unobtainable on the home number and an ansaphone on the mother's mobile. I leave a message.

She's Booked In and we take her to the Livescan machine. She seems a bit more relaxed.

"I don't like coppers" she tells us, as if it's unexpected information "but you two are nice".

"Hear that" I ask Nathaniel as he primes the computer to do fingerprints, "we're nice".

"I'm so glad to hear that" he says without looking up from the keyboard.

After all's done I put her in a kiddy cell. Her Custody sheet has 30 minute visits specified.

"Want a hot chocolate?" I offer.

She smiles. "Yes please".

"Sugar"

"Yes"

I hold up my fingers, one, two then three.

"Just one".

We spend the next hour doing the photocopying and form filling necessary for the handover to CID. My Arrest Statement included her various outbursts that fall within the remit of Significant Statement and the fact that handcuffing her was justified in light of her generally brattish behaviour and likelihood she'd do a runner if given half a chance.

This whole thing took about three hours. It would have taken more but there was no queue at Custody.

We knock off two hours late. Well aware that she is only going to get a Final Warning which is not a punishment, just a threat that further stupidity will get her in more trouble.

OLD GIT AND A TWENTY

A call is put out to me and Nathaniel. This time to investigate a report of a male being a nuisance in a boozer just round the corner from where we are. We make our way there in a couple of minutes and the barmaid tells us that the old codger we can see glaring at us across the bar, looking like Rab C Nesbitt's grandfather, is barred and knows it but is moaning that he was short changed on a twenty pound note three nights previously. She adds that he hasn't set foot in the pub in months until today.

When we approach him the old boy is incredibly scruffy. His hair is in the comb over position but is yellow to the point of a 'dog turd brown' and his skin is greasy and covered in liver spots. He has very few teeth left and the rest are brown and stained. He reeks of tobacco, his 'suit' is ill fitting and has clearly seen not only better days but looks like someone was buried in it.

"What seems to be the problem here?" Nathaniel asks him and he begins a self righteous monologue about putting a twenty pound note on the bar to pay for his beer last Saturday and only getting change for a fiver. Our Sergeant and a female officer turn up while he's in full flow but leave once they realise that the "threat" has been nullified.

"Well, come outside and we'll tell you what the score is".

Once out on the pavement he again begins lamenting his lack of proper change and when he pauses for breath Nathaniel reminds him that he's barred from the pub and furthermore this isn't the first time that he's claimed to have been short changed. In fact it's

332

happened at least three times this month in three different places.

The bloke replies that he has no memory of being banned from the pub, that it definitely hasn't happened before and what about that time two years ago that someone hit him twice on the back of the head and we STILL haven't done a thing about it? Furthermore he has a daughter who was attacked and we haven't done anything about that either and WHY not?

He rants, pisses and moans while Nathaniel occasionally and with complete calm reminds him that he's tried this before and that if he has a problem with the pub he should pursue a civil claim.

Eventually after being faced with our serenity and realising that his dribbly, spittle fuelled rantings aren't getting him anywhere he shouts "tell you what FORGET IT!".

He storms off and we start to walk in the same direction as him. He realises this and shouts out, flapping his arms like a seal "DON'T FOLLOW ME DOWN THE STREET!".

"Our car's in the same direction as you are walking Sir" Nathaniel calmly states to the rapidly disappearing back of this wretch.

I get on the radio and call in that he's gone on his way and is no longer causing a nuisance to the good folk of the boozer.

This example of "defusing the situation" was a text book case of being a British Bobby. The guy was allowed to stand there wasting ten minutes of our time until he'd vented his spleen. The best thing to have done would be to get him outside and then simply tell him to push off or get nicked. Not let him rage about an unfair world at two of Her Majesty's finest.

ACTION PLAN MEETING

Kerwan had arranged a meeting with me and Nathaniel to discuss my Action Plans. These had been renewed and increased substantially the previous September in the wake of his attempts to get me to jack it all in after I had the unmitigated cheek to go and complain about how he was behaving. They had expired three weeks ago and this meeting was to discuss where we went from here.

Inspector Gerva had assured me that he would 'personally oversee' my remaining probationary period, that Reg 13 would not even be considered for at least six months due to the amount of time I'd had off sick and that Kerwan and Esobé would only now be involved in 'ticking the boxes' and doing their jobs insofar as red tape and signing off NOS's. He was now going to be in charge of my development and would be in control of my path to becoming Confirmed.

Sergeant Rine had told me he would also be attending as I was part of his Section. It had been months since I'd clapped eyes on Kerwan and if it was up to me I would never have had to look at him again. Unfortunately it wasn't so I had to put up with it. I went into the meeting feeling confident though as I had been made promises that we would be 'starting afresh' and things would now be different.

Oh naive, trusting, little thing.

First of all he presented me, Nathaniel and Sergeant Rine with the Action Plan forms saying "they're more or less the same with just slight variations". I spent five minutes in silence reading them while he tapped his Biro on the desk impatiently and he was indeed right.

They were EXACTLY the same, only differences being the dates and the line managers I was to report to. When I'd finished reading he then went into a spiel about how, as the previous Superintendent had told me, if I did not achieve these Action Plans then Reg 13 would be invoked and I could be dismissed, completely ignoring what his own boss Inspector Gerva had told me.

I looked up. "I was told by Mr Gerva these Action Plans were going to be changed and I was under the impression most of them would be written off".

Kerwan looks at me defiantly and replies "The only thing Inspector Gerva told me to remove was the bit about 'receiving complaints from members of the public' so that's all I've removed".

He looks pissed off and stubborn, like a child who is determined not to let his brother play with his football, even though he can't play with it himself as he's grounded. He holds up a form, dated six weeks previously. Old feedback from Declan that Inspector Gerva had shown me during my meeting with him and Sergeant Vivanco. "It's all in here" he says, shaking the form "have you seen this?".

"Yes but that's an old form. There's another one that Declan's sent that I've seen. I know he sent it to the PDU because Inspector Gerva told me he'd received it. Have you seen it?"

He shakes his head.

"Declan also said that my Race & Diversity Action Plan should be written off. He emailed me to say that he'd told you that".

Kerwan raises himself up in his chair and replies "that's not up to him that's up to me. The thing with Diversity is it's SUCH a broad area. I've got evidence from Nathaniel that you didn't handle an incident last night very well which means this part of the Plan is still relevant".

The 'incident' he was referring to had happened in the early hours of the morning and involved an old woman who thought her neighbours were going to kill her 'with science'. We turned up there and even though I told Nathaniel on the doorstep that I'd never dealt with this type of thing before he insisted that I lead.

The poor woman was visibly scared and embarrassed and said that she knew we'd probably think she was crazy but she was convinced she'd heard her neighbours plotting to kill her through scientific means. She didn't elaborate on what those means were though and added that she knew she was probably just imagining things but was really scared they were going to come and 'get' her. I sat down and talked to her gently, reassuring her that it was indeed her imagination and asked her what she'd like me to do. She replied that she wanted me to call her nephew Cuthbert who lived nearby. As no crime had been committed and it was 2.30 in the morning I didn't know if this was appropriate so tried convincing her that she was perfectly safe. I went upstairs and checked her bedroom, the spare room and the toilet and returned downstairs and checked the kitchen before telling her that everything was safe. The entire time I did this Nathaniel simply stood there and watched me, not helping or contributing in any way. No matter what I said she wasn't having any of it and after about ten minutes I was getting embarrassed as I had run out of options. I then suggested she try and get some sleep to which she replied "well that's not going to happen is it?".

At that point Nathaniel took over, asked her what nephew Cuthbert's phone number was and offered her a cup of tea. He then called him, assured him nothing was amiss but could he come and visit his poor aunt and fifteen minutes later Cuthbert turned up, bleary eyed and clearly not happy to have been roused from his pit. Nathaniel also called paramedics out to see if she was physically sound and the whole thing was wrapped up in about half an hour.

While I didn't handle it well, it was simply due to lack of experience and not knowing what my options were.

While Diversity may indeed be SUCH a broad area, my Action Plan for Respect for Race & Diversity was specifically for invasion of other people's personal space and expressing adverse opinions about illegal immigrants. It had nothing whatsoever to do with not being able to soothe senile octogenarians who think their neighbours are going to murder them in their beds. Kerwan was determined to hold on to the Action Plan, without changing one word of it and prove to everyone and most importantly me that I was not up to The Job. He was deliberately twisting the incident to fit under the mantle of Diversity but was either too stupid or too determined to bin me to realise that it was as clear as the polish on his chevrons that he was grasping at straws and trying to make the facts fit his own opinions.

Anticipating that Kerwan might still behave like he used to I had printed off Declan's farewell email to me when I left CID where he had said "from what I've seen of you at work your Race and Diversity Action Plan can be written off" and had brought it along.

"I have a copy of Declan's email saying the Plan should be written off. Would you like to see it?" I proffer the folded sheet.

Kerwan looks down nose at it, shakes his head and sneers "NO".

There's a pause while me, Nathaniel and Sergeant Rine just stare at him then he adds "forward it to me by email".

I then say that in the latest feedback (which Kerwan conveniently hadn't seen, even though his department have received a copy) Declan stated that the only reason my Resilience got such a low score was because I was unable to prove I had it in sufficiency due to being on Restricted Duties and on a Non-Confrontational risk assessment, hence my always avoiding confrontation.

Kerwan then comes out with "this part of your Plan is also still relevant. Confrontation doesn't just mean violence. It can mean a verbal argument or even the way someone speaks. In my opinion you didn't assess the situations correctly".

While operating under Occ Health's RA I had been told that I was to remain completely Non-Confrontational. The letter they sent out was two pages long and amongst other things stated that I was absolutely NOT to escort prisoners or enter Custody for any reason and that I was to verify a situation was safe before dealing with it or continuing with it. This was later relaxed slightly to say I COULD enter Custody but had to check the area was safe before going in (i.e. opening the door and having a look). I once saw a guy having a heated row with the Custody skipper who was then sat next to me in the Holding Cell while I waited to use the LiveScan machine. Adhering to the RA I had asked one of the accompanying officers if the guy was likely to kick off. My colleague didn't know why I'd done this and went and told Declan.

I was later allowed to transport prisoners, but only non-aggressive ones. Clive had asked me to escort a 62 year old woman back to her car at a shopping mall. She'd been nicked for shoplifting and apparently her husband had died two weeks previously so we were being super nice to her. I complied with the RA by asking if she was likely to kick off to which Clive looked at me in disbelief and went "Lance, she's 62!".

We got back to the mall, dropped her off and while picking up the CCTV footage of her nicking a jumper we were casually told by the control room supervisor that the woman had punched the security guard in the face who'd detained her, but later claimed to have no memory of doing it.

Finally I had got back to the satellite Nick we worked out at about 10pm to find the alarm was going off. Noone else was there and I was alone so I let myself in and then rang Clive for the disarm code. He asked me if I'd checked the building and I replied I couldn't in case someone was there as I was still Non-Confrontational.

This was all written down and forwarded to Inspector Gerva who gave it to Kerwan. As my RA was very explicit, it was a bit tight of them to even mark these incidents down but I could also understand why they did it as they needed to report what I did or didn't do for written appraisals.

A fully fit PCSO would not be officially criticised for avoiding confrontation while on duty. A verbal argument can escalate in a second to physical aggression. My RA from Occ Health specifically stated 'Non-Confrontational' NOT 'A Bit Confrontational Provided It's Only A Verbal Row'.

I had done exactly what I had been told to do which was to keep myself out of harm's way through avoiding all possibility of getting hurt or getting into a situation that might leave me permanently paralysed. I had a slipped disc and had spent many months getting better. I had done nothing wrong by behaving in this way and was in fact acting under instructions from a higher authority (Occ Health) as to how to conduct myself.

Kerwan was judging my avoidance of confrontation as if I was fully fit, despite having evidence that I was far from it. Even turning around suddenly could worsen the pain and he was trying to retain an Action Plan, formulated when I was active and fully mobile, based on actions and inactions when I was partially paralysed.

I look at him and ask "have you seen my risk assessment? I had a herniated disc, I was in constant pain".

He just glares at me

I then offer "Declan stated how impressed he was that the day after being officially signed on again as Fully Fit I offered to attend a potentially violent arrest of a man who had ten minutes previously committed multiple criminal damage and GBH".

Kerwan shakes his head, looking irritated and holds up his hand. "It's no use arguing with me I'm just the messenger, you need to talk to the people who gave you the feedback".

I look down at the Action Plans and then back at him. "I'm NOT going to sign this. I'd like time to consult with the Federation".

He looks even more annoyed but replies "this isn't a Federation matter but if you want to seek advice then that's fine. Me, Nathaniel and Sergeant Rine now need to discuss this alone".

I get up, taking the form and my PNB with me. As I open the door to leave Kerwan calls after me "THANK YOU Lance".

"You're welcome" I say without turning round.

After all the hours I'd spent compiling dozens of documents to refute the validity of these Action Plans. After getting expert testimony, counter signatures in my PNB, evidence and statements. After hours of meetings to discuss this and being told things would now be different, they were exactly the same. Kerwan was determined I was going to fail and had ignored every piece of evidence I had put together (much of which had been acknowledged by his own boss Inspector Gerva) and tried to get me to sign a piece of paper which effectively said that all that effort didn't mean anything and that he was right and I was wrong.

I rang Declan the next day and told him what had happened. He laughed and said "he's not supposed to do that, Action Plans expire after six months". He then forwarded Kerwan his new appraisal of me with the high scores and noted improvement in all areas bar Resilience and Cc'd me onto the email.

Kerwan predictably, completely ignored it.

This and an argument I would have with Nathaniel five days later made me decide I'd had enough.

On what would be my penultimate Shift he went ballistic one night after finding out I hadn't done the lengthy and time consuming PNB entry he'd told me to always do for a Vehicle Defect Rectification Scheme ticket.

If you are driving a vehicle which is defective in some way, but still able to be driven without danger to yourself or other drivers, an easy piece of paper for a cop to issue is the VDRS. It is an acceptance of blame but means you don't have to go to Court for driving with a defective rear light or bald tyres, you just have to get the problem fixed within one week and bring the ticket, signed by the servicing mechanic to a specified Nick. There is no cost to you unless you fail to fix the problem or do not bring proof in within seven days.

The PNB entry was at least four pages of anal detail including why you stopped the vehicle. where, what time it was, who the driver was and a physical description, if there were any passengers, the driver's address, the state of the vehicle, any marks on the vehicle, its registration number, that you examined it for defects, that you Cautioned the driver and that you offered him the VDRS as an alternative to going to Court. As we had issued two it would take at least an hour to fill the PNB out. I had genuinely forgotten he'd told me this and once he'd finished ranting and swearing about how we would now have to waste more time if it was done a day late, I pointed out that my previous tutor Jacob had said a lengthy entry was not necessary for a VDRS and a cursory PNB note giving the ticket number and location was enough.

"If THAT'S what he told you then show me and I will take it up with him as a Training issue and negligence on his behalf" he replied, still furious at what he clearly perceived was laziness on my part.

About an hour later when he'd calmed down I asked "did you mean what you said about showing you proof or are you simply throwing down the gauntlet?"

He turned from his computer monitor and replied "No, if he told you that then show me and I will take it up with him".

He examines the proffered PNB.

"Fine. I will call him to discuss this. However it does NOT excuse the fact that you did not do it as I told you to". He then turns back to his PC, still blatantly annoyed.

Later that night I called Jacob, told him I was resigning and said "just so you know, if you haven't received a call already you may get one from Nathaniel". I elaborated on why and then added "don't want you to think I've been badmouthing you behind your back".

Without pausing Jacob replied "he's welcome to. THAT'S how I was trained to do it. VDRS is the original document so you only need to make a brief PNB entry".

So, a screaming fit from Nathaniel for what he perceived as an unacceptable lapse while Jacob had not advised me incorrectly, just differently.

That night I told Sergeant Rine I'd finally reached the end of my tether and had had enough. He listened to what I had to say, didn't flinch when I called Kerwan 'a right cunt' and said he was "really sorry, and in particular sorry that you've had such a bad experience". I asked if he wanted me to come in the following day as it was a Saturday Night Shift and I didn't want to leave him one down on Fight Night.

He replied "up to you. You don't have to. Neither me nor the Section will think any the less of you if you don't".

Nathaniel came up to me half an hour later with my daily feedback to sign. It mentioned in great detail the VDRS incident and how he'd already spoken to Sergeant Kerwan about this who wanted the feedback to be forwarded to Inspector Gerva.

I looked at it then handed it back. "I'm not signing that. I'm gone from tomorrow".

I extend my hand. "You're a good bloke Nathaniel".

He turns away, won't look me in the face but takes my hand and shakes it in silence then walks off with my unsigned feedback form.

At the end of the day Nathaniel was a decent man and a good officer. He unfortunately couldn't grasp the fact that not everyone in his position of responsibility is as attentive as he is to what they're doing or how they train Probies. He also couldn't understand that his way of doing things was not only not the only way, but not only the only right way.

I'd fought back against being bullied and refused to be forced out, now I could leave because I chose to and had a landmark to look back on and know that I had stood up for myself.

FINAL NIGHT.

The final night was a good one to bow out on.

I got to the Nick at 1530, got changed and met Sergeant Rine coming down the corridor.

"Hello Sergeant, same decision as last night. Are you happy for me to be here?

He stops and looks at me, then replies "as long as you're happy TO be here".

After Briefing, as Nathaniel had taken Annual Leave, he pairs me with a female constable called Doris, a year ahead of my Intake who's about to enter Fast Track, he states that he doesn't know the etiquette for someone resigning like this as he's never had it happen before and that he'll have a word with the Guv'nor and let me know what needs to be done later on.

Me and Doris pootle about in the car. She's a Basic driver so we stay in the housing estates waiting to see if anyone comes our way, or if anybody can be given a ticket.

"So" she says "what do you want to do tonight? Got anything you need to do for your NOS's?"

"Nope. This is my last night. I resigned yesterday".

She looks shocked. "Oh, well in that case we'd better keep you out of trouble then" she says laughing. "If you don't mind me asking why did you quit?"

"I've had enough. I've had hours of meetings about this and the Federation got involved and nothing's changed. If I tell you something will you keep it to yourself? It's not anything that falls under the remit of the sodding Classroom Contract exceptions".

"Sure" she replies. I look at her and think I can trust her... but then again I've thought that before and it's got me in a world of hurt. Still, it's not exactly a secret.

I tell her the whole story and she tuts and looks out the window "when did you decide to quit then?".

"Last night" I reply "I fought so hard for so long and it was like getting to the top of Everest, used up all my energy and then to have them point to an even bigger mountain and say 'didn't we tell you? You have to climb THAT one too".

She nods, marking a line on the windscreen with her left index finger. "This job will shaft you. Some people can take it and some people can't. It seems like they had it in for you".

"I can take it. I just about can take anything except being bullied and kicked to death by my own people. We're supposed to support each other, not stab each other in the back".

The night goes as normal. An abandoned 999 call to check out (nothing to deal with, his 5 year old daughter had done it), a traffic stop and then back to the Nick for some paperwork and change of shift as we handed the cars over to Night duty and prepared to climb in the Rowdy Van.

While filling out my PNB Sergeant Rine approached me.

"Lance" he said quietly, touching my arm "the Inspector's in the building. I told him what you'd said and he says he'd like to speak with you".

I am nervous at this vague statement. Is he going to try to talk me out of it? Is he going to want to know why I'm leaving?

We enter the Briefing Room and the Guy' is sitting there in uniform with his winter jacket on, pips on each shoulder. He's in his early 40s but looks about 32. Sandy hair with a floppy fringe, 6 feet 4 inches and broad shouldered. Very educated voice. Calls constables "mate" or "chap". Looks and sounds almost exactly like a character from a war movie with a name like 'Spitfire McGuire'. The kind of fellow that would run into the RAF officers' mess as the klaxon began blaring to signal the latest Luftwaffe bombing run. Goggles round his neck, lipstick on his collar and bomber jacket undone, rousing the men with banter such as "come on chaps, let's get the birds in the air and get the parcels delivered. Tuppeny ones are up to mischief again".

He smiles as I enter and greet him with "Sir".

"Hello mate, have a seat", me and the Sergeant sit down.

"I understand you've decided to resign. Difficult decision to have to make, I admire you for having the guts to do it. Not my business to ask why but sorry to lose you. The Sergeant's told me that you were unsure of what happens with regard to notice period" he gestures to the skipper. "Well I can tell you categorically that you DON'T have to work your notice period so don't worry about that".

I relax slightly, relieved to be told that this is the end after tonight.

"I also understand from the Sergeant that you were told you didn't have to come in tonight but you chose to anyway. I just want to say thank you for not letting us down on a busy night and for that you don't have to work tomorrow unless you want to. My gift to you".

He pauses. I use the gap in conversation to say my piece. "Thank you Sir, I appreciate that. I won't come in if it's all the same I just didn't want to leave you one down on Fight Night. I've met some good officers while I've been here such as Nathaniel and the Sergeant" I glance across at the Sarge and am surprised to see that he is looking at me and looking visibly upset. "I've also met some that weren't so good and may or may not take a grievance out against them at some point in the future. Once again I'd just like to say thanks and thanks for checking this out for me".

The Inspector stands up and extends his hand. I shake it. "Sorry it hasn't worked out for you chap. Good luck with whatever you do next". He smiles and leaves the Briefing Room. I go to leave but the Sergeant shuts the door. He turns to me.

"I just want to say Lance that you may feel it's a cowardly thing to resign but I know it must be difficult and I want you to know you've got nothing but respect from me". He still looks upset. I'd heard this before from Kerwan but somehow it's different.

"Thank you Sarge, that means a lot".

We do our patrol and they keep me out of arrests. When people need to be nicked it's one of the others that does it such as two gobby drunks outside a pub who'd assaulted a third man. One of them I'd nicked the week before for Drink Driving. They are both stuck in the back of the van and I'm on babysitting duty looking at them through the perspex screen. Two minutes down the road and I hear one say to the other in what he appears to think is a hushed whisper "listen mate, we've got to get our stories straight before we get to the pig shop".

I stand up and yell "SARRRRGE!"

He stops the van and we put the least pissed one in the back with us. He immediately begins moaning and complaining so I look at him and snap "SHUT! UP!" He mutters something so I add "I said SHUT! UP!" He glares at me in sullen silence the rest of the way.

Later we arrest an 18 stone female drunk who fights her way into the back of the van and it takes four of us to get her in. She was the first person I arrested with this Force so it's kind of poetic that I assist with nicking her on my final shift. Her jeans appear to be about a 45 inch waist and shoving her in the back takes a good minute of grunting and heaving while the half full Carlsberg Special Brew can she was drinking from rolls around in the road and she bucks and struggles, swearing her head off and lashing out at everyone. Just as she goes in I am momentarily distracted by a camera flash going off and look to my right to see a guy in a tweed jacket standing next to us smiling. His mate has just taken a photo of him. I can deal with violent, aggressive fat women but THIS is beyond belief. Doris grabs his mate and makes him delete the photo. I pull the grinning imbecile to one side.

"RIGHT" I bark at him "JUST WHAT THE BLOODY HELL DO YOU THINK YOU'RE PLAYING AT?"

"I am tourist" he replies still smiling.

"YOU'RE ALSO COMPLETELY STUPID!" I yell at him, "DO YOU WANT TO GET ARRESTED?"

"I am tourist, from Belgium"

"DO YOU WANT TO SPEND THE NIGHT IN A CELL?"

My NVCs and facial expression have finally sunk into his

retarded, alcohol sodden brain and his smile slowly fades. He still hasn't got a clue what I'm saying though. "Err...I no understand".

"DO YOU WANT TO GO TO PRISON FOR BEING AN IDIOT?"

"Err...no. Prison no thank you".

Just as the back doors to the van close I can see the arrestee violently head butting the back of the cage. The van literally shakes each time she does this. Trying to speak over the booming noises and the squeak of the axles as they reposition I grab a Special Constable who's nearby and say "watch him, I'm going to speak to the Sergeant". He nods and stands with the now slightly perturbed and terminally stupid tourist.

"Sarge that guy just stood next to us and had his photo taken during the arrest of your delightful passenger. Can I nick him for Obstruction?".

The Sarge glances over at the tourist, looks at me and smiles. "No, just bollock him and let him go, we're busy".

I walk back, the detained female is still going at it. The booming noises only slightly louder than her stream of swearing.

"RIGHT! You are VERY lucky. You obstructed an arrest and if it was up to me I'd arrest YOU but I've been told not to. Get out of my sight!"

He stammers "err... thanking you" and darts off to meet his photographer buddy and they slope away.

I thankfully didn't have to deal with the necessary Cell Exit performed on the Arrestee once she got to the Nick (who was sprayed in the face after kicking the Custody nurse) and at the end of the shift, around 3am the Sergeant and me counted off my equipment into a big Evidence bag, he noted it down in his PNB and got me to countersign it.

"Remember I told you that I'd complained to the Super' about the PDU but it was now resolved?"

He nods.

"Well that wasn't true. They did fuck all. The previous Super even sat there with Kerwan next to me and went 'I take it you don't have a problem with any of this feedback' meaning my Action Plans.

What the fuck am I s'posed to say to THAT? The person who gave me the feedback is sitting right next to me!"

"Puts you on the spot" the Sergeant says nodding.

"Still take care" I tell him "like I said I've got nothing against you or any of the Section. You're all good people".

We shake hands and I go home.

As sad as I was to go and as frustrating and upsetting as it was to have fought so hard for so long only to end up leaving anyway I drove home as the sun was coming up completely knackered but happy that I'd gone out with dignity and had not let people down. One thing I've learned in life is that the most important things are entrances and exits. I count my entrance as being on duty as a Special in central London on July 7th 2005 as that was when I decided to join full time. My exit was a night where I did what I'd joined up to do and had dealt with keeping the public safe and arresting criminals, NOT fannying about with mobile phone drivers or sodding Stop forms. Further I was with a Sergeant who was a decent man who was sad to see me go and a Section that were probably indifferent to my departure as I'd only known them 10 days but wished me well and even posed for a group photo (provided I promised not to put it on Facebook).

I went to bed feeling miserable but positive that I'd made the right decision and that I'd conducted myself as what would have been called 60 years ago a "gentleman". It was over and I could move on.

Or so I thought....

"You're supposed to work your notice" a PSE snaps at me as I sit next to her in the office she shares with two other, equally miserable looking women.

The following Wednesday I had gone into Area HQ for a meeting with the Fed Rep. We'd arranged it anyway and rather than waste the opportunity had agreed to use the appointment to discuss any options available for a grievance against Kerwan and Esobé or the Force as a whole.

While waiting to speak to him I had gone down to Personnel to hand in my Warrant Card.

"The Inspector says I don't have to"

"It's not up to him it's the Superintendent's decision" she says and then pauses as if I'm supposed to be awestruck at the word.

"He wasn't around. Do I need to remind you that the Inspector was the highest ranking officer on duty in the whole Area at the time he made that decision?"

On any Day Shift you will usually find all ranks up to Chief Constable, or on Area the Chief Super' dotted about. Come the later part of Late Turn or Night Duty they are tucked up in bed or doing whatever higher ranks do to unwind of an evening, so the Duty Governor for the Section on duty is the highest ranking Area officer. The only time his superiors are called out is in the event of something REALLY serious. He made the decision. Therefore it should stand.

She tuts and glares at me "it's not up to him. The Superintendent makes the decisions".

"He wasn't there. This is the first I've been told about it" I protest. As I have quit and have been told I am free I am slightly more confident and therefore cocky than I would have been a week ago.

"I'll have to check with the Superintendent and see what he thinks. If he's not prepared to back the decision you'll have to work".

As SMT are in their daily meeting this could take up to an hour or more.

"I have handed all my gear in bar this Warrant Card" I say, waving the black leather wallet at her.

"We can unpack all your stuff and give you back your Airwave" she says, completely oblivious to the obvious security, Integrity not to mention Health and Safety risks of forcing someone back on to the Beat and giving him the power to arrest people when he simply doesn't want to be there.

I sigh. "Fine I'll wait for you in the CID office".

I go back and tell my two former skippers Jarrod and Julian plus the Fed Rep James Wilne what happened.

"Typical" Jarrod chuckles.

An hour later James approaches and sits down opposite me.

"Lance the Superintendent has overruled the Inspector and says you have to work".

I am angry, pissed off and amazed at the lack of common good manners involved in this. Can't he tell me himself?

James looks at me, then "go and see Personnel again see what they have to say".

Back in the office and the PSE gets out a chart with my projected shifts on it, put down before I decided to quit. She has highlighted the relevant dates and says:

"Now you need to work today..."

I glare at her and then interrupt, pointing to the four days' worth of stubble on my chin and the ripped jeans I'm wearing. "I think we can both agree I'm NOT working today. You have overruled a management decision without any prior notice and it's not like I'm dressed to impress".

She pauses, flusters, realises I have a point and then says "Well, ok but you need to work tomorrow and then you have two days off and then three days on Lates and then two shifts the following week. Your remaining Annual Leave can be used to write off the other shifts if you want".

She hands me the form and I take it, suppressing the urge to shout "YOU FUCKING CUNTS!" at the top of my lungs.

"Can I see the Superintendent then?"

"He's probably in his office. That's up to you".

I approach the Secretary he shares with the Chief Super in the office between them.

"Can I see the Superintendent please?"

"Oh he's gone" she replies brightly, looking up from her typing. "Won't be back for a couple of hours".

Jesus Christ! He didn't have the decency to tell me to my face, even though he knew I was sitting in an office one floor down and now he's fucked off out.

I head back up to the CID office and show the Fed Rep the form.

"Is this guy for real?" I ask him.

"Yes, I'm afraid so. How do you think we feel? We have it all the time".

He ponders for a minute then says "go and see the Inspector who made the decision, I saw him downstairs about 15 minutes ago, he's in the Duty Manager's office on the Ground Floor"

I make my way down there and knock on the door, looking at Spitfire McGuire through the safety glass, who is standing talking to the PSE I was with only a few minutes ago. This has clearly created waves all through the levels of Command.

The Inspector sees me and I hear him say "he's standing in the doorway as we're speaking" and then walks over to open the door. He looks visibly embarrassed and uncomfortable.

"I'm really sorry chap, in a common sense world this decision would stand" he says shaking his head and patting my shoulder.

The PSE then pipes up "but normally it is standard practice to work your notice".

"Yes, but I wasn't told that AND the Inspector specifically said I didn't have to work AND we shook hands on it".

"It's normal practice" she insists again.

"Look mate I'm going to go and speak to the Superintendent now, this really shouldn't have happened".

I head back up to CID for the third time. I sit there and feel absolutely betrayed and hurt. Having done what was clearly acknowledged as the decent thing and come in on Saturday night, despite being told I didn't have to, solely in order to help out and not let other people down. My own sense of ethics and honour had told me to do this. Now not only has that been spat on by someone who appears to have neither quality but the Inspector has been humiliated and embarrassed in front of a resigning probationary Constable by his superior, who clearly has no sense of justice, common sense or decency.

I have had enough. Time to do something other than just piss and moan. I stand up and tell the Fed Rep and my two ex-skippers "sorry guys but in light of the undue stress and anxiety that this has put me under I am now signing myself off Sick. I'm gone".

I shake their hands and bolt for the door in case the Inspector comes back while I'm still here. "Take the back stairs" James shouts. I glance over my shoulder and he winks at me.

Driving home about 15 minutes later and the Inspector calls. Even though I'm wearing a headset I pull over as I'm not going to be able to concentrate on the road during this conversation.

"Hello chap" he says "really sorry, but the Superintendent is insisting you have to work".

"Is it really ethical to put someone back in a uniform and give them a Class 5 firearm if they don't want to be there?" I ask him.

"He doesn't want you back on Section. He just wants you to come in and do something for your remaining Shifts. Where are you now?"

"I've signed myself off with Stress and Anxiety about 15 minutes ago" I reply "I'm heading to the doctor's now to get a note to back it up"

"Ok, that's fine. Call me tomorrow and I'll let you know if they will want to rearrange your shifts in light of you officially being Sick".

I thank him and we hang up.

I got the doctor's note, photocopied it five times and then sent the original to Personnel. The next day I called the Inspector again.

"Hello?...Oh hello mate".

I can hear background noises which means he's outside. "Do you want me to call you back?" I ask.

"No it's alright chap, just leaving the scene. Had a firearms incident"

"WHAT!? You sure you don't want me to call you back later?"

"No mate, it's all wrapped up. Replica anyway. I still haven't found out about your shifts, I'll call you tomorrow".

I pause then say "He should have backed you and then simply told you in private not to do it again, not embarrassed you like that".

"I know mate, I was majorly fucked off. Still, I'll call you tomorrow ok?"

We hang up again.

Next day I'm still asleep at about 9am and the phone rings. It's not Spitfire McGuire but PDU Ma'am whose posh, dulcet tones are not what I need to wake me up. She says "it's Insp..." and then changes it to her first name, presumably realising that I am no longer required to call her by her title.

"Former Ma'am" I say groggily "how are you?"

"Were you asleep?" she says sharply, sounding like that's just NOT the done thing.

"I'm signed off Sick" I reply.

"Yes, but you should be out there doing something not lounging about in bed".

"Ok..errr in a minute I'm going to go out and do a five mile run and then do 200 press ups on my knuckles"

"Glad to hear it. Just to let you know that I'm ringing on the other Inspector's behalf as he's off due to a funeral. We've checked and you DON'T have to work your remaining Shifts at all now, even if you aren't signed off sick till the end of your notice period".

"Oh believe me I will be, but thanks for that" I reply then add "and the Super' was well out of order. He should have backed him and then bollocked him after, not shamed him in front of me"

"Hmm...well" she says, remaining predictably non committal.

There's another pause and she asks "what are you going to do now?"

"Oooh, I don't know. I'm a clever chap. I'll find something. Maybe travel for a bit first". I hesitate but then add "I'd just like to say that I never had a problem with you".

"That's good to know" she says flatly, in a tone that suggests she couldn't care less.

"I'd also like you to know that you reading all that disgusting filth during that meeting will live with me until the day I die".

"And why's that?"

"Errr...how do I put this? You're an Inspector, you're a woman and you're posh".

"Well it was on the Internet in public view. Anyway, get yourself up and about".

I chuckle. "Take care".

"Yes, you too".

We hang up.

I got signed off until the end of my notice period and was also given back my remaining Annual Leave. This meant I got twice the amount in my final pay packet than I would have had if I hadn't been off Sick.

Had the Guv'nor told me I had to work on that Saturday night where we shook hands and the Sergeant said he had nothing but respect for me then I would have happily agreed to. To have the Super overrule this without having the decency to tell me to my face and to anger and humiliate both me and a very good Inspector was just one further piece of evidence that this hugely important organisation lack fundamental standards which they can't even apply to each other. I left with promises and feelings of goodwill on all sides on what was supposed to be my final Shift and came back to tie up loose ends only to be told that the deputy area commander had wiped his feet on all the honour and dignity that I had mustered to bow out with and had had reciprocated by his own managers.

A week after leaving, the Fed Rep told me that Inspector Gerva had asked "why didn't Lance speak to me first?".

I rang him the next day and explained what had happened, apologising for not calling but that nothing had changed despite his promises. He still tried to polish the turd and stated "maybe Sergeant Kerwan was trying to be the manager, I mean, I was on Leave". I asked him to pass on my thanks to Sergeant Vivanco and then hung up.

A fortnight later I submitted my Exit Form to the Force. It had some lovely tick boxes on it including 'did you feel bullied?' and 'did you feel discriminated against due to disability?' to which I gleefully ticked 'yes' to both and elaborated in the 'Additional Info' box on exactly how badly Kerwan and Esobé had treated me. The box for Exit Interview was already marked 'Not Required' and after consulting the Federation again I requested an Exit Interview with the Area Commander.

A short time after I'd posted the form back James Wilne called to say that a Chief Inspector had intercepted it and had replied to my request to see the Big Boss with "PC Manley has made his feelings for leaving quite clear. We do not feel the need nor have the appetite to discuss this any further".

A week after this I received a certificate, hand signed by the Chief Constable saying what date I joined and my rank when I left (which was probationary Constable). It came in a "DO NOT BEND" cardboard envelope which the postman bent in half and then shoved through my letterbox. Still, it was only marginally creased and is in a big folder of stuff, including the 7/7 thank you from the Chief Super' of Snow Hill, my Law Degree and my Open Water Scuba Diving certificate.

The Police is not anything like it should be or what it used to be. We spent half a day on how to use our batons, an hour on how to use our pepper spray and at least six weeks on Race and Diversity training. While The Sweeney in 1975 was simply a gritty TV cop drama, Life on Mars and Ashes to Ashes are popular because they show a less complicated world where, despite their faults cops got the job done and while you might not have wanted them as mates they were there to protect you and would do that above all else. Gene Hunt (that's Glennister not Keitel) is a corrupt, homophobic, sexist bully but middle aged women I know love him because of his "unreconstructed-ness" and the fact that he "doesn't care what people think of him". Men think he's ace because he doesn't mess about, is loyal and brave and is ultimately there to protect the weak and helpless, like all good cops should. He is like Jack Sparrow. What we all want but pretend we hate.

In the distant mists of aeons past, English cops did their thing in the knowledge that they were upholding The Law. It was second to nothing. It reigned supreme. It was the glue of society. Regardless of who you were and where you came from you would be treated the same as everyone else. Then, one day there rode into town a nosey person called Lord Scarman. He was sent to investigate the Police by the politicians and his experience of The Law was as a Judge. He had no first hand evidence or experience of what being a Police officer was about. He probed and he fiddled and he interfered and months later he gave a report that accused the Police of being 'institutionally racist'. Instead of doing what anybody with any self respect would have done which was to have dealt with the specific issues and then carry on, the Police Senior Management crapped their collective trousers and allowed their Forces to be moulded and shaped beyond all recognition by the politicians. Judges' Rules were replaced by the complex minefield of PACE and over the next two decades and beyond, the Police began to let themselves be transformed more and more into caricatures of what they once were.

Now Police trainees only have to be average. Average fitness, average intelligence, average discipline, average appearance and average stamina. Except of course for the area of Race and Diversity where anyone who excels will rise like a chav's street cred upon receiving his first ASBO and anyone who is notably lacking will be used as the poster boy or girl for intolerance and prejudice.

CONFRONTING TOBY

The day after my notice period ended I went back to confront Toby.

It expired June 14th and I had waited patiently until it ran out before I went back to see him. As vindictive as Kerwan was I knew that even if I was signed off Sick during a resignation period he could, if he wanted to, have tried to do me for "bringing the Force into disrepute" if they were still paying me a wage and I did anything that reflected badly on them.

In an envelope I put two photocopies. One of the letter from COLP's Chief Super' for Snow Hill. The other was from my friend, stating what had happened to her, how she was on the cover of two national newspapers on July 8th and her contact details. I also put in a covering letter stating this was in response to what he'd put in writing about thinking I was lying. I included my email address. Then I wrote on the envelope flap "written, sealed and delivered on June 15th", signed it and then put sellotape over the writing.

I turned up at 10am and asked to speak to him. The building houses many Council organisations and departments, with Toby's crew on the first floor. The receptionist glances out into the car park. "Yes, his car's still here so he's in. Is he expecting you?"

"No".

"Just take a seat and I'll phone his office".

I choose a seat facing the door that I know he'll come out of and wait. I hear the receptionist call upstairs and say "there's a Lance Manley here for you.....no, he didn't say what he wanted...no, he's alone. No, he's definitely alone".

A few minutes later and he emerges, looks around and sees me. I stand up and walk towards him. He looks uncomfortable and embarrassed. He looks at me and then turns away and stammers "Lance?! Errr...I've only got two minutes, literally. I'm in a meeting".

I stop and wink at him theatrically and hold out the envelope. He appears startled, then takes it.

"This is for you" I say, winking again. "If you've got anything to say for yourself my contact details are in there. You take care" and walk off.

"You too" he says to my back as I head for the entrance.

I had rehearsed in my head what I would do when I saw him again. It ranged from going up to his office and simply walking in uninvited, to making him open the letter and demanding an apology. In the end I settled for just putting the envelope in his hand and seeing the look of discomfort and embarrassment on his face. He clearly knew why I'd come back even though he'd been caught off guard and was not the arrogant, bullying, aggressive man from the meeting but someone who looked scared that his past had come back to confront him.

I had consulted the Federation about any ramifications through doing this and the Fed Rep told me to go right ahead, adding "hopefully it will make him feel very stupid".

He now has proof that I was telling the truth.

He never wrote to the email address I had deliberately put in the letter or made any other attempt to contact me so I can only assume he's not sorry at all for what he did.

PHONE CALL TO MA'AM POSTLETHWAITE

I always had a lot of respect for Ma'am Postlethwaite. She wasn't as scary as she tried to make out and at her initial speech to all of us, as we sat there nervously fidgeting in our best suits, I wondered after if it would have been appropriate to have prompters like in a pantomime with 'Boo' and 'Hiss' cards to hold up at opportune moments.

She was however consistent, fair and compassionate, despite being the strictest officer I'd ever met.

A week or so after resigning I called her up. After being on hold for about five minutes she came on the line:

"Erika Postlethwaite speaking, sorry to keep you waiting".

"Hello Erika, it's Lance Manley"

(Slight pause, then): "Oh hello Lance"

"Did you know I've resigned?"

"Yes I had heard"

"I just wanted to say goodbye".

(Another pause, then): "Thank you, that was sweet of you".

"Also to have the luxury of being able to use your first name".

She laughs, "well, what can I say?"

"I just want to repeat what I said in that meeting that I always respected you and if every Police officer was the same as you then the Force would be a much better place".

(A longer pause then): "Well...thank you for saying that".

"Are you going to be a substantive CI?"

"Not certain yet, it's up to the ACC. I have submitted a portfolio and need to wait to see what he says".

"I hope you get it"

(An even longer pause, then she begins telling me all about the lengthy process of applying for the extra pips permanently and how, if she's promoted she doesn't want to leave responsibility for probationers to someone she doesn't trust).

I then tell her "some time ago you told me that you didn't think I had what it takes to do The Job and never had done".

"Yes, I remember"

"I still don't begrudge you saying that to me. You did it in private, to my face with respect for my feelings and weren't trying to humiliate me or make me cry. If Kerwan had done that I wouldn't have felt so angry after".

There's another long pause and rather than wait to see if she'll end it I decide to lighten the mood. "Do you remember that day we came in to the College. First fifteen minutes as Police officers and you came in and scared us all to death in the lecture theatre?"

She laughs and replies "I think you know me well enough by now Lance to know that my bark is much worse than my bite".

"Maybe, but once again, I wish every senior officer was like you".

She replies "you'll have to write a book and put us all in it."

Hmmm....

"What makes you say that?" I ask her.

"You have a lot of stories about your time with us. You could write some funny stories and base them on us".

"The thought had occurred to me. We'll see. Anyway, good luck with your promotion".

"Thank you Lance, you take care".

Ma'am Postlethwaite was what every probationer needed whether they wanted it or not and in a lot of ways was like my first Headmistress at Primary School. She was zero tolerance, set examples she expected followed and was consistent with everyone despite being incredibly intimidating and strict if reason demanded it.

Only difference was that Ma'am Postlethwaite wasn't a nun.

JUSTICE?

Five months after resigning I wrote to the Chief Constable, the Deputy Chief Constable and the three Assistant Chief Constables of my old Force, saying that I had been bullied and had suffered disability discrimination. I specifically named who was responsible. I used words like "immeasurably distressed" and "lack of dignity, integrity or fairness".

A reply came back three weeks later from the Head of Human Resources saying that after having interviewed all the people in my Area's SMT and the people I'd mentioned in my letter AND having looked at the files those same people had on me they had found no evidence that I had been bullied OR had suffered disability discrimination and now considered the matter closed.

I didn't know whether to laugh or cry.

GLOSSARY

10/8- Code for "being able to talk openly". This can be anything from answering the Job mobile on handsfree to having your earpiece in while using the Airwave radio. Those with any common sense will always say "are you 10/8?" when phoning a colleague before blurting out potentially sensitive information.

28 Days Later- Horror movie about England being wiped out by a virus which makes everyone very angry. A big chunk was filmed in the City of London.

ABH- Actual Bodily Harm. A serious physical assault.

Absolute Necessity- The test for whether popping a cap in some dude's arse....sorry, discharging a lethal projectile from a firearm into a Suspect, was justified.

Abstracting Electricity- Stealing someone's leccy. One way of dealing with squatters.

ACPO- Association of Chief Police Officers. A gentleman's club for anyone of Assistant Chief Constable rank and above. Make decisions that affect everyone below them.

Acting Up. Doing the next level up's job but for no extra money. The most senior person on a Section can Act Up in the absence of the skipper. While useful if you want the job full time a lot of Forces will take the piss and have you Acting for ages before pulling the plug.

Action Plan- Plan of action identifying developmental issues an officer (usually probationary) has and putting a time limit on them being rectified. Used to bully those that don't fit in or have an opinion different from their Sergeant's.

ADS- Acting Detective Sergeant.

Advanced Driver- The sexy stuff. Authorised to drive big, powerful, throbbing machines and run other vehicles off the road (with Inspector's authorisation of course). Also licensed for TPAC.

ADVOKATE- Mnemonic used to remember the key elements needed for a good Statement. Amount of Time, Distance, Visibility, Obstructions, Known, Anything out of the ordinary, Time Elapsed, Errors. PCSOs should have this tattooed on the inside of their eyelids.

AFO/Authorised Firearms Officer- Not quite the sexy stuff. Not cleared for a pistol but authorised to hold a machine gun outside the Old Bailey or at any function that requires an armed, visible deterrent. Can be seen at Heathrow Airport in times of increased security or looking miserable, soaked to the skin in the rain whenever anyone is going to or from court that the tabloids have made the public hate.

Affray- Fighting or threatening violence when two or more people are present.

Airwave- Police radio. Relatively recent addition to a PC's kit this is a two way radio, mobile phone and tracking device in one. Replaced those horrid kits still seen occasionally on The Bill.

Annual Leave- Holiday. Once booked, approved and signed off it cannot be taken away from you unless you offer it up.

App Add- Appropriate Adult- What is required for Interview for anyone who is under 17 or has mental issues. These can be relatives or friends or someone that the Police will bring in at taxpayer's expense if noone else is willing to/ can't be contacted. Good ones will sit there and look bored or embarrassed. Bad ones will have no conception of what is going on and attempt to engage their vile offspring in jovial banter.

Area- Each Constabulary has several Areas from two (City of London) to lots (Thames Valley).

Armed Response Unit- Imagine being a reserve England goalkeeper. You have to attend all the training sessions, know all the tactics and be as fit as the rest of the team but hardly ever get to play. Then one day you are called upon and have to be as good as the normal goalie. Kind of sums up these chaps, who very rarely get to draw their weapons let alone fire them but have a fitness test that the army would be proud of (and all coppers should have to do) and get cautioned for Murder if they ever shoot and kill someone in the line of duty. Also have to administer CPR to anyone they've just shot "once the threat it nullified" and prove they pulled the trigger in an act of 'absolute necessity'.

ASBO- Anti Social Behaviour Order- Labour government invention. When someone's behaviour is intolerable they are issued with this little beauty, supposedly shaming them into behaving like a decent human being. In reality it's the most toothless law ever conceived and the few chavs that can read regard getting one as proof of how hard they are.

Ashes to Ashes- Time travelling cop show sequel to Life on Mars, pitting a sensitive, intelligent, politically correct, 2008 female Inspector against a 1981 male bastion of Old School. Her line to him over dinner "even after 30 years of feminism there's thousands of women who would give their eye teeth to be sitting here with you" sums it up completely.

ASP- Piddly little baton that looks good when being opened like a light sabre and that's about it. Closing it means you have to bang it on a hard, unyielding surface which means anyone in The Lake District can't shut it in about 90% of their Area.

Assistant Chief Constable- Two to three in every Force. 3rd from top and head up entire areas of Force policy, training or duties. Usually only seen at passing out parades or queuing at the HQ canteen. Tend to shout at Chief Supers if the Crime Stats for their Areas are too high.

Assistant Commissioner- Metropolitan Police equivalent to Chief Constable, City of London Police equivalent to Deputy Chief Constable.

Barney- Violent or aggressive argument.

Basic Driver- Someone who has passed their test again with a Force Driving Instructor to ensure they can drive Police cars obeying the Highway Code at all times.

Basic Training- Getting to know the Law, Self Defence and most importantly how to be nice to those who are Diverse.

Beak- Magistrate.

Beat- An officer's normal zone of work.

Detail's Box- My attitude affects your reaction. Your reaction affects my attitude. This is the theory behind being able to talk someone down from heightened twattiness to calm compliance. Being "nice but firm" will however NOT work on the drunk, the mentally ill, the drugged up or even the very angry. "KNOCK IT OFF OR I'LL SPRAY YOU IN THE FACE" would be more effective but is not in line with the Conflict Resolution Model or the Human Rights Act.

Bilking- Making off without payment.

Bin- (1) Cell (2) Verb meaning to sack someone deemed unsuitable.

Bleep Test- Part of the fitness test in order to get in and used intermittently through Training. You run from one side of the gym to the other. The bleeps keep getting closer together. Reduced from 8.1 to 5.4 which means a pregnant woman carrying twins, 8 months gone would be able to walk it.

Blues and Twos- Sirens and lights on simultaneously. Usually while driving at excess speed.

Bobby's Bracelets- Handcuffs.

Body- Arrested person.

Body in the Bin- A prisoner in a cell.

Booking In- Being presented to the Custody skipper and the arresting officer explaining why you were deprived of your liberty. A cross between the Tower of London Changing of the Keys ceremony ("Why is the prisoner brought before me?" "Well Sergeant at 11.30pm while on routine patrol I was called to....etc, etc") and checking into a cheap hotel ("do you have any religious or dietary requirements we should know about?"). Those that comply will have a reasonably pleasant time of it. Anyone being larey will realise that Custody skippers can flip like a coin and make your stay quite depressing.

Breach of the Peace- BoP- Doing anything that upsets the tranquillity of the public karma. Used as a tool when attending Domestic Violence call outs.

Breakfast Club- 1980s cult movie about five teenagers who bond over a Saturday spent in school detention. Now used to describe any moment where people lower their barriers and interact as human beings.

Briefing/ Muster- The daily meeting of every Section that's on duty that day. Usually consist of photos of ugly people who are Wanted or Just Been Released From Prison and any Hot Spots to look out for. Led by a Sergeant and sometimes the Duty Governor. When there's only one officer on duty plus the Sergeant (i.e. everyone else is sick/ on Leave/ having Training) they tend to dispense with it to avoid really taking the piss.

Briefing Room- Where the above happens.

Bring the Force Into Disrepute- Doing anything that can be perceived as conduct unbecoming of an Officer of the Law. From wearing your uniform on a dating website to being nicked for getting too drunk to walk home.

Bronze Cordon- The furthest point out from a crime scene. Will be cordon tape and Police Constables and/ or PCSOs who will stand their for as long as it takes and have to argue with lippy members of the public who don't seem to realise the correlation between scene of serious crime and NOT being able to walk where it happened.

BTP- British Transport Police. One of a handful of unique UK Police Forces. Based in London although they control all public transport throughout Great Britain.

Bulling- Not a typo. This is the act of getting tennis elbow polishing your boots with 95 layers of Cherry Blossom Parade Gloss until they are able to dazzle low flying aircraft. Hard to do, easy to lose (like if some selfish git steps on your foot and rips off the first 5 layers). Sensible coppers keep one pair under the bed just for parades and the rare occasions that ACPO are in the vicinity.

Caution- (1) What you MUST give to a Suspect as soon as

reasonably practicable after Arrest. (2) Bit of paper a Suspect will sign to admit to whatever they did. Deemed to be a punishment all on its own.

Cell Exit- Oh the joys of the Duty of Care. Anyone who's violent upon arrival at Custody will be subjected to this little manoeuvre. At least 2 and preferably about 10 cops will take the wriggling, spitting, swearing Suspect from the van into the cell where the plastic-coated mattress will be flung onto the floor and they will be placed upon it and sat on. They will then be systematically searched, their clothes taken, apart from underwear and the people sitting on them will peel off one at a time. The conundrum is that the last person out, who's the Officer sitting on the suspect's back with their hands restrained, can't get out without the Suspect jumping up and thumping them. So....the Second to Last person out then walks up to them, takes their belt in one hand, taps them on the shoulder (as verbal signals would also tip off the wriggling wretch) and then pulls them out of the room backwards, before the door is slammed shut and the Suspect expends their energy by kicking it for the next two hours.

Challenge- What you are supposed to do if someone says or does something you don't like (e.g. "I challenge that"). The reality is that people will usually sneak off and winge to a senior officer behind your back.

CHAV- Council Housed and Violent. Noun used to describe a breed of people who are usually unemployed, have limited intelligence, zero fashion sense and children named after football teams. Collective noun is Vending Pack (e.g. "that window put through in WH Smith's was probably that Vending Pack of chavs we saw legging it through the park").

Chief Constable- Second only to the Home Secretary (isn't that terrifying?) and Commander in Chief of an entire Force. Range from brilliant (John Stephens, Mike Fuller, Mike Todd) to utterly awful (Ian Blair, Della Cannings, Timothy Brain).

Chief Inspector- A Guv'nor's Guv'nor. This is where the rot starts to set in as they are on the ladder of high achievement by this point and can see the ACPO annual dinner invite as a Golden Ticket of opportunity. Only usually seen by constables on special occasions (i.e. anything the CI thinks will get them noticed).

Chief Superintendent- Area Commander. Like feudal barons from the Dark Ages, each one jealously guards their own domain and tries to outdo the other barons while paying homage to the King (Chief Constable).

CID- Criminal Investigations Division. Suit wearing brethren of Uniform who investigate crimes after the initial Arrest and get issued with covert body armour.

COBRA- Emergency committee convened in times of severe national emergency. Led by the Prime Minister of the day.

Commander- Metropolitan and City of London rank equivalent to Assistant Chief Constable. City have only one while Met have loads.

Commissioner- Metropolitan and City of London top boys. Two levels above a Chief Constable. Most Met cops sing Sir John Stephens' praises while lamenting the day that Ian Blair ever got the job.

Compliant Cuffs- Rigid, nasty and painful handcuffs that are designed to stop people wriggling around after being nicked. Intended to hurt if you struggle.

Confirmed- Having passed probation you are now harder to sack.

Conflict Resolution Model- How to defuse a potentially violent situation in a way least likely to result in litigation against the Police.

Constable- Beat Bobby. The lowest level there is (unless you count PCSOs).

Constabulary- A Police Force. There are 43 in England and Wales controlled by the Home Office plus others that come under different remits (e.g. BTP, Battersea Parks, Dover Port Authority).

Constant- Everyone's fave chore. Someone has been nicked who may die in Custody so some poor sod has to sit and watch them while they are in the Cell, with the door open. About as fun as watching paint dry, but with the knowledge that you'll face criminal proceedings if they croak.

Control- The centre of communication for the entire Force.

Core Section- The main Section on duty at any time.

Cough- Admit in interview whatever naughty thing you are accused of. Beloved of CID is the Cough as it makes the interviewing Officer look molten as lava and means slightly less fannying about afterwards trying to prove it.

Crown Prosecution Service- CPS- Independent body that looks at the case file assembled by the Police and decides whether to prosecute the case in court or not. While this in theory means impartiality and objective judgment of evidence, in reality they are as target driven as the Fuzz and will only go with safe bets (e.g. one case I know of where an arrest for attempted murder was prosecuted as ABH).

CS Spray- Nasty, cross contaminating class five firearm that eight times out of ten also affects passers by, innocent bystanders or the officer using it. Like, durr!

Custody Suite- Cell area of a Nick. Usually contains the fingerprint machine, the DNA kits, the prisoner's property store and one or two fairly morose skippers.

Customers- What the Police now call the public...oh for fuck's sake!

Cycle Response Squad- Some time ago it was realised that no matter how high a volume you turned your siren up to and how fast you flashed the blue lights, in London and any congested city the sodding traffic will mean you are unable to get to that stabbing in double quick time. Sooo, some genius came up with these guys who look fairly comical in their "Police" cycle helmets, day-glo Body Armour and tight lycra shorts. Are trained in defensive tactics using their Rock Hopper stunt bikes (i.e. sticking it between themselves and the irate baddy) and how to ride down flights of steps without going arse over tit. Best way to get away from them is to simply run into a building you know has more than one exit.

Dawn of the Dead- 1978 horror movie (remade in 2004) about zombies taking over America.

Day Book- PNB for CID officers.

Deputy Assistant Commissioner- Metropolitan Police equivalent rank to Deputy Chief Constable.

Deputy Chief Constable- Second from top and basically a Chief Constable in waiting (although not necessarily of their own Force). Act up in the absence/ death/ promotion of the Chief and are seen even less than their boss.

Deputy Commissioner- Number two in the Metropolitan Police. One rank above a Chief Constable.

Designated Police Station- Whichever one in an Area has an active Custody Suite.

Ding Dong- Verbal argument. Usually involving shouting.

Dining In Night- Official dinner where you wear a suit and have a posh meal, sometimes with senior officers as waiters. Fines are given for elbows on table, using a mobile or gents taking their jackets off.

Div- Stupid or dim person. Derived from prison speak. Anyone too thick to do a job involving mental effort was given the task of sticking dividers into cardboard boxes.

DO- Divisional Officer- Another name for Special Chief Inspector.

Door Kickers- People who like to kick the cell door from the inside to vent their frustration at having been detained. As Interview Rooms in older nicks are situated in the Cell Block you can sometimes play a tape back and hear muffled booming in the background.

Double Crewed- Two people in the car. Useful and in some areas fundamental for officer safety. Unfortunately a lot of Forces don't do this due to bad management or lack of funding.

Drill Staff- Those in charge of parades and marching. Wear a red sash across the tunic, carry a riding crop and tend to bellow orders and/ or insults at the top of their lungs. Prone to amusing put downs such as "your trousers make you look like Charlie Chaplin. Have you been ill?" or "your helmet looks like a bucket, has your head shrunk?" etc, etc.

Drunk and Disorderly- Being drunk in public and behaving in a disorderly fashion. Usually an arrest will only be made on a D&D if he or she is too pissed to stand up straight or too pig headed to realise after repeated warnings that arguing with coppers isn't very sensible.

Drunk and Incapable- Drunk to the point of being unable to stand up at all. Usually don't realise they've been detained until they wake up in a cell with a headache.

Drunk in a Public Place- Technically an offence which means if someone is drunk but neither D&D nor D&I you can still nick them if you want to.

Dynamic Risk Assessment- Sizing up a scene to decide how much risk is involved. In theory this is common sense but there are reported occasions of this going far too far and the Police doing nothing until it's too late.

EAO- Evidence Assessment Officer.

EFPN- Endorsable Fixed Penalty Notice- A fine AND points on your driving licence.

ERB- Emergency Restraint Belt. Used to secure a violent or self harming prisoner's arms and legs if they are thrashing about too much. Olds ones would take ages to get on as you had to have someone else help you and you absolutely HAD to get them in the correct positions on the knees. Further you had to be trained before you could use one. Now they have been replaced with Fast Wraps which are basically a Judo belt with velcro. Only takes one person, no training and is on in a jiffy. Makes you want to weep.

ERV- Emergency Response Vehicle. The fast cars, used by Standard and Advanced drivers in order to blat it through red lights, exceed the speed limit and generally get there in quick order. Usually there's only one or two per Section which means anyone else is in the less powerful motors. The most grating thing about this is that if there's two Advanced drivers on a Section, only one gets the ERV and the other CANNOT attend an incident in breach of the Highway Code as their vehicle is deemed not to be up to the performance capabilities required.

Exit Interview- When you leave you are entitled see a senior officer or Personnel department employee. Your chance to suggest a few changes or slag off anyone who made your life a misery. Those retiring on full pensions get the right to be interviewed by the Chief Constable.

Fast Track- Being placed on an accelerated promotion scheme provided you make the required grades and fulfil the necessary criteria.

Federation- Police equivalent to a Union. Designed to protect the rights of its members for a small fee. A thorn in the side of both the Government and Senior Management.

Flash Call- Call in need of immediate response by Police.

Fight Night- Friday or Saturday Late Turn or Night Shift.

File Note- A note on your file for being a naughty Police person. The lower end of disciplinary proceedings. Usually consists of a meeting where you will then have a note for 6 months or 1 year, depending on seriousness. For confirmed officers this can be as grave as ABH. For probationers it can be losing equipment or chewing gum in briefings.

Final Warning- Final Reprimand for a Juvenile.

Foot Patrol- What it says on the tin.

FPN- Fixed Penalty Notice.

Front Stack- Being handcuffed with Compliant cuffs with your arms to the front.

Fuzz- Police. Also Pigs, Old Bill, Filth, Gavvers, Bobbies, Peelers, Bizzies, Traps, Boys in Blue, Rozzers, Cops and Unappreciated Masochists.

GBH- Grievous Bodily Harm. A very serious physical assault.

Gene Hunt- The Detective Chief Inspector from TV shows Life on Mars and Ashes to Ashes. Despite being a drunken, sexist, racist, bullying, chain smoking, homophobic, foul mouthed bully Mr Hunt has proved popular with many people including ACPO, Senior

Management, Old School, New School and the general public. Has become a sex symbol of a strain of masculinity that has long since been neutered by Political Correctness and Feminism over the years. Phillip Glennister who plays Hunt is apparently a regular guest at official Police dinners.

Going Equipped- Getting caught carrying something that could be used to commit a crime (e.g. bolt cutters or a crowbar).

GPV- General Purpose Vehicle- The normal patrol cars that are used to potter about town in. Not authorised for pursuit or anything remotely sexy.

Handcuff Hero- Someone who only gets argumentative and aggressive once they are wearing a pair of Bobby's Bracelets.

Handover Package- File of stuff given by arresting officers to CID so they can carry on with investigating the alleged offence.

Heartbeat- Rustic TV cop show set in the 1950s where the village Bobby is a pleasant, clean shaven chap and even the criminals are decent sorts in their own way.

High Viz- The bright yellow jackets you are given in order to protect you on busy roads, legally facilitate a traffic stop (as they can claim they didn't see you if they don't stop and it's night time) and mean that you are a visible presence on the streets. Also remove any last hope of getting respect from the public as it's hard for anyone to accept a bollocking from someone resembling Tinky Winky from the Teletubbies.

Hobby Bobby- Special Constable.

Holding Cell- Area where Prisoners are taken before they are presented to the Custody Sergeant. They are searched and their belongings bagged and they give their details in here, if compliant.

Unlike American gaols which have lovely big cages you just shove everyone into and call their names out when the system is ready to process them, ours are open to the outside world and if you've arrested two or more people for fighting then you have the nightmare of trying to keep them apart in one small room.

Hoody- Hooded sports top. Worn by chavs a great deal.

Hot Fuzz- Immensely popular, clever and funny movie about Nick Angel, an English cop who's too good for his own good. The reasons they push him off to Sandford are frighteningly believable.

Human Rights Act- Designed by the Labour government to ensure everyone is treated with a basic level of decency. Reality is that criminals now know how to play the system and will screech about their Human Rights if deprived of eight hours sleep or not allowed a cigarette.

IC- Identity Code- Used to describe someone's perceived ethnicity. IC1 being White European. IC3 being Black.

Inappropriate Language- Anything that someone else is annoyed you said. This can be obvious such as abusive language, racism or homophobia down to leaving silly remarks on your Facebook account.

Inspector- A Sir or a Ma'am. A skipper's line manager and the first rank you have to stand up for as they enter the room. Range from brilliant to utterly piss poor in equal measure.

Interview- The questioning of a Suspect, usually on tape. There can be up to four cassettes being used simultaneously depending on the Force (one for Court, one for the Case, one for the Suspect and one for the little boy who lives down the lane).

JAPAN- Mnemonic meaning Justified, Authorised, Proportionate,

Auditable and Necessary. Everything the Police do has to retrospectively fit in with this little beauty. Safety Trainers loathe it as there will be a lot of probationers getting a dig in the ear off role play actors during Arrest Scenarios as they were too busy attempting to mentally JAPAN their actions to notice the nasty bloke with the rubber knife had got within their reactionary gap.

Job, The- Being a Police Officer.

Juvenile- Anyone under 17.

Life on Mars- Time travelling cop show pitting a sensitive, intelligent, politically correct 2006 Chief Inspector against his 1973 counterpart. This and Ashes to Ashes proved to be immensely popular with both the frustrated cops of the 21st century and the disillusioned general public. At the ACPO general meeting of 2007, they voted anonymously on keypads for very serious issues. At the end to lighten the mood they voted for their favourite TV show and Life on Mars got 65%.

Livescan- The modern, less messy way of fingerprinting a Suspect by using a flat screen and scanning them in. Relies on the Suspect being totally compliant as you have to "roll" their digits onto the screen.

Load Belt- Same as American cops. Wide nylon belt with chunky rucksack buckle. Used to carry your spray, cuffs, torch, first aid kit and baton.

Load Vest- A brilliant invention designed to supersede the utility belt. Meant to make wearing heavy things like cuffs or batons or even radios better by distributing the weight over the upper torso and not the hips. This ultimately led to many officers on Sick Leave with bad backs as this thing and body armour do not do the spine any favours.

Lord Scarman- Well meaning, bumbling old fool who did more harm than good after his damning report on the Police in the mid 1980s. Jeffrey Palmer's interpretation of Scarman in TV show Ashes to Ashes is painfully wonderful, as is watching Gene Hunt fulfil many officers' fantasies by bringing Scarman down to Earth.

Magnums- Brand of Police issue boots.

Marquess of Queensbury Rules- How to fight fair in Boxing.

Mounted- The horse squad.

Mule- Drugs courier.

National Service- Forced conscription into the armed forces.

NCS/ Non Compliant Suspect Dog- Malonois. One step below Armed Response. Nasty, psychotic and bad tempered Belgian hound used to bring down the most aggressive of suspects in a flurry of teeth and fur. The fact that this creature is one level below getting shot at kind of sums it up.

NFA- (1) No further action. (2) No fixed abode.

Nick- (1) The act of performing an arrest on a Suspect. (2) A Police Station.

NIP- Notice of Intended Prosecution. Letter you get in the post for offences such as failing to stop your car when instructed to by the Police.

Noble Cause- Doing something wrong or illegal in order to prevent someone else getting hurt.

Nominal- Someone known to be a prolific criminal in a local Area.

NONCE- Paedophile. Prison speak for Not On Normal Courtyard Exercises.

Non-Specific Deity- What you are encouraged to say instead of "God" while on duty. No, I'm not making this up.

NOS- National Occupational Standard. Have to be filled out and signed off to prove competency in certain areas. Over 30 of these litter a probationer's email inbox like cow pats from the devil's own herd. While some are reasonably sensible (ability to deal with prisoners, performing an arrest) others are a waste of time (First Aid, which you can get signed off simply by having done the training or Proving Respect for Race and Diversity. This one is 9 points long and in my case consisted of being nice to a store manager who had not even heard alleged racist abuse being mumbled at him by an irate customer).

NVCs- Non Verbal Communications. Body language. Someone displaying aggressive NVCs may be about to lamp you one. It also means you can hit them first and then claim pre-emptive self defence.

Occupational Health- Unit responsible for dealing with sick Police staff.

Off Duty Intervention- Getting involved in something on a Rest Day or while going to or from work. While it is a requirement of The Job to at least make a witness Statement if you see something criminal, a lot of Forces get the heeby jeebies about this kind of thing and will rebuke their troops for getting stuck in. It does mean you can fulfil that long suppressed urge to pull the emergency handle on a train though.

Old Man, The- The Chief Constable or Commissioner.

Old School- This used to mean any copper who's been in more than 20 years. Since 1998 the Force has changed beyond recognition and it can mean 6 years or more. Many retired Old Schoolers say they would rather die than rejoin, but loved it when they were there.

OST- Officer Safety Training. The physical stuff. We spent 2 weeks on this and about 6 in total on Race and Diversity. You get 1- 2 hours on using your Pava spray (a class five firearm) and up to half a day on use of baton (an offensive weapon in a civilian's hands). The department will usually consist of ex-army types with broken noses and a penchant for 15 mile runs before breakfast.

PACE- Police and Criminal Evidence Act 1984. Brought in due to findings by Lord Scarman. Replaced Judges' Rules. Basically means that prisoners are all treated like hotel guests when in custody.

Panic Button- Orange knob on the top of a Police radio. Hold it for one and a half seconds it takes control of the channel it's on and means that the whole Area you work in will have to listen to you. It also makes every other Officer's radio vibrate repeatedly. Useful if you are getting a kicking off the friends of the local scrote you just tried to nick when you went out Single Crewed, but only if you know precisely where you are. Even if the unit is off the button will still work (which causes much embarrassment when people push it accidentally while putting a dormant radio into the leather holder).

Paper Sift- After filling out your application form to join it will be marked and those that pass are said to have "survived the sift".

Passing Out Parade- Marching in your best uniform to rousing, orchestral music around the Skid Pan in front of your relatives and senior officers before being inspected by an ACC. That is unless it's raining in which case it's in the gym. Signifies either the end of Basic Training or having made it through probation depending on which Force you're with.

Pava/ Pepper Spray- As CS gas is like a mild form of VX and will cross contaminate an entire room, some genius came up with this alternative which is great provided you manage to get it in the suspect's eyes, it's not windy and you are pointing it the right way. Due to Health and Safety and the poxy Human Rights Act we no longer get a dosage in the face during training. The training for using this lasts an hour, if that.

PCSO- Police Community Support Officer. Also known as Blunkett's Bobbies, Plastic Police or Burger Kings (i.e. they have as much legal power as a burger flipper). The invention of the 2nd most cretinous Labour Home Secretary David Blunkett (the first being Jackie Smith). Initially conceived to deal with low level crime and act as community liaisons. However they have no arrest powers, cannot physically act to detain you and are of no use whatsoever for anything except visual reassurance to little old ladies. Most famously let a 10 year old boy drown in a pond in front of his hysterical mother as they weren't trained to enter deep water.

PDA/ Public Display of Affection- Kissing in public. Inappropriate for an officer on duty even though it may not be your fault you came across a drunken Hen party on the High Street who like a bloke in uniform.

PDU- Professional Development Unit. A Sergeant and Constable overseen by a rarely seen Inspector. In charge of probationers for an entire Area. Kind of like having an uncle and aunt and not knowing if the next time you visit you're going to be favourite nephew or not.

PNB- Pocket Note Book. A Police officer's legal record of daily duties. Anything that you feel is relevant goes in here and you may be asked to bring it to Court to "refresh" your memory when that bicycle theft you dealt with a year ago finally ends up in front of the Judge. In this age of Blackberrys (which PCSOs get issued with) and mobile phones that can do Sat Nav it's amazing that cops still rely on these to document a Shift. Ones left lying carelessly around will have willies draw in them by sniggering colleagues. As you can't tear the page out the schoolboy joke will be on display for everyone to see (such as Barristers in Court, senior officers or even the Judiciary).

PNC- Police National Computer. All info on anyone who has ever been involved with the cops either as a complainant, victim or

Suspect. Great if used properly and if functioning at 100% capacity. Crap if faulty, if the operator is a bit of a div or it's noisy and you can't get half the info over the air due to static or the person you are dealing with (and possibly his mates) whingeing about Police harassment.

PND- Penalty Notice for Disorder.

POETS day. Not a chance to revel in the linguistic phraseology of Yeats or Blake but Piss Off Early, Tomorrow's Saturday. Usually used by CID, those in Training or Senior Management.

POLAC/ Police Accident- What the Guv'nor hates and the person involved in it had better hope wasn't their fault. Any vehicle involved in Police duties that is involved in an RTC falls under this one. It used to include officers on their way to or from duty but this has been dropped due to the cost of replacing PC Jones's brand new Ferrari that he drove into a wall after coming off a Night Shift with five hours overtime.

Police Service- What the Met changed their name to in order to appear less "aggressive" and more "people friendly". Can't have your cake and eat it.

Porridge- Prison.

Positive Intervention- Doing something constructive when you turn up at a Domestic Violence incident. If there is any sign whatsoever of more than a verbal argument then one of the people involved will be leaving, either willingly or after being arrested.

PPE/ Appointments- Personal Protective Equipment- Baton, Cuffs, Stabby and Pepper Spray.

Previous- Prior criminal record.

Priority One- Highest grade there is for a Flash Call. If you want Police attendance quickly when phoning 999 then talk in the present continuous tense, say your life is in danger and for good measure say the crime is racially motivated.

Probation- The preliminary two years of an officer's life in The Job. Easier to do before Political Correctness reared it's ghastly head as you will be watched like a hawk for your ability to fit in and picked up on Diversity issues if you don't.

PSD- Professional Standards Department. The Spanish Inquisition of the Police. Feared by most, despised by more. Mainly because you may end up meeting them through no fault of your own.

PSE- Police Support Employee- Anyone who's not a cop but works for the Force.

Public Order- Catch all expression that can be holding a shield and batting off petrol bombs during a riot to making sure people stay the right side of the cordon at a crime scene or public event.

Public Order 1, 2 & 3- Most Forces train cadets up to level 3 which is basically forming a line by grasping each other's utility belts to prevent anyone getting past. Levels 1 and 2 are the hardcore with the visored helmets, asbestos suits and see through shields.

PubWatch- A zero tolerance approach to drunken loutishness. Get banned from one pub then you get banned from all the pubs in town and possibly the neighbouring towns as well.

Push/ Pull- The second bit of the fitness test. A rowing machine that they spin you around on after you've pulled, to see how much you can push. Designed to test your ability to push away someone trying to fight you while simultaneously trying to hang onto them. Due to their non-confrontational job role, PCSOs only do the Push bit.

Race & Diversity- The current focus of attention within the English and Welsh Police at the expense of baton training, self defence, driving skills or even common sense. All training now incorporates R&D somewhere.

Reactionary Gap- 4 to 6 feet. The distance you are supposed to keep between yourself and anyone you are dealing with. This in theory means they will find it harder to attack you. I bet BTP love this little rule, particularly at rush hour on the London Underground.

Red Bull Rooster- Drunken, aggressive male who walks towards you in a threatening manner bobbing his head like a bird. Usually has his shirt off.

Red Key- Dynamic entry tool that lets you bosh down people's front doors in the advent of a dawn raid or old Elsie Bagthorpe having 14 bottles of milk on the doorstep and not being seen for two weeks. Heavy lump of concrete, surrounded by a bright red metal casing with two handles on the top that is swung like a Medieval battering ram into the weak point of a door in order to facilitate cops swarming all over the place and checking for trouble. While the motion is simply one half of "A Leg and a Wing to See the King" they will make you do an entire days' training before signing you off to use it. This ultimately means that you may have one in your car but will have to call up a trained colleague to use it for you. The first time I did this the colleague took an hour to arrive meaning we stood about twiddling our thumbs outside an address that it was suspected had the rotting corpse of a suicide in it.

Refs- Food break for cops.

Refuse Charge- No charges brought against an arrested person.

Regulation 9- A complaint against an officer by a member of the public. While Old School coppers realised you had to have a few in order to be doing a good job, modern bobbies quite rightly cack their trousers when one arrives as they can drag on for months and may result in dismissal.

Regulation 13- Dismissal of probationer before probation has ended. Once Confirmed it is much harder to get rid of someone, so anyone clocked as being a nuisance will find themselves being dragged over the coals with this little tool in their first two years.

Relief- Replacement for an officer doing a duty that needs round the clock monitoring (e.g. a Constant or standing on a cordon).

Remand- Make a Suspect remain in Custody instead of bailing them.

Reprimand- Caution for a Juvenile.

Rest Days- A copper's weekend. As the Police are out and about 24/7 rest days need to be fitted in to account for this and you may find yourself off on Monday and Tuesday. This is fine in theory but a right dog end if you have just come off Nights as your first day off will be halved through sleeping in till 3pm.

Riot- The pinnacle of the Public Order Act. Officially acknowledging that a riot occurred means the Constabulary whose remit it happened in are admitting they lost control. They are then liable to pay for all damage caused. Therefore if 200 people gather to trash the high street in Chelsea you will get multiple arrests for Violent Disorder.

Risk Assessment- Anything from sizing up the pub brawl you have just attended to being told in writing what you can and can't do while on duty if recovering from being Sick.

Role Plays- Strutting your funky stuff to an assessor with one or more role play actors in anything from a vehicle stop to dealing with a violent prisoner. Are totally unrealistic, particularly as the actor will react to gentle persuasion the way you want them to and not laugh in your face, gob on you or stab you.

Rowdy Van- Also known as the Pub Van. The mini bus with the cage in the back. Can have up to eight testosterone fuelled gavvers in it spoiling for a rumble.

RTC/ Road Traffic Collision- A car crash. Renamed from RTA as it has been dictated that the word 'accident' suggests noone was to blame.

Rudolph Giuliani- Not an Italian reindeer but the Zero Tolerance Mayor of New York who, through his tough stance on law breaking managed to reduce violent crime and theft by around 75% in the space of a year. Stood for the Republican nomination for President of the USA in 2008.

Rural/ Village Warden. Basically a PCSO but in a green fleece and not employed by the Fuzz but the local council. About as much use as a condom in monastery.

Sandford- Originally the fictional town used for role plays and exams in the world of Police training. Has since shown up in the movie Hot Fuzz.

Section- The constables, Sergeant and Inspector of a particular duty squad.

Section 1, PACE- Searching someone for anything illegal you have reasonable grounds to suspect they have on them. They are not under arrest at this point, only 'detained'.

Section 32, PACE- Searching someone after arrest for evidence, items that could cause harm or anything they could use to 'facilitate an escape' (such as those concealed handcuff keys that crop up on Ebay occasionally).

Section 4a Public Order Act- Intentional harassment, alarm or distress.

Section 5, Public Order Act- Behaviour likely to cause harassment, alarm or distress. Means you can be nicked for swearing.

Section 44, Terrorism Act- Draconian power utilised in times of severe threat. Means you do not need to have, give or state a reason for stopping someone and searching them. Your Force will still warn you not to single people out though. Last I heard, Al Qaeda weren't yet an equal opportunities employer.

Section 47, Offences Against the Person Act- ABH or Actual Bodily Harm.

Self Harm- Hurting yourself deliberately.

Sergeant- A skipper. Wear chevrons on their shoulders and are the first promotion from the rank of Constable. Those in charge of Custody are non-specific deities in their own kingdoms. Those in charge of Response teams tend to get ulcers.

Shoeing- Being beaten up. Usually involving a lot of kicking.

Shout- A radio call from Control to attend an incident.

Significant Silence- Anything a Suspect DOESN'T say while in Interview (e.g. remaining mum when the question "why were you carrying that human head in your lunch box?" is put to you).

Significant Statement- Anything a Suspect says after Caution and before being Interviewed.

Single Crewed- One person in the car. Highly dangerous if you are anywhere except the town centre and are expected to respond to emergency calls.

Six Feet- The distance a severed head has to be from a corpse before an officer on scene can declare the person dead without the coroner's opinion. Anyone with any sense would just boot it across the floor.

Skid Pan- Large area of flat land at the Police college where Standard and Advanced drivers practice throwing expensive vehicles around in controlled skids or weaving between bollards.

SMT/ Senior Management Team- The bigwigs of an Area. CIs and above. Have regular meetings (either daily or weekly depending on where you are) and worry about the crime stats for their area. If there's too many crimes and not enough nicking then the Area Commander will bollock the Deputy Area Commander. The Deputy will bollock his CI and the CI will bollock the Duty Inspectors. They will in turn take it out on their Section. Gotta love performance based policing.

SO- Section Officer- Another name for Special Sergeant.

SO13- Royal Armed Protection. Can be seen at Buckingham Palace and Clarence House (amongst others) holding machine guns and looking fierce.

SO19- Metropolitan Police Firearms unit.

S.O.P.H.I.E- Charity set up by the parents of murdered Goth Sophie Lancaster. Stands for Stamp Out Prejudice, Hatred and Intolerance Everywhere

Special Constable- The volunteers. Full Police powers and a warrant card plus free travel if they work in London. Minimum of 200 hours per year, average 4 a week. Despite being unpaid they outrank any PCSO even if off duty. Alternately even the Chief Commandant (Special Chief Constable) is outranked by any Regular officer. Range from the brilliant and genuinely motivated to people who like to ponse about in a uniform on a Friday night.

Stab Proof Vest- Kevlar body armour. Great with knives, useless against ballistics more powerful than an air rifle.

Standard Driver- Someone who IS allowed to break the speed limit in an ERV up to a certain level but, if pursuing a Suspect who goes over that level, has to hand over to Advanced or break off completely.

Stand Down- To be relieved of a duty or to be told to leave a scene. Frustrating in the extreme if you know it's way past knocking off time but the Guv'nor's approval is needed before you can go.

Statement- Written account of what you saw. Good ones will be detailed in the extreme but as they are invariably hand written will take ages.

Stop Form- Vary from Force to Force but have to be filled out every time you stop someone to ask more than "how are you?". An attempt to make coppers accountable for why they are detaining people for a chat. Take a minimum of ten minutes to fill out even if you are experienced. Most Forces use them as an easy way of fulfilling paperwork quotas.

Substantive. A confirmed officer of the rank he or she currently holds. A substantive constable has made it through probation. A Substantive Superintendent has moved into a bigger office.

Superintendent- Deputy Area Commander (well they were in my Force). If substantive they tend to be decent. If acting up they are invariably putting a portfolio together and are about as useful as a stab proof vest at a crack house raid.

Superintendent's Association- The Federation for Supers and Chief Supers. Why the hell they have their own organisation remains a mystery.

Suspect- Person suspected of committing a crime. If nicked guaranteed a solicitor (at taxpayer's expense), a meal or two (at taxpayer's expense) and help with any drug or alcohol issues (at taxpayer's expense). Also, if they can't speak English they will be provided with a translator over the Custody skipper's speakerphone at between 9 and 12 per minute (at taxpayers' expense).

TAC Team- Tactical Team- Usually big blokes in black combat gear and shin pads who are used for dramatic entries and putting in doors.

Take Down- Bringing a Non Compliant Suspect to the floor.

Tazer- Stun gun that fires electric barbs into an assailant, incapacitating them while the trigger is held. Despite being more effective than both batons or spray only a handful of Forces issue them to anyone except the Firearms unit.

TDS- Temporary Detective Sergeant.

Temporary. Doing the next level up's job but getting that level's wage and knowing that unless you REALLY fart on your Weetabix you are guaranteed to keep it and become Substantive.

The Bill- Fictional TV Police show set at Sun Hill Nick in London. Totally unrealistic, not only for the fact that their body armour sleeves clearly have no Kevlar in them (they bend) but also because everyone is good looking and the cops have regular verbal arguments that would result in disciplinary action in any real Force.

TPAC- Tactical Pursuit and Containment and not a quick fix of Typhoo. The art of boxing in a vehicle (you need a friend in another car who's Advanced too to do this) and forcing it to slow down. Less fun than simply ramming the bastard into a ditch.

Traffic- Road Police.

Training Club- Monthly meeting of Specials to bring them up to speed on changes in Force policy or Law.

Travelling Fraternity- As Romany Gypsies are a protected ethnic minority, anyone who travels but isn't a Gypsy comes under this politically correct moniker.

TWOC- Taking Without Owner's Consent- Joyriding- Taking someone's vehicle for a spin without their express permission. Has now become a verb (e.g. "if you've got one of them, some chav'll definitely twoc it").

Uniform- (1) What Beat cops wear on duty. (2) Any Beat officer or senior rank who wears the tie and epaulettes.

Village Warden- Equivalent of a PCSO (i.e. a uniform and no power) but employed by the local council.

Violent Disorder- Section 2 of the Public Order Act. A little riot.

Wanted on Warrant- Someone who has been naughty and not yet arrested for their naughtiness. These show up regularly when you stop someone and then find out after the requisite PNC check that they are needed for a chat about some previous bad behaviour.

Warrant Card- Badge of office for a cop. The leather holder with the force shield ranges from impressive, golden and large (City of London) to tiny (Met) to a sheriff's badge (most other Forces).

Whiskey Mikes- Phonetic term for Warning Markers. If a Stop Check reveals that the person you are talking about has Previous for stabbing coppers and dancing a jig over their still twitching corpses, the Control Centre operator is supposed say " Several Whiskey Mikes. Are you 10/ 8?" Used by more Airwave savvy Controllers who realise that blurting out sensitive info may result in the Suspect doing a bunk or the officer getting attacked.

Wibble- Insane or of questionable mental health.

Wife Beater- Stella Artois lager (pronounced 'ar-twah').

WPC- Woman Police Constable- Politically incorrect and now defunct moniker for lady cops. Also called Woopsies.

Writing Room- Where cops fill out paperwork and check their email.

RANK STRUCTURE OF ENGLISH AND WELSH POLICE FORCES

Commissioner (Metropolitan and City of London only) (Crown over one pip, over laurel wreath)

II

Deputy Commissioner (Metropolitan only) (Crown over two pips, over laurel wreath)

II

Chief Constable (Assistant Commissioner Metropolitan Police) (Crown over laurel wreath)

II

Deputy Chief Constable (Deputy Assistant Commissioner Metropolitan Police, Assistant Commissioner City of London Police) (Pip over laurel wreath)

II

Assistant Chief Constable (Commander Metropolitan and City of London Police) (Laurel wreath)

II

Chief Superintendent (Crown over pip)

II

Superintendent (Crown)

II

Chief Inspector (Three pips)

II

Inspector (Two pips)

II

Sergeant (3 chevrons over divisional letter and shoulder number)

II

Constable (Divisional letter and shoulder number)

RANK STRUCTURE OF CITY OF LONDON SPECIAL CONSTABULARY

Special Commandant (SC logo, laurel wreath with four bars inside)

II

Special Superintendent (SC logo, four bars)

II

Special Chief Inspector/ Divisional Officer (SC logo, three bars)

II

Special Inspector/ Assistant Divisional Officer (SC logo, two bars)

II

Special Sergeant/ Section Officer (SC logo, divisional letter, shoulder number and one bar)

II

Special Constable (SC logo, divisional letter and shoulder number)